Robert William Lowe, Colley Cibber, James Wright, Anthony Ashton

An Apology for the Life of Mister Colley Cibber

Vol. 1

Robert William Lowe, Colley Cibber, James Wright, Anthony Ashton

An Apology for the Life of Mister Colley Cibber
Vol. 1

ISBN/EAN: 9783337415358

Printed in Europe, USA, Canada, Australia, Japan

Cover: Foto ©Raphael Reischuk / pixelio.de

More available books at **www.hansebooks.com**

AN APOLOGY FOR THE LIFE OF

MR. COLLEY CIBBER

WRITTEN BY HIMSELF

A NEW EDITION WITH NOTES AND SUPPLEMENT

BY

ROBERT W. LOWE

WITH TWENTY-SIX ORIGINAL MEZZOTINT PORTRAITS BY

R. B. PARKES, AND EIGHTEEN ETCHINGS

BY ADOLPHE LALAUZE

IN TWO VOLUMES

VOLUME THE FIRST

LONDON

JOHN C. NIMMO

14, KING WILLIAM STREET, STRAND

MDCCCLXXXIX

PREFACE.

COLLEY CIBBER'S famous Autobiography has always been recognized as one of the most delightful books of its class ; but, to students of theatrical history, the charm of its author's ingenuous frankness has been unable altogether to overweigh the inaccuracy and vagueness of his treatment of matters of fact. To remove this cause of complaint is the principal object of the present edition. But correcting errors is only one of an editor's duties, and by no means the most difficult. More exacting, and almost equally important, are the illustration of the circumstances surrounding the author, the elucidation of his references to current events, and the comparison of his statements and theories with those of judicious contemporaries. In all these particulars I have interpreted my duty in the widest sense, and have aimed at giving, as far as in me lies, an exhaustive commentary on the "Apology."

I am fortunate in being able to claim that my work contains much information which has never before been made public. A careful investigation

of the MSS. in the British Museum, and of the
Records of the Lord Chamberlain's Office (to which
my access was greatly facilitated by the kindness of
Mr. Edward F. S. Pigott, the Licenser of Plays),
has enabled me to give the exact dates of many
transactions which were previously uncertain, and to
give references to documents of great importance
in stage history, whose very existence was before
unknown. How important my new matter is, may
be estimated by comparing the facts given in my
notes regarding the intricate transactions of the years
1707 to 1721, with any previous history of the same
period. Among other sources of information, I
may mention the Cibber Collections in the Forster
Library at South Kensington, to which my attention
was drawn by the kindness of the courteous keeper,
Mr. R. F. Sketchley; and I have also, of course,
devoted much time to contemporary newspapers.

In order to illustrate the "Apology," two tracts of
the utmost rarity, the "Historia Histrionica" and
Anthony Aston's "Brief Supplement" to Cibber's
Lives of the Actors, are reprinted in this edition.
The "Historia Histrionica" was written, all authorities agree, by James Wright, Barrister-at-Law,
whose "History and Antiquities of the County of
Rutland" is quoted by Cibber in his first chapter
(vol. i. p. 8). The historical value of this pamphlet
is very great, because it contains the only formal
account in existence of the generation of actors who
preceded Betterton, and because it gives many curious

and interesting particulars regarding the theatres and plays, as well as the actors, before and during the Civil Wars. As Cibber begins his account of the stage (see chap. iv.) at the Restoration, there is a peculiar propriety in prefacing it by Wright's work; a fact which has already been recognized, for the publisher of the third edition (1750) of the "Apology" appended to it "A Dialogue on Old Plays and Old Players," which is simply a reprint of the "Historia Histrionica" under another title, and without the curious preface.

Following the "Historia Histrionica" will be found a copy of the Patent granted to Sir William Davenant, one of the most important documents in English stage history. A similar grant was made to Thomas Killigrew, as is noted on page 87 of this volume.

These documents form a natural introduction to Cibber's History of the Stage and of his own career, which commences, as has been said, at the Restoration, and ends, somewhat abruptly, with his retirement from the regular exercise of his profession in 1733. To complete the record of Cibber's life, I have added a Supplementary Chapter to the "Apology," in which I have also noted briefly the chief incidents of theatrical history up to the time of his death. In this, too, I have told with some degree of minuteness the story of his famous quarrel with Pope; and to this chapter I have appended a list of Cibber's dramatic productions, and a Bibliography of works by, or relating to him.

Anthony Aston's " Brief Supplement to Colley Cibber, Esq; his Lives of the late famous Actors and Actresses," of which a reprint is given with this edition, is almost, if not quite, the rarest of theatrical books. Isaac Reed, says Genest, "wrote his name in his copy of Aston's little book, with the date of 1769—he says—'this Pamphlet contains several circumstances concerning the Performers of the last century, which are no where else to be found—it seems never to have been published'—he adds— 'Easter Monday, 1795—though I have now possessed this pamphlet 26 years, it is remarkable that I never have seen another copy of it.'" Of Aston himself, little is known. According to his own account he came on the stage about 1700, and we know that he was a noted stroller; but as to when he was born, or when he died, there is no information. He is supposed, and probably with justice, to be the "trusty Anthony, who has so often adorned both the theatres in England and Ireland," mentioned in Estcourt's advertisement of his opening of the Bumper Tavern, in the "Spectator" of 28th and 29th December, 1711; and he was no doubt a well-known character among actors and theatre-goers. He would thus be well qualified for his undertaking as biographer of the actors of his time; and, indeed, his work bears every mark of being the production of a writer thoroughly well acquainted with his subject. This valuable pamphlet has been, until now practically a sealed book to theatrical students.

The three works which make up this edition—
Cibber's "Apology," Wright's "Historia Histrionica,"
and Aston's "Brief Supplement"—are reprinted
verbatim et literatim; the only alterations made being
the correction of obvious errors. Among obvious
errors I include the avalanche of commas with which
Cibber's printers overwhelmed his text. A more
grotesque misuse of punctuation I do not know, and
I have struck out a large number of these points,
not only because they were unmeaning, but also
because, to a modern reader, they were irritating in
the highest degree. The rest of the punctuation I
have not interfered with, and with the single exception of these commas the present edition reproduces
not only the matter of the works reprinted, but the
very manner in which they originally appeared, the
use of italics and capitals having especially been carefully observed.

The "Apology" of Cibber has gone through six
editions. I have reprinted the text of the second,
because it was certainly revised by the author, and
many corrections made. But I have carefully compared my text with that of the first edition, and,
wherever the correction is more than merely verbal,
I have indicated the fact in a note (*c. g.* vol. i. p. 72).
The only edition which has been annotated is that
published in 1822, under the editorship of Edmund
Bellchambers. Whether the Notes were written by
the Editor or by Jacob Henry Burn, who annotated
Dickens's "Grimaldi," is a point which I have raised

in my "Bibliographical Account of English Theatrical Literature" (p. 373). I have been unable to
obtain any authentic information on the subject, so
give Burn's claim for what it is worth. The statement as to the latter's authorship was made in his
own handwriting on the back of the title-page of
a copy of the book, sold by a well-known book-
seller some years ago. It was in the following
terms :—

"In 1821, while residing at No. 28, Maiden Lane, Covent
Garden, the elder Oxberry, who frequently called in as he passed,
found me one day adding notes in MS. to Cibber's 'Apology.'
Taking it up, he said he should like to reprint it; he wanted
something to employ the spare time of his hands, and preferred
to buy my copy, thus annotated. I think it was two pounds I
said he should have it for; this sum he instantly paid, and the
notes throughout are mine, not Bellchambers's, who having seen
it through the press or corrected the proofs whilst printing, added
his name as the editor.—J. H. BURN."

Whether Burn or Bellchambers be the author, the
notes, I find, are by no means faultlessly accurate.
I have made little use of them, except that the Biographies, which are by far the most valuable of the
annotations, are reprinted at the end of my second
volume. Even in these, it will be seen, I have
corrected many blunders. Some of the memoirs I
have condensed slightly; and, as the Biographies of
Booth, Dogget, and Wilks were in all essential
points merely a repetition of Cibber's narrative, I
have not reprinted them. In all cases where I have
made any use of Bellchambers's edition, or have had

a reference suggested to me by it, I have carefully acknowledged my indebtedness.

Among the works of contemporary writers which I have quoted, either in illustration, in criticism, or in contradiction of Cibber, it will be noticed that I make large drafts upon the anonymous pamphlet entitled " The Laureat : or, the right side of Colley Cibber, Esq ; " (1740). I have done this because it furnishes the keenest criticism upon Cibber's statements, and gives, in an undeniably clever style, the views of Cibber's enemies upon himself and his works. I am unable even to guess who was the author of this work, but he must have been a man well acquainted with theatrical matters.

Another pamphlet from which I quote, " The Egotist: or, Colley upon Cibber" (1743), is interesting as being, I think without doubt, the work of Cibber himself, although not acknowledged by him.

Many of the works which I quote in my notes have gone through only one edition, and my quotations from these are easily traced ; but, for the convenience of those who may wish to follow up any of my references to books which have been more than once issued, I may mention that in the case of Davies's "Dramatic Miscellanies" I have referred throughout to the edition of 1785; that Dr. Birkbeck Hill's magnificent edition of Boswell's " Life of Johnson " is that which I have quoted ; and that the references to Nichols's reprint of Steele's " Theatre," the " Anti-Theatre," &c., are to the scarce and valuable

edition in 2 vols. 12mo, 1791.   My quotations from
the "Tatler" have been made from a set of the
original folio numbers, which I am fortunate enough
to possess; and I have made my extracts from the
"Roscius Anglicanus" from Mr. Joseph Knight's
beautiful facsimile edition.   The index, which will
be found at the end of the second volume, has been
the object of my special attention, and I have spared
no pains to make it clear and exhaustive.

ROBERT W. LOWE.

LONDON, *September*, 1888.

PUBLISHER'S PREFACE.

THE twenty-six portraits and eighteen chapter headings in this new edition of Colley Cibber's "Apology" are all newly engraved. The portraits are copperplate mezzotints, engraved by R. B. Parkes from the best and most authentic originals, in the selection of which great care has been taken. Where more than one portrait exists, the least hackneyed likeness has been chosen, and pains have been taken to secure those pictures which are likely to be esteemed as rarities. The chapter headings are etched by Adolphe Lalauze, and the subjects represent scenes from plays illustrating the costumes, manner, and appearance of the actors of Cibber's period, from contemporary authorities.

LONDON, *October*, 1888.

CONTENTS.

LIST OF MEZZOTINT PORTRAITS.

NEWLY ENGRAVED BY R. B. PARKES.

VOLUME THE FIRST.

b

LIST OF CHAPTER HEADINGS.

NEWLY ETCHED FROM CONTEMPORARY DRAWINGS BY ADOLPHE LALAUZE.

[1] Colley Cibber's "brazen brainless brothers." According to Horace Walpole, "one of the Statues was the portrait of Oliver Cromwell's porter, then in Bedlam."

HISTORIA HISTRIONICA:

AN
Hiſtorical Account
OF THE
Engliſh-Stage,
SHEWING

The ancient Uſe, Improvement, and Perfection, of Dramatick Repreſentations, in this Nation.

IN A

Dialogue, of *PLAYS* and *PLAYERS*.

—— *Olim meminiſſe juvabit.*

LONDON.

Printed by *G. Croom*, for *William Haws* at the Roſe in *Ludgate-ſtreet.* 1699.

THE PREFACE.

MUCH has been Writ of late pro *and* con, *about the Stage, yet the Subject admits of more, and that which has not been hetherto toucht upon ; not only what that is, but what it was, about which some People have made such a Busle. What it is we see, and I think it has been sufficiently display'd in Mr.* Collier's *Book; What it was in former Ages, and how used in this Kingdom, so far back as one may collect any Memorialls, is the Subject of the following Dialogue. Old Plays will be always read by the* Curious, *if it were only to discover the Manners and Behaviour of several Ages ; and how they alter'd. For Plays are exactly like* Portraits *Drawn in the Garb and Fashion of the time when Painted. You see one Habit in the time of King* Charles I. *another quite different from that, both for Men and Women, in Queen* Elizabeths *time; another under* Henry *the Eighth different from both; and so backward all various. And in the several Fashions of Behaviour and Conversation, there is as much Mutability as in that of cloaths. Religion and Religious matters was once as much the Mode in publick Entertainments, as the Contrary has been in*

*some times since. This appears in the different Plays
of several Ages: And to evince this, the following
Sheets are an Essay or Specimen.*

*Some may think the Subject of this Discourse
trivial, and the persons herein mention'd not worth
remembering. But besides that I could name some
things contested of late with great heat, of as little, or
less Consequence, the Reader may know that the Profession of Players is not so totally scandalous, nor all
of them so reprobate, but that there has been found
under that Name, a Canonized Saint in the primitive Church; as may be seen in the* Roman
Martyrology *on the* 29th *of* March; *his name*
Masculas *a Master of Interludes, (the Latin is*
Archimimus, *and the French translation* un Maitre
Comedien) *who under the Persecution of the* Vandals
in Africa, *by* Geisericus *the* Arian *King, having
endured many and greivious Torments and Reproaches
for the Confession of the Truth, finisht the Course of
this glorious Combat. Saith the said* Martyrology.

*It appears from this, and some further Instances in
the following Discourse, That there have been Players
of worthy Principles as to Religion, Loyalty, and other
Virtues; and if the major part of them fall under a
different Character, it is the general unhappiness of
Mankind, that the* Most *are the* Worst.

A

DIALOGUE

OF

PLAYS and PLAYERS.

Lovewit, Truman.

Lovew. Honest Old Cavalier! well met, 'faith I'm glad to see thee.

Trum. Have a care what you call me. Old, is a Word of Disgrace among the Ladies; to be Honest is to be Poor, and Foolish, (as some think) and Cavalier is a Word as much out of Fashion as any of 'em.

Lovew. The more's the pity: But what said the Fortune-Teller in *Ben. Johnson*'s Mask of *Gypsics*, to the then *Lord Privy Seal,*

Honest and Old !
In those the Good *Part of a Fortune is told.*

Trum. *Ben. Johnson?* How dare you name *Ben. Johnson* in these times? When we have such a crowd of Poets of a quite different Genius; the least of which thinks himself as well able to correct *Ben. Johnson*, as he could a Country School Mistress that taught to Spell.

Lovew. We have indeed, Poets of a different Genius; so are the Plays: but in my Opinion, they

are all of 'em (some few excepted) as much inferior
to those of former Times, as the Actors now in being
(generally speaking) are, compared to *Hart*, *Mohun*,
Burt, *Lacy*, *Clun*, and *Shatterel* ; for I can reach no
farther backward.

TRUM. I can ; and dare assure you, if my Fancy
and Memory are not partial (for Men of my Age
are apt to be over indulgent to the Thoughts of their
youthful Days) I say the Actors that I have seen
before the Wars, *Lowin*, *Tayler*, *Pollard*, and some
others, were almost as far beyond *Hart* and his
Company, as those were beyond these now in being.

LOVEW. I am willing to believe it, but cannot
readily ; because I have been told, That those whom
I mention'd, were Bred up under the others of your
Acquaintance, and follow'd their manner of Action,
which is now lost.   So far, that when the Question
has been askt, Why these Players do not revive
the *Silent Woman*, and some other of *Johnson*'s
Plays, (once of highest esteem) they have answer'd,
truly, Because there are none now Living who can
rightly Humour those Parts ; for all who related
to the *Black-friers*, (where they were Acted in perfection) are now Dead, and almost forgotten.

TRUM. 'Tis very true, *Hart* and *Clun*, were
bred up Boys at the *Black-friers*, and acted Womens
Parts, *Hart* was *Robinson*'s Boy or Apprentice : He
acted the Dutchess in the Tragedy of *the Cardinal*,
which was the first Part that gave him Reputation.
Cartwright, and *Wintershal* belong'd to the private

House in *Salisbury-court*, *Burt* was a Boy first under *Shank* at the *Black-friers*, then under *Beeston* at the *Cockpit*; and *Mohun*, and *Shatterel* were in the same Condition with him, at the last Place. There *Burt* used to Play the principal Women's Parts, in particular *Clariana* in *Love's Cruelty*; and at the same time *Mohun* acted *Bellamente*, which Part he retain'd after the Restauration.

LOVEW. That I have seen, and can well remember. I wish they had Printed in the last Age (so I call the times before the Rebellion) the Actors Names over against the Parts they Acted, as they have done since the Restauration. And thus one might have guest at the Action of the Men, by the Parts which we now Read in the Old Plays.

TRUM. It was not the Custome and Usage of those Days, as it hath been since. Yet some few Old Plays there are that have the Names set against the Parts, as, *The Dutchess of Malfy*; *the Picture*; *the Roman Actor*; *the deserving Favourite*; *the Wild Goose Chace*, (at the Black-friers) *the Wedding*; *the Renegado*; *the fair Maid of the West*; *Hannibal and Scipio*; *King John and Matilda*; (at the Cockpit) and *Holland's Leaguer*, (at Salisbury Court).

LOVEW. These are but few indeed : But pray Sir, what Master-Parts can you remember the Old *Black-friers* Men to Act, in *Johnson*, *Shakespear*, and *Fletcher's* Plays.

TRUM. What I can at present recollect I'll tell you; *Shakespear*, (who as I have heard, was a much better Poet, than Player) *Burbadge*, *Hemmings*, and others of the Older sort, were Dead before I knew the Town; but in my time, before the Wars, *Lowin* used to Act, with mighty Applause, *Falstaffe*, *Morose*, *Volpone*, and *Mammon* in the *Alchymist*; *Melancius*, in the *Maid's* Tragedy, and at the same time *Amyntor* was Play'd by *Stephen Hammerton*, (who was at first a most noted and beautiful Woman Actor, but afterwards he acted with equal Grace and Applause, a Young Lover's Part); *Tayler* Acted *Hamlet* incomparably well, *Jago*, *Truewit* in the *Silent Woman*, and *Face* in the *Alchymist*; *Swanston* used to Play *Othello*; *Pollard*, and *Robinson* were Comedians, so was *Shank* who us'd to Act Sir *Roger*, in *the Scornful Lady*. These were of the *Black-friers*. Those of principal Note at the *Cockpit*, were, *Perkins*, *Michael Bowyer*, *Sumner*, *William Allen*, and *Bird*, eminent Actors, and *Robins* a Comedian. Of the other Companies I took little notice.

Lovew. Were there so many Companies?

Trum. Before the Wars, there were in being all these Play-houses at the same time. The *Black-friers*, and *Globe* on the *Bankside*, a Winter and Summer House, belonging to the same Company, called the King's Servants; the *Cockpit* or *Phœnix*, in *Drury-lane*, called the Queen's Servants; the private House in *Salisbury-court*, called the Prince's Servants; the *Fortune* near *White-cross-street*, and the *Red Bull* at the upper end of St. *John's-street*:

The two last were mostly frequented by Citizens, and the meaner sort of People. All these Companies got Money, and Liv'd in Reputation, especially those of the *Black-friers*, who were Men of grave and sober Behaviour.

LOVEW. Which I admire at; That the Town much less than at present, could then maintain Five Companies, and yet now Two can hardly subsist.

TRUM. Do not wonder, but consider, That tho' the Town was then, perhaps, not much more than half so Populous as now, yet then the Prices were small (there being no Scenes) and better order kept among the Company that came; which made very good People think a Play an Innocent Diversion for an idle Hour or two, the Plays themselves being then, for the most part, more Instructive and Moral. Whereas of late, the Play-houses are so extreamly pestered with Vizard-masks and their Trade, (occasioning continual Quarrels and Abuses) that many of the more Civilized Part of the Town are uneasy in the Company, and shun the Theater as they would a House of Scandal. It is an Argument of the worth of the Plays and Actors, of the last Age, and easily inferr'd, that they were much beyond ours in this, to consider that they cou'd support themselves meerly from their own Merit; the weight of the Matter, and goodness of the Action, without Scenes and Machines: Whereas the present Plays with all that shew, can hardly draw an Audience, unless there be the additional Invitation of a *Signior Fideli*, a *Monsieur*

L'abbe, or some such Foreign Regale exprest in the bottom of the Bill.

LOVEW. To wave this Digression, I have Read of one *Edward Allin*, a Man so famed for excellent Action, that among *Ben. Johnson*'s epigrams, I find one directed to him, full of Encomium, and concluding thus

> *Wear this Renown, 'tis just that who did give*
> *So many Poets Life, by one should Live.*

Was he one of the *Black-friers*?

TRUM. Never, as I have heard; (for he was Dead before my time). He was Master of a Company of his own, for whom he Built the *Fortune* Playhouse from the Ground, a large, round Brick Building. This is he that grew so Rich that he purchased a great estate in *Surrey* and elsewhere; and having no Issue, He built and largely endow'd *Dulwich* College, in the Year 1619, for a Master, a Warden, Four Fellows, Twelve aged poor People, and Twelve poor Boys, &c. A noble Charity.

LOVEW. What kind of Play houses had they before the Wars?

TRUM. The *Black-friers*, *Cockpit*, and *Salisburycourt*, were called Private Houses, and were very small to what we see now. The *Cockpit* was standing since the Restauration, and *Rhode*'s Company Acted there for some time.

LOVEW. I have seen that.

TRUM. Then you have seen the other two, in effect; for they were all three Built almost exactly alike, for Form and Bigness. Here they had Pits for the Gentry, and Acted by Candle-light. The *Globe,* *Fortune* and *Bull,* were large Houses, and lay partly open to the Weather, and there they alwaies Acted by Daylight.

LOVEW. But, prithee, *Truman,* what became of these Players when the Stage was put down, and the Rebellion rais'd ?

TRUM. Most of 'em, except *Lowin, Tayler* and *Pollard* (who were superannuated) went into the King's Army, and like good Men and true, Serv'd their Old Master, tho' in a different, yet more honourable, Capacity. *Robinson* was Kill'd at the Taking of a Place, (I think *Basing House*) by *Harrison,* he that was after Hang'd at *Charing-cross,* who refused him Quarter, and Shot him in the Head when he had laid down his Arms ; abusing Scripture at the same time, in saying, *Cursed is he that doth the Work of the Lord negligently. Mohun* was a Captain, (and after the Wars were ended here, served in *Flanders,* where he received Pay as a Major) *Hart* was a Lieutenant of Horse under Sir *Thomas Dallison,* in *Prince Rupert's* Regiment, *Burt* was Cornet in the same Troop, and *Shatterel* Quarter-master. *Allen* of the *Cockpit,* was a Major, and Quarter Master General at *Oxford.* I have not heard of one of these Players of any Note that sided with the other Party, but only *Swanston,* and he profest himself a Presbyterian, took up the Trade of a Jeweller, and liv'd in *Alder-manbury,* within the Territory of Father *Calamy.* The rest either Lost, or expos'd their Lives for their King. When the Wars were over, and the Royalists totally Subdued, most of 'em who were left alive gather'd to *London*, and for a Subsistence endeavour'd to revive their Old Trade, privately. They made up one Company out of all the Scatter'd Members of Several; and in the Winter before the King's Murder, 1648, they ventured to Act some Plays with as much caution and privacy as cou'd be, at the *Cockpit*. They continu'd undisturbed for three or four Days; but at last as they were presenting the Tragedy of the *Bloudy Brother* (in which *Lowin* Acted Aubrey, *Tayler* Rollo, *Pollard* the Cook, *Burt* Latorch, and I think *Hart* Otto) a Party of Foot Souldiers beset the House, surpriz'd 'em about the midle of the Play, and carried 'em away in their habits, not admitting them to shift, to *Hatton-house*, then a Prison, where having detain'd them some time, they Plunder'd them of their Cloths and let 'em loose again. Afterwards in *Oliver*'s time, they used to Act privately, three or four Miles, or more, out of Town, now here, now there, sometimes in Noblemens Houses, in particular *Holland-house* at *Kensington*, where the Nobility and Gentry who met (but in no great Numbers) used to make a Sum for them, each giving a broad Peice, or the like. And *Alexander Goffe*, the Woman Actor at *Black-friers* (who had made himself known to Persons of Quality) used to be the Jackal, and give notice of Time and Place. At Christmass, and Bartlemew-fair, they used to Bribe the Officer who Commanded the Guard at *Whitehall*, and were thereupon connived at to Act for a few Days, at the *Red Bull*; but were sometimes notwithstanding Disturb'd by Soldiers. Some pickt up a little Money by publishing the Copies of Plays never before Printed, but kept up in Manuscript. For instance, in the Year 1652, *Beaumont* and *Fletcher*'s *Wild Goose Chace* was Printed in Folio, *for the Public use of all the Ingenious*, (as the Title-page says) *and private Benefit of* John Lowin *and* Joseph Tayler, *Servants to his late Majesty*; and by them Dedicated *To the Honour'd few Lovers of Dramatick Poesy*: Wherein they modestly intimate their Wants. And that with sufficient Cause; for whatever they were before the Wars, they were, after, reduced to a necessitous Condition. *Lowin* in his latter Days, kept an Inn (the three Pidgions) at *Brentford*, where he dyed very Old, (for he was an Actor of eminent Note in the Reign of K. *James* the first) and his Poverty was as great as his Age. *Tayler* Dyed at *Richmond* and was there Buried. *Pollard* who Lived Single, and had a Competent Estate; Retired to some Relations he had in the Country, and there ended his Life. *Perkins* and *Sumner* of the *Cockpit*, kept House together at *Clerkenwel*, and were there Buried. These all Dyed some Years before the Restauration. What follow'd after, I need not tell you: You can easily Remember.

LOVEW. Yes, presently after the Restauration, the King's Players Acted publickly at the *Red Bull* for some time, and then Removed to a New-built Play-

house in *Vere-street*, by *Claremarket*. There they
continued for a Year or two, and then removed to
the *Theater Royal* in *Drury-lane*, where they first
made use of Scenes, which had been a little before
introduced upon the publick Stage by Sir *William
Davenant* at the *Duke's Old Theater* in *Lincolns-
Inn-fields*, but afterwards very much improved, with
the Addition of curious Machines, by Mr. *Betterton*
at the New *Theater* in *Dorset-Garden*, to the great
Expence and continual Charge of the Players. This
much impair'd their Profit o'er what it was before;
for I have been inform'd, (by one of 'em) That for
several Years next after the Restauration, every whole
Sharer in Mr. *Hart's* Company, got 1000*l. per an.*
About the same time that Scenes first enter'd upon
the Stage at *London*, Women were taught to Act their
own Parts ; since when, we have seen at both Houses
several excellent Actresses, justly famed as well for
Beauty, as perfect good Action. And some Plays (in
particular *The Parson's Wedding*) have been Presented all by Women, as formerly all by Men. Thus
it continued for about 20 Years, when Mr. *Hart* and
some of the Old Men began to grow weary, and were
minded to leave off ; then the two Companies thought
fit to Unite ; but of late, you see, they have thought it
no less fit to Divide again, though both Companies
keep the same Name of his Majesty's Servants. All
this while the Play-house Musick improved Yearly,
and is now arrived to greater Perfection than ever I
knew it. Yet for all these Advantages, the Reputation

of the Stage, and Peoples Affection to it, are much Decay'd. Some were lately severe against it, and would hardly allow Stage-Plays fit to be longer permitted. Have you seen Mr. *Collier's* book ?

TRUM. Yes, and his Opposer's.

LOVEW. And what think you ?

TRUM. In my mind Mr. *Collier's* Reflections are Pertinent, and True in the Main ; the Book ingeniously Writ, and well Intended : But he has overshot himself in some Places ; and his Respondents, perhaps, in more. My Affection inclines me not to Engage on either side, but rather Mediate. If there be Abuses relating to the Stage ; (which I think is too apparent) let the Abuse be Reformed, and not the use, for that Reason only, Abolish'd. 'Twas an Old saying when I was a Boy,

Absit Abusus, non desit totaliter Usus.

I shall not run through Mr. *Collier's* Book ; I will only touch a little on two or three general Notions, in which, I think he may be mistaken. What he urges out of the Primitive Councils, and Fathers of the Church, seems to me to be directed against the Heathen Plays, which were a sort of Religious Worship with them, to the Honour of *Ceres*, *Flora*, or some of their false Deities ; they had always a little Altar on their Stages, as appears plain enough from some places in *Plautus*. And Mr. *Collier* himself, p. 235, tells us out of *Livy*, that Plays were brought in upon the Score of Religion, to pacify the Gods. No wonder

c

then, they forbid Christians to be present at them,
for it was almost the same as to be present at their
Sacrifices. We must also observe that this was in
the Infancy of Christianity, when the Church was
under severe, and almost continual Persecutions, and
when all its true Members were of most strict and
exemplary Lives, not knowing when they should be
call'd to the Stake, or thrown to Wild-Beasts. They
communicated Daily, and expected Death hourly ;
their thoughts were intent upon the next World, they
abstain'd almost wholly from all Diversions and pleasures (though lawfull and Innocent) in this. Afterwards when Persecution ceased, and the church
flourisht, Christians being then freed from their
former Terrors, allow'd themselves, at proper times,
the lawfull Recreations of Conversation, and among
other (no doubt) this of Shewes and Representations.
After this time, the Censures of the Church indeed,
might be continued, or revived, upon occasion,
against Plays and Players ; tho' (in my Opinion) it
cannot be understood generally, but only against such
Players who were of Vicious and Licencious Lives,
and represented profane Subjects, inconsistant with
the Morals and probity of Manners requisite to
Christians ; and frequented chiefly by such loose and
Debaucht People, as were much more apt to Corrupt
than Divert those who associated with them. I say, I
cannot think the Canons and Censures of the Fathers
can be applyed to all Players, *qualenus* Players ; for
if so how could Plays be continued among the Chris-

tians, as they were, of Divine Subjects, and Scriptural
Stories? A late French Author, speaking of the
Original of the *Hotel de Bourgogne* (a Play-house in
Paris) says that the ancient Dukes of that Name
gave it to the Brotherhood of the Passion, established in the Church of Trinity-Hospital in the
Rue S. Denis, on condition that they should represent here Interludes of Devotion: And adds that
there have been public Shews in this Place 600
Years ago. The Spanish and Portuguize continue
still to have, for the most part, such Ecclesiastical
Stories, for the Subject of their Plays: And, if we
may believe *Gage*, they are Acted in their Churches
in *Mexico*, and the Spanish *West-Indies*.

LOVEW. That's a great way off, *Truman*; I had
rather you would come nearer Home, and confine
your discourse to Old *England*.

TRUM. So I intend. The same has been done
here in *England*; for otherwise how comes it to be
prohibited in the 88*th* Canon, among those past in
Convocation, 1603. Certain it is that our ancient
Plays were of Religious Subjects, and had for their
Actors, (if not Priests) yet Men relating to the Church.

LOVEW. How does that appear?

TRUM. Nothing clearer. *Stow* in his Survey of
London, has one Chapter *of the Sports and Pas-
times of old time used in this City*; and there he
tells us, That in the Year 1391 (which was 15
R. 2.) a Stage-Play was play'd by the Parish-
Clerks of *London*,. at the *Skinner's-well* beside

Smithfield, which Play continued three Days together, the King, Queen, and Nobles of the Realm
being present.   And another was play'd in the Year
1409, (11 *H.* 4.) which lasted eight Days, and was
of Matter from the Creation of the World ; whereat
was present most part of the Nobility and Gentry of
England. Sir *William Dugdale*, in his Antiquities
of *Warwickshire*, p. 116, speaking of the *Gray-friers*
(or *Franciscans*) at *Coventry*, says, Before the suppression of the Monasteries, this City was very
famous for the Pageants that were play'd therein
upon *Corpus-Christi* Day ; which Pageants being
acted with mighty State and Reverence by the Friers
of this House, had Theatres for the several Scenes
very large and high, plac'd upon Wheels, and drawn
to all the eminent Parts of the City, for the better
advantage of the Spectators ; and contain'd the Story
of the New Testament, composed in old English
Rhime.   An ancient Manuscript of the same is now
to be seen in the *Cottonian* Library, *Sub Effig.*
Vespat. D. 8.   Since the Reformation, in Queen
Elizabeth's time, Plays were frequently acted by
Quiristers and Singing Boys ; and several of our old
Comedies have printed in the Title Page, *Acted by*
the Children of Paul's, (not the School, but the
Church) others, *By the Children of Her Majesty's*
Chappel ; in particular, *Cinthias Revels*, and the
Poetaster were play'd by them ; who were at that
time famous for good Action.   Among *Ben. John-*
son's Epigrams you may find *An Epitaph on S. P.*

(Sal Pavy) *one of the Children of Queen* Elizabeth's *Chappel*, part of which runs thus,

> *Years he counted scarce Thirteen*
> *When Fates turn'd Cruel,*
> *Yet three fill'd Zodiacks he had been*
> *The Stages Jewell;*
> *And did act (what now we moan)*
> *Old Men so duly,*
> *As, sooth, the* Parcæ *thought him one,*
> *He play'd so truly.*

Some of these Chappel Boys, when they grew Men, became Actors at the *Black-friers*; such were *Nathan Feild*, and *John Underwood*. Now I can hardly imagine that such Plays and Players as these, are included in the severe Censure of the Councils and Fathers; but such only who are truly within the Character given by *Didacus de Tapia*, cited by Mr. *Collier*, p. 276, *viz. The Infamous Playhouse; a place of contradiction to the strictness and sobriety of Religion; a place hated by God, and haunted by the Devil.* And for such I have as great an abhorrance as any man.

LOVEW. Can you guess of what Antiquity the representing of Religious Matters, on the Stage, hath been in *England?*

TRUM. How long before the Conquest I know not, but that it was used in *London* not long after, appears by *Fitz-Stevens*, an Author who wrote in the reign of King *Henry* the Second. His words are, *Londonia pro spectaculis theatralibus, pro ludis scenicis, ludos habet sanctiores, Representationes mira-*

culorum, quæ sancti Confessores operati sunt, seu Representationes passionum quibus claruit constantia Martyrum. Of this, the Manuscript which I lately mention'd, in the *Cottonian* Library, is a notable instance. Sir *William Dugdale* cites this Manuscript, by the Title of *Ludus Coventriæ* ; but in the printed Catalogue of that Library, p. 113, it is named thus, *A Collection of Plays in old English Metre.* h. e. *Dramata sacra in quibus exhibentur historiæ Veteris & N. Testamenti, introductis quasi in Scenam personis illic memoratis, quas secum invicem colloquentes pro ingenio fingit Poeta. Videntur olim coram populo, sive ad instruendum sive ad placendum, a fratribus mendicantibus repræsentata.* It appears by the latter end of the Prologue, that these Plays or Interludes, were not only play'd at *Coventry*, but in other Towns and Places upon occasion. And possibly this may be the same Play which *Stow* tells us was play'd in the reign of King *Henry* IV., which lasted for Eight Days. The Book seems by the Character and Language to be at least 300 Years old. It begins with a general Prologue, giving the arguments of 40 Pageants or Gesticulations (which were as so many several Acts or Scenes) representing all the Histories of both Testaments, from the Creation, to the choosing of St. *Mathias* to be an Apostle. The Stories of the New Testament are more largely exprest, *viz.* The Annunciation, Nativity, Visitation ; but more especially all Matters relating to the Passion very particularly, the Resurrection, Ascention, the choice of St. *Mathias* : After which is also represented the Assumption, and last Judgment. All these things were treated of in a very homely style, (as we now think) infinitely below the Dignity of the Subject : But it seems the Gust of that Age was not so nice and delicate in these Matters ; the plain and incurious Judgment of our Ancestors, being prepared with favour, and taking every thing by the right and easiest Handle : For example, in the Scene relating to the Visitation :

Maria. But husband of oo thyng pray you most mekely,
I haue knowing that our Cosyn Elizabeth with childe is,
That it please yow to go to her hastyly,
If ought we myth comfort her it wer to me blys.

Joseph. A Gods sake, is she with child, sche ?
Than will her husband Zachary be mery.
In Montana they dwelle, fer hence, so moty the,
In the city of Juda, I know it verily ;
It is hence I trowe myles two a fifty,
We ar like to be wery or we come at the same.
I wole with a good will, blessyd wyff Mary ;
Now go we forth then in goddys name, &c.

A little before the Resurrection :

Nunc dormient milites, & veniet anima Christi de inferno, cum Adam & Eva, Abraham, John Baptist, & *aliis.*

Anima Christi. Come forth Adam, and Eve with the,
And all my fryndes that herein be,
In Paradys come forth with me
    In blysse for to dwelle.
The fende of hell that is yowr foo
He shall be wrappyd and woundyn in woo :
Fro wo to welth now shall ye go,
    With myrth euer mor to melle.

> *Adam.* I thank the Lord of thy grete grace
> That now is forgiuen my gret trespace,
> Now shall we dwellyn in blyssful pace, &c.

The last Scene or Pageant, which represents the Day of Judgment, begins thus:

> *Michael. Surgite,* All men aryse,
> *Venite ad judicium,*
> For now is set the High Justice,
> And hath assignyd the day of Dome:
> Kepe you redyly to this grett assyse,
> Both gret and small, all and sum,
> And of yowr answer you now advise,
> What you shall say when that yow com, &c.

These and such like, were the Plays which in former Ages were presented publickly: Whether they had any settled and constant Houses for that purpose, does not appear; I suppose not. But it is notorious that in former times there was hardly ever any Solemn Reception of Princes, or Noble Persons, but Pageants (that is Stages Erected in the open Street) were part of the Entertainment. On which there were Speeches by one or more Persons, in the nature of Scenes; and be sure one of the Speakers must be some Saint of the same Name with the Party to whom the Honour is intended. For instance, there is an ancient Manuscript at *Coventry*, call'd the *Old Leet Book*, wherein is set down in a very particular manner, (fo. 168) the reception of Queen *Margaret*, wife of *H.* 6, who came to *Coventry* (and I think, with her, her young Son, Prince *Edward*) on the Feast of the Exaltation of the Holy-Cross, 35

II. 6. (1456). Many Pageants and Speeches were made for her Welcome; out of all which, I shall observe but two or three, in the Old English, as it is Recorded.

St. Edward. Moder of mekenes, Dame Margarete, princes most excellent,
I King Edward wellcome you with affection cordial,
Certefying to your highnes mekely myn entent,
For the wele of the King and you hertily pray I shall,
And for prince Edward my gostly chylde, who I love principal.
Praying the, John Evangelist, my help therein to be,
On that condition right humbly I giue this Ring to the.

John Evangelist. Holy Edward crowned King, Brother in Verginity,
My power plainly I will prefer thy will to amplefy.
Most excellent princes of wymen mortal, your Bedeman will I be.
I know your Life so vertuous that God is pleased thereby.
The birth of you unto this Reme shall cause great Melody :
The vertuous voice of Prince Edward shall dayly well encrease,
St. Edward his Godfader and I shall pray therefore doubtlese.

St. Margaret. Most notabul princes of wymen earthle,
Dame Margarete, the chefe myrth of this Empyre,
Ye be hertely welcome to this Cyte.
To the plesure of your highnesse I wyll set my desyre ;
Both nature and gentlenesse doth me require,
Seth we be both of one name, to shew you kindnesse ;
Wherefore by my power ye shall have no distresse.

I shall pray to the Prince that is endlese
To socour you with solas of his high grace ;
He will here my petition this is doubtlesse,
For I wrought all my life that his will wace.
Therefore, Lady, when you be in any dredfull case,
Call on me boldly, thereof I pray you,
And trust in me feythfully, I will do that may pay you.

In the next Reign (as appears in the same Book,

fo. 221) an other Prince *Edward*, Son of King *Edward* the 4, came to *Coventry* on the 28 of *April*, 14 *E*. 4, (1474) and was entertain'd with many Pageants and Speeches, among which I shall observe only two : one was of St. *Edward* again, who was then made to speak thus,

> Noble Prince Edward, my Cousin and my Knight,
> And very Prince of our Line com yn dissent,
> I Saint Edward have pursued for your faders imperial Right,
> Whereof he was excluded by full furious intent.
> Unto this your Chamber as prince full excellent
> Ye be right welcome. Thanked be Crist of his sonde,
> For that that was ours is now in your faders honde.

The other Speech was from St. *George*; and thus saith the Book.

> ———— Also upon the Condite in the Croscheping was St. George armed, and a kings daughter kneling afore him with a Lamb, and the fader and the moder being in a Towre aboven beholding St. George saving their daughter from the Dragon, and the Condite renning wine in four places, and Minstralcy of Organ playing, and St. George hauing this Speech under-written.

> O mighty God our all succour celestiall,
> Which this Royme hast given in dower
> To thi moder, and to me George protection perpetuall
> It to defend from enimys fer and nere,
> And as this mayden defended was here
> By thy grace from this Dragons devour,
> So, Lord preserve this noble prince, and ever be his socour.

Lovew. I perceive these holy Matters consisted very much of Praying ; but I pitty poor St. *Edward* the Confessor, who in the compass of a few Years, was made to promise his favour and assistance to two young Princes of the same Name indeed, but of as different and opposite Interests as the two Poles. I know not how he could perform to both.

TRUM. Alas! they were both unhappy, notwith-standing these fine Shews and seeming caresses of Fortune, being both murder'd, one by the Hand, the other by the procurement of *Rich.* Duke of *Glocester.* I will produce but one Example more of this sort of Action, or Representations, and that is of later time, and an instance of much higher Nature than any yet mentioned, it was at the marriage of Prince *Arthur,* eldest Son of king *Henry* 7. to the Princess *Catherine* of *Spain, An.* 1501. Her passage through *London* was very magnificent, as I have read it described in an old M.S. Chronicle of that time. The Pageants and Speeches were many; the Persons represented St. *Catherine,* St. *Ursula,* a Senator, Noblesse, Virtue, an Angel, King *Alphonse, Job, Boetius,* &c. among others one is thus described.

When this Spech was ended, she held on her way tyll she cam unto the Standard in Chepe, where was ordeyned the fifth Pagend made like an hevyn, theryn syttyng a Personage represent-ing the fader of hevyn, beyng all formyd of Gold, and brennying beffor his trone vii Candyilis of wax standyng in vii Candyl-stykis of Gold, the said personage beyng environed wyth sundry Hyrarchies off Angelis, and sytting in a Cope of most rich cloth of Tyssu, garnishyd wyth stoon and perle in most sumptuous wyse. Foragain which said Pagend upon the sowth syde of the strete stood at that tyme, in a hows wheryn that tyme dwellyd *William Geffrey* habyrdasher, the king, the Quene, my Lady the Kingys moder, my Lord of *Oxynfford,* with many othir Lordys and Ladys, and Perys of this Realm, wyth also certayn Ambas-sadors of France lately sent from the French King; and so

passyng the said Estatys, eyther guyvyng to other due and con-
venyent Saluts and Countenancs, so sone as hyr grace was
approachid unto the sayd Pagend, the fadyr began his Spech as
folowyth :

Hunc veneram locum, septeno lumine septum.
Dignumque Arthuri *totidem astra micant.*

I am begynyng and ende, that made ech creature
My sylfe, and for my sylfe, but man esspecially
Both male and female, made aftyr myne aun fygure,
Whom I joyned togydyr in Matrimony
And that in Paradyse, declaring opynly
That men shall weddyng in my Chyrch solempnize,
Fygurid and signifyed by the erthly Paradyze.

In thys my Chyrch I am allway recydent
As my chyeff tabernacle, and most chosyn place,
Among these goldyn candylstikkis, which represent
My Catholyk Chyrch, shynyng affor my face,
With lyght of feyth, wisdom, doctryne, and grace,
And mervelously eke enflamyd toward me
Wyth the extyngwible fyre of Charyte.

Wherefore, my welbelovid dowgthyr Katharyn,
Syth I have made yow to myne awn semblance
In my Chyrch to be maried, and your noble Childryn
To regn in this land as in their enherytance,
Se that ye have me in speciall remembrance :
Love me and my Chyrch yowr spiritual modyr,
For ye dispysing that oon, dyspyse that othyr.

Look that ye walk in my precepts, and obey them well :
And here I give you the same blyssyng that I
Gave my well beloved chylder of Israell;
Blyssyd be the fruyt of your bely;
Yower substance and frutys I shall encrease and multyply;
Yower rebellious Enimyes I shall put in yowr hand,
Encreasing in honour both yow and yowr land.

LOVEW. This would be censured now a days as
profane to the highest degree.

TRUM. No doubt on't : Yet you see there was a time when People were not so nicely censorious in these Matters, but were willing to take things in the best sence : and then this was thought a noble Entertainment for the greatest King in *Europe* (such I esteem King *H*. 7. at that time) and proper for that Day of mighty Joy and Triumph. And I must farther observe out of the Lord *Bacon*'s History of *H*. 7. that the chief Man who had the care of that Days Proceedings was Bishop *Fox*, a grave Councelor for War or Peace, and also a good Surveyor of Works, and a good Master of Cerimonies, and it seems he approv'd it. The said Lord *Bacon* tells us farther, That whosoever had those Toys in compiling, they were not altogether Pedantical.

LOVEW. These things however are far from that which we understand by the name of a Play.

TRUM. It may be so ; but these were the Plays of those times. Afterwards in the Reign of K. *H*. 8. both the Subject and Form of these Plays began to alter, and have since varied more and more. I have by me, a thing called *A merry Play between the Pardoner and the Frere, the Curate and Neybour Pratte*. Printed the 5 of *April* 1533, which was 24 *H*. 8. (a few Years before the Dissolution of Monasteries). The design of this Play was to redicule Friers and Pardoners. Of which I'll give you a taste. To begin it, the Fryer enters with these Words,

Deus hic ; the holy Trynyte
Preserue all that now here be.

> Dere bretherne, yf ye will consyder
> The Cause why I am com hyder,
> Ye wolde be glad to knowe my entent ;
> For I com not hyther for mony nor for rent,
> I com not hyther for meat nor for meale,
> But I com hyther for your Soules heale, &c.

After a long Preamble, he addresses himself to Preach, when the Pardoner enters with these Words,

> God and St. Leonarde send ye all his grace
> As many as ben assembled in this place, &c.

And makes a long Speech, shewing his Bulls and his Reliques, in order to sell his Pardons for the raising some Money towards the rebuilding,

> Of the holy Chappell of sweet saynt Leonarde,
> Which late by fyre was destroyed and marde.

Both these speaking together, with continual interruption, at last they fall together by the Ears. Here the Curate enters (for you must know the Scene lies in the Church)

> Hold your hands ; a vengeance on ye both two
> That euer ye came hyther to make this ado,
> To polute my Chyrche, &c.

> *Fri.* Mayster Parson, I marvayll ye will give Lycence
> To this false knaue in this Audience
> To publish his ragman rolles with lyes.
> I desyred hym ywys more than ones or twyse
> To hold his peas tyll that I had done,
> But he would here no more than the man in the mone.

> *Pard.* Why sholde I suffre the, more than thou me ?
> Mayster parson gaue me lycence before the.
> And I wolde thou knowest it I have relykes here,
> Other maner stuffe than thou dost bere :

I wyll edefy more with the syght of it,
Than will all thy pratynge of holy wryt;
For that except that the precher himselfe lyve well,
His predycacyon wyll helpe never a dell, &c.

Pars. No more of this wranglyng in my Chyrch:
I shrewe your hertys bothe for this lurche.
Is there any blood shed here between these knaues?
Thanked be god they had no stauys,
Nor egotoles, for then it had ben wronge.
Well, ye shall synge another songe.

Here he calls his Neighbour *Prat* the Constable, with design to apprehend 'em, and set 'em in the Stocks. But the Frier and Pardoner prove sturdy, and will not be stockt, but fall upon the poor Parson and Constable, and bang 'em both so well-favour'dly, that at last they are glad to let 'em go at liberty: And so the Farce ends with a drawn Battail. Such as this were the Plays of that Age, acted in Gentlemens Halls at Christmas, or such like festival times, by the Servants of the Family, or Strowlers who went about and made it a Trade. It is not unlikely that* Lords in those days, and Persons of eminent Quality, had their several Gangs of Players, as some have now of Fidlers, to whom they give Cloaks and Badges. The first Comedy that I have seen that looks like regular, is *Gammer Gurton's Needle*, writ I think in the reign of King *Edward* 6. This is composed of five Acts, the Scenes unbroken, and the unities of Time and Place duly

* Till the 25 Year of Queen *Elizabeth*, the Queen had not any Players; but in that Year 12 of the best of all those who belonged to several Lords, were chosen & sworn her Servants, as Grooms of the Chamber. Stow's *Annals*, p. 698.

observed.   It was acted at *Christ* Colledge in *Cambridge*; there not being as yet any settled and publick Theaters.

LOVEW. I observe, *Truman*, from what you have said, that Plays in *England* had a beginning much like those of *Greece*, the Monologues and the Pageants drawn from place to place on Wheels, answer exactly to the Cart of *Thespis*, and the Improvements have been by such little steps and degrees as among the Ancients, till at last, to use the Words of Sir *George Buck* (in his *Third University of* England) *Dramatick Poesy is so lively exprest and represented upon the publick Stages and Theatres of this City*, as Rome *in the* Auge (*the highest pitch*) *of her Pomp and Glory, never saw it better perform'd, I mean* (says he) *in respect of the Action and Art, and not of the Cost and Sumptiousness.*   This he writ about the Year 1631.   But can you inform me *Truman*, when publick Theaters were first erected for this purpose in *London*?

TRUM. Not certainly; but I presume about the beginning of Queen *Elizabeths* Reign.   For *Stow* in his Survey of *London* (which Book was first printed in the Year 1598) says, *Of late Years, in place of these Stage-plays* (i. e. those of Religious Matters) *have been used Comedies, Tragedies, Interludes, and Histories, both true and feigned; for the acting whereof certain publick Places, as the Theatre, the Curtine, &c. have been erected.*   And the continuator of *Stows* Annals, p. 1004, says, That in Sixty Years

before the publication of that Book, (which was *An.
Dom.* 1629) no less than 17 publick Stages, or
common Playhouses, had been built in and about
London. In which number he reckons five Inns or
Common Osteries, to have been in his time turned
into Play-houses, one Cock-pit, St. *Paul's* singing
School, one in the *Blackfriers,* one in the *Whitefriers,*
and one in former time at *Newington* Buts; and
adds, before the space of 60 years past, I never
knew, heard, or read, of any such Theaters, set
Stages, or Playhouses, as have been purposely built
within Man's Memory.

LOVEW. After all, I have been told, that Stage-
Plays are inconsistant with the Laws of this Kingdom, and Players made Rogues by Statute.

TRUM. He that told you so strain'd a point of
Truth. I never met with any Law wholly to sup-
press them : Sometimes indeed they have been pro-
hibited for a Season; as in times of *Lent,* general
Mourning or publick Calamities, or upon other
occasions, when the Government saw fit. Thus by
Proclamation, 7 of *April,* in the first Year of Queen
Elizabeth, Plays and Interludes were forbid till *All
hallow-tide* next following. *Hollinshed,* p. 1184. Some
Statutes have been made for their Regulation or
Reformation, not general suppression. By the Stat.
39 *Eliz.* c. 4, (which was made *for the suppressing of
Rogues, Vagabonds and sturdy Beggars*) it is enacted,

S. 2, That all persons that be, or utter themselves to be,
Proctors, Procurers, Patent gatherers, or Collectors for Gaols,

d

Prisons or Hospitals, or Fencers, Barewards, common players of
Interludes and Ministrels, wandering abroad, (other than Players
of Interludes belonging to any Baron of this Realm, or any other
honourable Personage of greater Degree, to be authoriz'd to play
under the Hand and Seal of Arms of such Baron or Personage)
All Juglers, Tinkers, Pedlers, and Petty chapmen, wandering
abroad, all wandring Persons, &c. able in Body, using loytering,
and refusing to work for such reasonable Wages as is commonly
given, &c. These shall be ajudged and deemed Rogues, Vagabonds and sturdy Beggars, and punished as such.

LOVEW. But this priviledge of Authorizing or
Licensing, is taken away by the Stat. 1 *Ja*. 1. ch. 7, S. 1,
and therefore all of them (as Mr. *Collier* says, p. 242)
are expresly brought under the foresaid Penalty,
without distinction.

TRUM. If he means all Players, without distinction, 'tis a great Mistake. For the force of the
Queens Statute extends only to *wandring Players*,
and not to such as are the King or Queen's Servants, and establisht in settled Houses by Royal
Authority. On such, the ill Character of vagrant
Players (or as they are now called, Strolers) can
cast no more aspersion, than the wandring Proctors,
in the same Statute mentioned, on those of *Doctors-
Commons*. By a Stat. made 3 *Ja*. I. ch. 21. It
was enacted,

That if any person shall in any Stage-play, Enterlude, Shew,
Maygame, or Pageant, jestingly or prophanely speak or use the
holy name of God, Christ Jesus, the holy Ghost, or of the Trinity,
he shall forfeit for every such offence, 10*l*.

The Stat. 1 *Char*. I. ch. 1, enacts,

That no Meetings, Assemblies, or concourse of People shall be out of their own Parishes, on the Lords day, for any Sports or Pastimes whatsoever, nor any Bear-bating, Bull-bating, Enterludes, Common Plays, or other unlawful Exercises and Pastimes used by any person or persons within their own Parishes.

These are all the Statutes that I can think of relating to the Stage and Players; but nothing to suppress them totally, till the two Ordinances of the Long Parliament, one of the 22 of *October* 1647, the other of the 11 of *Feb.* 1647. By which all Stage-Plays and Interludes are absolutely forbid; the Stages, Seats, Galleries, *&c.* to be pulled down; all Players tho' calling themselves the King or Queens Servants, if convicted of acting within two Months before such Conviction, to be punished as Rogues according to Law; the Money received by them to go to the Poor of the Parish; and every Spectator to Pay 5*s.* to the use of the Poor. Also Cock-fighting was prohibited by one of *Oliver*'s Acts of 31 *Mar.* 1654. But I suppose no body pretends these things to be Laws; I could say more on this Subject, but I must break off here, and leave you, *Lovewit* ; my Occasions require it.

LOVE. Farewel, Old *Cavalier*.

TRUM. 'Tis properly said ; we are almost all of us, now, gone and forgotten.

A Copy of the LETTERS PATENTS then granted by King Charles II. under the Great Seal of England, to SIR WILLIAM D'AVENANT, KNT. his Heirs and Assigns, for erecting a new Theatre, and establishing of a company of actors in any place within London or Westminster, or the Suburbs of the same : And that no other but this company, and one other company, by virtue of a like Patent, to THOMAS KILLIGREW, ESQ. ; should be permitted within the said liberties.

CHARLES the second, by the Grace of God, king of England, Scotland, France, and Ireland, defender of the faith, &c. to all to whom all these presents shall come, greeting.

Whereas our royal father of glorious memory, by his letters patents under his great seal of England bearing date at Westminster the 26th day of March, in the 14th year of his reign, did give and grant unto Sir William D'avenant (by the name of William D'avenant, gent.) his heirs, executors, administrators,

Recites former patents, 14 Car. I. ann. 1639, to Sir Will. D'avenant.

and assigns, full power, licence, and authority, That he, they, and every of them, by him and themselves, and by all and every such person and persons as he or they should depute or appoint, and his and their laborers, servants, and workmen, should and might, lawfully, quietly, and peaceably, frame, erect, new build, and set up, upon a parcel of ground, lying near unto or behind the Three Kings ordinary in Fleet-street, in the parishes of St. Dunstan's in the West, London; or in St. Bride's, London; or in either of them, or in any other ground in or about that place, or in the whole street aforesaid, then allotted to him for that use; or in any other place that was, or then after should be assigned or allotted out to the said Sir William D'avenant by Thomas Earl of Arundel and Surry, then Earl Marshal of England, or any other commissioner for building, for the time being in that behalf, a theatre or play-house, with necessary tiring and retiring rooms, and other places convenient, containing in the whole forty yards square at the most, wherein plays, musical entertainments, scenes, or other the like presentments might be presented. And our said royal father did grant unto the said Sir William D'avenant, his heirs, executors, and administrators and assignes, that it should and might be lawful·to and for him the said Sir William D'avenant, his heirs, executors, administrators, and assignes, from time to time, to gather together, entertain, govern, privilege, and keep, such and so many players and persons to exercise actions, musical presentments, scenes, dancing, and the like, as he the said Sir William D'avenant, his heirs, executors, administrators, or assignes, should think fit and approve for the said house. And such persons to permit and continue, at and during the pleasure of the said Sir William D'avenant, his heirs, executors, administrators, or assignes, from time to time, to act plays in such house so to be by him or them erected, and exercise musick, musical presentments, scenes, dancing, or other the like, at the same or other houses or times, or after plays are ended, peaceably and quietly, without the impeachment or impediment of any person or persons whatsoever, for the honest recreation of such as should desire to see the same ; and that it should and might be lawful to and for the said Sir William D'avenant, his heirs, executors, administrators, and assigns, to take and receive of such as should resort to see or hear any such plays, scenes, and entertainments whatsoever, such sum or sums of money as was or then after, from time to time, should be accustomed to be given or taken in other play-houses and places for the like plays, scenes, presentments, and entertainments as in and by the said letters patents, relation being thereunto had, more at large may appear.

And whereas we did, by our letters patents under the great seal of England, bearing date the 16th day of May, in the 13th year of our reign, exemplifie

13 Car. II. exemplification of said letters patents.

the said recited letters patents granted by our royal
father, as in and by the same, relation being thereunto had, at large may appear.

Surrender of
both to the king
in the court of
Chancery.
And whereas the said Sir William
D'avenant hath surrendered our letters
patents of exemplification, and also the
said recited letters patents granted by
our royal father, into our Court of Chancery, to be
cancelled; which surrender we have accepted, and
do accept by these presents.

New grant to Sir
William D'ave-
nant, his heirs
and assignes.
Know ye that we of our especial
grace, certain knowledge, and meer
motion, and upon the humble petition
of the said Sir William D'avenant, and
in consideration of the good and faithful service
which he the said Sir William D'avenant hath done
unto us, and doth intend to do for the future; and
in consideration of the said surrender, have given
and granted, and by these presents, for us, our heirs
and successors, do give and grant, unto the said Sir
William D'avenant, his heirs, executors, administrators, and assigns, full power, licence, and authority,
that he, they, and every one of them, by him and
themselves, and by all and every such person and
persons as he or they should depute or appoint, and
his or their labourers, servants, and workmen, shall

To erect a thea-
tre in London
or Westmister,
or the suburbs.
and may lawfully, peaceably, and quietly,
frame, erect, new build, and set up, in
any place within our cities of London
and Westminster, or the suburbs thereof,

where he or they shall find best accommodation for
that purpose; to be assigned and allotted out by the
surveyor of our works; one theatre or play-house,
with necessary tiring and retiring rooms, and other
places convenient, of such extent and dimention as
the said Sir William D'avenant, his heirs or assigns
shall think fitting : wherein tragedies, comedies,
plays, operas, musick, scenes, and all other entertainments of the stage whatsoever, may be shewed
and presented.

And we do hereby, for us, our heirs and successors,
grant unto the said Sir William D'avenant, his heirs
and assigns, full power, licence, and authority, from
time to time, to gather together, entertain, govern,
priviledge and keep, such and so many
players and persons to exercise and act
tragedies, comedies, plays, operas, and
other performances of the stage, within
the house to be built as aforesaid, or
within the house in Lincoln's-Inn-Fields, wherein
the said Sir William D'avenant doth now exercise
the premises ; or within any other house, where he
or they can best be fitted for that purpose, within
our cities of London and Westminster, or the
suburbs thereof; which said company shall be the
servants of our dearly beloved brother, James Duke
of York, and shall consist of such number as the
said Sir William D'avenant, his heirs or assigns,
shall from time to time think meet.   And such persons to permit and continue at and during the

*And to enter-
tain players, &c.
to act without
the impeach-
ment of any
person.*

pleasure of the said Sir William D'avenant, his heirs
or assigns, from time to time, to act plays and entertainments of the stage, of all sorts, peaceably and
quietly, without the impeachment or impediment of
any person or persons whatsoever, for the honest
recreation of such as shall desire to see the same.

And that it shall and may be lawful to and for the
said Sir William D'avenant, his heirs and assigns, to
take and receive of such our subjects as shall resort
to see or hear any such plays, scenes and entertainments whatsoever, such sum or sums of money, as
either have accustomably been given and taken in
the like kind, or as shall be thought reasonable by
him or them, in regard of the great expences of
scenes, musick, and such new decorations, as have
not been formerly used.

And further, for us, our heirs, and successors, we
do hereby give and grant unto the said Sir William
D'avenant, his heirs and assigns, full power to make
such allowances out of that which he shall so receive,
by the acting of plays and entertainments of the
stage, as aforesaid, to the actors and other persons
imployed in acting, representing, or in any quality
whatsoever, about the said theatre, as he or they
shall think fit ; and that the said company shall be
under the sole government and authority of the said
Sir William D'avenant, his heirs and assigns.   And
all scandalous and mutinous persons shall from time
to time be by him and them ejected and disabled
from playing in the said theatre.

And for that we are informed that divers companies of players have taken upon them to act plays publicly in our said cities of London and Westminster, or the suburbs thereof, without any authority for that purpose; we do hereby declare our dislike of the same, and will *That no other company but this, and one other under Mr. Killigrew, be permitted to act within London or Westminster or the suburbs.* and grant that only the said company erected and set up, or to be erected and set up by the said Sir William D'avenant, his heirs and assigns, by virtue of these presents, and one other company erected and set up, or to be erected and set up by Thomas Killigrew, Esq., his heirs or assigns, and none other, shall from henceforth act or represent comedies, tragedies, plays, or entertainments of the stage, within our said cities of London and Westminster, or the suburbs thereof; which said company to be erected by the said Thomas Killigrew, his heirs or assigns, shall be subject to his and their government and authority, and shall be stiled the Company of Us and our Royal Consort.

And the better to preserve amity and correspondency betwixt the said companies, and that the one may not incroach upon the other by any indirect means, we will and ordain, That no actor or other person employed about either of the said theatres, erected by the said Sir William D'avenant and Thomas Killigrew, or either of them, or deserting his company, shall be received by the governor or any of the said *No actor to go from one company to the other.*

other company, or any other person or persons, to
be employed in acting, or in any matter relating to
the stage, without the consent and approbation of
the governor of the company, whereof the said
person so ejected or deserting was a member, signi-
fied under his hand and seal. And we do by these
presents declare all other company and companies,
saving the two companies before mentioned, to be
silenced and suppressed.

And forasmuch as many plays, formerly acted, do
contain several prophane, obscene, and scurrilous
passages ; and the womens parts therein have been
acted by men in the habits of women, at which some
have taken offence : for the preventing of these
abuses for the future, we do hereby straitly charge
and command and enjoyn, that from henceforth no
new play shall be acted by either of the said companies, containing any passages offensive to piety
and good manners, nor any old or revived play,
containing any such offensive passages as aforesaid,
until the same shall be corrected and
To correct plays,
&c.   purged, by the said masters or governors
of the said respective companies, from
all such offensive and scandalous passages, as aforesaid. And we do likewise permit and give leave
that all the womens parts to be acted in either of
the said two companies for the time to come, may
be performed by women, so long as these recreations, which, by reason of the abuses aforesaid,
were scandalous and offensive, may by such reforma-

tion be esteemed, not only harmless delights, but useful and instructive representations of humane life, to such of our good subjects as shall resort to see the same.

And these our letters patents, or the inrolment thereof, shall be in all things good and effectual in the law, according to the true intent and meaning of the same, any thing in these presents contained, or any law, statute, act, ordinance, proclamation, provision, restriction, or any other matter, cause, or thing whatsoever to the contrary, in any wise notwithstanding; although express mention of the true yearly value, or certainty of the premises, or of any of them, or of any other gifts or grants by us, or by any of our progenitors or predecessors, heretofore made to the said Sir William D'avenant in these presents, is not made, or any other statute, act, ordinance, ·provision, proclamation, or restriction heretofore had, made, enacted, ordained, or provided, or any other matter, cause, or thing whatsoever to the contrary thereof, in any wise notwithstanding. In witness whereof, we have caused these our letters to be made patents. Witness our self at Westminster, the fifteenth day of January, in the fourteenth year of our reign.

These letters patents to be good and effectual in the law, according to the true meaning of the same, although, &c.

By the King.

HOWARD.

A N

A P O L O G Y

FOR THE

L I F E

O F

Mr. COLLEY CIBBER, *Comedian,*

A N D

Late PATENTEE of the *Theatre-Royal.*

With an Hiſtorical View of the STAGE *during his* OWN TIME.

WRITTEN BY HIMSELF.

—————————— *Hoc eſt*
Vivere bis, vitâ poſſe priore frui.   Mart. lib. 2.

When Years no more of active Life retain,
'Tis Youth renew'd, to laugh 'em o'er again. Anonym.

The SECOND EDITION.

L O N D O N:

Printed by JOHN WATTS for the AUTHOR:
And Sold by W. LEWIS in *Ruſſel-Street,* near
Convent - Garden.

MDCCXL.

TO A
CERTAIN GENTLEMAN.[1]

SIR,

BECAUSE I know it would give you less Concern to find your Name in an impertinent Satyr, than before the daintiest Dedication of a modern Author, I conceal it.

Let me talk never so idly to you, this way ; you are, at least, under no necessity of taking it to yourself : Nor when I boast of your favours, need you blush to have bestow'd them. Or I may now give you

---

[1] The Right Honourable Henry Pelham. Davies ("Life of Garrick," ii. 377) says that the "Apology" was dedicated to "that wise and honest minister," Pelham. John Taylor ("Records of my Life," i. 263) writes : "The name of the person to whom the Dedication to the 'Apology' was addressed is not mentioned, but the late Mr. John Kemble assured me that he had authority for saying it was Mr. Pelham, brother to the Duke of Newcastle." From the internal evidence it seems quite clear that this is so. In the Verses to Cibber quoted in "The Egotist," p. 69, the authoress writes :—

> " *Some praise a Patron and reveal him :*
> *You paint so true, you can't conceal him.*
> *Their gaudy Praise undue but shames him,*
> *While your's by Likeness only names him.*"

c

all the Attributes that raise a wise and good-natur'd
Man to Esteem and Happiness, and not be cen-
sured as a Flatterer by my own or your Enemies.
—— I place my own first ; because as they are the
greater Number, I am afraid of not paying the
greater Respect to them. Yours, if such there are,
I imagine are too well-bred to declare themselves :
But as there is no Hazard or visible Terror in an
Attack upon my defenceless Station, my Censurers
have generally been Persons of an intrepid Sincerity.
Having therefore shut the Door against them while
I am thus privately addressing you, I have little to
apprehend from either of them.

Under this Shelter, then, I may safely tell you,
That the greatest Encouragement I have had to
publish this Work, has risen from the several Hours
of Patience you have lent me at the Reading it. It
is true, I took the Advantage of your Leisure in the
Country, where moderate Matters serve for Amusement ; and there, indeed, how far your Good-nature
for an old Acquaintance, or your Reluctance to put
the Vanity of an Author out of countenance, may
have carried you, I cannot be sure; and yet Appearances give me stronger Hopes : For was not the
Complaisance of a whole Evening's Attention as
much as an Author of more Importance ought to
have expected ? Why then was I desired the next
Day to give you a second Lecture ? Or why was I
kept a third Day with you, to tell you more of the
same Story ? If these Circumstances have made

me vain, shall I say, Sir, you are accountable for them? No, Sir, I will rather so far flatter myself as to suppose it possible, That your having been a Lover of the Stage (and one of those few good Judges who know the Use and Value of it, under a right Regulation) might incline you to think so copious an Account of it a less tedious Amusement, than it may naturally be to others of different good Sense, who may have less Concern or Taste for it. But be all this as it may; the Brat is now born, and rather than see it starve upon the Bare Parish Provision, I chuse thus clandestinely to drop it at your Door, that it may exercise One of your Many Virtues, your Charity, in supporting it.

If the World were to know into whose Hands I have thrown it, their Regard to its Patron might incline them to treat it as one of his Family: But in the Consciousness of what I *am*, I chuse not, Sir, to say who you *are*. If your Equal in Rank were to do publick Justice to your Character, then, indeed, the Concealment of your Name might be an unnecessary Diffidence: But am I, Sir, of Consequence enough, in any Guise, to do Honour to Mr. ———? Were I to set him in the most laudable Lights that Truth and good Sense could give him, or his own Likeness would require, my officious Mite would be lost in that general Esteem and Regard which People of the first Consequence, even of different Parties, have a Pleasure in paying him. Encomiums to Superiors from Authors of lower Life, as they are naturally liable to Suspicion, can add very little Lustre to what before was visible to the publick Eye : Such Offerings (to use the Stile they are generally dressed in) like *Pagan* Incense, evaporate on the Altar, and rather gratify the Priest than the Deity.

But you, Sir, are to be approached in Terms within the Reach of common Sense : The honest Oblation of a chearful Heart is as much as you desire or I am able to bring you : A Heart that has just Sense enough to mix Respect with Intimacy, and is never more delighted than when your rural Hours of Leisure admit me, with all my laughing Spirits, to be my idle self, and in the whole Day's Possession of you ! Then, indeed, I have Reason to be vain ; I am, then, distinguish'd by a Pleasure too great to be conceal'd, and could almost pity the Man of graver Merit that dares not receive it with the same unguarded Transport ! This Nakedness of Temper the World may place in what Rank of Folly or Weakness they please ; but 'till Wisdom can give me something that will make me more heartily happy, I am content to be gaz'd at as I am, without lessening my Respect for those whose Passions may be more soberly covered.

Yet, Sir, will I not deceive you ; 'tis not the Lustre of your publick Merit, the Affluence of your Fortune, your high Figure in Life, nor those honourable Distinctions, which you had rather deserve than be told of, that have so many Years made my plain

Heart hang after you : These are but incidental
Ornaments, that, 'tis true, may be of Service to you
in the World's Opinion ; and though, as one among
the Crowd, I may rejoice that Providence has so
deservedly bestow'd them; yet my particular Attach-
ment has risen from a meer natural and more
engaging Charm, The Agreeable Companion ! Nor
is my Vanity half so much gratified in the *Honour*,
as my Sense is in the *Delight* of your Society!
When I see you lay aside the Advantages of Superiority, and by your own Chearfulness of Spirits
call out all that Nature has given me to meet them ;
then 'tis I taste you! then Life runs high! I desire!
I possess you !

Yet, Sir, in this distinguish'd Happiness I give
not up my farther Share of that Pleasure, or of that
Right I have to look upon you with the publick
Eye, and to join in the general Regard so unani-
mously pay'd to that uncommon Virtue, your *Integrity!* This, Sir, the World allows so conspicuous
a Part of your Character, that, however invidious
the Merit, neither the rude License of Detraction,
nor the Prejudice of Party, has ever once thrown
on it the least Impeachment or Reproach. This is
that commanding Power that, in publick Speaking,
makes you heard with such Attention! This it is
that discourages and keeps silent the Insinuations
of Prejudice and Suspicion; and almost renders
your Eloquence an unnecessary Aid to your Asser-
tions : Even your Opponents, conscious of your *Inte-*

grity, hear you rather as a Witness than an Orator—
But this, Sir, is drawing you too near the Light,
Integrity is too particular a Virtue to be cover'd
with a general Application. Let me therefore only
talk to you, as at *Tusculum* (for so I will call that
sweet Retreat, which your own Hands have rais'd)
where like the fam'd Orator of old, when publick
Cares permit, you pass so many rational, unbending
Hours : There! and at such Times, to have been
admitted, still plays in my Memory more like a
fictitious than a real Enjoyment! How many
golden Evenings, in that Theatrical Paradise of
water'd Lawns and hanging Groves, have I walk'd
and prated down the Sun in social Happiness!
Whether the Retreat of *Cicero*, in Cost, Magnificence, or curious Luxury of Antiquities, might
not out-blaze the *simplex Munditiis*, the modest
Ornaments of your *Villa*, is not within my reading
to determine : But that the united Power of Nature,
Art, or Elegance of Taste, could have thrown so
many varied Objects into a more delightful Harmony, is beyond my Conception.

When I consider you in this View, and as the
Gentleman of Eminence surrounded with the general
Benevolence of Mankind ; I rejoice, Sir, for you
and for myself; to see *You* in this particular Light
of Merit, and myself sometimes admitted to my
more than equal Share of you.

If this *Apology* for my past Life discourages you
not from holding me in your usual Favour, let me

quit this greater Stage, the World, whenever I may, I shall think This the best-acted Part of any I have undertaken, since you first condescended to laugh with,

  SIR,

   Your most obedient,

    most obliged, and

     most humble Servant,

      COLLEY CIBBER.

Novemb. 6.
1739.

AN APOLOGY FOR THE LIFE OF
MR. COLLEY CIBBER, &c.[1]

CHAPTER I.

The Introduction. The Author's Birth. Various Fortune at School. Not lik'd by those he lov'd there. Why. A Digression upon Raillery. The Use and Abuse of it. The Comforts of Folly. Vanity of Greatness. Laughing, no bad Philosophy.

YOU know, Sir, I have often told you that one time or other I should give the Publick some Memoirs of my own Life; at which you have never fail'd to laugh, like a Friend, without saying a word to

[1] Cibber, in Chapter ix., mentions that he is writing his Apology at Bath, and Fielding, in the mock trial of " *Col. Apol.*"

dissuade me from it ; concluding, I suppose, that such
a wild Thought could not possibly require a serious
Answer. But you see I was in earnest. And now
you will say the World will find me, under my own
Hand, a weaker Man than perhaps I may have pass'd
for, even among my Enemies.—With all my Heart!
my Enemies will then read me with Pleasure, and
you, perhaps, with Envy, when you find that Follies,
without the Reproach of Guilt upon them, are not
inconsistent with Happiness.—But why make my
Follies publick ? Why not ? I have pass'd my Time
very pleasantly with them, and I don't recollect that
they have ever been hurtful to any other Man living.
Even admitting they were injudiciously chosen,
would it not be Vanity in me to take Shame to myself
for not being found a Wise Man ? Really, Sir, my
Appetites were in too much haste to be happy, to
throw away my Time in pursuit of a Name I was
sure I could never arrive at.

Now the Follies I frankly confess I look upon as
in some measure discharged ; while those I conceal
are still keeping the Account open between me and

given in "The Champion" of 17th May, 1740, indicts the Prisoner "for that you, not having the Fear of Grammar before your
Eyes, on the   of   at a certain Place, called the
Bath, in the County of *Somerset*, in *Knights-Bridge*, in the County
of *Middlesex*, in and upon the *English* Language an Assault did
make, and then and there, with a certain Weapon called a Goose-
quill, value one Farthing, which you in your left Hand then held,
several very broad Wounds but of no Depth at all, on the said
English Language did make, and so you the said Col. *Apol.* the
said *English* Language did murder."

my Conscience. To me the Fatigue of being upon a continual Guard to hide them is more than the Reputation of being without them can repay. If this be Weakness, *defendit numerus*, I have such comfortable Numbers on my side, that were all Men to blush that are not Wise, I am afraid, in Ten, Nine Parts of the World ought to be out of Countenance :[1] But since that sort of Modesty is what they don't care to come into, why should I be afraid of being star'd at for not being particular? Or if the Particularity lies in owning my Weakness, will my wisest Reader be so inhuman as not to pardon it? But if there should be such a one, let me at least beg him to shew me that strange Man who is perfect! Is any one more unhappy, more ridiculous, than he who is always labouring to be thought so, or that is impatient when he is not thought so? Having brought myself to be easy under whatever the World may say of my Undertaking, you may still ask me why I give myself all this trouble? Is it for Fame, or Profit to myself,[2] or Use or Delight to others? For all these

---

[1] This seems to be a favourite argument of Cibber. In his "Letter" to Pope, 1742, he answers Pope's line, "And has not Colley still his Lord and Whore?" at great length, one of his arguments being that the latter accusation, "without some particular Circumstances to aggravate the Vice, is the flattest Piece of Satyr that ever fell from the formidable Pen of Mr. *Pope:* because (*defendit numerus*) take the first ten thousand Men you meet, and I believe, you would be no Loser, if you betted ten to one that every single Sinner of them, one with another, had been guilty of the same Frailty."—p. 46.

[2] Cibber's "Apology" must have been a very profitable book.

Considerations I have neither Fondness nor Indifference : If I obtain none of them, the Amusement, at worst, will be a Reward that must constantly go along with the Labour.   But behind all this there is something inwardly inciting, which I cannot express in few Words ; I must therefore a little make bold with your Patience.

A Man who has pass'd above Forty Years of his Life upon a Theatre, where he has never appear'd to be Himself, may have naturally excited the Curiosity of his Spectators to know what he really was when in no body's Shape but his own ; and whether he, who by his Profession had so long been ridiculing his Benefactors, might not, when the Coat

It was published in one volume quarto in 1740, and in the same year the second edition, one volume octavo, was issued. A third edition appeared in 1750, also in one volume octavo. Davies ("Dramatic Miscellanies," iii. 506) says : "Cibber must have raised considerable contributions on the public by his works. To say nothing of the sums accumulated by dedications, benefits, and the sale of his plays singly, his dramatic works, in quarto, by subscription, published 1721, produced him a considerable sum of money. It is computed that he gained, by the excellent Apology for his Life, no less than the sum of £1,500." "The Laureat" (1740) is perhaps Davies's authority for his computation. "*Ingenious indeed*, who from such a Pile of indigested incoherent Ideas huddled together by the *Misnomer* of a History, could raise a Contribution on the Town (if Fame says true) of Fifteen hundred Pounds."—"Laureat," p. 96.

Cibber no doubt kept the copyright of the first and second editions in his own hands. In 1750 he sold his copyright to Robert Dodsley for the sum of fifty guineas. The original assignment, which bears the date "March ye 24th, 1749/50," is in the collection of Mr. Julian Marshall.

of his Profession was off, deserve to be laugh'd at
himself; or from his being often seen in the most
flagrant and immoral Characters, whether he might
not see as great a Rogue when he look'd into the
Glass himself as when he held it to others.

It was doubtless from a Supposition that this sort
of Curiosity wou'd compensate their Labours that so
many hasty Writers have been encourag'd to publish
the Lives of the late Mrs. *Oldfield*, Mr. *Wilks*, and
Mr. *Booth*, in less time after their Deaths than one
could suppose it cost to transcribe them.[1]

Now, Sir, when my Time comes, lest they shou'd
think it worth while to handle my Memory with the
same Freedom, I am willing to prevent its being so
oddly besmear'd (or at best but flatly white-wash'd)
by taking upon me to give the Publick This, as true
a Picture of myself as natural Vanity will permit me
to draw : For to promise you that I shall never be
vain, were a Promise that, like a Looking-glass too
large, might break itself in the making : Nor am I
sure I ought wholly to avoid that Imputation, because if Vanity be one of my natural Features, the

---

[1] Of Mrs. Oldfield there was a volume of " Authentick Memoirs" published in 1730, the year she died; and in 1731
appeared Egerton's " Faithful Memoirs," and " The Lover's Miscellany," in which latter are memoirs of Mrs. Oldfield's " Life and
Amours." Three memoirs of Wilks immediately followed his
death, the third of which was written by Curll, who denounces the
other two as frauds. Benjamin Victor wrote a memoir of Booth
which was published in the year of his death, and there was one
unauthorized memoir issued in the same year. Bellchambers
instances the Life of Congreve as another imposition.

Portrait wou'd not be like me without it. In a Word, I may palliate and soften as much as I please; but upon an honest Examination of my Heart, I am afraid the same Vanity which makes even homely People employ Painters to preserve a flattering Record of their Persons, has seduced me to print off this *Chiaro Oscuro* of my Mind.

And when I have done it, you may reasonably ask me of what Importance can the History of my private Life be to the Publick? To this, indeed, I can only make you a ludicrous Answer, which is, That the Publick very well knows my Life has not been a private one; that I have been employ'd in their Service ever since many of their Grandfathers were young Men; And tho' I have voluntarily laid down my Post, they have a sort of Right to enquire into my Conduct (for which they have so well paid me) and to call for the Account of it during my Share of Administration in the State of the Theatre. This Work, therefore, which I hope they will not expect a Man of hasty Head shou'd confine to any regular Method: (For I shall make no scruple of leaving my History when I think a Digression may make it lighter for my Reader's Digestion.) This Work, I say, shall not only contain the various Impressions of my Mind, (as in *Louis the Fourteenth* his Cabinet you have seen the growing Medals of his Person from Infancy to Old Age,) but shall likewise include with them the *Theatrical History of my Own Time*, from my first Appearance on the Stage to my last *Exit*.[1]

[1] From this expression it appears that Cibber did not con-

If then what I shall advance on that Head may any ways contribute to the Prosperity or Improvement of the Stage in Being, the Publick must of consequence have a Share in its Utility.

This, Sir, is the best Apology I can make for being my own Biographer. Give me leave therefore to open the first Scene of my Life from the very Day I came into it; and tho' (considering my Profession) I have no reason to be asham'd of my Original; yet I am afraid a plain dry Account of it will scarce admit of a better Excuse than what my brother *Bays* makes for Prince *Prettyman* in the *Rehearsal*, viz. *I only do it for fear I should be thought to be no body's Son at all*;[1] for if I have led a worthless Life, the Weight of my Pedigree will not add an Ounce to my intrinsic Value. But be the Inference what it will, the simple Truth is this.

I was born in *London*, on the 6*th* of *November* 1671,[2] in *Southampton-Street*, facing *Southampton-House.*[3]

template again returning to the stage. He did, however, make a few final appearances, his last being to support his own adaptation of Shakespeare's "King John," which he called "Papal Tyranny in the Reign of King John," and which was produced at Covent Garden on 15th February, 1745.

[1] "The Rehearsal," act iii. sc. 4.

[2] The christening of Colley Cibber is recorded in the Baptismal Register of the Church of St. Giles-in-the-Fields. The entry reads :—

"November 1671   Christnings

20. Colly sonne of Caius Gabriell Sibber and Jane ux "

[3] Mr. Laurence Hutton, in his "Literary Landmarks of London," page 52, says: "Southampton House, afterwards Bedford House, taken down in the beginning of the present century, occupied the north side of Bloomsbury Square. Evelyn speaks of it

My Father, *Caius Gabriel Cibber*,[1] was a Native
of *Holstein*, who came into *England* some time
before the Restoration of King *Charles* II. to follow
his Profession, which was that of a Statuary, &c.
The *Basso Relievo* on the Pedestal of the Great
Column in the City, and the two Figures of the
Lunaticks, the *Raving* and the *Melancholy*, over the
Gates of *Bethlehem-Hospital*,[2] are no ill Monuments
of his Fame as an artist. My Mother was the
Daughter of *William Colley*, Esq; of a very ancient
Family of *Glaiston* in *Rutlandshire*, where she was
born. My Mother's Brother, *Edward Colley*, Esq;
(who gave me my Christian Name) being the last
Heir Male of it, the Family is now extinct. I shall
only add, that in *Wright's* History of *Rutlandshire*,
publish'd in 1684, the *Colley's* are recorded as Sheriffs

in his Diary, October, 1664, as in course of construction. Another
and an earlier Southampton House in Holborn, 'a little above
Holborn Bars,' was removed some twenty years before Cibber's
birth. He was, therefore, probably born at the upper or north
end of Southampton Street, facing Bloomsbury Square, where now
are comparatively modern buildings, and not in Southampton
Street, Strand, as is generally supposed."

[1] Caius Gabriel Cibber, born at Flensborg in Holstein in 1630;
married, as his second wife, Jane Colley, on 24th November, 1670;
died in 1700. He was, as Colley Cibber states, a sculptor of
some note.

[2] "Where o'er the gates, by his fam'd father's hand,
Great Cibber's brazen, brainless brothers stand."
(Final edition of "The Dunciad," i. verses 31-2.)
Bellchambers notes that these figures were removed to the New
Hospital in St. George's Fields. They are now in South Ken-
sington Museum.

and Members of Parliament from the Reign of *Henry* VII. to the latter End of *Charles* I., in whose Cause chiefly Sir *Antony Colley*, my Mother's Grandfather, sunk his Estate from Three Thousand to about Three Hundred *per Annum*.[1]

In the Year 1682, at little more than Ten Years of Age, I was sent to the Free-School of *Grantham* in *Lincolnshire*, where I staid till I got through it, from the lowest Form to the uppermost. And such Learning as that School could give me is the most I pretend to (which, tho' I have not utterly forgot, I cannot say I have much improv'd by Study) but even there I remember I was the same inconsistent Creature I have been ever since! always in full Spirits, in some small Capacity to do right, but in a more frequent Alacrity to do wrong; and consequently often under a worse Character than I wholly deserv'd : A giddy Negligence always possess'd me, and so much, that I remember I was once whipp'd for my *Theme*, tho' my Master told me, at the same

---

[1] "It was found by office taken in the 13th year of H. 8. that *John Colly* deceased, held the Mannour and Advowson of Glaiston of *Edward* Duke of Buckingham, as of his Castle of Okeham by knights service."—Wright's "History and Antiquities of the County of Rutland," p. 64.

"In the 26. *Car.* 1. (1640) Sir *Anthony Colly* Knight, then Lord of this Mannor, joyned with his Son and Heir apparent, *William Colly* Esquire, in a Conveyance of divers parcels of Land in Glaiston, together with the Advowson of the Church there, to *Edward Andrews* of Bisbroke in this County, Esquire : Which Advowson is since conveyed over to *Peterhouse* in Cambridge." *Ibid.* p. 65.

time, what was good of it was better than any Boy's
in the Form.   And (whatever Shame it may be to
own it) I have observ'd the same odd Fate has frequently attended the course of my later Conduct in
Life.   The unskilful openness, or in plain Terms,
the Indiscretion I have always acted with from my
Youth, has drawn more ill-will towards me, than
Men of worse Morals and more Wit might have
met with.   My Ignorance and want of Jealousy of
Mankind has been so strong, that it is with Reluctance I even yet believe any Person I am acquainted with can be capable of Envy, Malice, or Ingratitude:[1]   And to shew you what a Mortification it
was to me, in my very boyish Days, to find myself
mistaken, give me leave to tell you a School Story.

A great Boy, near the Head taller than myself, in
some wrangle at Play had insulted me; upon which
I was fool-hardy enough to give him a Box on the
Ear; the Blow was soon return'd with another that
brought me under him and at his Mercy.   Another
Lad, whom I really lov'd and thought a good-natur'd
one, cry'd out with some warmth to my Antagonist
(while I was down) Beat him, beat him soundly!
This so amaz'd me that I lost all my Spirits to

---

[1] Fielding ("Joseph Andrews," chap. iii.), writing of Parson
Adams, says: "Simplicity was his characteristic: he did, no more
than Mr. Colley Cibber, apprehend any such passions as malice
and envy to exist in mankind; which was indeed less remarkable
in a country parson, than in a gentleman who has passed his life
behind the scenes—a place which has been seldom thought the
school of innocence."

resist, and burst into Tears! When the Fray was
over I took my Friend aside, and ask'd him, How
he came to be so earnestly against me ? To which,
with some glouting[1] Confusion, he reply'd, Because
you are always jeering and making a Jest of me to
every Boy in the School. Many a Mischief have I
brought upon myself by the same Folly in riper Life.
Whatever Reason I had to reproach my Companion's
declaring against me, I had none to wonder at it
while I was so often hurting him: Thus I deserv'd
his Enmity by my not having Sense enough to know
I *had* hurt him; and he hated me because he had
not Sense enough to know that I never *intended* to
hurt him.

As this is the first remarkable Error of my Life I
can recollect, I cannot pass it by without throwing
out some further Reflections upon it; whether flat or
spirited, new or common, false or true, right or wrong,
they will be still my own, and consequently like me;
I will therefore boldly go on; for I am only oblig'd
to give you my *own*, and not a *good* Picture, to shew
as well the Weakness as the Strength of my Understanding. It is not on what I write, but on my
Reader's Curiosity I relie to be read through: At
worst, tho' the Impartial may be tir'd, the Ill-natur'd
(no small number) I know will see the bottom of me.

What I observ'd then, upon my having unde-
signedly provok'd my School-Friend into an Enemy,
is a common Case in Society; Errors of this kind

---

[1] Glout is an obsolete word signifying " to pout, to look sullen.'

often sour the Blood of Acquaintance into an inconceivable Aversion, where it is little suspected.   It is
not enough to say of your Raillery that you intended
no offence ; if the Person you offer it to has either a
wrong Head, or wants a Capacity to make that distinction, it may have the same effect as the Intention
of the grossest Injury : And in reality, if you know
his Parts are too slow to return it in kind, it is a
vain and idle Inhumanity, and sometimes draws the
Aggressor into difficulties not easily got out of : Or
to give the Case more scope, suppose your Friend
may have a passive Indulgence for your Mirth, if
you find him silent at it ; tho' you were as intrepid as
Cæsar, there can be no excuse for your not leaving
it off.   When you are conscious that your Antagonist
can give as well as take, then indeed the smarter the
Hit the more agreeable the Party : A Man of chearful Sense among Friends will never be grave upon
an Attack of this kind, but rather thank you that you
have given him a Right to be even with you : There
are few Men (tho' they may be Masters of both) that
on such occasions had not rather shew their Parts
than their Courage, and the Preference is just ; a
Bull-Dog may have one, and only a Man can have
the other.   Thus it happens that in the coarse
Merriment of common People, when the Jest begins
to swell into earnest ; for want of this Election you
may observe, he that has least wit generally gives the
first Blow.   Now, as among the Better sort, a readiness of Wit is not always a Sign of intrinsick Merit ;

so the want of that readiness is no Reproach to a
Man of plain Sense and Civility, who therefore
(methinks) should never have these lengths of Liberty
taken with him. Wit there becomes absurd, if not
insolent; ill-natur'd I am sure it is, which Imputation
a generous Spirit will always avoid, for the same
Reason that a Man of real Honour will never send a
Challenge to a Cripple. The inward Wounds that
are given by the inconsiderate Insults of Wit to
those that want it, are as dangerous as those given
by Oppression to Inferiors; as long in healing, and
perhaps never forgiven. There is besides (and little
worse than this) a mutual Grossness in Raillery that
sometimes is more painful to the Hearers that are
not concern'd in it than to the Persons engaged. I
have seen a couple of these clumsy Combatants drub
one another with as little Manners or Mercy as if
they had two Flails in their Hands; Children at
Play with Case-knives could not give you more
Apprehension of their doing one another a Mischief.
And yet, when the Contest has been over, the
Boobys have look'd round them for Approbation, and
upon being told they were admirably well match'd,
have sat down (bedawb'd as they were) contented at
making it a drawn Battle. After all that I have said,
there is no clearer way of giving Rules for Raillery
than by Example.

There are two Persons now living, who tho' very
different in their manner, are, as far as my Judgment
reaches, complete Masters of it; one of a more polite

and extensive Imagination, the other of a Knowledge
more closely useful to the Business of Life : The
one gives you perpetual Pleasure, and seems always
to be taking it ; the other seems to take none till his
Business is over, and then gives you as much as if
Pleasure were his only Business. The one enjoys
his Fortune, the other thinks it first necessary to
make it ; though that he will enjoy it then I cannot
be positive, because when a Man has once pick'd up
more than he wants, he is apt to think it a Weakness
to suppose he has enough. But as I don't remember
ever to have seen these Gentlemen in the same
Company, you must give me leave to take them
separately.[1]

The first of them, then, has a Title, and —— no
matter what ; I am not to speak of the great, but the
happy part of his Character, and in this one single
light ; not of his being an illustrious, but a delightful
Companion.

In Conversation he is seldom silent but when he
is attentive, nor ever speaks without exciting the
Attention of others ; and tho' no Man might with less
Displeasure to his Hearers engross the Talk of the
Company, he has a Patience in his Vivacity that

[1] Bellchambers suggests that these two persons were the Earl
of Chesterfield and " Bubb Doddington."   As to the former he is
no doubt correct, but I cannot see a single feature of resemblance
between the second portrait and Lord Melcombe. "The Laureat"
says (p. 18) that the portraits were "L—d C—d and Mr. E—e"
[probably Erskine]. Bellchambers seems to have supposed that
" Bubb " was a nickname.

chuses to divide it, and rather gives more Freedom
than he takes; his sharpest Replies having a mixture
of Politeness that few have the command of; his
Expression is easy, short, and clear; a stiff or studied
Word never comes from him; it is in a simplicity of
Style that he gives the highest Surprize, and his
Ideas are always adapted to the Capacity and Taste
of the Person he speaks to : Perhaps you will understand me better if I give you a particular Instance
of it. A Person at the University, who from being
a Man of Wit easily became his Acquaintance there,
from that Acquaintance found no difficulty in being
made one of his Chaplains : This Person afterwards
leading a Life that did no great Honour to his Cloth,
obliged his Patron to take some gentle notice of it;
but as his Patron knew the Patient was squeamish,
he was induced to sweeten the Medicine to his Taste,
and therefore with a smile of good humour told him,
that if to the many Vices he had already, he would
give himself the trouble to add one more, he did not
doubt but his Reputation might still be set up again.
Sir *Crape*, who could have no Aversion to so pleasant
a Dose, desiring to know what it might be, was
answered, *Hypocrisy, Doctor, only a little Hypocrisy !*
This plain Reply can need no Comment; but *ex pede
Herculem*, he is every where proportionable. I think
I have heard him since say, the Doctor thought
Hypocrisy so detestable a Sin that he dy'd without
committing it. In a word, this Gentleman gives
Spirit to Society the Moment he comes into it, and

whenever he leaves it they who have Business have
then leisure to go about it.

Having often had the Honour to be my self the
But of his Raillery, I must own I have received
more Pleasure from his lively manner of raising the
Laugh against me, than I could have felt from the
smoothest flattery of a serious Civility. Tho' Wit
flows from him with as much ease as common Sense
from another, he is so little elated with the Advantage
he may have over you, that whenever your good
Fortune gives it against him, he seems more pleas'd
with it on your side than his own. The only advantage he makes of his Superiority of Rank is,
that by always waving it himself, his inferior finds he
is under the greater Obligation not to forget it.

When the Conduct of social Wit is under such
Regulations, how delightful must those *Convivia*,
those Meals of Conversation be, where such a Member presides ; who can with so much ease (as *Shakespear* phrases it) *set the Table in a roar*.[1] I am in no
pain that these imperfect Out-lines will be apply'd
to the Person I mean, because every one who has
the Happiness to know him must know how much
more in this particular Attitude is wanting to be like
him.

The other Gentleman, whose bare Interjections of
Laughter have humour in them, is so far from having
a Title that he has lost his real name, which some
Years ago he suffer'd his Friends to railly him out

---

[1] "Set the table on a roar."—"Hamlet," act v. sc. 1.

of; in lieu of which they have equipp'd him with one they thought had a better sound in good Company. He is the first Man of so sociable a Spirit that I ever knew capable of quitting the Allurements of Wit and Pleasure for a strong Application to Business; in his Youth (for there was a Time when he was young) he set out in all the hey-day Expences of a modish Man of Fortune ; but finding himself over-weighted with Appetites, he grew restiff, kick'd up in the middle of the Course, and turn'd his back upon his Frolicks abroad, to think of improving his Estate at home : In order to which he clapt Collars upon his Coach-Horses, and that their Mettle might not run over other People, he ty'd a Plough to their Tails, which tho' it might give them a more slovenly Air, would enable him to keep them fatter in a foot pace, with a whistling Peasant beside them, than in a full trot, with a hot-headed Coachman behind them. In these unpolite Amusements he has laugh'd like a Rake and look'd about him like a Farmer for many Years. As his Rank and Station often find him in the best Company, his easy Humour, whenever he is called to it, can still make himself the Fiddle of it.

And tho' some say he looks upon the Follies of the World like too severe a Philosopher, yet he rather chuses to laugh than to grieve at them ; to pass his time therefore more easily in it, he often endeavours to conceal himself by assuming the Air and Taste of a Man in fashion ; so that his only Uneasiness seems to be, that he cannot quite prevail with his

Friends to think him a worse Manager than he really is; for they carry their Raillery to such a height that it sometimes rises to a Charge of downright Avarice against him. Upon which Head it is no easy matter to be more merry upon him than he will be upon himself. Thus while he sets that Infirmity in a pleasant Light, he so disarms your Prejudice, that if he has it not, you can't find in your Heart to wish he were without it. Whenever he is attack'd where he seems to lie so open, if his Wit happens not to be ready for you, he receives you with an assenting Laugh, till he has gain'd time enough to whet it sharp enough for a Reply, which seldom turns out to his disadvantage. If you are too strong for him (which may possibly happen from his being oblig'd to defend the weak side of the Question) his last Resource is to join in the Laugh till he has got himself off by an ironical Applause of your Superiority.

If I were capable of Envy, what I have observ'd of this Gentleman would certainly incline me to it; for sure to get through the necessary Cares of Life with a Train of Pleasures at our Heels in vain calling after us, to give a constant Preference to the Business of the Day, and yet be able to laugh while we are about it, to make even Society the subservient Reward of it, is a State of Happiness which the gravest Precepts of moral Wisdom will not easily teach us to exceed. When I speak of Happiness, I go no higher than that which is contain'd in the World we

now tread upon ; and when I speak of Laughter, I
don't simply mean that which every Oaf is capable
of, but that which has its sensible Motive and proper
Season, which is not more limited than recommended
by that indulgent Philosophy,

Cum ratione insanire.[1]

When I look into my present Self, and afterwards
cast my Eye round all my Hopes, I don't see any one
Pursuit of them that should so reasonably rouze me
out of a Nod in my Great Chair, as a call to those
agreeable Parties I have sometimes the Happiness
to mix with, where I always assert the equal Liberty
of leaving them, when my Spirits have done their
best with them.

Now, Sir, as I have been making my way for
above Forty Years through a Crowd of Cares, (all
which, by the Favour of Providence, I have honestly
got rid of) is it a time of Day for me to leave off
these Fooleries, and to set up a new Character ?
Can it be worth my while to waste my Spirits, to
bake my Blood, with serious Contemplations, and
perhaps impair my Health, in the fruitless Study of
advancing myself into the better Opinion of those
very—very few Wise Men that are as old as I am ?
No, the Part I have acted in real Life shall be all
of a piece,

——Servetur ad imum,
Qualis ab incepto processerit. Hor.[2]

---

[1] Ter. *Eun.* i. 1, 18.   [2] *Ars Poetica,* 126.

C

I will not go out of my Character by straining to be
wiser than I *can* be, or by being more affectedly pen-
sive than I *need* be; whatever I am, Men of Sense will
know me to be, put on what Disguise I will; I can
no more put off my Follies than my Skin; I have
often try'd, but they stick too close to me; nor am I
sure my Friends are displeased with them; for, besides that in this Light I afford them frequent matter
of Mirth, they may possibly be less uneasy at their
own Foibles when they have so old a Precedent to
keep them in Countenance : Nay, there are some
frank enough to confess they envy what they laugh
at; and when I have seen others, whose Rank and
Fortune have laid a sort of Restraint upon their
Liberty of pleasing their Company by pleasing themselves, I have said softly to myself,——Well, there
is some Advantage in having neither Rank nor
Fortune! Not but there are among them a third
Sort, who have the particular Happiness of unbending into the very Wantonness of Good-humour without depreciating their Dignity : He that is not
Master of that Freedom, let his Condition be never
so exalted, must still want something to come up to
the Happiness of his Inferiors who enjoy it. If
Socrates cou'd take pleasure in playing at *Even or
Odd* with his Children, or *Agesilaus* divert himself in
riding the Hobby-horse with them, am I oblig'd to
be as eminent as either of them before I am as
frolicksome? If the Emperor *Adrian*, near his
death, cou'd play with his very Soul, his *Animula*,

&c. and regret that it cou'd be no longer companion-
able ; if Greatness at the same time was not the
Delight he was so loth to part with, sure then these
chearful Amusements I am contending for must
have no inconsiderable share in our Happiness ; he
that does not chuse to live his own way, suffers
others to chuse for him.   Give me the Joy I always
took in the End of an old Song,

My Mind, my Mind is a Kingdom to me ! [1]

If I can please myself with my own Follies, have
not I a plentiful Provision for Life ?   If the World
thinks me a Trifler, I don't desire to break in upon
their Wisdom ; let them call me any Fool but an
Unchearful one ; I live as I write ; while my Way
amuses me, it's as well as I wish it ; when another
writes better, I can like him too, tho' he shou'd not
like me.   Not our great Imitator of *Horace* himself
can have more Pleasure in writing his Verses than
I have in reading them, tho' I sometimes find myself
there (as *Shakespear* terms it) *dispraisingly* [2] spoken
of : [3] If he is a little free with me, I am generally in

---

[1] In William Byrd's collection, entitled " Psalmes, Sonets, &
songs of sadnes and pietie," 1588, 4to., is the song to which
Cibber probably refers :—
    " My Minde to me a Kingdome is."
Mr. Bullen, in his " Lyrics from Elizabethan Song-books " (p. 78),
quotes it.

[2]   " And so many a time,
    When I have spoke of you dispraisingly,
    Hath ta'en your part."—" Othello," act iii. sc. 3.

[3] This is Cibber's first allusion to Pope's enmity.   It was after

good Company, he is as blunt with my Betters; so
that even here I might laugh in my turn. My
Superiors, perhaps, may be mended by him; but, for
my part, I own myself incorrigible : I look upon my
Follies as the best part of my Fortune, and am more
concern'd to be a good Husband of Them, than of
That; nor do I believe I shall ever be rhim'd out of
them.   And, if I don't mistake, I am supported in
my way of thinking by *Horace* himself, who, in excuse
of a loose Writer, says,

> *Prætulerim scriptor delirus, inersque videri,*
> *Dum mea delectent mala me, vel denique fallant,*
> *Quam sapere, et ringi——*[1]

which, to speak of myself as a loose Philosopher, I
have thus ventur'd to imitate :

> *Me, while my laughing Follies can deceive,*
> *Blest in the dear Delirium let me live,*
> *Rather than wisely know my Wants and grieve.*

We had once a merry Monarch of our own, who thought
chearfulness so valuable a Blessing, that he would
have quitted one of his Kingdoms where he cou'd not
enjoy it ; where, among many other Conditions they
had ty'd him to, his sober Subjects wou'd not suffer
him to laugh on a *Sunday;* and tho' this might not
be the avow'd Cause of his Elopement,[2] I am not

the publication of the "Apology" that Pope's attacks became
more bitter.
[1] Horace, *Epis.* ii. 2, 126.
[2] Charles II.'s flight from his Scottish Presbyterian subjects, at

sure, had he had no other, that this alone might not have serv'd his turn; at least, he has my hearty Approbation either way; for had I been under the same Restriction, tho' my staying were to have made me his Successor, I shou'd rather have chosen to follow him.

How far his Subjects might be in the right is not my Affair to determine; perhaps they were wiser than the Frogs in the Fable, and rather chose to have a Log than a Stork for their King; yet I hope it will be no Offence to say that King *Log* himself must have made but a very simple Figure in History.

The Man who chuses never to laugh, or whose becalm'd Passions know no Motion, seems to me only in the quiet State of a green Tree; he vegetates, 'tis true, but shall we say he lives? Now, Sir, for Amusement.—Reader, take heed! for I find a strong impulse to talk impertinently; if therefore you are not as fond of seeing, as I am of shewing myself in all my Lights, you may turn over two Leaves together, and leave what follows to those who have more Curiosity, and less to do with their Time, than you have.—As I was saying then, let us, for Amusement, advance this, or any other Prince, to the most glorious Throne, mark out his Empire in what Clime

the end of 1650, to take refuge among his wild Highland supporters, was caused by the insolent invectives of the rigid Presbyterian clergymen, who preached long sermons at him, on his own wickedness and that of his father and mother, and made his life generally a burden.

you please, fix him on the highest Pinnacle of un-
bounded Power; and in that State let us enquire
into his degree of Happiness; make him at once the
Terror and the Envy of his Neighbours, send his
Ambition out to War, and gratify it with extended
Fame and Victories; bring him in triumph home,
with great unhappy Captives behind him, through
the Acclamations of his People, to repossess his
Realms in Peace. Well, when the Dust has been
brusht from his Purple, what will he do next? Why,
this envy'd Monarch (who we will allow to have a more
exalted Mind than to be delighted with the trifling
Flatteries of a congratulating Circle) will chuse to
retire, I presume, to enjoy in private the Contempla-
tion of his Glory; an Amusement, you will say, that
well becomes his Station! But there, in that pleasing
Rumination, when he has made up his new Account
of Happiness, how much, pray, will be added to the
Balance more than as it stood before his last Expedi-
tion? From what one Article will the Improvement
of it appear? Will it arise from the conscious Pride
of having done his weaker Enemy an Injury? Are
his Eyes so dazzled with false Glory that he thinks
it a less Crime in him to break into the Palace of his
Princely Neighbour, because he gave him time to
defend it, than for a Subject feloniously to plunder
the House of a private Man? Or is the Outrage of
Hunger and Necessity more enormous than the
Ravage of Ambition? Let us even suppose the
wicked Usage of the World as to that Point may

keep his Conscience quiet; still, what is he to do
with the infinite Spoil that his imperial Rapine has
brought home ? Is he to sit down and vainly deck
himself with the Jewels which he has plunder'd from
the Crown of another, whom Self-defence had compell'd to oppose him ? No, let us not debase his Glory
into so low a Weakness. What Appetite, then, are
these shining Treasures food for ? Is their vast
Value in seeing his vulgar Subjects stare at them,
wise Men smile at them, or his Children play with
them ? Or can the new Extent of his Dominions
add a Cubit to his Happiness ? Was not his Empire
wide enough before to do good in ? And can it add
to his Delight that now no Monarch has such room
to do mischief in ? But farther; if even the great
Augustus, to whose Reign such Praises are given,
cou'd not enjoy his Days of Peace free from the
Terrors of repeated Conspiracies, which lost him
more Quiet to suppress than his Ambition cost him
to provoke them : What human Eminence is secure ?
In what private Cabinet then must this wondrous
Monarch lock up his Happiness that common Eyes
are never to behold it ? Is it, like his Person, a
Prisoner to its own Superiority ? Or does he at last
poorly place it in the Triumph of his injurious De-
vastations ? One Moment's Search into himself will
plainly shew him that real and reasonable Happiness
can have no Existence without Innocence and
Liberty. What a Mockery is Greatness without
them ? How lonesome must be the Life of that

Monarch who, while he governs only by being fear'd, is restrain'd from letting down his Grandeur sometimes to forget himself and to humanize him into the Benevolence and Joy of Society? To throw off his cumbersome Robe of Majesty, to be a Man without disguise, to have a sensible Taste of Life in its Simplicity, till he confess from the sweet Experience that *dulce est desipere in loco*[1] was no Fool's Philosophy. Or if the gawdy Charms of Pre-eminence are so strong that they leave him no Sense of a less pompous, tho' a more rational Enjoyment, none sure can envy him but those who are the Dupes of an equally fantastick Ambition.

My Imagination is quite heated and fatigued in dressing up this Phantome of Felicity; but I hope it has not made me so far misunderstood, as not to have allow'd that in all the Dispensations of Providence the Exercise of a great and virtuous Mind is the most elevated State of Happiness: No, Sir, I am not for setting up Gaiety against Wisdom; nor for preferring the Man of Pleasure to the Philosopher; but for shewing that the Wisest or greatest Man is very near an unhappy Man, if the unbending Amusements I am contending for are not sometimes admitted to relieve him.

How far I may have over-rated these Amusements let graver Casuists decide; whether they affirm or reject what I have asserted hurts not my

---

[1] Hor. *Od.* iv. 12, 28.

Purpose ; which is not to give Laws to others ; but to shew by what Laws I govern myself : If I am misguided, 'tis Nature's Fault, and I follow her from this Persuasion ; That as Nature has distinguish'd our Species from the mute Creation by our Risibility, her Design must have been by that Faculty as evidently to raise our Happiness, as by our *Os Sublime* [1] (our erected Faces) to lift the Dignity of our Form above them.

Notwithstanding all I have said, I am afraid there is an absolute Power in what is simply call'd our Constitution that will never admit of other Rules for Happiness than her own ; from which (be we never so wise or weak) without Divine Assistance we only can receive it ; So that all this my Parade and Grimace of Philosophy has been only making a mighty Merit of following my own Inclination. A very natural Vanity ! Though it is some sort of Satisfaction to know it does not impose upon me. Vanity again ! However, think It what you will that has drawn me into this copious Digression, 'tis now high time to drop it : I shall therefore in my next Chapter return to my School, from whence I fear I have too long been Truant.

---

[1] "Os homini sublime dedit."—Ovid, *Met.* i. 85.

CHAPTER II.

He that writes of himself not easily tir'd. Boys may give Men Lessons. The Author's Preferment at School attended with Misfortunes. The Danger of Merit among Equals. Of Satyrists and Backbiters. What effect they have had upon the Author. Stanzas publish'd by himself against himself.

IT often makes me smile to think how contentedly I have set myself down to write my own Life; nay, and with less Concern for what may be said of it than I should feel were I to do the same for a deceased Acquaintance. This you will easily account for when you consider that nothing gives a Coxcomb more delight than when you suffer him to talk of himself; which sweet Liberty I here enjoy for a whole Volume together! A Privilege which neither cou'd be allow'd me, nor wou'd become me to take, in the Company I am generally admitted to;[1] but here, when I have all the Talk to myself, and have no body to interrupt or contradict me, sure, to say whatever I have a mind other People shou'd know of me is a Pleasure which none but Authors as vain as myself can conceive.——But to my History.

However little worth notice the Life of a School-boy may be supposed to contain, yet, as the Passions of Men and Children have much the same Motives and differ very little in their Effects, unless where the elder Experience may be able to conceal them: As therefore what arises from the Boy may possibly be a Lesson to the Man, I shall venture to relate a Fact or two that happen'd while I was still at School.

In *February*, 1684-5, died King *Charles* II. who being the only King I had ever seen, I remember (young as I was) his Death made a strong Impression upon me, as it drew Tears from the Eyes of Multitudes, who looked no further into him than I

---

[1] Cibber is pardonably vain throughout at the society he moved in. His greatest social distinction was his election as a member of White's. His admission to such society was of course the subject of lampoons, such as the following :—

" *The* BUFFOON, *An* EPIGRAM.

Don't boast, prithee *Cibber*, so much of thy State,
That like *Pope* you are blest with the smiles of the Great;
With both they Converse, but for different Ends,
And 'tis easy to know their Buffoons from their Friends."

did : But it was, then, a sort of School-Doctrine to regard our Monarch as a Deity; as in the former Reign it was to insist he was accountable to this World as well as to that above him. But what, perhaps, gave King *Charles* II. this peculiar Possession of so many Hearts, was his affable and easy manner in conversing; which is a Quality that goes farther with the greater Part of Mankind than many higher Virtues, which, in a Prince, might more immediately regard the publick Prosperity. Even his indolent Amusement of playing with his Dogs and feeding his Ducks in St. *James's Park*, (which I have seen him do) made the common People adore him, and consequently overlook in him what, in a Prince of a different Temper, they might have been out of humour at.

I cannot help remembring one more Particular in those Times, tho' it be quite foreign to what will follow. I was carry'd by my Father to the Chapel in *Whitehall;* where I saw the King and his royal Brother the then Duke of *York*, with him in the Closet, and present during the whole Divine Service. Such Dispensation, it seems, for his Interest, had that unhappy Prince from his real Religion, to assist at another to which his Heart was so utterly averse. ———I now proceed to the Facts I promis'd to speak of.

King *Charles* his Death was judg'd by our Schoolmaster a proper Subject to lead the Form I was in into a higher kind of Exercise ; he therefore enjoin'd

us severally to make his Funeral Oration : This
sort of Task, so entirely new to us all, the Boys receiv'd with Astonishment as a Work above their
Capacity ; and tho' the Master persisted in his Command, they one and all, except myself, resolved to
decline it. But I, Sir, who was ever giddily forward
and thoughtless of Consequences, set myself roundly
to work, and got through it as well as I could. I
remember to this Hour that single Topick of his
Affability (which made me mention it before) was
the chief Motive that warm'd me into the Undertaking; and to shew how very childish a Notion I
had of his Character at that time, I raised his
Humanity, and Love of those who serv'd him, to
such Height, that I imputed his Death to the Shock
he receiv'd from the Lord *Arlington's* being at the
point of Death about a Week before him.[1] This
Oration, such as it was, I produc'd the next Morning :
All the other Boys pleaded their Inability, which the
Master taking rather as a mark of their Modesty
than their Idleness, only seem'd to punish by setting
me at the Head of the Form : A Preferment dearly
bought ! Much happier had I been to have sunk
my Performance in the general Modesty of declining it. A most uncomfortable Life I led among
them for many a Day after ! I was so jeer'd, laugh'd
at, and hated as a pragmatical Bastard (School-boys
Language) who had betray'd the whole Form, that

---

[1] Arlington did not, however, die till the 28th July, 1685,
surviving Charles II. by nearly six months.

scarce any of 'em wou'd keep me company; and tho'
it so far advanc'd me into the Master's Favour that
he wou'd often take me from the School to give me
an Airing with him on Horseback, while they were
left to their Lessons ; you may be sure such envy'd
Happiness did not encrease their Good-will to me :
Notwithstanding which my Stupidity cou'd take no
warning from their Treatment.   An Accident of the
same nature happen'd soon after, that might have
frighten'd a Boy of a meek Spirit from attempting
any thing above the lowest Capacity.   On the 23d
of *April* following, being the Coronation-Day of the
new King, the School petition'd the Master for leave
to play; to which he agreed, provided any of the
Boys would produce an *English* Ode upon that
Occasion.————The very Word, *Ode*, I know makes
you smile already; and so it does me; not only
because it still makes so many poor Devils turn Wits
upon it, but from a more agreeable Motive; from a
Reflection of how little I then thought that, half a
Century afterwards, I shou'd be call'd upon twice a
year, by my Post,[1] to make the same kind of Obla-
tions to an *unexceptionable* Prince, the serene Happiness of whose Reign my halting Rhimes are still so
unequal to————This, I own, is Vanity without Disguise; but *Hæc olim meminisse juvat :*[2] The remembrance of the miserable prospect we had then before

[1] Cibber was appointed Poet-Laureate on the death of Eusden.
His appointment was dated 3rd December, 1730.

[2] " Forsan et hæc olim meminisse juvabit."—Virg. *Æneid*, i. 207.

us, and have since escaped by a Revolution, is now a Pleasure which, without that Remembrance, I could not so heartily have enjoy'd.[1] The Ode I was speaking of fell to my Lot, which in about half an Hour I produc'd. I cannot say it was much above the merry Style of *Sing! Sing the Day, and sing the Song*, in the Farce : Yet bad as it was, it serv'd to get the School a Play-day, and to make me not a little vain upon it ; which last Effect so disgusted my Play-fellows that they left me out of the Party I had most a mind to be of in that Day's Recreation. But their Ingratitude serv'd only to increase my Vanity ; for I consider'd them as so many beaten Tits that had just had the Mortification of seeing my Hack of a *Pegasus* come in before them. This low Passion is so rooted in our Nature that some-times riper Heads cannot govern it. I have met with much the same silly sort of Coldness, even from my Contemporaries of the Theatre, from having the superfluous Capacity of writing myself the Characters I have acted.

Here, perhaps, I may again seem to be vain ; but if all these Facts are true (as true they are) how can I help it? Why am I oblig'd to conceal them ? The Merit of the best of them is not so extraordinary as to have warn'd me to be nice upon it ; and the Praise due to them is so small a Fish, it was scarce worth while to throw my Line into the Water for it.

[1] As Laureate, and as author of "The Nonjuror," Cibber is bound to be extremely loyal to the Protestant dynasty.

If I confess my Vanity while a Boy, can it be Vanity, when a Man, to remember it? And if I have a tolerable Feature, will not that as much belong to my Picture as an Imperfection? In a word, from what I have mentioned, I wou'd observe only this; That when we are conscious of the least comparative Merit in ourselves, we shou'd take as much care to conceal the Value we set upon it, as if it were a real Defect: To be elated or vain upon it is shewing your Money before People in want; ten to one but some who may think you to have too much may borrow, or pick your Pocket before you get home. He who assumes Praise to himself, the World will think overpays himself. Even the Suspicion of being vain ought as much to be dreaded as the Guilt itself. *Cæsar* was of the same Opinion in regard to his Wife's Chastity. Praise, tho' it may be our due, is not like a *Bank-Bill*, to be paid upon Demand; to be valuable it must be voluntary. When we are dun'd for it, we have a Right and Privilege to refuse it. If Compulsion insists upon it, it can only be paid as Persecution in Points of Faith is, in a counterfeit Coin: And who ever believ'd Occasional Conformity to be sincere? *Nero*, the most vain Coxcomb of a Tyrant that ever breath'd, cou'd not raise an unfeigned Applause of his Harp by military Execution; even where Praise is deserv'd, Ill-nature and Self-conceit (Passions that poll a majority of Mankind) will with less reluctance part with their Mony than their Approbation. Men of the greatest

Merit are forced to stay 'till they die before the
World will fairly make up their Account: Then indeed you have a Chance for your full Due, because
it is less grudg'd when you are incapable of enjoying
it: Then perhaps even Malice shall heap Praises
upon your Memory; tho' not for your sake, but that
your surviving Competitors may suffer by a Comparison.[1] 'Tis from the same Principle that *Satyr*
shall have a thousand Readers where *Panegyric* has
one. When I therefore find my Name at length in
the Satyrical Works of our most celebrated living
Author, I never look upon those Lines as Malice
meant to me, (for he knows I never provok'd it) but
Profit to himself: One of his Points must be, to have
many Readers: He considers that my Face and
Name are more known than those of many thousands
of more consequence in the Kingdom: That therefore, right or wrong, a Lick at the *Laureat*[2] will

---

[1] Curiously enough, Cibber's praise of his deceased companion-
actors has been attributed to something of this motive.

[2] Bellchambers prints these words thus: "Lick at the Laureat,"
as if Cibber had referred to the title of a book; and notes: "This
is the title of a pamphlet in which some of Mr. Cibber's peculi-
arities have been severely handled." But I doubt this, for there
is nothing in Cibber's arrangement of the words to denote that
they represent the title of a book; and, besides, I know no work
with such a title published before 1740. Bellchambers, in a note
on page 114, represents that he quotes from "Lick at the Laureat,
1730;" but I find the quotation he gives in "The Laureat," 1740
(p. 31), almost *verbatim*. As it stands in the latter there is no hint
that it is quoted from a previous work, nor, indeed, do the terms
of it permit of such an interpretation. I can, therefore, only

always be a sure Bait, *ad captandum vulgus*, to catch
him little Readers: And that to gratify the Un-
learned, by now and then interspersing those merry
Sacrifices of an old Acquaintance to their Taste, is a
piece of quite right Poetical Craft.[1]

But as a little bad Poetry is the greatest Crime
he lays to my charge, I am willing to subscribe to his
opinion of *it*.[2] That this sort of Wit is one of the

suppose that Bellchambers is wrong in attributing the sentence to
a work called "A Lick at the Laureat."

[1] The principal allusions to Cibber which, up to the time of the
publication of the "Apology," Pope had made, were in the
"Dunciad":—

> "How, with less reading than makes felons 'scape,
> Less human genius than God gives an ape,
> Small thanks to France and none to Rome or Greece,
> A past, vamp'd, future, old, reviv'd, new piece,
> 'Twixt Plautus, Fletcher, Congreve, and Corneille,
> Can make a Cibber, Johnson, or Ozell."
>
> > Second edition, Book i. 235-240.

> "Beneath his reign, shall Eusden wear the bays,
> Cibber preside, Lord-Chancellor of Plays."
>
> > Second edition, Book iii. 319, 320.

In the "Epistle to Dr. Arbuthnot" there were one or two
passing allusions to Cibber, one of them being the line :—

> "And has not Colley still his Lord and whore?"

for which Cibber retaliated in his "Letter" of 1742.

In the "First Epistle of the Second Book of Horace" (1737),
Cibber is scurvily treated. In it occur the lines :—

> "And idle Cibber, how he breaks the laws,
> To make poor Pinkey eat with vast applause!"

[2] Cibber's Odes were a fruitful subject of banter. Fielding in
"Pasquin," act ii. sc. 1, has the following passage :—

> "*2nd Voter.* My Lord, I should like a Place at Court too; I

easiest ways too of pleasing the generality of
Readers, is evident from the comfortable subsistence
which our weekly Retailers of Politicks have been
known to pick up, merely by making bold with a
Government that had unfortunately neglected to find
their Genius a better Employment.

Hence too arises all that flat Poverty of Censure
and Invective that so often has a Run in our publick Papers upon the Success of a new Author;
when, God knows, there is seldom above one Writer
among hundreds in Being at the same time whose
Satyr a Man of common Sense ought to be mov'd at.
When a Master in the Art is angry, then indeed we
ought to be alarm'd! How terrible a Weapon is
Satyr in the Hand of a great Genius? Yet even

don't much care what it is, provided I wear fine Cloaths, and have
something to do in the Kitchen, or the Cellar; I own I should
like the Cellar, for I am a divilish Lover of Sack.

Lord Place. Sack, say you? Odso, you shall be Poet-Laureat.

2nd Voter. Poet! no, my Lord, I am no Poet, I can't make
verses.

Lord Place. No Matter for that—you'll be able to make Odes.

2nd Voter. Odes, my Lord! what are those?

Lord Place. Faith, Sir, I can't tell well what they are; but I
know you may be qualified for the Place without being a Poet."

Boswell (" Life of Johnson," i. 402) reports that Johnson said,
" His [Cibber's] friends give out that he *intended* his birth-day *Odes*
should be bad : but that was not the case, Sir; for he kept them
many months by him, and a few years before he died he shewed
me one of them, with great solicitude to render it as perfect as
might be."

In "The Egotist" (p. 63) Cibber is made to say: "As bad
Verses are the Devil, and good ones I can't get up to——"

there, how liable is Prejudice to misuse it? How
far, when general, it may reform our Morals, or what
Cruelties it may inflict by being angrily particular,[1]
is perhaps above my reach to determine. I shall
therefore only beg leave to interpose what I feel for
others whom it may personally have fallen upon.
When I read those mortifying Lines of our most
eminent Author, in his Character of *Atticus*[2] (*Atticus*, whose Genius in Verse and whose Morality in
Prose has been so justly admir'd) though I am
charm'd with the Poetry, my Imagination is hurt at
the Severity of it; and tho' I allow the Satyrist to
have had personal Provocation, yet, methinks, for
that very Reason he ought not to have troubled the
Publick with it : For, as it is observed in the 242d
Tatler, "In all Terms of Reproof, when the Sen-
" tence appears to arise from Personal Hatred or
" Passion, it is not then made the Cause of Man-
" kind, but a Misunderstanding between two Per-
" sons." But if such kind of Satyr has its incontestable Greatness ; if its exemplary Brightness may
not mislead inferior Wits into a barbarous Imitation
of its Severity, then I have only admir'd the Verses,
and expos'd myself by bringing them under so scrupulous a Reflexion : But the Pain which the Acri-
mony of those Verses gave me is, in some measure,

---

[1] "Champion," 29th April, 1740: "When he says (*Fol.* 23)
Satire is *angrily* particular, every Dunce of a Reader knows that
he means angry with a particular Person."

[2] Cibber's allusion to Pope's treatment of Addison is a fair hit.

allay'd in finding that this inimitable Writer, as he advances in Years, has since had Candour enough to celebrate the same Person for his visible Merit. Happy Genius! whose Verse, like the Eye of Beauty, can heal the deepest Wounds with the least Glance of Favour.

Since I am got so far into this Subject, you must give me leave to go thro' all I have a mind to say upon it; because I am not sure that in a more proper Place my Memory may be so full of it. I cannot find, therefore, from what Reason Satyr is allow'd more Licence than Comedy, or why either of them (to be admir'd) ought not to be limited by Decency and Justice. Let *Juvenal* and *Aristophanes* have taken what Liberties they please, if the Learned have nothing more than their Antiquity to justify their laying about them at that enormous rate, I shall wish they had a better excuse for them! The Personal Ridicule and Scurrility thrown upon *Socrates*, which *Plutarch* too condemns; and the Boldness of *Juvenal*, in writing real Names over guilty Characters, I cannot think are to be pleaded in right of our modern Liberties of the same kind. *Facit indignatio versum*[1] may be a very spirited Expression, and seems to give a Reader hopes of a lively Entertainment: But I am afraid Reproof is in unequal Hands when Anger is its Executioner; and tho' an outrageous Invective may carry some Truth in it, yet it will never have that natural, easy Credit

---

[1] Juvenal, i. 79.

with us which we give to the laughing Ironies of a
cool Head. The Satyr that can smile *circum præ-
cordia ludit*, and seldom fails to bring the Reader
quite over to his Side whenever Ridicule and folly
are at variance. But when a Person satyriz'd is us'd
with the extreamest Rigour, he may sometimes meet
with Compassion instead of Contempt, and throw
back the Odium that was designed for him, upon
the Author. When I would therefore disarm the
Satyrist of this Indignation, I mean little more than
that I would take from him all private or personal
Prejudice, and wou'd still leave him as much general
Vice to scourge as he pleases, and that with as much
Fire and Spirit as Art and Nature demand to enliven
his Work and keep his Reader awake.

Against all this it may be objected, That these are
Laws which none but phlegmatick Writers will observe, and only Men of Eminence should give. I
grant it, and therefore only submit them to Writers
of better Judgment. I pretend not to restrain others
from chusing what I don't like; they are welcome (if
they please too) to think I offer these Rules more from
an Incapacity to break them than from a moral Humanity. Let it be so! still, That will not weaken the
strength of what I have asserted, if my Assertion be
true. And though I allow that Provocation is not
apt to weigh out its Resentments by Drachms and
Scruples, I shall still think that no publick Revenge
can be honourable where it is not limited by Justice; and if Honour is insatiable in its Revenge it

loses what it contends for and sinks itself, if not into Cruelty, at least into Vain-glory.

This so singular Concern which I have shewn for others may naturally lead you to ask me what I feel for myself when I am unfavourably treated by the elaborate Authors of our daily Papers.[1] Shall I be sincere? and own my frailty? Its usual Effect is to make me vain! For I consider if I were quite good for nothing these Pidlers in Wit would not be concern'd to take me to pieces, or (not to be quite so vain) when they moderately charge me with only Ignorance or Dulness, I see nothing in That which an honest Man need be asham'd of:[2] There is many a good Soul who from those sweet Slumbers of the Brain are never awaken'd by the least harmful Thought; and I am

---

[1] Davies ("Dram. Misc.," iii. 511) says: "If we except the remarks on plays and players by the authors of the Tatler and Spectator, the theatrical observations in those days were coarse and illiberal, when compared to what we read in our present daily and other periodical papers."

[2] "*Frankly.* Is it not commendable in a Man of Parts, to be warmly concerned for his Reputation?

Author [*Cibber*]. In what regards his Honesty or Honour, I will make you some Allowances: But for the Reputation of his Parts, not one Tittle!"—"The Egotist: or, Colley upon Cibber," p. 13.

Bellchambers notes here: "When Cibber was charged with moral offences of a deeper dye, he thought himself at liberty, I presume, to relinquish his indifference, and bring the libeller to account. On a future page will be found the public advertisement in which he offered a reward of ten pounds for the detection of Dennis."

sometimes tempted to think those Retailers of Wit
may be of the same Class; that what they write pro-
ceeds not from Malice, but Industry; and that I
ought no more to reproach them than I would a
Lawyer that pleads against me for his Fee; that
their Detraction, like Dung thrown upon a Meadow,
tho' it may seem at first to deform the Prospect, in a
little time it will disappear of itself and leave an involuntary Crop of Praise behind it.

When they confine themselves to a sober Criticism
upon what I write; if their Censure is just, what
answer can I make to it?   If it is unjust, why should
I suppose that a sensible Reader will not see it, as
well as myself?   Or, admit I were able to expose
them by a laughing Reply, will not that Reply beget
a Rejoinder?   And though they might be Gainers
by having the worst on't in a Paper War, that is no
Temptation for me to come into it.   Or (to make
both sides less considerable) would not my bearing
Ill-language from a Chimney-sweeper do me less
harm than it would be to box with him, tho' I were
sure to beat him?   Nor indeed is the little Reputation I have as an Author worth the trouble of a Defence.   Then, as no Criticism can possibly make me
worse than I really am; so nothing I can say of myself can possibly make me better: When therefore
a determin'd Critick comes arm'd with Wit and Outrage to take from me that small Pittance I have, I
wou'd no more dispute with him than I wou'd resist
a Gentleman of the Road to save a little Pocket-

Money.[1] Men that are in want themselves seldom make a Conscience of taking it from others. Whoever thinks I have too much is welcome to what share of it he pleases : Nay, to make him more merciful (as I partly guess the worst he can say of what I now write) I will prevent even the Imputation of his doing me Injustice, and honestly say it myself, *viz.* That of all the Assurances I was ever guilty of, this of writing my own Life is the most hardy. I beg his Pardon ! ——— Impudent is what I should have said ! That through every Page there runs a Vein of Vanity and Impertinence which no *French Ensigns memoires* ever came up to ; but, as this is a common Error, I presume the Terms of *Doating Trifler*, *Old Fool*, or *Conceited Coxcomb* will carry Contempt enough for an impartial Censor to bestow on me ; that my style is unequal, pert, and frothy, patch'd and party-colour'd like the Coat of an *Harlequin* ; low and pompous, cramm'd with Epithets, strew'd with Scraps of second-hand *Latin* from common Quotations ; frequently aiming at Wit, without ever hitting the Mark ; a mere Ragoust toss'd up from the offals of other authors : My Subject below all Pens but my own, which, whenever I keep to, is flatly daub'd by one eternal Egotism : That I want

---

[1] " *Frankly*. It will be always natural for Authors to defend their Works.

Author [*Cibber*]. And would it not be as well, if their Works defended themselves ? "—"The Egotist : or, Colley upon Cibber," p. 15.

nothing but Wit to be as accomplish'd a Coxcomb
here as ever I attempted to expose on the Theatre:
Nay, that this very Confession is no more a Sign of
my Modesty than it is a Proof of my Judgment,
that, in short, you may roundly tell me, that ——
Cinna (or *Cibber*) *vult videri Pauper, et est Pauper.*

> *When humble* Cinna *cries,* I'm poor and low,
> *You may believe him——he is really so.*

Well, Sir Critick! and what of all this? Now I
have laid myself at your Feet, what will you do with
me? Expose me? Why, dear Sir, does not every
Man that writes expose himself? Can you make
me more ridiculous than Nature has made me? You
cou'd not sure suppose that I would lose the Pleasure of Writing because you might possibly judge
me a Blockhead, or perhaps might pleasantly tell
other People they ought to think me so too. Will
not they judge as well from what *I* say as what *You*
say? If then you attack me merely to divert yourself, your Excuse for writing will be no better than
mine. But perhaps you may want Bread: If that
be the Case, even go to Dinner, i' God's name![1]

If our best Authors, when teiz'd by these Triflers,
have not been Masters of this Indifference, I should
not wonder if it were disbeliev'd in me; but when it
is consider'd that I have allow'd my never having

---

[1] In his "Letter to Pope," 1742, p. 7, Cibber says: "After near
twenty years having been libell'd by our Daily-paper Scriblers, I
never was so hurt, as to give them one single Answer."

been disturb'd into a Reply has proceeded as much from Vanity as from Philosophy,[1] the Matter then may not seem so incredible : And tho' I confess the complete Revenge of making them Immortal Dunces in Immortal Verse might be glorious ; yet, if you will call it Insensibility in me never to have winc'd at them, even that Insensibility has its happiness, and what could Glory give me more ?[2] For my part, I have always had the comfort to think, whenever they design'd me a Disfavour, it generally flew back into their own Faces, as it happens to Children when they squirt at their Play-fellows against the Wind. If a Scribbler cannot be easy because he fancies I have too good an Opinion of my own Productions, let him write on and mortify ; I owe him not the Charity to be out of temper myself merely to keep him quiet or give him Joy : Nor, in reality, can I see why any thing misrepresented, tho' believ'd of me by Persons to whom I am unknown, ought to give me any more Concern than what may be thought of me in *Lapland :* 'Tis with those with whom I am to *live* only, where my Character can affect me ; and I will ven-

---

[1] "*Frankly.* I am afraid you will discover yourself ; and your Philosophical Air will come out at last meer Vanity in Masquerade.
Author [*Cibber*]. O ! if there be Vanity in keeping one's Temper ; with all my Heart."—"The Egotist : or, Colley upon Cibber," p. 13.

[2] In his "Letter to Pope," 1742, p. 9, Cibber says : " I would not have even your merited Fame in Poetry, if it were to be attended with half the fretful Solicitude you seem to have lain under to maintain it."

ture to say, he must find out a new way of Writing
that will make me pass my Time *there* less agreeably.

You see, Sir, how hard it is for a Man that is
talking of himself to know when to give over; but if
you are tired, lay me aside till you have a fresh Appetite; if not, I'll tell you a Story.

In the Year 1730 there were many Authors
whose Merit wanted nothing but Interest to recommend them to the vacant *Laurel*, and who took it ill
to see it at last conferred upon a Comedian; insomuch, that they were resolved at least to shew
specimens of their superior Pretensions, and accordingly enliven'd the publick Papers with ingenious
Epigrams and satyrical Flirts at the unworthy Successor:[1] These Papers my Friends with a wicked
Smile would often put into my Hands and desire
me to read them fairly in Company: This was a
Challenge which I never declin'd, and, to do my
doughty Antagonists Justice, I always read them

---

[1] The best epigram is that which Cibber ("Letter," 1742, p.
39) attributes to Pope :—
  "In merry Old England, it once was a Rule,
  The King had his Poet, and also his Fool.
  But now we're so frugal, I'd have you to know it,
  That Cibber can serve both for Fool and for Poet."
  Dr. Johnson also wrote an epigram, of which he seems to have
been somewhat proud :—
  "Augustus still survives in Maro's strain,
  And Spenser's verse prolongs Eliza's reign;
  Great George's acts let tuneful Cibber sing;
  For Nature form'd the Poet for the King."
                                        Boswell, i. 149.

with as much impartial Spirit as if I had writ them myself. While I was thus beset on all sides, there happen'd to step forth a poetical Knight-Errant to my Assistance, who was hardy enough to publish some compassionate Stanzas in my Favour. These, you may be sure, the Raillery of my Friends could do no less than say I had written to myself. To deny it I knew would but have confirmed their pretended Suspicion : I therefore told them, since it gave them such Joy to believe them my own, I would do my best to make the whole Town think so too. As the Oddness of this Reply was I knew what would not be easily comprehended, I desired them to have a Days patience, and I would print an Explanation to it : To conclude, in two Days after I sent this Letter, with some doggerel Rhimes at the Bottom,

To the Author of the Whitehall Evening-Post.

S I R,

THE Verses to the Laureat in yours of Saturday *last have occasion'd the following Reply, which I*

In "Certain Epigrams, in Laud and Praise of the Gentlemen of the Dunciad," p. 8, is :—

EPIGRAM XVI.

A Question by ANONYMUS.

" Tell, if you can, which did the worse,
    Caligula, or *Gr—n's* [Grafton's] Gr—ce ?
That made a Consul of a *Horse*,
    And this a Laureate of an *Ass*."

In " The Egotist : or, Colley upon Cibber," p. 49, Cibber is

*hope you'll give a Place in your next, to shew that we
can be quick as well as smart upon a proper Occasion:
And, as I think it the lowest Mark of a Scoundrel to
make bold with any Man's Character in Print without subscribing the true Name of the Author; I therefore desire, if the Laureat is concern'd enough to ask
the Question, that you will tell him my Name and
where I live; till then, I beg leave to be known by no
other than that of,*

Your Servant,

Monday, Jan. 11, 1730.   FRANCIS FAIRPLAY.

These were the Verses.[1]

I.

Ah, hah! Sir Coll, *is that thy Way,
   Thy own dull Praise to write?
And wou'd'st thou stand so sure a Lay?
   No, that's too stale a Bite.*

II.

*Nature and Art in thee combine,
   Thy Talents here excel:
All shining Brass thou dost outshine,
   To play the Cheat so well.*

III.

Who sees thee in Iago's *Part,
   But thinks thee such a Rogue?*

made to say: "An *Ode* is a Butt, that a whole Quiver of Wit is
let fly at every Year!"

[1] "The Laureat" says: "The Things he calls Verses, carry the
most evident Marks of their Parent *Colley.*"—p. 24.

And is not glad, with all his Heart,
　To hang so sad a Dog?

IV.

When Bays *thou play'st, Thyself thou art;*
　For that by Nature fit,
No Blockhead better suits the Part,
　Than such a Coxcomb Wit.

V.

In Wronghead *too, thy Brains we see,*
　Who might do well at Plough;
As fit for Parliament was he,
　As for the Laurel, Thou.

VI.

Bring thy protected Verse from Court,
　And try it on the Stage;
There it will make much better Sport,
　And set the Town in Rage.

VII.

There Beaux and Wits and Cits and Smarts,
　Where Hissing's not uncivil,
Will shew their Parts to thy Deserts,
　And send it to the Devil.

VIII.

But, ah! in vain 'gainst Thee we write,
　In vain thy Verse we maul!
Our sharpest Satyr's thy Delight,
　* *For*——Blood! thou'lt stand it all.

　　* *A Line in the Epilogue to the* Nonjuror.

IX.

Thunder, 'tis said, the Laurel spares;
Nought but thy Brows could blast it:
And yet——O curst, provoking Stars!
Thy Comfort is, thou hast *it.*

This, Sir, I offer as a Proof that I was seven
Years ago[1] the same cold Candidate for Fame
which I would still be thought; you will not easily
suppose I could have much Concern about it, while,
to gratify the merry Pique of my Friends, I was
capable of seeming to head the Poetical Cry then
against me, and at the same Time of never letting
the Publick know 'till this Hour that these Verses
were written by myself: Nor do I give them you as
an Entertainment, but merely to shew you this particular Cast of my Temper.

When I have said this, I would not have it thought
Affectation in me when I grant that no Man worthy
the Name of an Author is a more faulty Writer than
myself; that I am not Master of my own Language[2]

---

[1] This allusion to time shows that Cibber began his "Apology"
about 1737.

[2] Fielding has many extremely good attacks on Cibber's style
and language. For instance :—

"I shall here only obviate a flying Report . . . that whatever
Language it was writ in, it certainly could not be *English*. . . .
Now I shall prove it to be *English* in the following Manner.
Whatever Book is writ in no other Language, is writ in *English*.
This Book is writ in no other Language, *Ergo*, It is writ in
English."—"Champion," 22nd April, 1740.

Again ("Joseph Andrews," book iii. chap. vi.), addressing the

I too often feel when I am at a loss for Expression: I know too that I have too bold a Disregard for that Correctness which others set so just a Value upon: This I ought to be ashamed of, when I find that Persons, perhaps of colder Imaginations, are allowed to write better than myself. Whenever I speak of any thing that highly delights me, I find it very difficult to keep my Words within the Bounds of Common Sense: Even when I write too, the same Failing will sometimes get the better of me; of which I cannot give you a stronger Instance than in that wild Expression I made use of in the first Edition of my Preface to the *Provok'd Husband;* where, speaking of Mrs. *Oldfield's* excellent Performance in the Part of Lady *Townly*, my Words ran thus, *viz. It is not enough to say, that here she outdid her usual Outdoing.*[1]—A most vile Jingle, I grant it! You may, well ask me, How could I possibly commit such a Wantonness to Paper? And I owe myself the Shame of confessing I have no Excuse for it but that, like a Lover in the Fulness of his Content, by endeavouring to be floridly grateful I talk'd Nonsense. Not but it makes me smile to remember how many flat Writers have made themselves brisk upon this single Expression; wherever the

Muse or Genius that presides over Biography, he says: "Thou, who, without the assistance of the least spice of literature, and even against his inclination, hast, in some pages of his book, forced Colley Cibber to write English."

[1] In later editions the expression was changed to "She here out-did her usual excellence."

Verb, *Outdo,* could come in, the pleasant Accusative, *Outdoing,* was sure to follow it. The provident Wags knew that *Decies repetita placeret :*[1] so delicious a Morsel could not be serv'd up too often! After it had held them nine times told for a Jest, the Publick has been pester'd with a tenth Skull thick enough to repeat it. Nay, the very learned in the Law have at last facetiously laid hold of it! Ten Years after it first came from me it served to enliven the elo-quence of an eloquent Pleader before a House of Parliament! What Author would not envy me so frolicksome a Fault that had such publick Honours paid to it?

After this Consciousness of my real Defects, you will easily judge, Sir, how little I presume that my Poetical Labours may outlive those of my mortal *Cotemporaries.*[2]

At the same time that I am so humble in my Pre-tensions to Fame, I would not be thought to under-value it; Nature will not suffer us to despise it, but she may sometimes make us too fond of it. I have known more than one good Writer very near ridicu-lous from being in too much Heat about it. Who-ever intrinsically deserves it will always have a pro-

---

[1] "Decies repetita placebit."—Horace, *Ars Poetica,* 365.
[2]   "For instance : when you rashly think,
     No rhymer can like Welsted sink,
     His merits balanc'd, you shall find,
     The laureat leaves him far behind."
          Swift, *On Poetry : a Rhapsody,* l. 393.

portionable Right to it. It can neither be resign'd
nor taken from you by Violence. Truth, which is
unalterable, must (however his Fame may be contested) give every Man his Due : What a Poem
weighs it will be worth ; nor is it in the Power of
Human Eloquence, with Favour or Prejudice, to
increase or diminish its Value. Prejudice, 'tis true,
may a while discolour it ; but it will always have its
Appeal to the Equity of good Sense, which will
never fail in the End to reverse all false Judgment
against it. Therefore when I see an eminent Author
hurt, and impatient at an impotent Attack upon his
Labours, he disturbs my Inclination to admire him ;
I grow doubtful of the favourable Judgment I have
made of him, and am quite uneasy to see him so
tender in a Point he cannot but know he ought not
himself to be judge of ; his Concern indeed at
another's Prejudice or Disapprobation may be natural ; but to own it seems to me a natural Weakness.
When a Work is apparently great it will go without
Crutches ; all your Art and Anxiety to heighten the
Fame of it then becomes low and little.[1] He that
will bear no Censure must be often robb'd of his
due Praise. Fools have as good a Right to be
Readers as Men of Sense have, and why not to give

[1] "*Frankly.* Then for your Reputation, if you won't bustle
about it, and now and then give it these little Helps of Art, how
can you hope to raise it?

Author [*Cibber*]. If it can't live upon simple Nature, let it die,
and be damn'd ! I shall give myself no further Trouble about
it."—"The Egotist : or, Colley upon Cibber," p. 9.

their Judgments too ?   Methinks it would be a sort of Tyranny in Wit for an Author to be publickly putting every Argument to death that appear'd against him ; so absolute a Demand for Approbation puts us upon our Right to dispute it ; Praise is as much the Reader's Property as Wit is the Author's ; Applause is not a Tax paid to him as a Prince, but rather a Benevolence given to him as a Beggar ; and we have naturally more Charity for the dumb Beggar than the sturdy one.   The Merit of a Writer and a fine Woman's Face are never mended by their talk- ing of them : How amiable is she that seems not to know she is handsome !

To conclude ; all I have said upon this Subject is much better contained in six Lines of a Reverend Author, which will be an Answer to all critical Cen- sure for ever.

Time is the Judge ; Time has nor Friend nor Foe ;
False Fame must wither, and the True will grow.
Arm'd with this Truth all Criticks I defy ;
For, if I fall, by my own Pen I die ;
While Snarlers strive with proud but fruitless Pain,
To wound Immortals, or to slay the Slain.[1]

[1] Young's second "Epistle to Mr. Pope."

CHAPTER III.

The Author's several Chances for the Church, the Court, and the Army. Going to the University. Met the Revolution at Nottingham. Took Arms on that Side. What he saw of it. A few Political Thoughts. Fortune willing to do for him. His Neglect of her. The Stage preferr'd to all her Favours. The Profession of an Actor consider'd. The Misfortunes and Advantages of it.

I AM now come to that Crisis of my Life when Fortune seem'd to be at a Loss what she should do with me. Had she favour'd my Father's first Designation of me, he might then, perhaps, have had as sanguine Hopes of my being a Bishop as I afterwards conceived of my being a General when I first took Arms at the Revolution. Nay, after that I

had a third Chance too, equally as good, of becoming
an Under-propper of the State. How at last I came
to be none of all these the Sequel will inform you.

About the Year 1687 I was taken from School to
stand at the Election of Children into *Winchester*
College ; my being by my Mother's Side a Descen-
dant[1] of *William* of *Wickam*, the Founder, my Father
(who knew little how the World was to be dealt with)
imagined my having that Advantage would be Security enough for my Success, and so sent me simply
down thither, without the least favourable Recommendation or Interest, but that of my naked Merit
and a pompous Pedigree in my Pocket. Had he
tack'd a Direction to my Back, and sent me by the
Carrier to the Mayor of the Town, to be chosen
Member of Parliament there, I might have had just as
much Chance to have succeeded in the one as the
other. But I must not omit in this Place to let you
know that the Experience which my Father then
bought, at my Cost, taught him some Years after to
take a more judicious Care of my younger Brother,
Lewis Cibber, whom, with the Present of a Statue of
the Founder, of his own making, he recommended
to the same College. This Statue now stands (I
think) over the School Door there,[2] and was so well

[1] Indirectly surely, William of Wykeham being a priest.

[2] I am indebted to the courtesy of the Head Master of Winchester College, the Rev. Dr. Fearon, for the information that
this statue, a finely designed and well-executed work, still stands
over the door of the big school. A Latin inscription states that
it was presented by Caius Gabriel Cibber in 1697.

executed that it seem'd to speak——for its Kinsman. It was no sooner set up than the Door of Preferment was open to him.

Here one would think my Brother had the Advantage of me in the Favour of Fortune, by this his first laudable Step into the World. I own I was so proud of his Success that I even valued myself upon it ; and yet it is but a melancholy Reflection to observe how unequally his Profession and mine were provided for ; when I, who had been the Outcast of Fortune, could find means, from my Income of the Theatre, before I was my own Master there, to supply in his highest Preferment his common Necessities. I cannot part with his Memory without telling you I had as sincere a Concern for this Brother's Well-being as my own. He had lively Parts and more than ordinary Learning, with a good deal of natural Wit and Humour ; but from too great a disregard to his Health he died a Fellow of *New College* in *Oxford* soon after he had been ordained by Dr. *Compton*, then Bishop of *London*. I now return to the State of my own Affair at *Winchester*.

After the Election, the Moment I was inform'd that I was one of the unsuccessful Candidates, I blest myself to think what a happy Reprieve I had got from the confin'd Life of a School-boy ! and the same Day took Post back to *London*, that I might arrive time enough to see a Play (then my darling Delight) before my Mother might demand an Account of my travelling Charges. When I look back to that Time, it almost makes me tremble to think what Miseries, in fifty Years farther in Life, such an unthinking Head was liable to! To ask why Providence afterwards took more Care of me than I did of myself, might be making too bold an Enquiry into its secret Will and Pleasure: All I can say to that Point is, that I am thankful and amazed at it![1]

'Twas about this time I first imbib'd an Inclination, which I durst not reveal, for the Stage; for besides that I knew it would disoblige my Father, I had no Conception of any means practicable to make my way to it. I therefore suppress'd the bewitching Ideas of so sublime a Station, and compounded with my Ambition by laying a lower Scheme, of only getting the nearest way into the immediate Life of a Gentleman-Collegiate. My Father being at this time employ'd at *Chattsworth* in *Derbyshire* by the

[1] Bellchambers finds in this sentence "a levity, which accords with the charges so often brought against Cibber of impiety and irreligion;" and he quotes from Davies ("Dram. Misc.," iii. 506) two stories—one, that Cibber spat at a picture of our Saviour; and the other, that he endeavoured to enter into discussion with "honest Mr. William Whiston" with the intention of insulting him. Both anecdotes seem to me rather foolish. I do not suppose Cibber was in any sense a religious man, but his works are far from giving any offence to religion; and, as a paid supporter of a Protestant succession, I think he was too prudent to be an open scoffer. A sentence in one of Victor's "Letters" (i. 72), written from Tunbridge, would seem to show that Cibber at least preserved appearances. He says, "Every one complies with what is called the *fashion*—*Cibber* goes constantly to *prayers* —and the *Curate* (to return the compliment) as constantly, when prayers are over, to the *Gaming table!*"

(then) Earl of *Devonshire*, who was raising that Seat from a *Gothick* to a *Grecian* Magnificence, I made use of the Leisure I then had in *London* to open to him by Letter my Disinclination to wait another Year for an uncertain Preferment at *Winchester*, and to entreat him that he would send me, *per saltum*, by a shorter Cut, to the University. My Father, who was naturally indulgent to me, seem'd to comply with my Request, and wrote word that as soon as his Affairs would permit, he would carry me with him and settle me in some College, but rather at *Cambridge*, where (during his late Residence at that Place, in making some Statues that now stand upon *Trinity* College New Library) he had contracted some Acquaintance with the Heads of Houses, who might assist his Intentions for me.[1] This I lik'd

---

[1] By the kindness of a friend at Cambridge I am enabled to give the following interesting extracts from a letter written by Mr. William White, of Trinity College Library, regarding the statues here referred to: "They occupy the four piers, subdividing the balustrade on the east side of the Library, overlooking Neville's Court. The four Statues represent Divinity, Law, Physic, and Mathematics. That these were executed by Mr. Gabriel Cibber our books will prove. I will give you two or three extracts from Grumbold's Account Book, kept in the Library. He was Foreman of the Works when the Library was built. I think Cibber cut the Statues here. It is quite certain he and his men were here some time : no doubt they superintended the placing of them in their positions, at so great a height.

'Payd for the Carridg of a Larg Block Stone Given by John Manning to yᵉ Coll. for one of yᵉ Figures 01 : 00 : 00.'

'May 7, 1681. Pᵈ to Mʳ Gabriell Cibber for cutting four statues 80 : 00 : 00.'

better than to go discountenanc'd to *Oxford*, to which
it would have been a sort of Reproach to me not to
have come elected. After some Months were elaps'd,
my Father, not being willing to let me lie too long
idling in *London*, sent for me down to *Chattsworth*,
to be under his Eye, till he cou'd be at leisure to
carry me to *Cambridge*. Before I could set out on
my Journey thither, the Nation fell in labour of the
Revolution, the News being then just brought to
London That the Prince of *Orange* at the Head
of an Army was landed in the *West*.[1] When I
came to *Nottingham*, I found my Father in Arms
there, among those Forces which the Earl of
Devonshire had rais'd for the Redress of our violated
Laws and Liberties. My Father judg'd this a proper
Season for a young Strippling to turn himself loose
into the Bustle of the World; and being himself too
advanc'd in Years to endure the Winter Fatigue
which might possibly follow, entreated that noble
Lord that he would be pleas'd to accept of his Son
in his room, and that he would give him (my Father)
leave to return and finish his Works at *Chattsworth*.
This was so well receiv'd by his Lordship that he
not only admitted of my Service, but promis'd my

' **27** June. P^d to ye Widdo Bats for Mr Gabriel Cibbers and
his mens diatt 05 : 18 : 11. P^d to Mr Martin [for the same]
12 : 03 : 03.' "

In connection with these statues an amusing practical joke was
played while Byron was an undergraduate, which was attributed to
him—unjustly, however, I believe.

[1] 5th November, 1688.

Father in return that when Affairs were settled he would provide for me. Upon this my Father return'd to *Derbyshire*, while I, not a little transported, jump'd into his Saddle. Thus in one Day all my Thoughts of the University were smother'd in Ambition ! A slight Commission for a Horse-Officer was the least View I had before me. At this Crisis you cannot but observe that the Fate of King *James* and of the Prince of *Orange*, and that of so minute a Being as my self, were all at once upon the Anvil : In what shape they wou'd severally come out, tho' a good *Guess* might be made, was not then *demonstrable* to the deepest Foresight ; but as my Fortune seem'd to be of small Importance to the Publick, Providence thought fit to postpone it 'till that of those great Rulers of Nations was justly perfected. Yet, had my Father's Business permitted him to have carried me one Month sooner (as he intended) to the University, who knows but by this time that purer Fountain might have wash'd my Imperfections into a Capacity of writing (instead of Plays and Annual Odes) Sermons and Pastoral Letters. But whatever Care of the Church might so have fallen to my share, as I dare say it may be now in better Hands, I ought not to repine at my being otherwise disposed of.[1]

---

[1] Fielding, in " Joseph Andrews," book i. chap. 1 : " How artfully does the former [Cibber] by insinuating that he escaped being promoted to the highest stations in the Church and State, teach us a contempt of worldly grandeur ! how strongly does he inculcate an absolute submission to our Superiors !"

You must now consider me as one among those desperate Thousands, who, after a Patience sorely try'd, took Arms under the Banner of Necessity, the natural Parent of all Human Laws and Government. I question if in all the Histories of Empire there is one Instance of so bloodless a Revolution as that in *England* in 1688, wherein Whigs, Tories, Princes, Prelates, Nobles, Clergy, common People, and a Standing Army, were unanimous. To have seen all *England* of one Mind is to have liv'd at a very particular Juncture. Happy Nation! who are never divided among themselves but when they have least to complain of! Our greatest Grievance since that Time seems to have been that we cannot all govern; and 'till the Number of good Places are equal to those who think themselves qualified for them there must ever be a Cause of Contention among us. While Great Men want great Posts, the Nation will never want real or seeming Patriots; and while great Posts are fill'd with Persons whose Capacities are but Human, such Persons will never be allow'd to be without Errors; not even the Revolution, with all its Advantages, it seems, has been able to furnish us with unexceptionable Statesmen! for from that time I don't remember any one Set of Ministers that have not been heartily rail'd at; a Period long enough one would think (if all of them have been as bad as they have been call'd) to make a People despair of ever seeing a good one: But as it is possible that Envy, Prejudice, or Party may sometimes have a share in what is generally thrown upon 'em, it is not easy for a private Man to know who is absolutely in the right from what is said against them, or from what their Friends or Dependants may say in their Favour: Tho' I can hardly forbear thinking that they who have been *longest* rail'd at, must from that Circumstance shew in some sort a Proof of Capacity. ——But to my History.

It were almost incredible to tell you, at the latter end of King *James's* Time (though the Rod of Arbitrary Power was always shaking over us) with what Freedom and Contempt the common People in the open Streets talk'd of his wild Measures to make a whole Protestant Nation Papists; and yet, in the height of our secure and wanton Defiance of him, we of the Vulgar had no farther Notion of any Remedy for this Evil than a satisfy'd Presumption that our Numbers were too great to be master'd by his mere Will and Pleasure; that though he might be too hard for our Laws, he would never be able to get the better of our Nature; and that to drive all *England* into Popery and Slavery he would find would be teaching an old Lion to dance.[1]

---

[1] Fielding ("Champion," 6th May, 1740): "Not to mention our Author's Comparisons of himself to King *James*, the Prince of *Orange*, *Alexander the Great*, *Charles* the XIIth, and *Harry* IV. of *France*, his favourite Simile is a Lion, thus *page* 39, we have a SATISFIED PRESUMPTION, that *to drive* England *into slavery is like teaching* AN OLD LION TO DANCE. 104. *Our new critics are like Lions Whelps that dash down the Bowls of Milk &c.* besides a third Allusion to the same Animal: and this brings into my Mind

But happy was it for the Nation that it had then wiser Heads in it, who knew how to lead a People so dispos'd into Measures for the Publick Preservation.

Here I cannot help reflecting on the very different Deliverances *England* met with at this Time and in the very same Year of the Century before : Then (in 1588) under a glorious Princess, who had at heart the Good and Happiness of her People, we scatter'd and destroy'd the most formidable Navy of Invaders that ever cover'd the Seas : And now (in 1688) under a Prince who had alienated the Hearts of his People by his absolute Measures to oppress them, a foreign Power is receiv'd with open Arms in defence of our Laws, Liberties, and Religion, which our native Prince had invaded! How widely different were these two Monarchs in their Sentiments of Glory! But, *Tantum religio potuit suadere malorum.*[1]

When we consider in what height of the Nation's Prosperity the Successor of Queen *Elizabeth* came to this Throne, it seems amazing that such a Pile of *English* Fame and Glory, which her skilful Admini-

a Story which I once heard from *Booth*, that our Biographer had, in one of his Plays in a Local Simile, introduced this generous Beast in some Island or Country where Lions did not grow; of which being informed by the learned *Booth*, the Biographer replied, *Prithee tell me then, where there is a Lion, for God's Curse, if there be a Lion in* Europe, Asia, Africa, *or* America, *I will not lose my simile.*"

[1] Lucretius, i. 102.

stration had erected, should in every following
Reign down to the Revolution so unhappily moulder
away in one continual Gradation of Political Errors :
All which must have been avoided, if the plain Rule
which that wise Princess left behind her had been
observed, *viz. That the Love of her People was the
surest Support of her Throne.* This was the Principle by which she so happily govern'd herself and
those she had the Care of. In this she found
Strength to combat and struggle thro' more Difficulties and dangerous Conspiracies than ever *English*
Monarch had to cope with. At the same time that
she profess'd to *desire* the People's Love, she took
care that her Actions shou'd *deserve* it, without the
least Abatement of her Prerogative ; the Terror of
which she so artfully covered that she sometimes
seem'd to flatter those she was determin'd should
obey. If the four following Princes had exercis'd
their Regal Authority with so visible a Regard to
the Publick Welfare, it were hard to know whether
the People of *England* might have ever complain'd
of them, or even felt the want of that Liberty they
now so happily enjoy. 'Tis true that before her
Time our Ancestors had many successful Contests
with their Sovereigns for their *ancient Right* and
Claim to it ; yet what did those Successes amount
to ? little more than a Declaration that there was
such a Right in being ; but who ever saw it enjoy'd ?
Did not the Actions of almost every succeeding
Reign shew there were still so many Doors of

Oppression left open to the Prerogative that (whatever Value our most eloquent Legislators may have set upon those ancient Liberties) I doubt it will be difficult to fix the Period of their having a real Being before the Revolution : Or if there ever was an elder Period of our unmolested enjoying them, I own my poor Judgment is at a loss where to place it. I will boldly say then, it is to the Revolution only we owe the full Possession of what, 'till then, we never had more than a perpetually contested Right to : And, from thence, from the Revolution it is that the Protestant Successors of King *William* have found their Paternal Care and Maintenance of that Right has been the surest Basis of their Glory.[1]

These, Sir, are a few of my Political Notions, which I have ventur'd to expose that you may see what sort of an *English* Subject I am ; how wise or weak they may have shewn me is not my Concern ; let the weight of these Matters have drawn me never so far out of my Depth, I still flatter myself that I have kept a simple, honest Head above Water. And it is a solid Comfort to me to consider that how insignificant soever my Life was at the Revolution, it had still the good Fortune to make one among the many who brought it about ; and that I now, with

---

[1] John Dennis, in an advertisement to "The Invader of his Country," 1720, says, " 'tis as easy for Mr. *Cibber* at this time of Day to make a Bounce with his Loyalty, as 'tis for a Bully at Sea, who had lain hid in the Hold all the time of the Fight, to come up and swagger upon the Deck after the Danger is over."

my Coævals, as well as with the Millions since born, enjoy the happy Effects of it.

But I must now let you see how my particular Fortune went forward with this Change in the Government; of which I shall not pretend to give you any farther Account than what my simple Eyes saw of it.

We had not been many Days at *Nottingham* before we heard that the Prince of *Denmark*, with some other great Persons, were gone off from the King to the Prince of *Orange*, and that the Princess *Anne*, fearing the King her Father's Resentment might fall upon her for her Consort's Revolt, had withdrawn her self in the Night from *London*, and was then within half a Days Journey of *Nottingham*; on which very Morning we were suddenly alarm'd with the News that two thousand of the King's Dragoons were in close pursuit to bring her back Prisoner to *London*: But this Alarm it seems was all Stratagem, and was but a part of that general Terror which was thrown into many other Places about the Kingdom at the same time, with design to animate and unite the People in their common defence; it being then given out that the *Irish* were every where at our Heels to cut off all the Protestants within the Reach of their Fury. In this Alarm our Troops scrambled to Arms in as much Order as their Consternation would admit of, when, having advanc'd some few Miles on the *London* Road, they met the Princess in a Coach, attended only by the Lady *Churchill* (now

Dutchess Dowager of *Marlborough*) and the Lady
Fitzharding, whom they conducted into *Nottingham*
through the Acclamations of the People : The same
Night all the Noblemen and the other Persons of
Distinction then in Arms had the Honour to sup
at her Royal Highness's Table ; which was then furnish'd (as all her necessary Accommodations were)
by the Care and at the Charge of the Lord *Devonshire*. At this Entertainment, of which I was a
Spectator, something very particular surpriz'd me :
The noble Guests at the Table happening to be
more in number than Attendants out of Liveries
could be found for, I being well known in the Lord
Devonshire's Family, was desired by his Lordship's
Maitre d'Hotel to assist at it : The Post assign'd me
was to observe what the Lady *Churchill* might call
for. Being so near the Table, you may naturally
ask me what I might have heard to have pass'd in
Conversation at it ? which I should certainly tell you
had I attended to above two Words that were utter'd
there, and those were, *Some Wine and Water*. These
I remember came distinguish'd and observ'd to my
Ear, because they came from the fair Guest whom I
took such Pleasure to wait on : Except at that single
Sound, all my Senses were collected into my Eyes,
which during the whole Entertainment wanted no
better Amusement, than of stealing now and then
the Delight of gazing on the fair Object so near me :
If so clear an Emanation of Beauty, such a commanding Grace of Aspect struck me into a Regard that

had something softer than the most profound Respect
in it, I cannot see why I may not without Offence
remember it; since Beauty, like the Sun, must sometimes lose its Power to chuse, and shine into equal
Warmth the Peasant and the Courtier.[1] Now to
give you, Sir, a farther Proof of how good a Taste
my first hopeful Entrance into Manhood set out
with, I remember above twenty Years after, when
the same Lady had given the World four of the
loveliest Daughters that ever were gaz'd on, even
after they were all nobly married, and were become
the reigning Toasts of every Party of Pleasure, their
still lovely Mother had at the same time her Votaries,
and her Health very often took the Lead in those
involuntary Triumphs of Beauty. However pre-
sumptuous or impertinent these Thoughts might
have appear'd at my first entertaining them, why
may I not hope that my having kept them decently
secret for full fifty Years may be now a good round
Plea for their Pardon? Were I now qualify'd to
say more of this celebrated Lady, I should conclude
it thus: That she has liv'd (to all Appearance) a
peculiar Favourite of Providence; that few Examples
can parallel the Profusion of Blessings which have
attended so long a Life of Felicity. A Person so

---

[1] "Champion," 29th April, 1740: "When in *page* 42, we read,
Beauty SHINES *into equal Warmth the Peasant and the Courtier*,
do we not know what he means though he hath made a Verb
active of SHINE, as in *Page* 117, he hath of REGRET, *nothing could
more painfully regret a judicious Spectator*."

attractive! a Husband so memorably great! an Offspring so beautiful! a Fortune so immense! and a
Title which (when Royal Favour had no higher to
bestow) she only could receive from the Author of
Nature; a great Grandmother without grey Hairs!
These are such consummate Indulgencies that we
might think Heaven has center'd them all in one
Person, to let us see how far, with a lively Understanding, the full Possession of them could contribute
to human Happiness.—I now return to our Military
Affairs.

From *Nottingham* our Troops march'd to *Oxford;*
through every Town we pass'd the People came out,
in some sort of Order, with such rural and rusty
Weapons as they had, to meet us, in Acclamations of
Welcome and good Wishes. This I thought promis'd a favourable End of our Civil War, when the
Nation seem'd so willing to be all of a Side! At
Oxford the Prince and Princess of *Denmark* met for
the first time after their late Separation, and had all
possible Honours paid them by the University.
Here we rested in quiet Quarters for several Weeks,
till the Flight of King *James* into *France;* when the
Nation being left to take care of it self, the only
Security that could be found for it was to advance
the Prince and Princess of *Orange* to the vacant
Throne. The publick Tranquillity being now settled,
our Forces were remanded back to *Nottingham.*
Here all our Officers who had commanded them
from their first Rising receiv'd Commissions to con-

firm them in their several Posts; and at the same time such private Men as chose to return to their proper Business or Habitations were offer'd their Discharges. Among the small number of those who receiv'd them, I was one; for not hearing that my Name was in any of these new Commissions, I thought it time for me to take my leave of Ambition, as Ambition had before seduc'd me from the imaginary Honours of the Gown, and therefore resolv'd to hunt my Fortune in some other Field.[1]

[1] One of the commonest imputations made against Cibber was that he was of a cowardly temper. In "Common Sense" for 11th June, 1737, a paper attributed to Lord Chesterfield, there is a dissertation on kicking as a humorous incident on the stage. The writer adds: "Of all the Comedians who have appeared upon the Stage within my Memory, no one has taking (*sic*) a Kicking with so much Humour as our present most excellent Laureat, and I am inform'd his Son does not fall much short of him in this Excellence; I am very glad of it, for as I have a Kindness for the young Man, I hope to see him as well kick'd as his Father was before him."

I confess that I am not quite sure how far this sentence is ironically meant, but Bellchambers refers to it as conveying a serious accusation of cowardice. He also quotes from Davies ("Dram. Misc.," iii. 487), who relates, on the authority of Victor, that Cibber, having reduced Bickerstaffe's salary by one-half, was waited upon by that actor, who "flatly told him, that as he could not subsist on the small sum to which he had reduced his salary, he must call the author of his distress to an account, for that it would be easier for him to lose his life than to starve. The affrighted Cibber told him, he should receive an answer from him on Saturday next. Bickerstaffe found, on that day, his usual income was continued." This story rests only on Victor's authority, but is, of course, not improbable. There is also a vague report that Gay, in revenge for Cibber's banter of "Three Hours

From *Nottingham* I again return'd to my Father
at *Chattsworth*, where I staid till my Lord came
down, with the new Honours [1] of Lord Steward of his
Majesty's Houshold and Knight of the Garter! a
noble turn of Fortune! and a deep Stake he had
play'd for! which calls to my Memory a Story we
had then in the Family, which though too light for
our graver Historians notice, may be of weight
enough for my humble Memoirs.   This noble Lord
being in the Presence-Chamber in King *James*'s
time, and known to be no Friend to the Measures
of his Administration, a certain Person in favour
there, and desirous to be more so, took occasion to
tread rudely upon his Lordship's Foot, which was
return'd with a sudden Blow upon the Spot: For
this Misdemeanour his Lordship was fin'd thirty
thousand Pounds; but I think had some time allow'd
him for the Payment.[2]   In the Summer preceding the
Revolution, when his Lordship was retir'd to *Chattsworth*, and had been there deeply engag'd with other
Noblemen in the Measures which soon after brought
it to bear, King *James* sent a Person down to him
with Offers to mitigate his Fine upon Conditions of
ready Payment, to which his Lordship reply'd, That
if his Majesty pleas'd to allow him a little longer

---

after Marriage," personally chastised him, but I know no good
authority for the story.

   [1] Cibber (1st ed.) wrote: "new Honours of Duke of *Devonshire*, Lord Steward," &c.   He corrected his blunder in 2nd ed.

   [2] See Macaulay ("History," 1858, vol. ii. p. 251).

time, he would rather chuse to play *double* or *quit* with him : The time of the intended Rising being then so near at hand, the Demand, it seems, came too late for a more serious Answer.

However low my Pretensions to Preferment were at this time, my Father thought that a little Court-Favour added to them might give him a Chance for saving the Expence of maintaining me, as he had intended, at the University: He therefore order'd me to draw up a Petition to the Duke, and, to give it some Air of Merit, to put it into *Latin*, the Prayer of which was, That his Grace would be pleas'd to do something (I really forget what) for me.——How-ever the Duke, upon receiving it, was so good as to desire my Father would send me to *London* in the Winter, where he would consider of some Provision for me. It might, indeed, well require time to con-sider it; for I believe it was then harder to know what I was really fit for, than to have got me any thing I was not fit for : However, to *London* I came, where I enter'd into my first State of Attendance and Dependance for about five Months, till the *February* following. But alas ! in my Intervals of Leisure, by frequently seeing Plays, my wise Head was turn'd to higher Views, I saw no Joy in any other Life than that of an Actor, so that (as before, when a Candidate at *Winchester*) I was even afraid of succeeding to the Preferment I sought for : 'Twas on the Stage alone I had form'd a Happiness prefer-able to all that Camps or Courts could offer me ! and there was I determin'd, let Father and Mother take it as they pleas'd, to fix my *non ultra*.[1] Here I think my self oblig'd, in respect to the Honour of that noble Lord, to acknowledge that I believe his real Intentions to do well for me were prevented by my own inconsiderate Folly; so that if my Life did not then take a more laudable Turn, I have no one but my self to reproach for it; for I was credibly inform'd by the Gentlemen of his Houshold, that his Grace had, in their hearing, talk'd of recommending me to the Lord *Shrewsbury*, then Secretary of State, for the first proper Vacancy in that Office. But the distant Hope of a Reversion was too cold a Temptation for a Spirit impatient as mine, that wanted immediate Possession of what my Heart was so differently set upon. The Allurements of a Theatre are still so strong in my Memory, that perhaps few, except those who have felt them, can conceive: And I am yet so far willing to excuse my Folly, that I am convinc'd, were it possible to take off that Disgrace and Prejudice which Custom has thrown upon the Profession of an Actor, many a well-born younger Brother and Beauty of low Fortune would gladly have adorn'd the Theatre, who by their not being able to brook such Dishonour to their Birth, have

[1] Davies (" Dram. Misc.," iii. 444) says : " Cibber and Verbruggen were two dissipated young fellows, who determined, in opposition to the advice of friends, to become great actors. Much about the same time, they were constant attendants upon Downes, the prompter of Drury-Lane, in expectation of employment."

pass'd away their Lives decently unheeded and forgotten.

Many Years ago, when I was first in the Menagement of the Theatre, I remember a strong Instance, which will shew you what degree of Ignominy the Profession of an Actor was then held at.—A Lady, with a real Title, whose female Indiscretions had occasion'd her Family to abandon her, being willing, in her Distress, to make an honest Penny of what Beauty she had left, desired to be admitted as an Actress ; when before she could receive our Answer, a Gentleman (probably by her Relation's Permission) advis'd us not to entertain her, for Reasons easy to be guess'd. You may imagine we cou'd not be so blind to our Interest as to make an honourable Family our unnecessary Enemies by not taking his Advice ; which the Lady, too, being sensible of, saw the Affair had its Difficulties, and therefore pursu'd it no farther. Now, is it not hard that it should be a doubt whether this Lady's Condition or ours were the more melancholy ? For here you find her honest Endeavour to get Bread from the Stage was look'd upon as an Addition of new Scandal to her former Dishonour ! so that I am afraid, according to this way of thinking, had the same Lady stoop'd to have sold Patches and Pomatum in a Band-box from Door to Door, she might in that Occupation have starv'd with less Infamy than had she reliev'd her Necessities by being famous on the Theatre. Whether this Prejudice may have arisen from the

Abuses that so often have crept in upon the Stage,
I am not clear in ; tho' when that is grossly the
Case, I will allow there ought to be no Limits set to
the Contempt of it; yet in its lowest Condition in
my time, methinks there could have been no Pretence
of preferring the Band-box to the Buskin. But this
severe Opinion, whether merited or not, is not the
greatest Distress that this Profession is liable to.

I shall now give you another Anecdote, quite the
reverse of what I have instanc'd, wherein you will
see an Actress as hardly us'd for an Act of Modesty
(which without being a Prude, a Woman, even upon
the Stage, may sometimes think it necessary not to
throw off.) This too I am forc'd to premise, that the
Truth of what I am going to tell you may not be
sneer'd at before it be known. About the Year 1717,
a young Actress of a desirable Person, sitting in an
upper Box at the Opera, a military Gentleman
thought this a proper Opportunity to secure a little
Conversation with her, the Particulars of which were
probably no more worth repeating than it seems the
Damoiselle then thought them worth listening to;
for, notwithstanding the fine Things he said to her,
she rather chose to give the Musick the Preference
of her Attention : This Indifference was so offensive
to his high Heart, that he began to change the
Tender into the Terrible, and, in short, proceeded at
last to treat her in a Style too grosly insulting for
the meanest Female Ear to endure unresented :
Upon which, being beaten too far out of her Discre-

tion, she turn'd hastily upon him with an angry Look, and a Reply which seem'd to set his Merit in so low a Regard, that he thought himself oblig'd in Honour to take his time to resent it : This was the full Extent of her Crime, which his Glory delay'd no longer to punish than 'till the next time she was to appear upon the Stage : There, in one of her best Parts, wherein she drew a favourable Regard and Approbation from the Audience, he, dispensing with the Respect which some People think due to a polite Assembly, began to interrupt her Performance with such loud and various Notes of Mockery, as other young Men of Honour in the same Place have sometimes made themselves undauntedly merry with : Thus, deaf to all Murmurs or Entreaties of those about him, he pursued his Point, even to throwing near her such Trash as no Person can be suppos'd to carry about him unless to use on so particular an Occasion.

A Gentleman then behind the Scenes, being shock'd at his unmanly Behaviour, was warm enough to say, That no Man but a Fool or a Bully cou'd be capable of insulting an Audience or a Woman in so monstrous a manner. The former valiant Gentleman, to whose Ear the Words were soon brought by his Spies, whom he had plac'd behind the Scenes to observe how the Action was taken there, came immediately from the Pit in a Heat, and demanded to know of the Author of those Words if he was the Person that spoke them ? to which he calmly reply'd,

That though he had never seen him before, yet, since he seem'd so earnest to be satisfy'd, he would do him the favour to own, That indeed the Words were his, and that they would be the last Words he should chuse to deny, whoever they might fall upon. To conclude, their Dispute was ended the next Morning in *Hyde-Park*, where the determin'd Combatant who first ask'd for Satisfaction was oblig'd afterwards to ask his Life too; whether he mended it or not, I have not yet heard; but his Antagonist in a few Years after died in one of the principal Posts of the Government.[1]

Now, though I have sometimes known these gallant Insulters of Audiences draw themselves into Scrapes which they have less honourably got out of, yet, alas! what has that avail'd? This generous publick-spirited Method of silencing a few was but repelling the Disease in one Part to make it break out in another: All Endeavours at Protection are new Provocations to those who pride themselves in pushing their Courage to a Defiance of Humanity. Even when a Royal Resentment has shewn itself in the behalf of an injur'd Actor, it has been unable to defend him from farther Insults! an Instance of which happen'd in the late King *James*'s time. Mr. *Smith*[2] (whose Character as a Gentleman could have

[1] "The Laureat" states that Miss Santlow (afterwards Mrs. Barton Booth) was the actress referred to; that Captain Montague was her assailant, and Mr. Secretary Craggs her defender.

[2] See memoir of William Smith at end of second volume.

been no way impeach'd had he not degraded it by
being a celebrated Actor) had the Misfortune, in a
Dispute with a Gentleman behind the Scenes, to receive a Blow from him : The same Night an Account
of this Action was carry'd to the King, to whom the
Gentleman was represented so grosly in the wrong,
that the next Day his Majesty sent to forbid him the
Court upon it. This Indignity cast upon a Gentleman only for having maltreated a Player, was look'd
upon as the Concern of every Gentleman ; and a
Party was soon form'd to assert and vindicate their
Honour, by humbling this favour'd Actor, whose
slight Injury had been judg'd equal to so severe a
Notice. Accordingly, the next time *Smith* acted he
was receiv'd with a Chorus of Cat-calls, that soon
convinc'd him he should not be suffer'd to proceed
in his Part ; upon which, without the least Discom-
posure, he order'd the Curtain to be dropp'd ; and,
having a competent Fortune of his own, thought the
Conditions of adding to it by his remaining upon the
Stage were too dear, and from that Day entirely
quitted it.[1] I shall make no Observation upon the
King's Resentment, or on that of his good Subjects ; how far either was or was not right, is not the
Point I dispute for : Be that as it may, the unhappy
Condition of the Actor was so far from being reliev'd
by this Royal Interposition in his favour, that it was
the worse for it.

While these sort of real Distresses on the Stage

[1] See memoir.

are so unavoidable, it is no wonder that young
People of Sense (though of low Fortune) should be
so rarely found to supply a Succession of good Actors.
Why then may we not, in some measure, impute the
Scarcity of them to the wanton Inhumanity of those
Spectators, who have made it so terribly mean to appear there? Were there no ground for this Question, where could be the Disgrace of entring into a
Society whose Institution, when not abus'd, is a delightful School of Morality; and where to excel
requires as ample Endowments of Nature as any one
Profession (that of holy Institution excepted) whatsoever? But, alas! as *Shakespear* says,

*Where's that Palace, whereinto, sometimes
Foul things intrude not?* [1]

Look into St. *Peter*'s at *Rome*, and see what a
profitable Farce is made of Religion there! Why
then is an Actor more blemish'd than a Cardinal?
While the Excellence of the one arises from his
innocently seeming what he is not, and the Eminence of the other from the most impious Fallacies
that can be impos'd upon human Understanding? If
the best things, therefore, are most liable to Corruption, the Corruption of the Theatre is no Disproof
of its innate and primitive Utility.

In this Light, therefore, all the Abuses of the
Stage, all the low, loose, or immoral Supplements to

[1]   " As where's that palace whereinto foul things
Sometimes intrude not ? "—" Othello," act iii. sc. 3.

wit, whether in making Virtue ꞏridiculous or Vice
agreeable, or in the decorated Nonsense and Absurdities of Pantomimical Trumpery, I give up to the
Contempt of every sensible Spectator, as so much
rank Theatrical Popery.   But cannot still allow these
Enormities to impeach the Profession, while they are
so palpably owing to the deprav'd Taste of the Multitude.   While Vice and Farcical Folly are the
most profitable Commodities, why should we wonder
that, time out of mind, the poor Comedian, when real
Wit would bear no Price, should deal in what would
bring him most ready Money?   But this, you will
say, is making the Stage a Nursery of Vice and
Folly, or at least keeping an open Shop for it.——
I grant it: But who do you expect should reform
it? The Actors? Why so? If People are permitted
to buy it without blushing, the Theatrical Merchant
seems to have an equal Right to the Liberty of sell-
ing it without Reproach.   That this Evil wants a
Remedy is not to be contested; nor can it be denied
that the Theatre is as capable of being preserv'd by
a Reformation as Matters of more Importance;
which, for the Honour of our National Taste, I could
wish were attempted; and then, if it could not subsist under decent Regulations, by not being permitted to present any thing there but what were
worthy to be there, it would be time enough to consider, whether it were necessary to let it totally fall,
or effectually support it.

Notwithstanding all my best Endeavours to re-

commend the Profession of an Actor to a more
general Favour, I doubt, while it is liable to such
Corruptions, and the Actor himself to such unlimited
Insults as I have already mention'd, I doubt, I
say, we must still leave him a-drift, with his intrinsick
Merit, to ride out the Storm as well as he is able.

However, let us now turn to the other side of this
Account, and see what Advantages stand there to
balance the Misfortunes I have laid before you. There
we shall still find some valuable Articles of Credit,
that sometimes overpay his incidental Disgraces.

First, if he has Sense, he will consider that as
these Indignities are seldom or never offer'd him by
People that are remarkable for any one good Quality,
he ought not to lay them too close to his Heart : He
will know too, that when Malice, Envy, or a brutal
Nature, can securely hide or fence themselves in a
Multitude, Virtue, Merit, Innocence, and even sovereign Superiority, have been, and must be equally
liable to their Insults ; that therefore, when they fall
upon him in the same manner, his intrinsick Value
cannot be diminish'd by them : On the contrary, if,
with a decent and unruffled Temper, he lets them
pass, the Disgrace will return upon his Aggressor,
and perhaps warm the generous Spectator into a Partiality in his Favour.

That while he is conscious, That, as an Actor, he
must be always in the Hands of Injustice, it does
him at least this involuntary Good, that it keeps him
in a settled Resolution to avoid all Occasions of provoking it, or of even offending the lowest Enemy,

who, at the Expence of a Shilling, may publickly
revenge it.

That, if he excells on the Stage, and is irreproach-
able in his Personal Morals and Behaviour, his Profession is so far from being an Impediment, that it
will be oftner a just Reason for his being receiv'd
among People of condition with Favour; and sometimes with a more social Distinction, than the best,
though more profitable Trade he might have follow'd,
could have recommended him to.

That this is a Happiness to which several Actors
within my Memory, as *Betterton*, *Smith*, *Montfort*,
Captain *Griffin*,[1] and Mrs. *Braccgirdle* (yet living)
have arriv'd at; to which I may add the late cele-

---

[1] Captain Griffin was, no doubt, the Griffin who is mentioned
by Downes as entering the King's Company "after they had
begun at Drury Lane." This is of course very indefinite as regards
time.   Drury Lane was opened in 1663, but the first character
for which we can find Griffin's name mentioned, is that of Varnish
in "The Plain-Dealer," which was produced in 1674.   At the
Union in 1682, Griffin took a good position in the amalgamated
company, and continued on the stage till about 1688, when
his name disappears from the bills.   During this time he
is not called *Captain*, but in 1701 the name of Captain Griffin
appears among the Drury Lane actors.   Genest says it is more
probable that this should be Griffin returned to the stage after
thirteen years spent in the army, than that Captain Griffin
should have gone on the stage without having previously been
connected with it.   In this Genest is quite correct, for the anecdote of Goodman and Griffin, which Cibber tells in Chap. XII.
shows conclusively that *Captain* Griffin was an actor during
Goodman's stage-career, which ended certainly before 1690.   He
appears to have finally retired about the beginning of 1708.
Downes says " *Mr.* Griffin *so Excell'd in* Surly. Sir Edward Belfond,
The Plain Dealer, *none succeeding in the 2 former have Equall'd him,*

brated Mrs. *Oldfield.* Now let us suppose these
Persons, the Men, for example, to have been all
eminent Mercers, and the Women as famous Milli-
ners, can we imagine that merely as such, though
endow'd with the same natural Understanding, they
could have been call'd into the same honourable
Parties of Conversation ? People of Sense and Condition could not but know it was impossible they
could have had such various Excellencies on the
Stage, without having something naturally valuable
in them : And I will take upon me to affirm, who
knew them all living, that there was not one of the
Number who were not capable of supporting a
variety of Spirited Conversation, tho' the Stage were
never to have been the Subject of it.

That to have trod the Stage has not always been
thought a Disqualification from more honourable
Employments ; several have had military Commis-
sions ; *Carlisle* [1] and *Wiltshire* [2] were both kill'd Cap-

---

[nor any] *except his Predecessor Mr.* Hart *in the latter*" (p. 40). I
have ventured to supply the two words "nor any" to make clear
what Downes must have meant.

[1] The "Biographia Dramatica" (i. 87) gives an account of
James Carlile. He was a native of Lancashire, and in his youth
was an actor ; but he left the stage for the army, and was killed at
the battle of Aughrim, 11th July, 1691. Nothing practically is
known of his stage career. Downes (p. 39) notes that at the
Union of the Patents in 1682, "Mr. *Monfort* and Mr. *Carlile*,
were grown to the Maturity of good *Actors.*" I cannot trace Carlile's name in the bills any later than 1685.

[2] Wiltshire seems to have been a very useful actor of the
second rank. In 1685 he also appears for the last time.

tains; one in King *William*'s Reduction of *Ireland*; and the other in his first War in *Flanders*; and the famous *Ben. Johnson*, tho' an unsuccessful Actor, was afterwards made Poet-Laureat.[1]

To these laudable Distinctions let me add one more; that of Publick Applause, which, when truly merited, is perhaps one of the most agreeable Gratifications that venial Vanity can feel. A Happiness almost peculiar to the Actor, insomuch that the best Tragick Writer, however numerous his separate Admirers may be, yet, to unite them into one general Act of Praise, to receive at once those thundring Peals of Approbation which a crouded Theatre throws out, he must still call in the Assistance of the skilful Actor to raise and partake of them.

In a Word, 'twas in this flattering Light only, though not perhaps so thoroughly consider'd, I look'd upon the Life of an Actor when but eighteen Years of Age; nor can you wonder if the Temptations were too strong for so warm a Vanity as mine to resist; but whether excusable or not, to the Stage at length I came, and it is from thence, chiefly, your Curiosity, if you have any left, is to expect a farther Account of me.

---

[1] That Ben Jonson was an unsuccessful actor is gravely doubted by Gifford and by his latest editor, Lieut.-Col. Cunningham, who give excellent reasons in support of their view. See memoir prefixed to edition of Jonson, 1870, i. xi.

CHAPTER IV.

A short View of the Stage, from the Year 1660 to the Revolution.
The King's and Duke's Company united, composed the best Set of
English *Actors yet known.   Their several Theatrical Characters.*

THO' I have only promis'd you an Account of
all the material Occurrences of the Theatre
during my own Time, yet there was one which happen'd not above seven Years before my Admission
to it, which may be as well worth notice as the first
great Revolution of it, in which, among numbers, I
was involv'd.   And as the one will lead you into a
clearer View of the other, it may therefore be previously necessary to let you know that

King *Charles* II. at his Restoration granted two
Patents, one to Sir *William Davenant*,[1] and the
other to *Thomas Killigrew*, Esq.,[2] and their several
Heirs and Assigns, for ever, for the forming of two
distinct Companies of Comedians : The first were

[1] Sir William Davenant was the son of a vintner and innkeeper
at Oxford.   It was said that Shakespeare used frequently to stay
at the inn, and a story accordingly was manufactured that William
Davenant was in fact the son of the poet through an amour with
Mrs. Davenant.   But of this there is no shadow of proof.   Davenant went to Oxford, but made no special figure as a scholar,
winning fame, however, as a poet and dramatist.   On the death of
Ben Jonson in 1637 he was appointed Poet-Laureate, and in 1639
received a licence from Charles I. to get together a company of
players.   In the Civil War he greatly distinguished himself, and
was knighted by the King for his bravery.   Before the Restoration
Davenant was permitted by Cromwell to perform some sort of
theatrical pieces at Rutland House, in Charter-House Yard,
where "The Siege of Rhodes" was played about 1656.   At the
Restoration a Patent was granted to him in August, 1660, and he
engaged Rhodes's company of Players, including Betterton,
Kynaston, Underhill, and Nokes.   Another Patent was granted
to him, dated 15th January, 1663, (see copy of Patent given *ante*,)
under which he managed the theatre in Lincoln's Inn Fields till
his death in 1668.   Davenant's company were called the Duke's
Players.   The changes which were made in the conduct of the
stage during Davenant's career, such as the introduction of elaborate scenery and the first appearance of women in plays, make it
one of the first interest and importance.   (See Mr. Joseph Knight's
Preface to his recent edition of the " Roscius Anglicanus.")

[2] Thomas Killigrew (not " Henry " Killigrew, as Cibber erro-
neously writes) was a very noted and daring humorist.   He was a
faithful adherent of King Charles I., and at the Restoration was
made a Groom of the Bedchamber.   He also received a Patent,
dated 25th April, 1662, to raise a company of actors to be
called the King's Players.   These acted at the Theatre Royal in
Drury Lane.   Killigrew survived the Union of the two Companies

call'd the *King's Servants*, and acted at the Theatre-Royal in *Drury-Lane ;*[1] and the other the *Duke's Company*, who acted at the Duke's Theatre in *Dorset-Garden.*[2] About ten of the King's Company were on the Royal Houshold-Establishment, having each ten Yards of Scarlet Cloth, with a proper quantity of Lace allow'd them for Liveries ; and in their Warrants from the Lord Chamberlain were stiled *Gentlemen of the Great Chamber.*[3] Whether the like Appointments were extended to the Duke's Company, I am not certain ; but they were both in high Estimation with the Publick, and so much the

in 1682, dying on the 19th of March, 1683. He cannot be said to have made much mark in theatrical history. The best anecdote of Killigrew is that related by Granger, how he waited on Charles II. one day dressed like a Pilgrim bound on a long journey. When the King asked him whither he was going, he replied, "To Hell, to fetch back Oliver Cromwell to take care of England, for his successor takes none at all."

[1] It is curious to note that this theatre, which occupied the same site as the present Drury Lane, was sometimes described as Drury Lane, sometimes as Covent Garden.

[2] Should be Lincoln's Inn Fields. Dorset Garden, which was situated in Salisbury Court, Fleet Street, was not opened till 1671.

[3] Genest (ii. 302) remarks on this : "How long this lasted does not appear—it appears however that it lasted to Queen Anne's time, as the alteration of 'Wit without Money' is dedicated to Thomas Newman, Servant to her Majesty, one of the Gentlemen of the Great Chamber, and Book-keeper and Prompter to her Majesty's Company of Comedians in the Haymarket." Dr. Doran in his "Their Majesties' Servants" (1888 edition, iii. 419), says that he was informed by Benjamin Webster that Baddeley was the last actor who wore the uniform of scarlet and gold prescribed for the Gentlemen of the Household, who were patented actors.

Delight and Concern of the Court, that they were
not only supported by its being frequently present at
their publick *Presentations*, but by its taking cogni-
zance even of their private Government, insomuch
that their particular Differences, Pretentions, or
Complaints were generally ended by the *King* or
Duke's Personal Command or Decision. Besides
their being thorough Masters of their Art, these
Actors set forwards with two critical Advantages,
which perhaps may never happen again in many
Ages. The one was, their immediate opening after
the so long Interdiction of Plays during the Civil
War and the Anarchy that followed it. What eager
Appetites from so long a Fast must the Guests of
those Times have had to that high and fresh variety
of Entertainments which *Shakespear* had left prepared
for them ? Never was a Stage so provided! A hundred Years are wasted, and another silent Century
well advanced, and yet what unborn Age shall say
Shakespear has his equal! How many shining Actors
have the warm Scenes of his Genius given to Posterity? without being himself in his Action equal to
his Writing! A strong Proof that Actors, like
Poets, must be born such. Eloquence and Elocution are quite different Talents : *Shakespear* could
write *Hamlet*, but Tradition tells us That the *Ghost*,
in the same Play, was one of his best Performances
as an Actor : Nor is it within the reach of Rule or
Precept to complete either of them. Instruction, 'tis
true, may guard them equally against Faults or Ab-

surdities, but there it stops; Nature must do the
rest : To excel in either Art is a self-born Happiness
which something more than good Sense must be the
Mother of.

The other Advantage I was speaking of is, that
before the Restoration no Actresses had ever been
seen upon the *English* Stage.[1] The Characters of
Women on former Theatres were perform'd by Boys,
or young Men of the most effeminate Aspect. And
what Grace or Master-strokes of Action can we conceive such ungain Hoydens to have been capable of?
This Defect was so well considered by *Shakespear*,
that in few of his Plays he has any greater Dependance upon the Ladies than in the Innocence and
Simplicity of a *Desdemona*, an *Ophelia*, or in the
short Specimen of a fond and virtuous *Portia*. The
additional Objects then of real, beautiful Women

---

[1] The question of the identity of the first English actress is a
very intricate one. Mr. Percy Fitzgerald, in his "New History
of the English Stage," seems to incline to favour Anne Marshall,
while Mr. Joseph Knight, in his edition of the "Roscius Anglicanus," pronounces for Mrs. Coleman. Davies says positively
that "the first woman actress was the mother of Norris, commonly
called Jubilee Dicky." Thomas Jordan wrote a Prologue "to
introduce the first woman that came to act on the stage," but as
the lady's name is not given, this does not help us. The distinction is also claimed for Mrs. Saunderson (afterwards Mrs. Betterton) and Margaret Hughes. But since Mr. Knight has shown
that the performances in 1656 at Rutland House, where Mrs.
Coleman appeared, were for money, I do not see that we can
escape from the conclusion that this lady was the first English
professional actress. Who the first actress after the Restoration
was is as yet unsettled.

could not but draw a Proportion of new Admirers to the Theatre. We may imagine, too, that these Actresses were not ill chosen, when it is well known that more than one of them had Charms sufficient at their leisure Hours to calm and mollify the Cares of Empire.[1] Besides these peculiar Advantages, they had a private Rule or Agreement, which both Houses were happily ty'd down to, which was, that no Play acted at one House should ever be attempted at the other. All the capital Plays therefore of *Shakespear*, *Fletcher*, and *Ben. Johnson* were divided between them by the Approbation of the Court and their own alternate Choice.[2] So that when *Hart*[3] was famous for *Othello*, *Betterton* had no less a Reputation for *Hamlet*. By this Order the Stage was supply'd with a greater Variety of Plays than could possibly have been shewn had both Companies been employ'd at the same time upon the same Play; which Liberty, too, must have occasion'd such frequent Repetitions of 'em, by their opposite Endeavours to forestall and anticipate one another, that the best Actors in the World must have grown tedious and tasteless to the Spectator: For what Pleasure is not languid to Satiety?[4] It was therefore one of our

[1] Meaning, no doubt, Nell Gwyn and Moll Davis.

[2] Genest points out (i. 404) that Cibber is not quite accurate here. Shakespeare's and Fletcher's plays *may* have been shared; Jonson's certainly were not.

[3] See memoir of Hart at end of second volume.

[4] Genest says that this regulation "might be very proper at the first restoration of the stage; but as a perpetual rule it was absurd.

greatest Happinesses (during my time of being in
the Menagement of the Stage) that we had a certain
Number of select Plays which no other Company
had the good Fortune to make a tolerable Figure in,
and consequently could find little or no Account by
acting them against us. These Plays therefore for
many Years, by not being too often seen, never fail'd
to bring us crowded Audiences ; and it was to this
Conduct we ow'd no little Share of our Prosperity.
But when four Houses [1] are at once (as very lately
they were) all permitted to act the same Pieces, let
three of them perform never so ill, when Plays
come to be so harrass'd and hackney'd out to the
common People (half of which too, perhaps, would as
lieve see them at' one House as another) the best
Actors will soon feel that the Town has enough of
them.

I know it is the common Opinion, That the more
Play-houses the more Emulation ; I grant it ; but
what has this Emulation ended in ?   Why, a daily

Cibber approves of it, not considering that Betterton could never
have acted Othello, Brutus, or Hotspur (the very parts for which
Cibber praises him so much) if there had not been a junction of
the companies." Bellchambers, in a long note, also contests
Cibber's opinion.

[1] In the season 1735-6, in addition to the two Patent Theatres,
Drury Lane and Covent Garden, Giffard was playing at Goodman's
Fields Theatre, and Fielding, with his Great Mogul's Company of
Comedians, occupied the Haymarket.   In 1736-7 Giffard played
at the Lincoln's-Inn-Fields Theatre, and Goodman's Fields was
unused. The Licensing Act of 1737 closed the two irregular
houses, leaving only Drury Lane and Covent Garden open.

Contention which shall soonest surfeit you with the best Plays; so that when what *ought* to please can no *longer* please, your Appetite is again to be raised by such monstrous Presentations as dishonour the Taste of a civiliz'd People.[1] If, indeed, to our several Theatres we could raise a proportionable Number of good Authors to give them all different Employment, then perhaps the Publick might profit from their Emulation: But while good Writers are so scarce, and undaunted Criticks so plenty, I am afraid a good Play and a blazing Star will be equal Rarities. This voluptuous Expedient, therefore, of indulging the Taste with several Theatres, will amount to much the same variety as that of a certain Oeconomist, who, to enlarge his Hospitality, would have two Puddings and two Legs of Mutton for the same Dinner.[2]—But to resume the Thread of my History.

These two excellent Companies were both prosperous for some few Years, 'till their Variety of Plays began to be exhausted: Then of course the better Actors (which the King's seem to have been

---

[1] Cibber here refers to the Pantomimes, which he deals with at some length in Chapter XV.

[2] Fielding ("Champion," 6th May, 1740): "Another Observation which I have made on our Author's Similies is, that they generally have an Eye towards the Kitchen. Thus, *page 56, Two Play-Houses are like two* PUDDINGS *or two* LEGS OF MUTTON. 224. *To plant young Actors is not so easy as to plant* CABBAGES. To which let me add a Metaphor in *page 57*, where *unprofitable Praise can hardly give Truth a* SOUP MAIGRE."

allowed) could not fail of drawing the greater
Audiences. Sir *William Davenant*, therefore, Master
of the Duke's Company, to make Head against their
Success, was forced to add Spectacle and Musick to
Action ; and to introduce a new Species of Plays,
since call'd Dramatick Opera's, of which kind were
the *Tempest, Psyche, Circe*, and others, all set off
with the most expensive Decorations of Scenes and
Habits, with the best Voices and Dancers.[1]

This sensual Supply of Sight and Sound coming
in to the Assistance of the weaker Party, it was no
Wonder they should grow too hard for Sense and
simple Nature, when it is consider'd how many more
People there are, that can see and hear, than think
and judge. So wanton a Change of the publick
Taste, therefore, began to fall as heavy upon the
King's Company as their greater Excellence in
Action had before fallen upon their Competitors : Of
which Encroachment upon Wit several good Prologues in those Days frequently complain'd.[2]

---

[1] "Dramatic Operas" seem to have been first produced about
1672. In 1673 "The Tempest," made into an opera by Shadwell,
was played at Dorset Garden ; "Pysche" followed in the next
year, and "Circe" in 1677. "Macbeth," as altered by Davenant,
was produced in 1672, "in the nature of an Opera," as Downes
phrases it.

[2] Dryden, in his "Prologue on the Opening of the New House"
in 1674, writes :—

"'Twere folly now a stately pile to raise,
To build a playhouse while you throw down plays ;
While scenes, machines, and empty operas reign——"

But alas! what can Truth avail, when its Dependance is much more upon the Ignorant than the
sensible Auditor? a poor Satisfaction, that the due
Praise given to it must at last sink into the cold
Comfort of—*Laudatur & Alget.*[1] Unprofitable
Praise can hardly give it a *Soup maigre*. Taste and
Fashion with us have always had Wings, and fly
from one publick Spectacle to another so wantonly,
that I have been inform'd by those who remember it,
that a famous Puppet-shew[2] in *Salisbury* Change
(then standing where *Cecil-Street* now is) so far distrest these two celebrated Companies, that they were
reduced to petition the King for Relief against it :
Nor ought we perhaps to think this strange, when,
if I mistake not, *Terence* himself reproaches the
Roman Auditors of his Time with the like Fondness
for the *Funambuli*, the Rope-dancers.[3] Not to dwell
too long therefore upon that Part of my History
which I have only collected from oral Tradition, I

and the Prologue concludes with the lines :—

> "'Tis to be feared——
> That, as a fire the former house o'erthrew,
> Machines and Tempests will destroy the new."

The allusion in the last line is to the opera of " The Tempest,"
which I have mentioned in the previous note.

[1]   " Probitas laudatur et alget."
Juvenal, i. 74.

[2] In the Prologue to "The Emperor of the Moon," 1687, the
line occurred : "'There's nothing lasting but the Puppet-show."

[3]   " Ita populus studio stupidus in funambulo
      Animum occuparat."
Terence, *Prol. to "Hecyra,"* line 4.

shall content myself with telling you that *Mohun* [1]
and *Hart* now growing old (for, above thirty Years
before this Time, they had severally born the King's
Commission of Major and Captain in the Civil Wars),
and the younger Actors, as *Goodman,* [2] *Clark,* [3] and
others, being impatient to get into their Parts, and
growing intractable, [4] the Audiences too of both
Houses then falling off, the Patentees of each, by the
King's Advice, which perhaps amounted to a Command, united their Interests and both Companies
into one, exclusive of all others, in the Year 1682. [5]
This Union was, however, so much in favour of the
Duke's Company, that *Hart* left the Stage upon it,
and *Mohun* survived not long after.

One only Theatre being now in Possession of the
whole Town, the united Patentees imposed their own

[1] See memoir of Michael Mohun at end of second volume.

[2] See memoir of Cardell Goodman at end of second volume.

[3] Of Clark very little is known. The earliest play in which his
name is given by Downes is "The Plain-Dealer," which was produced at the Theatre Royal in 1674, Clark playing Novel, a part
of secondary importance. His name appears to Massina in
"Sophonisba," Hephestion in "Alexander the Great," Dolabella
in "All for Love," Aquitius in "Mythridates," and (his last recorded part) the Earl of Essex, the principal character in "The
Unhappy Favourite," Theatre Royal, 1682. After the Union of
the Companies in 1682 his name does not occur. Bellchambers
has several trifling errors in the memoir he gives of this actor.

[4] Curll ("History of the English Stage," p. 9) says: "The
Feuds and Animosities of the KING'S *Company* were so well improved, as to produce an Union betwixt the two Patents."

[5] Cibber gives the year as 1684, but this is so obviously a slip
that I venture to correct the text.

Terms upon the Actors; for the Profits of acting were then divided into twenty Shares, ten of which went to the Proprietors, and the other Moiety to the principal Actors, in such Sub-divisions as their different Merit might pretend to. These Shares of the Patentees were promiscuously sold out to Money-making Persons, call'd Adventurers,[1] who, tho' utterly ignorant of Theatrical Affairs, were still admitted to a proportionate Vote in the Menagement of them; all particular Encouragements to Actors were by them, of Consequence, look'd upon as so many Sums deducted from their private Dividends. While therefore the Theatrical Hive had so many Drones in it, the labouring Actors, sure, were under the highest Discouragement, if not a direct State of Oppression. Their Hardship will at least appear in a much stronger Light when compar'd to our later Situation, who with scarce half their Merit succeeded to be Sharers under a Patent upon five times easier Conditions: For as they had but half the Profits divided among ten or more of them; we had three fourths of the whole Profits divided only among three of us: And as they might be said to have ten Task-masters over them, we never had but one Assistant Menager (not an Actor) join'd with us;[2] who, by the

[1] Genest (ii. 62) remarks: "The theatre in Dorset Garden had been built by subscription—the subscribers were called Adventurers—of this Cibber seems totally ignorant—that there were any new Adventurers, added to the original number, rests solely on his authority, and in all probability he is not correct."

[2] Cibber afterwards relates the connection of Owen Swiney,

Crown's Indulgence, was sometimes too of our own chusing. Under this heavy Establishment then groan'd this United Company when I was first admitted into the lowest Rank of it. How they came to be relieved by King *William*'s Licence in 1695, how they were again dispersed early in Queen *Anne*'s Reign, and from what Accidents Fortune took better care of Us, their unequal Successors, will be told in its Place: But to prepare you for the opening so large a Scene of their History, methinks I ought (in Justice to their Memory too) to give you such particular Characters of their Theatrical Merit as in my plain Judgment they seem'd to deserve. Presuming then that this Attempt may not be disagreeable to the Curious or the true Lovers of the Theatre, take it without farther Preface.

In the Year 1690, when I first came into this Company, the principal Actors then at the Head of it were,

Of Men.	Of Women.
Mr. *Betterton*,	Mrs. *Betterton*,
Mr. *Monfort*,	Mrs. *Barry*,
Mr. *Kynaston*,	Mrs. *Leigh*,
Mr. *Sandford*,	Mrs. *Butler*,
Mr. *Nokes*,	Mrs. *Monfort*, and
Mr. *Underhil*, and	Mrs. *Bracegirdle*.
Mr. *Leigh*.	

These Actors whom I have selected from their

William Collier, M.P., and Sir Richard Steele, with himself and his actor-partners.

Cotemporaries were all original Masters in their different Stile, not meer auricular Imitators of one another, which commonly is the highest Merit of the middle Rank, but Self-judges of Nature, from whose various Lights they only took their true Instruction. If in the following Account of them I may be obliged to hint at the Faults of others, I never mean such Observations should extend to those who are now in Possession of the Stage ; for as I design not my Memoirs shall come down to their Time, I would not lie under the Imputation of speaking in their Disfavour to the Publick, whose Approbation they must depend upon for Support.[1] But to my Purpose.

Betterton was an Actor, as *Shakespear* was an Author, both without Competitors ! form'd for the mutual Assistance and Illustration of each others Genius ! How *Shakespear* wrote, all Men who have a Taste for Nature may read and know—but with what higher Rapture would he still be *read* could they conceive how *Betterton play'd* him ! Then might they know the one was born alone to speak what the other only knew to write ! Pity it is that the momentary Beauties flowing from an harmonious Elocution cannot, like those of Poetry, be their own Record ! That the animated Graces of the Player can live no longer than the instant Breath and

---

[1] The only one of Cibber's contemporaries of any note who was alive when the "Apology" was published, was Benjamin Johnson. This admirable comedian died in August, 1742, in his seventy-seventh year, having played as late as the end of May of that year.

Motion that presents them, or at best can but faintly
glimmer through the Memory or imperfect Attes-
tation of a few surviving Spectators. Could *how*
Betterton spoke be as easily known as *what* he
spoke, then might you see the Muse of *Shakespear*
in her Triumph, with all her Beauties in their best
Array rising into real Life and charming her Beholders. But alas! since all this is so far out of the
reach of Description, how shall I shew you *Betterton?*
Should I therefore tell you that all the *Othellos,*
Hamlets, Hotspurs, Mackbeths, and *Brutus's* whom
you may have seen since his Time, have fallen far
short of him; this still would give you no Idea of
his particular Excellence.   Let us see then what a
particular Comparison may do! whether that may
yet draw him nearer to you?

You have seen a *Hamlet* perhaps, who, on the
first Appearance of his Father's Spirit, has thrown
himself into all the straining Vociferation requisite to
express Rage and Fury, and the House has thunder'd
with Applause; tho' the mis-guided Actor was all
the while (as *Shakespear* terms it) tearing a Passion
into Rags [1]——I am the more bold to offer you this
particular Instance, because the late Mr. *Addison,*
while I sate by him to see this Scene acted, made

[1] The actor pointed at is, no doubt, Wilks. In the last chapter
of this work Cibber, in giving the theatrical character of Wilks,
says of his Hamlet: "I own the Half of what he spoke was as
painful to my Ear, as every Line that came from Betterton was
charming."

the same Observation, asking me, with some Surprize,
if I thought *Hamlet* should be in so violent a Passion
with the Ghost, which, tho' it might have astonish'd,
it had not provok'd him ? for you may observe that
in this beautiful Speech the Passion never rises beyond an almost breathless Astonishment, or an Impatience, limited by filial Reverence, to enquire into
the suspected Wrongs that may have rais'd him from
his peaceful Tomb! and a Desire to know what a
Spirit so seemingly distrest might wish or enjoin a
sorrowful Son to execute towards his future Quiet in
the Grave ? This was the Light into which *Betterton*
threw this Scene ; which he open'd with a Pause of
mute Amazement! then rising slowly to a solemn,
trembling Voice, he made the Ghost equally terrible
to the Spectator as to himself![1] and in the descriptive
Part of the natural Emotions which the ghastly
Vision gave him, the boldness of his Expostulation
was still govern'd by Decency, manly, but not brav-
ing ; his Voice never rising into that seeming Outrage
or wild Defiance of what he naturally rever'd.[2]   But
alas! to preserve this medium, between mouthing

[1] Barton Booth, who was probably as great in the part of the
Ghost as Betterton was in Hamlet, said, "When I acted the Ghost
with Betterton, instead of my awing him, he terrified me. But
divinity hung round that man !"—" Dram. Misc.," iii. 32.

[2] "The Laureat " repeats the eulogium of a gentleman who had
seen Betterton play Hamlet, and adds: "And yet, the same
Gentleman assured me, he has seen Mr. *Betterton*, more than
once, play this Character to an Audience of twenty Pounds, or
under " (p. 32).

and meaning too little, to keep the Attention more pleasingly awake by a temper'd Spirit than by meer Vehemence of Voice, is of all the Master-strokes of an Actor the most difficult to reach. In this none yet have equall'd *Betterton*. But I am unwilling to shew his Superiority only by recounting the Errors of those who now cannot answer to them, let their farther Failings therefore be forgotten! or rather, shall I in some measure excuse them? For I am not yet sure that they might not be as much owing to the false Judgment of the Spectator as the Actor. While the Million are so apt to be transported when the Drum of their Ear is so roundly rattled; while they take the Life of Elocution to lie in the Strength of the Lungs, it is no wonder the Actor, whose end is Applause, should be also tempted at this easy rate to excite it. Shall I go a little farther? and allow that this Extreme is more pardonable than its opposite Error? I mean that dangerous Affectation of the Monotone, or solemn Sameness of Pronounciation, which, to my Ear, is insupportable; for of all Faults that so frequently pass upon the Vulgar, that of Flatness will have the fewest Admirers. That this is an Error of ancient standing seems evident by what *Hamlet* says, in his Instructions to the Players, *viz.*

Be not too tame, neither, &c.

The Actor, doubtless, is as strongly ty'd down to the Rules of *Horace* as the Writer.

Si vis me flere, dolendum est
Primum ipsi tibi————[1]

He that feels not himself the Passion he would raise, will talk to a sleeping Audience : But this never was the Fault of *Betterton;* and it has often amaz'd me to see those who soon came after him throw out, in some Parts of a Character, a just and graceful Spirit which *Betterton* himself could not but have applauded. And yet in the equally shining Passages of the same Character have heavily dragg'd the Sentiment along like a dead Weight, with a long-ton'd Voice and absent Eye, as if they had fairly forgot what they were about : If you have never made this Observation, I am contented you should not know where to apply it.[2]

A farther Excellence in *Betterton* was, that he could vary his Spirit to the different Characters he acted. Those wild impatient Starts, that fierce and flashing Fire, which he threw into *Hotspur*, never came from the unruffled Temper of his *Brutus* (for I have more than once seen a *Brutus* as warm as *Hotspur*) : when the *Betterton Brutus* was provok'd in his Dispute with *Cassius*, his Spirit flew only to his Eye ; his steady Look alone supply'd that Terror

---

[1] *Ars Poetica*, 102. This is the much discussed question of Diderot's " Paradoxe sur le Comédien," which has recently been revived by Mr. Henry Irving and M. Coquelin, and has formed the subject of some interesting studies by Mr. William Archer.

[2] This is doubtless directed at Booth, who was naturally of an indolent disposition, and seems to have been, on occasions, apt to drag through a part.

which he disdain'd an Intemperance in his Voice
should rise to.   Thus, with a settled Dignity of
Contempt, like an unheeding Rock he repelled upon
himself the Foam of *Cassius*.   Perhaps the very
Words of *Shakespear* will better let you into my
Meaning :

> *Must I give way and room to your rash Choler?*
> *Shall I be frighted when a Madman stares?*

And a little after,

> *There is no Terror*, Cassius, *in your Looks !* &c.

Not but in some part of this Scene, where he reproaches *Cassius*, his Temper is not under this Suppression, but opens into that Warmth which becomes
a Man of Virtue; yet this is that *Hasty Spark* of
Anger which *Brutus* himself endeavours to excuse.

But with whatever strength of Nature we see the
Poet shew at once the Philosopher and the Heroe,
yet the Image of the Actor's Excellence will be still
imperfect to you unless Language could put Colours
in our Words to paint the Voice with.

Et, si vis similem pingere, pinge sonum,[1] is enjoyn-
ing an impossibility.   The most that a *Vandyke* can
arrive at, is to make his Portraits of great Persons
seem to *think*; a *Shakespear* goes farther yet, and
tells you *what* his Pictures thought; a *Betterton* steps
beyond 'em both, and calls them from the Grave to
breathe and be themselves again in Feature, Speech,

---

[1] Ausonius, 11, 8 (*Epigram.* xi.).

and Motion. When the skilful Actor shews you all these Powers at once united, and gratifies at once your Eye, your Ear, your Understanding : To conceive the Pleasure rising from such Harmony, you must have been present at it ! 'tis not to be told you !

There cannot be a stronger Proof of the Charms of harmonious Elocution than the many even unnatural Scenes and Flights of the false Sublime it has lifted into Applause. In what Raptures have I seen an Audience at the furious Fustian and turgid Rants in *Nat. Lee's Alexander the Great !* For though I can allow this Play a few great Beauties, yet it is not without its extravagant Blemishes. Every Play of the same Author has more or less of them. Let me give you a Sample from this. *Alexander*, in a full crowd of Courtiers, without being occasionally call'd or provok'd to it, falls into this Rhapsody of Vainglory.

Can none remember ?   Yes, I know all must !

And therefore they shall know it agen.

When Glory, like the dazzling Eagle, stood
Perch'd on my Beaver, in the Granic Flood,
When Fortune's Self my Standard trembling bore,
And the pale Fates stood frighted on the Shore,
When the Immortals on the Billows rode,
And I myself appear'd the leading God.[1]

[1] "Alexander the Great ; or, the Rival Queens," act ii. sc. 1.

When these flowing Numbers came from the Mouth
of a *Betterton* the Multitude no more desired Sense
to them than our musical *Connoisseurs* think it essential in the celebrate Airs of an *Italian* Opera. Does
not this prove that there is very near as much Enchantment in the well-govern'd Voice of an Actor as
in the sweet Pipe of an Eunuch? If I tell you there
was no one Tragedy, for many Years, more in favour
with the Town than *Alexander*, to what must we
impute this its command of publick Admiration?
Not to its intrinsick Merit, surely, if it swarms with
passages like this I have shewn you! If this Passage
has Merit, let us see what Figure it would make upon
Canvas, what sort of Picture would rise from it. If
Le Brun, who was famous for painting the Battles of
this Heroe, had seen this lofty Description, what one
Image could he have possibly taken from it? In
what Colours would he have shewn us *Glory perch'd
upon a Beaver?* How would he have drawn *Fortune
trembling?* Or, indeed, what use could he have
made of *pale Fates* or *Immortals* riding upon *Billows*,
with this blustering *God* of his own making at the
head of them?[1]   Where, then, must have lain the
Charm that once made the Publick so partial to this

[1] Bellchambers notes on this passage: "The criticisms of
Cibber upon a literary subject are hardly worth the trouble of
confuting, and yet it may be mentioned that Bishop Warburton
adduced these lines as containing not only the most sublime, but
the most judicious imagery that poetry can conceive. If Le Brun,
or any other artist, could not succeed in pourtraying the terrors of
fortune, it conveys, perhaps, the highest possible compliment to

Tragedy ? Why plainly, in the Grace and Harmony of the Actor's Utterance. For the Actor himself is not accountable for the false Poetry of his Author; That the Hearer is to judge of; if it passes upon him, the Actor can have no Quarrel to it ; who, if the Periods given him are round, smooth, spirited, and high-sounding, even in a false Passion, must throw out the same Fire and Grace as may be required in one justly rising from Nature ; where those his Excellencies will then be only more pleasing in proportion to the Taste of his Hearer. And I am of opinion that to the extraordinary Success of this very Play we may impute the Corruption of so many Actors and Tragick Writers, as were immediately misled by it. The unskilful Actor who imagin'd all the Merit of delivering those blazing Rants lay only in the Strength and strain'd Exertion of the Voice, began to tear his Lungs upon every false or slight Occasion to arrive at the same Applause. And it is from hence I date our having seen the same Reason prevalent for above fifty Years. Thus equally misguided, too, many a barren-brain'd Author has stream'd into a frothy flowing Style, pompously rolling into sounding Periods signifying——roundly nothing ; of which Number, in some of my former

the powers of Lee, to admit that he has mastered a difficulty beyond the most daring aspirations of an accomplished painter." With all respect to Warburton and Bellchambers, I cannot help remarking that this last sentence seems to me perilously like nonsense.

Labours, I am something more than suspicious that I may myself have made one. But to keep a little closer to *Betterton*.

When this favourite Play I am speaking of, from its being too frequently acted, was worn out, and came to be deserted by the Town, upon the sudden Death of *Monfort*, who had play'd *Alexander* with Success for several Years, the Part was given to *Betterton*, which, under this great Disadvantage of the Satiety it had given, he immediately reviv'd with so new a Lustre that for three Days together it fill'd the House ;¹ and had his then declining Strength been equal to the Fatigue the Action gave him, it probably might have doubled its Success ; an uncommon Instance of the Power and intrinsick Merit of an Actor. This I mention not only to prove what irresistable Pleasure may arise from a judicious Elocution, with scarce Sense to assist it ; but to shew you too, that tho' *Betterton* never wanted Fire and Force when his Character demanded it ; yet, where it was not demanded, he never prostituted his Power to the low Ambition of a false Applause. And further, that when, from a too advanced Age, he resigned that toilsome Part of *Alexander*, the Play for many Years after never was able to impose upon the Publick ;² and I look upon his so particularly support-

¹ I can find no record of this revival, nor am I aware that any other authority than Cibber mentions it. I am unable therefore even to guess at a date.

² In 1706, in Betterton's own company at the Haymarket

ing the false Fire and Extravagancies of that Character to be a more surprizing Proof of his Skill
than his being eminent in those of *Shakespear;* because there, Truth and Nature coming to his Assistance, he had not the same Difficulties to combat, and
consequently we must be less amaz'd at his Success
where we are more able to account for it.

Notwithstanding the extraordinary Power he
shew'd in blowing *Alexander* once more into a blaze
of Admiration, *Betterton* had so just a sense of what
was true or false Applause, that I have heard him
say, he never thought any kind of it equal to an attentive Silence; that there were many ways of deceiving
an Audience into a loud one; but to keep them
husht and quiet was an Applause which only Truth
and Merit could arrive at: Of which Art there never
was an equal Master to himself. From these various
Excellencies, he had so full a Possession of the
Esteem and Regard of his Auditors, that upon his
Entrance into every Scene he seem'd to seize upon
the Eyes and Ears of the Giddy and Inadvertent!
To have talk'd or look'd another way would then
have been thought Insensibility or Ignorance.[1]   In
all his Soliloquies of moment, the strong Intelligence
of his Attitude and Aspect drew you into such an
impatient Gaze and eager Expectation, that you

Verbruggen played Alexander.   At Drury Lane, in 1704, Wilks
had played the part.

[1] Anthony Aston says that his voice "enforced universal attention even from the Fops and Orange girls."

almost imbib'd the Sentiment with your Eye before
the Ear could reach it.

As *Betterton* is the Centre to which all my Observations upon Action tend, you will give me leave,
under his Character, to enlarge upon that Head. In
the just Delivery of Poetical Numbers, particularly
where the Sentiments are pathetick, it is scarce cre-
dible upon how minute an Article of Sound depends
their greatest Beauty or Inaffection. The Voice of
a Singer is not more strictly ty'd to Time and Tune,
than that of an Actor in Theatrical Elocution:[1] The
least Syllable too long or too slightly dwelt upon in
a Period depreciates it to nothing; which very Syllable if rightly touch'd shall, like the heightening
Stroke of Light from a Master's Pencil, give Life

---

[1] Anthony Aston says of Mrs. Barry: "Neither she, nor any of
the Actors of those Times, had any Tone in their Speaking, (too
much, lately, in Use.)" But the line of criticism which Cibber
takes up here would lead to the conclusion that Aston is not
strictly accurate; and, moreover, I can scarcely imagine how, if
these older actors used no "tone," the employment of it should
have been so general as it certainly was a few years after Betterton's death. Victor ("History," ii. 164) writes of "the good old
Manner of singing and quavering out their tragic Notes," and on
the same page mentions Cibber's "quavering Tragedy Tones."
My view, also, is confirmed by the facts that in the preface to
"The Fairy Queen," 1692, it is said: "he must be a very ignorant Player, who knows not there is a Musical Cadence in speaking; and that a Man may as well speak out of Tune, as sing out
of Tune;" and that Aaron Hill, in his dedication of "The Fatal
Vision," 1716, reprobates the "affected, vicious, and unnatural tone
of voice, so common on the stage at that time." See Genest, iv. 16-
17. An admirable description of this method of reciting is given

and Spirit to the whole. I never heard a Line in
Tragedy come from *Betterton* wherein my Judgment,
my Ear, and my Imagination were not fully satisfy'd;
which, since his Time, I cannot equally say of any
one Actor whatsoever: Not but it is possible to be
much his Inferior, with great Excellencies; which I
shall observe in another Place. Had it been practicable to have ty'd down the clattering Hands of all
the ill judges who were commonly the Majority
of an Audience, to what amazing Perfection might
the *English* Theatre have arrived with so just
an Actor as *Betterton* at the Head of it! If what
was Truth only could have been applauded, how
many noisy Actors had shook their Plumes with
shame, who, from the injudicious Approbation of the
Multitude, have bawl'd and strutted in the place of
Merit? If therefore the bare speaking Voice has such
Allurements in it, how much less ought we to wonder,
however we may lament, that the sweeter Notes of
Vocal Musick should so have captivated even the

by Cumberland (" Memoirs," 2nd edition, i. 80): " Mrs. Cibber
in a key, high-pitched but sweet withal, sung, or rather recitatived
Rowe's harmonious strain, something in the manner of the Impro-
visatories: it was so extremely wanting in contrast, that, though it
did not wound the ear, it wearied it." Cumberland is writing of
Mrs. Cibber in the earlier part of her career (1746), when the
teaching of her husband's father, Colley Cibber, influenced her
acting: no doubt Garrick, who exploded the old way of speaking,
made her ultimately modify her style. Yet as she was, even in
1746, a very distinguished pathetic actress, we are forced to the
conclusion that the old style must have been more effective than
we are disposed to believe.

politer World into an Apostacy from Sense to an
Idolatry of Sound. Let us enquire from whence this
Enchantment rises. I am afraid it may be too naturally accounted for : For when we complain that the
finest Musick, purchas'd at such vast Expence, is so
often thrown away upon the most miserable Poetry,
we seem not to consider, that when the Movement of
the Air and Tone of the Voice are exquisitely harmonious, tho' we regard not one *Word* of what we hear,
yet the Power of the Melody is so busy in the Heart,
that we naturally annex Ideas to it of our own Creation, and, in some sort, become our selves the Poet
to the Composer ; and what Poet is so dull as not to
be charm'd with the Child of his own Fancy? So
that there is even a kind of Language in agreeable
Sounds, which, like the Aspect of Beauty, without
Words speaks and plays with the Imagination.
While this Taste therefore is so naturally prevalent,
I doubt to propose Remedies for it were but giving
Laws to the Winds or Advice to Inamorato's : And
however gravely we may assert that Profit ought
always to be inseparable from the Delight of the
Theatre ; nay, admitting that the Pleasure would be
heighten'd by the uniting them ; yet, while Instruc-
tion is so little the Concern of the Auditor, how can
we hope that so choice a Commodity will come to a
Market where there is so seldom a Demand for it?

It is not to the Actor, therefore, but to the vitiated
and low Taste of the Spectator, that the Corruptions
of the Stage (of what kind soever) have been owing.

If the Publick, by whom they must live, had Spirit enough to discountenance and declare against all the Trash and Fopperies they have been so frequently fond of, both the Actors and the Authors, to the best of their Power, must naturally have serv'd their daily Table with sound and wholesome Diet.[1]—— But I have not yet done with my Article of Elocution.

As we have sometimes great Composers of Musick who cannot sing, we have as frequently great Writers that cannot read ; and though without the nicest Ear no Man can be Master of Poetical Numbers, yet the best Ear in the World will not always enable him to pronounce them. Of this Truth *Dryden*, our first great Master of Verse and Harmony, was a strong Instance : When he brought his Play of *Amphytrion* to the Stage,[2] I heard him give it his first Reading to the Actors, in which, though it is true he deliver'd the plain Sense of every Period, yet the whole was in so cold, so flat, and unaffecting a manner, that I am afraid of not being believ'd when I affirm it.

On the contrary, *Lee*, far his inferior in Poetry, was so pathetick a Reader of his own Scenes, that I have been inform'd by an Actor who was present,

[1] As Dr. Johnson puts it in his famous Prologue (1747) :—

"Ah ! let no Censure term our Fate our Choice,
The Stage but echoes back the public Voice ;
The Drama's Laws the Drama's Patrons give,
For we, that live to please, must please to live."

[2] "Amphytrion" was played in 1690. The Dedication is dated 24th October, 1690.

that while *Lee* was reading to Major *Mohun* at a
Rehearsal, *Mohun*, in the Warmth of his Admiration,
threw down his Part and said, Unless I were able to
play it as well as you *read* it, to what purpose should
I undertake it?   And yet this very Author, whose
Elocution rais'd such Admiration in so capital an
Actor, when he attempted to be an Actor himself,
soon quitted the Stage in an honest Despair of ever
making any profitable Figure there.[1]   From all this
I would infer, That let our Conception of what we
are to speak be ever so just, and the Ear ever so
true, yet, when we are to deliver it to an Audience
(I will leave Fear out of the question) there must
go along with the whole a natural Freedom and becoming Grace, which is easier to conceive than to
describe : For without this inexpressible Somewhat
the Performance will come out oddly disguis'd, or
somewhere defectively unsurprizing to the Hearer.
Of this Defect, too, I will give you yet a stranger
Instance, which you will allow Fear could not be the
Occasion of : If you remember *Estcourt*,[2] you must
have known that he was long enough upon the Stage
not to be under the least Restraint from Fear in his
Performance : This Man was so amazing and extra-

[1] Downes ("Roscius Anglicanus," p. 34) relates Lee's mis-
adventure, which he attributes to stage-fright.   He says of Otway
the poet, that on his first appearance "*the full House put him to
such a Sweat and Tremendous Agony, being dash't, spoilt him for an
Actor.   Mr. Nat. Lee, had the same Fate in Acting Duncan in
Macbeth, ruin'd him for an Actor too.*"

[2] See memoir of Estcourt at end of second volume.

ordinary a Mimick, that no Man or Woman, from the
Coquette to the Privy-Counsellor, ever mov'd or
spoke before him, but he could carry their Voice,
Look, Mien, and Motion, instantly into another
Company : I have heard him make long Harangues
and form various Arguments, even in the manner of
thinking of an eminent Pleader at the Bar,[1] with
every the least Article and Singularity of his Utterance so perfectly imitated, that he was the very *alter
ipse*, scarce to be distinguish'd from his Original.
Yet more; I have seen upon the Margin of the
written Part of *Falstaff* which he acted, his own
Notes and Observations upon almost every Speech of
it, describing the true Spirit of the Humour, and with
what Tone of Voice, Look, and Gesture, each of
them ought to be delivered. Yet in his Execution
upon the Stage he seem'd to have lost all those just
Ideas he had form'd of it, and almost thro' the
Character labour'd under a heavy Load of Flatness :
In a word, with all his Skill in Mimickry and Knowledge of what ought to be done, he never upon the
Stage could bring it truly into Practice, but was upon
the whole a languid, unaffecting Actor.[2] After I

[1] It will be remembered that the Elder Mathews, the most
extraordinary mimic of modern times, had this same power in
great perfection. See his " Memoirs," iii. 153-156.

[2] Cibber has been charged with gross unfairness to Estcourt,
and his unfavourable estimate of him has been attributed to envy;
but Estcourt's ability seems to have been at least questionable.
This matter will be found treated at some length in the memoir
of Estcourt in the Appendix to this work.

have shewn you so many necessary Qualifications, not one of which can be spar'd in true Theatrical Elocution, and have at the same time prov'd that with the Assistance of them all united, the whole may still come forth defective; what Talents shall we say will infallibly form an Actor? This I confess is one of Nature's Secrets, too deep for me to dive into; let us content our selves therefore with affirming, That *Genius*, which Nature only gives, only can complete him. This *Genius* then was so strong in *Betterton*, that it shone out in every Speech and Motion of him. Yet Voice and Person are such necessary Supports to it, that by the Multitude they have been preferr'd to *Genius* itself, or at least often mistaken for it. *Betterton* had a Voice of that kind which gave more Spirit to Terror than to the softer Passions; of more Strength than Melody.[1] The Rage and Jealousy of *Othello* became him better than the Sighs and Tenderness of *Castalio*:[2] For though in *Castalio* he only excell'd others, in *Othello* he excell'd himself; which you will easily believe when you consider that, in spite of his Complexion, *Othello* has more natural Beauties than the best Actor can find in all the Magazine of Poetry to animate his Power and delight his Judgment with.

The Person of this excellent Actor was suitable to his Voice, more manly than sweet, not exceeding the

---

[1] "His voice was low and grumbling."—Anthony Aston.

[2] In Otway's tragedy of "The Orphan," produced at Dorset Garden in 1680, Betterton was the original Castalio.

middle Stature, inclining to the corpulent; of a
serious and penetrating Aspect; his Limbs nearer
the athletick than the delicate Proportion ; yet however form'd, there arose from the Harmony of the
whole a commanding Mien of Majesty, which the
fairer-fac'd or (as *Shakespear* calls 'em) the *curled*
Darlings of his Time ever wanted something to be
equal Masters of.   There was some Years ago to be
had, almost in every Print-shop, a *Metzotinto* from
Kneller, extremely like him.[1]

In all I have said of *Betterton*, I confine myself to
the Time of his Strength and highest Power in
Action, that you may make Allowances from what
he was able to execute at Fifty, to what you might
have seen of him at past Seventy; for tho' to the
last he was without his Equal, he might not then be
equal to his former Self; yet so far was he from
being ever overtaken, that for many Years after his
Decease I seldom saw any of his Parts in *Shakespear* supply'd by others, but it drew from me the
Lamentation of *Ophelia* upon *Hamlet*'s being unlike
what she had seen him.

————*Ah ! woe is me !*
T'have seen what I have *seen, see what I see !*

The last Part this great Master of his Profession
acted was *Melantius* in the *Maid's Tragedy*, for his
own Benefit ;[2] when being suddenly seiz'd by the

[1] See memoir of Betterton at end of second volume.
[2] 13th April, 1710.

Gout, he submitted, by extraordinary Applications, to have his Foot so far reliev'd that he might be able to walk on the Stage in a Slipper, rather than wholly disappoint his Auditors. He was observ'd that Day to have exerted a more than ordinary Spirit, and met with suitable Applause ; but the unhappy Consequence of tampering with his Distemper was, that it flew into his Head, and kill'd him in three Days, (I think) in the seventy-fourth Year of his Age.[1]

I once thought to have fill'd up my Work with a select Dissertation upon Theatrical Action,[2] but I find, by the Digressions I have been tempted to make in this Account of *Betterton*, that all I can say upon that Head will naturally fall in, and possibly be less tedious if dispers'd among the various Characters of the particular Actors I have promis'd to treat of ; I shall therefore make use of those several Vehicles, which you will find waiting in the next Chapter, to carry you thro' the rest of the Journey at your Leisure.

[1] In the "Tatler," No. 167, in which the famous criticism of Betterton's excellencies is given, his funeral is stated to have taken place on 2nd May, 1710.

[2] I do not know whether Cibber in making this remark had in view Gildon's Life of Betterton, in which there are twenty pages of memoir to one hundred and fifty of dissertation on acting.

CHAPTER V.

The Theatrical Characters of the Principal Actors in the Year 1690,
continu'd.

A few Words to Critical Auditors.

THO', as I have before observ'd, Women were not admitted to the Stage 'till the Return of King *Charles*, yet it could not be so suddenly supply'd with them but that there was still a Necessity, for some time, to put the handsomest young Men into Petticoats;[1] which *Kynaston* was then said to have

[1] This seems to have been done to a very limited extent. The first unquestionable date on which, after 1660, women appeared is 3rd January, 1661, when Pepys saw "The Beggar's Bush" at the Theatre, that is, Killigrew's house, and notes, "and here the

worn with Success; particularly in the Part of *Evadne*
in the *Maid's Tragedy*, which I have heard him
speak of, and which calls to my Mind a ridiculous
Distress that arose from these sort of Shifts which
the Stage was then put to.——The King coming a
little before his usual time to a Tragedy, found the
Actors not ready to begin, when his Majesty, not
chusing to have as much Patience as his good Subjects, sent to them to know the Meaning of it; upon
which the Master of the Company came to the Box,
and rightly judging that the best Excuse for their
Default would be the true one, fairly told his Majesty
that the Queen was not *shav'd* yet : The King, whose
good Humour lov'd to laugh at a Jest as well as to
make one, accepted the Excuse, which serv'd to
divert him till the male Queen cou'd be effeminated.
In a word, *Kynaston* at that time was so beautiful a
Youth that the Ladies of Quality prided themselves

first time that ever I saw women come upon the stage." At the
same theatre he had seen the same play on 20th November, 1660,
the female parts being then played by men. Thomas Jordan
wrote "*A Prologue, to introduce the first woman that came to act on
the stage, in the tragedy called* The Moor of Venice" (quoted by
Malone, "Shakespeare," 1821, iii. 128), and Malone supposes
justly as I think, that this was on 8th December, 1660; on which
date, in all probability, the first woman appeared on the stage after
the Restoration. Who she was we do not know. See *ante*, p. 90.
On 7th January, 1661, Kynaston played Epicœne in "The Silent
Woman," and on 12th January, 1661, Pepys saw "The Scornful
Lady," "now done by a woman." On the 4th of the same month
Pepys had seen the latter play with a man in the chief part, so
that it is almost certain that the "boy-actresses" disappeared
about the beginning of 1661.

in taking him with them in their Coaches to *Hyde-Park* in his Theatrical Habit, after the Play; which in those Days they might have sufficient time to do, because Plays then were us'd to begin at four a-Clock : The Hour that People of the same Rank are now going to Dinner.——Of this Truth I had the Curiosity to enquire, and had it confirm'd from his own Mouth in his advanc'd Age : And indeed, to the last of him, his Handsomeness was very little abated ; even at past Sixty his Teeth were all sound, white, and even, as one would wish to see in a reigning Toast of Twenty. He had something of a formal Gravity in his Mien, which was attributed to the stately Step he had been so early confin'd to, in a female Decency. But even that in Characters of Superiority had its proper Graces ; it misbecame him not in the Part of *Leon*, in *Fletcher's Rule a Wife*, &c. which he executed with a determin'd Manliness and honest Authority well worth the best Actor's Imitation. He had a piercing Eye, and in Characters of heroick Life a quick imperious Vivacity in his Tone of Voice that painted the Tyrant truly terrible. There were two Plays of *Dryden* in which he shone with uncommon Lustre ; in *Aurenge-Zebe* he play'd *Morat*, and in *Don Sebastian*, *Mulcy Moloch;* in both these Parts he had a fierce, Lionlike Majesty in his Port and Utterance that gave the Spectator a kind of trembling Admiration !

Here I cannot help observing upon a modest Mistake which I thought the late Mr. *Booth* committed

in his acting the Part of *Moral*. There are in this
fierce Character so many Sentiments of avow'd Bar-
barity, Insolence, and Vain-glory, that they blaze
even to a ludicrous Lustre, and doubtless the Poet
intended those to make his Spectators laugh while
they admir'd them ; but *Booth* thought it depreciated
the Dignity of Tragedy to raise a Smile in any part
of it, and therefore cover'd these kind of Sentiments
with a scrupulous Coldness and unmov'd Delivery,
as if he had fear'd the Audience might take too
familiar a notice of them.[1]   In Mr. *Addison's Cato*,
Syphax[2] has some Sentiments of near the same nature,

[1] "The Laureat" (p. 33) : " I am of Opinion, *Booth* was not
wrong in this. There are many of the Sentiments in this Character,
where Nature and common Sense are outraged ; and an Actor,
who shou'd give the full comic Utterance to them in his Delivery,
would raise what they call a *Horse-Laugh*, and turn it into
Burlesque."

On the other hand, Theophilus Cibber, in his Life of Booth,
p. 72, supports his father's opinion, saying :—

"The Remark is just—Mr. *Booth* would sometimes slur over
such bold Sentiments, so flightily delivered by the Poet. As he
was good-natured—and would ' hear each Man's Censure, yet
reserve his Judgment,'—I once took the Liberty of observing, that
he had neglected (as I thought) giving that kind of spirited Turn
in the afore-mentioned Character—He told me I was mistaken ;
it was not Negligence, but Design made him so slightly pass them
over :—For though, added he, in these places one might raise a
Laugh of Approbation in a few,—yet there is nothing more unsafe
than exciting the Laugh of Simpletons, who never know when or
where to stop ; and, as the Majority are not always the wisest
Part of an Audience,—I don't chuse to run the hazard."

[2] A long account of the production of "Cato" is given by
Cibber in Chap. XIV. From the cast quoted in a note, it will be
seen that Cibber himself was the original Syphax.

which I ventur'd to speak as I imagin'd *Kynaston* would have done had he been then living to have stood in the same Character. Mr. *Addison*, who had something of Mr. *Booth*'s Diffidence at the Rehearsal of his Play, after it was acted came into my Opinion, and own'd that even Tragedy on such particular Occasions might admit of a *Laugh* of *Approbation*.[1] In *Shakespear* Instances of them are frequent, as in *Mackbeth*, *Hotspur*, *Richard the Third*, and *Harry the Eighth*,[2] all which Characters, tho' of a tragical

[1] " The Laureat " (p. 33) : " I have seen the Original *Syphax* in *Cato*, use many ridiculous Distortions, crack in his Voice, and wreathe his Muscles and his Limbs, which created not a Smile of Approbation, but a loud Laugh of Contempt and Ridicule on the Actor." On page 34 : " In my Opinion, the Part of *Syphax*, as it was originally play'd, was the only Part in *Cato* not tolerably executed."

[2] Bellchambers on this passage has one of those aggravating notes, in which he seems to try to blacken Cibber as much as possible. I confess that I can see nothing of the " venom " he resents so vigorously. He says :—

" Theophilus Cibber, in the tract already quoted, expressly states, that Booth ' was not so scrupulously nice or timerous ' in this character, as in that to which our author has invidiously referred. I shall give the passage, for its powerful antidote to Colley's venom :—

' Mr. *Booth*, in this part, though he gave full Scope to the Humour, never dropped the Dignity of the Character—You laughed at *Henry*, but lost not your Respect for him.—When he appeared most familiar, he was by no means vulgar.—The People most about him felt the Ease they enjoyed was owing to his Condescension.—He maintained the Monarch.—*Hans Holbein* never gave a higher Picture of him than did the actor (*Booth*) in his Representation. When angry, his Eye spoke majestic Terror ; the noblest and the bravest of his Courtiers were awe-struck—He

I

Cast, have sometimes familiar Strokes in them so highly natural to each particular Disposition, that it is impossible not to be transported into an honest Laughter at them : And these are those happy Liberties which, tho' few Authors are qualify'd to take, yet, when justly taken, may challenge a Place among their greatest Beauties.   Now, whether *Dryden*, in his *Morat, feliciter Audet,*[1]——or may be allow'd the Happiness of having hit this Mark, seems not necessary to be determin'd by the Actor, whose Business, sure, is to make the best of his Author's Intention, as in this Part *Kynaston* did, doubtless not without *Dryden's* Approbation.   For these Reasons then, I thought my good Friend, Mr. *Booth* (who certainly had many Excellencies) carry'd his Reverence for the Buskin too far, in not following the bold Flights of the Author with that Wantonness of Spirit which the Nature of those Sentiments demanded : For Example ! *Morat* having a criminal Passion for *Indamora*, promises, at her Request, for one Day to spare the Life of her Lover *Aurenge-Zebe :* But not chusing to make known the real Motive of his Mercy, when *Nourmahal* says to him,

'Twill not be safe to let him live an Hour !

gave you the full Idea of that arbitrary Prince, who thought himself born to be obeyed ;—the boldest dared not to dispute his Commands :—He appeared to claim a Right Divine to exert the Power he imperiously assumed.' (p. 75)."

[1]   " Spirat Tragicum satis et feliciter audet."

Hor. *Epis.* ii. 1, 166.

Morat silences her with this heroical *Rhodomontade*,

> *I'll do't, to shew my Arbitrary Power.*[1]

Risum teneatis? It was impossible not to laugh and reasonably too, when this Line came out of the Mouth of *Kynaston*,[2] with the stern and haughty Look that attended it. But above this tyrannical, tumid Superiority of Character there is a grave and rational Majesty in *Shakespear's Harry the Fourth*, which, tho' not so glaring to the vulgar Eye, requires thrice the Skill and Grace to become and support. Of this real Majesty *Kynaston* was entirely Master; here every Sentiment came from him as if it had been his own, as if he had himself that instant conceiv'd it, as if he had lost the Player and were the real King he personated! a Perfection so rarely found, that very often, in Actors of good Repute, a certain Vacancy of Look, Inanity of Voice, or superfluous Gesture, shall unmask the Man to the judicious Spectator, who, from the least of those Errors, plainly sees the whole but a Lesson given him to be got by Heart from some great Author whose Sense is deeper than the Repeater's Understanding. This true Majesty *Kynaston* had so entire a Command of, that when he whisper'd the following plain Line to *Hotspur*,

> *Send us your Prisoners, or you'll hear of it!*[3]

---

[1] "Aurenge-Zebe; or, the Great Mogul," act iv.

[2] Kynaston was the original Morat at the Theatre Royal in 1675; Hart the Aurenge-Zebe.

[3] "King Henry IV.," First Part, act i. sc. 3.

He convey'd a more terrible Menace in it than the loudest Intemperance of Voice could swell to. But let the bold Imitator beware, for without the Look and just Elocution that waited on it an Attempt of the same nature may fall to nothing.

But the Dignity of this Character appear'd in *Kynaston* still more shining in the private Scene between the King and Prince his Son : There you saw Majesty in that sort of Grief which only Majesty could feel! there the paternal Concern for the Errors of the Son made the Monarch more rever'd and dreaded : His Reproaches so just, yet so unmix'd with Anger (and therefore the more piercing) opening as it were the Arms of Nature with a secret Wish, that filial Duty and Penitence awak'd, might fall into them with Grace and Honour. In this affecting Scene I thought *Kynaston* shew'd his most masterly Strokes of Nature ; expressing all the various Motions of the Heart with the same Force, Dignity and Feeling, they are written ; adding to the whole that peculiar and becoming Grace which the best Writer cannot inspire into any Actor that is not born with it. What made the Merit of this Actor and that of *Betterton* more surprizing, was that though they both observ'd the Rules of Truth and Nature, they were each as different in their manner of acting as in their personal Form and Features. But *Kynaston* staid too long upon the Stage, till his Memory and Spirit began to fail him. I shall not therefore say any thing of his Imperfections, which, at that time, were visibly not his own, but the Effects of decaying Nature.[1]

Monfort,[2] a younger Man by twenty Years, and at this time in his highest Reputation, was an Actor of a very different Style: Of Person he was tall, well made, fair, and of an agreeable Aspect: His Voice clear, full, and melodious: In Tragedy he was the most affecting Lover within my Memory. His Addresses had a resistless Recommendation from the very Tone of his Voice, which gave his Words such Softness that, as *Dryden* says,

> —— *Like Flakes of feather'd Snow,*
> *They melted as they fell !*[3]

All this he particularly verify'd in that Scene of *Alexander*, where the Heroe throws himself at the Feet of *Statira* for Pardon of his past Infidelities. There we saw the Great, the Tender, the Penitent, the Despairing, the Transported, and the Amiable, in the highest Perfection. In Comedy he gave the truest Life to what we call the *Fine Gentleman ;* his Spirit shone the brighter for being polish'd with Decency: In Scenes of Gaiety he never broke into the Regard that was due to the Presence of equal or superior Characters, tho' inferior Actors play'd them ; he fill'd the Stage, not by elbowing and crossing it before others, or disconcerting their Action, but by surpassing them in true masterly Touches of

---

[1] See memoir of Kynaston at end of second volume.

[2] Downes spells Mountfort's name Monfort and Mounfort.

[3] "Spanish Friar," act ii. sc. 1.

Nature.   He never laugh'd at his own Jest, unless
the Point of his Raillery upon another requir'd it.—
He had a particular Talent in giving Life to *bons
Mots* and *Repartees :* The Wit of the Poet seem'd
always to come from him *extempore*, and sharpen'd
into more Wit from his brillant manner of delivering
it; he had himself a good Share of it, or what is
equal to it, so lively a Pleasantness of Humour, that
when either of these fell into his Hands upon the
Stage, he wantoned with them to the highest Delight
of his Auditors.   The *agreeable* was so natural to
him, that even in that dissolute Character of the
Rover [1] he seem'd to wash off the Guilt from Vice,
and gave it Charms and Merit.   For tho' it may be
a Reproach to the Poet to draw such Characters not
only unpunish'd but rewarded, the Actor may still
be allow'd his due Praise in his excellent Performance.   And this is a Distinction which, when this
Comedy was acted at *Whitehall*, King *William*'s
Queen *Mary* was pleas'd to make in favour of *Monfort*, notwithstanding her Disapprobation of the Play.

He had, besides all this, a Variety in his Genius
which few capital Actors have shewn, or perhaps
have thought it any Addition to their Merit to arrive
at; he could entirely change himself; could at once
throw off the Man of Sense for the brisk, vain, rude,
and lively Coxcomb, the false, flashy Pretender to
Wit, and the Dupe of his own Sufficiency: Of

---

[1] Willmore, in Mrs. Behn's "Rover," of which Smith was the
original representative.

this he gave a delightful Instance in the Character of
Sparkish in *Wycherly's Country Wife.* In that of
Sir *Courtly Nice*[1] his Excellence was still greater :
There his whole Man, Voice, Mien, and Gesture
was no longer *Monfort*, but another Person.   There,
the insipid, soft Civility, the elegant and formal
Mien, the drawling Delicacy of Voice, the stately
Flatness of his Address, and the empty Eminence of
his Attitudes were so nicely observ'd and guarded
by him, that he had not been an entire Master of
Nature had he not kept his Judgment, as it were, a
Centinel upon himself, not to admit the least Likeness of what he us'd to be to enter into any Part of
his Performance, he could not possibly have so completely finish'd it.   If, some Years after the Death of
Monfort, I my self had any Success in either of these
Characters, I must pay the Debt I owe to his
Memory, in confessing the Advantages I receiv'd
from the just Idea and strong Impression he had
given me from his acting them.   Had he been
remember'd when I first attempted them my Defects
would have been more easily discover'd, and consequently my favourable Reception in them must have
been very much and justly abated.   If it could be
remembred how much he had the Advantage of me
in Voice and Person, I could not here be suspected
of an affected Modesty or of over-valuing his Excellence : For he sung a clear Counter-tenour, and had

[1] In Crowne's "Sir Courtly Nice," produced at the Theatre
Royal in 1685.

a melodious, warbling Throat, which could not but
set off the last Scene of Sir *Courtly* with an uncommon Happiness; which I, alas! could only struggle
thro' with the faint Excuses and real Confidence of
a fine Singer under the Imperfection of a feign'd and
screaming Trebble, which at best could only shew
you what I would have done had Nature been more
favourable to me.

This excellent Actor was cut off by a tragical
Death in the 33d Year of his Age, generally lamented
by his Friends and all Lovers of the Theatre. The
particular Accidents that attended his Fall are to be
found at large in the Trial of the Lord *Mohun*,
printed among those of the State, in *Folio.*[1]

Sandford might properly be term'd the *Spagnolet*
of the Theatre, an excellent Actor in disagreeable

---

[1] William Mountfort was born in 1659 or 1660. He became
a member of the Duke's Company as a boy, and Downes says
that in 1682 he had grown to the maturity of a good actor.
In the "Counterfeits," licensed 29th August, 1678, the Boy is
played by Young *Mumford*, and in "The Revenge," produced in
1680, the same name stands to the part of Jack, the Barber's Boy.
After the Union in 1682 he made rapid progress, for he played
his great character of Sir Courtly Nice as early as 1685. In this
Cibber gives him the highest praise; and Downes says, "Sir
Courtly was so nicely Perform'd, that not any succeeding, but Mr.
Cyber has Equall'd him." Mountfort was killed by one Captain
Hill, aided, it is supposed, by the Lord Mohun who died in
that terrible duel with the Duke of Hamilton, in 1712, in which
they hacked each other to death. Whether Hill murdered
Mountfort or killed him in fair fight is a doubtful point. (See
Doran's "Their Majesties' Servants," 1888 edition, i. 169-172;
see also memoir at end of second volume.)

Characters : For as the chief Pieces of that famous
Painter were of Human Nature in Pain and Agony,
so *Sandford* upon the Stage was generally as flagi-
tious as a *Creon*, a *Maligni*, an *Iago*, or a *Machiavil*[1]
could make him. The Painter, 'tis true, from the
Fire of his Genius might think the quiet Objects of
Nature too tame for his Pencil, and therefore chose
to indulge it in its full Power upon those of Violence
and Horror : But poor *Sandford* was not the Stage-
Villain by Choice, but from Necessity; for having a
low and crooked Person, such bodily Defects were
too strong to be admitted into great or amiable Characters; so that whenever in any new or revived
Play there was a hateful or mischievous Person,
Sandford was sure to have no Competitor for it :
Nor indeed (as we are not to suppose a Villain or
Traitor can be shewn for our Imitation, or not for
our Abhorrence) can it be doubted but the less
comely the Actor's Person the fitter he may be to perform them. The Spectator too, by not being misled
by a tempting Form, may be less inclin'd to excuse
the wicked or immoral Views or Sentiments of
them. And though the hard Fate of an *Oedipus*
might naturally give the Humanity of an Audience
thrice the Pleasure that could arise from the wilful
Wickedness of the best acted *Creon*, yet who could
say that *Sandford* in such a Part was not Master of
as true and just Action as the best Tragedian could

[1] Creon (Dryden and Lee's "Œdipus"); Malignii (Porter's
"Villain"); Machiavil (Lee's "Cæsar Borgia").

be whose happier Person had recommended him to
the virtuous Heroe, or any other more pleasing
Favourite of the Imagination? In this disadvan-
tageous Light, then, stood *Sandford* as an Actor;
admir'd by the Judicious, while the Crowd only
prais'd him by their Prejudice.[1] And so unusual had
it been to see *Sandford* an innocent Man in a Play,
that whenever he was so, the Spectators would
hardly give him credit in so gross an Improbability.
Let me give you an odd Instance of it, which I heard
Monfort say was a real Fact. A new Play (the Name
of it I have forgot) was brought upon the Stage,
wherein *Sandford* happen'd to perform the Part of
an honest Statesman: The Pit, after they had sate
three or four Acts in a quiet Expectation that the
well-dissembled Honesty of *Sandford* (for such of
course they concluded it) would soon be discover'd,
or at least, from its Security, involve the Actors in
the Play in some surprizing Distress or Confusion,
which might raise and animate the Scenes to come;
when, at last, finding no such matter, but that the
Catastrophe had taken quite another Turn, and that

---

[1] The "Tatler," No. 134: "I must own, there is something
very horrid in the publick Executions of an *English* Tragedy.
Stabbing and Poisoning, which are performed behind the Scenes
in other Nations, must be done openly among us to gratify the
Audience.

When poor *Sandford* was upon the Stage, I have seen him
groaning upon a Wheel, stuck with Daggers, impaled alive, calling
his Executioners, with a dying Voice, Cruel Dogs, and Villains!
And all this to please his judicious Spectators, who were wonderfully delighted with seeing a Man in Torment so well acted."

Sandford was really an honest Man to the end of the Play, they fairly damn'd it, as if the Author had impos'd upon them the most frontless or incredible Absurdity.[1]

It is not improbable but that from *Sandford*'s so masterly personating Characters of Guilt, the inferior Actors might think his Success chiefly owing to the Defects of his Person ; and from thence might take occasion, whenever they appear'd as Bravo's or Murtherers, to make themselves as frightful and as inhuman Figures as possible. In King *Charles*'s time, this low Skill was carry'd to such an Extravagance, that the King himself, who was black-brow'd and of a swarthy Complexion, pass'd a pleasant Remark upon his observing the grim Looks of the Murtherers in *Mackbeth ;* when, turning to his People in the Box about him, *Pray, what is the Meaning*, said he, *that we never see a Rogue in a Play, but, Godsfish ! they always clap him on a black Perriwig ? when it is well known one of the greatest Rogues in* England *always wears a fair one ?* Now, whether or no Dr. *Oates* at that time wore his own Hair I

---

[1] Bellchambers notes : "This anecdote has more vivacity than truth, for the audience were too much accustomed to see Sandford in parts of even a comic nature, to testify the impatience or disappointment which Mr. Cibber has described." I may add that I have been unable to discover any play to which the circumstances mentioned by Cibber would apply. But it must not be forgotten that, if the play were damned as completely as Cibber says, it would probably not be printed, and we should thus in all probability have no record of it.

cannot be positive : Or, if his Majesty pointed at some greater Man then out of Power, I leave those to guess at him who may yet remember the changing Complexion of his Ministers.[1] This Story I had from *Betterton*, who was a Man of Veracity : And I confess I should have thought the King's Observation a very just one, though he himself had been fair as *Adonis*. Nor can I in this Question help voting with the Court; for were it not too gross a Weakness to employ in wicked Purposes Men whose very suspected Looks might be enough to betray them ? Or are we to suppose it unnatural that a Murther should be thoroughly committed out of an old red Coat and a black Perriwig ?

For my own part, I profess myself to have been an Admirer of *Sandford*, and have often lamented that his masterly Performance could not be rewarded with that Applause which I saw much inferior Actors met with, merely because they stood in more laudable Characters. For, tho' it may be a Merit in an Audience to applaud Sentiments of Virtue and Honour; yet there seems to be an equal Justice that no Distinction should be made as to the Excellence of an Actor, whether in a good or evil Character; since neither the Vice nor the Virtue of it is his own, but given him by the Poet : Therefore, why is not the Actor who shines in either equally commendable ?— No, Sir; this may be Reason, but that is not always a Rule with us; the Spectator will tell you, that when

[1] Probably the Earl of Shaftesbury.

Virtue is applauded he gives part of it to himself; because his Applause at the same time lets others about him see that he himself admires it. But when a wicked Action is going forward; when an *Iago* is meditating Revenge and Mischief; tho' Art and Nature may be equally strong in the Actor, the Spectator is shy of his Applause, lest he should in some sort be look'd upon as an Aider or an Abettor of the Wickedness in view; and therefore rather chuses to rob the Actor of the Praise he may merit, than give it him in a Character which he would have you see his Silence modestly discourages. From the same fond Principle many Actors have made it a Point to be seen in Parts sometimes even flatly written, only because they stood in the favourable Light of Honour and Virtue.[1]

I have formerly known an Actress carry this Theatrical Prudery to such a height, that she was very near keeping herself chaste by it: Her Fondness for Virtue on the Stage she began to think might perswade the World that it had made an Impression on her private Life; and the Appearances of it actually went so far that, in an Epilogue to an obscure Play, the Profits of which were given to her, and wherein she acted a Part of impregnable Chas-

---

[1] Macready seems to have held something like this view regarding "villains." At the present time we have no such prejudices, for one of the most popular of English actors, Mr. E. S. Willard, owes his reputation chiefly to his wonderfully vivid presentation of villainy.

tity, she bespoke the Favour of the Ladies by a Pro-
testation that in Honour of their Goodness and
Virtue she would dedicate her unblemish'd Life to
their Example.   Part of this Vestal Vow, I remember, was contain'd in the following Verse :

Study to live the Character I play.[1]

But alas! how weak are the strongest Works of Art
when Nature besieges it? for though this good
Creature so far held out her Distaste to Mankind
that they could never reduce her to marry any one
of 'em; yet we must own she grew, like *Cæsar*,
greater by her Fall!   Her first heroick Motive to a
Surrender was to save the Life of a Lover who in
his Despair had vow'd to destroy himself, with
which Act of Mercy (in a jealous Dispute once in my
Hearing) she was provoked to reproach him in these
very Words: *Villain! did not I save your Life?*
The generous Lover, in return to that first tender
Obligation, gave Life to her First-born,[2] and that
pious Offspring has since raised to her Memory
several innocent Grandchildren.

---

[1] The play in question is "The Triumphs of Virtue," produced
at Drury Lane in 1697, and the actress is Mrs. Rogers, who afterwards lived with Wilks.   The lines in the Epilogue are :—

> "I'll pay this duteous gratitude; I'll do
> That which the play has done—I'll copy you.
> At your own virtue's shrine my vows I'll pay,
> Study to live the character I play."

[2] Chetwood gives a short memoir of this "first-born," who became the wife of Christopher Bullock, and died in 1739. Mrs.
Dyer was the only child of Mrs. Bullock's mentioned by Chetwood.

So that, as we see, it is not the Hood that makes
the Monk, nor the Veil the Vestal ; I am apt to think
that if the personal Morals of an Actor were to be
weighed by his Appearance on the Stage, the Advantage and Favour (if any were due to either side)
might rather incline to the Traitor than the Heroe,
to the *Sempronius* than the *Cato*, or to the *Syphax*
than the *Juba :* Because no Man can naturally desire
to cover his Honesty with a wicked Appearance ;
but an ill Man might possibly incline to cover his
Guilt with the Appearance of Virtue, which was the
Case of the frail Fair One now mentioned.   But be
this Question decided as it may, *Sandford* always
appear'd to me the honester Man in proportion to
the Spirit wherewith he exposed the wicked and
immoral Characters he acted : For had his Heart
been unsound, or tainted with the least Guilt of
them, his Conscience must, in spite of him, in any too
near a Resemblance of himself, have been a Check
upon the Vivacity of his Action.   *Sandford* therefore might be said to have contributed his equal
Share with the foremost Actors to the true and
laudable Use of the Stage : And in this Light too,
of being so frequently the Object of common Distaste, we may honestly stile him a Theatrical Martyr
to Poetical Justice : For in making Vice odious or
Virtue amiable, where does the Merit differ ?   To
hate the one or love the other are but leading Steps
to the same Temple of Fame, tho' at different Portals.[1]

[1] See memoir of Sandford at end of second volume.

This Actor, in his manner of Speaking, varied
very much from those I have already mentioned.
His Voice had an acute and piercing Tone, which
struck every Syllable of his Words distinctly upon
the Ear. He had likewise a peculiar Skill in his
Look of marking out to an Audience whatever he
judg'd worth their more than ordinary Notice. When
he deliver'd a Command, he would sometimes give it
more Force by seeming to slight the Ornament of
Harmony. In *Dryden*'s Plays of Rhime, he as little
as possible glutted the Ear with the Jingle of it,
rather chusing, when the Sense would permit him, to
lose it, than to value it.

Had *Sandford* liv'd in *Shakespear*'s Time, I am
confident his Judgment must have chose him above
all other Actors to have play'd his *Richard the Third:*
I leave his Person out of the Question, which, tho'
naturally made for it, yet that would have been the
the least Part of his Recommendation ; *Sandford*
had stronger Claims to it ; he had sometimes an
uncouth Stateliness in his Motion, a harsh and sullen
Pride of Speech, a meditating Brow, a stern Aspect,
occasionally changing into an almost ludicrous Triumph over all Goodness and Virtue : From thence
falling into the most asswasive Gentleness and sooth-
ing Candour of a designing Heart. These, I say,
must have preferr'd him to it ; these would have
been Colours so essentially shining in that Character,
that it will be no Dispraise to that great Author to
say, *Sandford* must have shewn as many masterly

Strokes in it (had he ever acted it) as are visible in the Writing it.[1]

When I first brought *Richard the Third*[2] (with such Alterations as I thought not improper) to the Stage, *Sandford* was engaged in the Company then acting under King *William's* Licence in *Lincoln's-Inn-Fields;* otherwise you cannot but suppose my Interest must have offer'd him that Part. What encouraged me, therefore, to attempt it myself at the *Theatre-Royal,* was that I imagined I knew how *Sandford* would have spoken every Line of it: If, therefore, in any Part of it I succeeded, let the Merit be given to him : And how far I succeeded in that Light, those only can be Judges who remember him. In order, therefore, to give you a nearer Idea of *Sandford,* you must give me leave (compell'd as I am to be vain) to tell you that the late Sir *John Vanbrugh,* who was an Admirer of *Sandford,* after

---

[1] It is a very common mistake to state that Cibber founded his playing of Richard III. on that of Sandford. He merely says that he tried to act the part as he knew Sandford *would* have played it.

[2] Cibber's adaptation, which has held the stage ever since its production, was first played at Drury Lane in 1700. Genest (ii. 195-219) gives an exhaustive account of Cibber's mutilation. His opinion of it may be gathered from these sentences : " One has no wish to disturb Cibber's own Tragedies in their tranquil graves, but while our indignation continues to be excited by the frequent representation of Richard the 3d in so disgraceful a state, there can be no peace between the friends of unsophisticated Shakspeare and Cibber." "To the advocates for Cibber's Richard I only wish to make one request—that they would never say a syllable in favour of Shakspeare."

he had seen me act it, assur'd me That he never knew any one Actor so particularly profit by another as I had done by *Sandford* in *Richard the Third: You have*, said he, *his very Look, Gesture, Gait, Speech, and every Motion of him, and have borrow'd them all only to serve you in that Character.* If, therefore, Sir *John Vanbrugh's* Observation was just, they who remember me in *Richard the Third* may have a nearer Conception of *Sandford* than from all the critical Account I can give of him.[1]

I come now to those other Men Actors, who at this time were equally famous in the lower Life of Comedy. But I find myself more at a loss to give you them in their true and proper Light, than those I have already set before you. Why the Tragedian warms us into Joy or Admiration, or sets our Eyes on flow with Pity, we can easily explain to another's Apprehension : But it may sometimes puzzle the

---

[1] "The Laureat" (p. 35): "This same Mender of *Shakespear* chose the principal Part, *viz. the King*, for himself; and accordingly being invested with the purple Robe, he screamed thro' four Acts without Dignity or Decency. The Audience ill-pleas'd with the Farce, accompany'd him with a smile of Contempt, but in the fifth Act, he degenerated all at once into Sir *Novelty*; and when in the Heat of the Battle at *Bosworth Field*, the King is dismounted, our Comic-Tragedian came on the Stage, really breathless, and in a seeming Panick, screaming out this Line thus—*A Harse, a Harse, my Kingdom for a Harse.* This highly delighted some, and disgusted others of his Auditors; and when he was kill'd by *Richmond*, one might plainly perceive that the good People were not better pleas'd that so *execrable a Tyrant* was destroy'd, than that so *execrable an Actor* was silent."

gravest Spectator to account for that familiar Violence of Laughter that shall seize him at some particular Strokes of a true Comedian. How then shall
I describe what a better Judge might not be able to
express ? The Rules to please the Fancy cannot so
easily be laid down as those that ought to govern
the Judgment. The Decency, too, that must be observed in Tragedy, reduces, by the manner of speaking it, one Actor to be much more like another than
they can or need be supposed to be in Comedy :
There the Laws of Action give them such free and
almost unlimited Liberties to play and wanton with
Nature, that the Voice, Look, and Gesture of a
Comedian may be as various as the Manners and
Faces of the whole Mankind are different from one
another. These are the Difficulties I lie under.
Where I want Words, therefore, to describe what I
may commend, I can only hope you will give credit
to my Opinion : And this Credit I shall most stand in
need of, when I tell you, that

Nokes[1] was an Actor of a quite different Genius
from any I have ever read, heard of, or seen, since
or before his Time ; and yet his general Excellence
may be comprehended in one Article, *viz.* a plain

---

[1] James Noke, or Nokes—not *Robert*, as Bellchambers states.
Of Robert Nokes little is known. Downes mentions both actors
among Rhodes's original Company, Robert playing male characters, and James being one of the "boy-actresses." Downes does
not distinguish between them at all, simply mentioning " Mr.
Nokes" as playing particular parts. Robert Nokes died about
1673, so that we are certain that the famous brother was James.

and palpable Simplicity of Nature, which was so
utterly his own, that he was often as unaccountably
diverting in his common Speech as on the Stage.   I
saw him once giving an Account of some Table-talk
to another Actor behind the Scenes, which a Man
of Quality accidentally listening to, was so deceived
by his Manner, that he ask'd him if that was a new
Play he was rehearsing?   It seems almost amazing
that this Simplicity, so easy to *Nokes*, should never
be caught by any one of his Successors.   *Leigh* and
Underhil have been well copied, tho' not equall'd by
others.   But not all the mimical Skill of *Estcourt*
(fam'd as he was for it) tho' he had often seen *Nokes*,
could scarce give us an Idea of him.   After this perhaps it will be saying less of him, when I own, that
though I have still the Sound of every Line he spoke
in my Ear, (which us'd not to be thought a bad one)
yet I have often try'd by myself, but in vain, to
reach the least distant Likeness of the *Vis Comica* of
Nokes.   Though this may seem little to his Praise,
it may be negatively saying a good deal to it, because
I have never seen any one Actor, except himself,
whom I could not at least so far imitate as to give
you a more than tolerable Notion of his manner.
But *Nokes* was so singular a Species, and was so
form'd by Nature for the Stage, that I question if
(beyond the trouble of getting Words by Heart) it
ever cost him an Hour's Labour to arrive at that
high Reputation he had, and deserved.

The Characters he particularly shone in, were Sir

Martin Marr-all, *Gomez* in the *Spanish Friar*, Sir *Nicolas Cully* in *Love in a Tub*,[1] *Barnaby Brittle* in the *Wanton Wife*, Sir *Davy Dunce* in the *Soldier's Fortune*, *Sosia* in *Amphytrion*,[2] &c. &c. &c. To tell you how he acted them is beyond the reach of Criticism: But to tell you what Effect his Action had upon the Spectator is not impossible: This then is all you will expect from me, and from hence I must leave you to guess at him.

He scarce ever made his first Entrance in a Play but he was received with an involuntary Applause, not of Hands only, for those may be, and have often been partially prostituted and bespoken, but by a General Laughter which the very Sight of him provoked and Nature cou'd not resist; yet the louder the Laugh the graver was his Look upon it; and sure, the ridiculous Solemnity of his Features were enough to have set a whole Bench of Bishops into a Titter, cou'd he have been honour'd (may it be no Offence to suppose it) with such grave and right reverend Auditors. In the ludicrous Distresses which, by the Laws of Comedy, Folly is often involv'd in, he sunk into such a mixture of piteous Pusillanimity and a Consternation so ruefully ridiculous and inconsolable, that when he had shook you to a Fatigue of Laughter it became a moot point whether you ought not to have pity'd him. When he debated

---

[1] "The Comical Revenge; or, Love in a Tub."

[2] Of these plays, "The Spanish Friar," "The Soldier's Fortune," and "Amphytrion" were produced after Robert Nokes's death.

any matter by himself, he would shut up his Mouth with a dumb studious Powt, and roll his full Eye into such a vacant Amazement, such a palpable Ignorance of what to think of it, that his silent Perplexity (which would sometimes hold him several Minutes) gave your Imagination as full Content as the most absurd thing he could say upon it. In the Character of Sir *Martin Marr-all*, who is always committing Blunders to the Prejudice of his own Interest, when he had brought himself to a Dilemma in his Affairs by vainly proceeding upon his own Head, and was afterwards afraid to look his governing Servant and Counsellor in the Face, what a copious and distressful Harangue have I seen him make with his Looks (while the House has been in one continued Roar for several Minutes) before he could prevail with his Courage to speak a Word to him! Then might you have at once read in his Face *Vexation*—that his own Measures, which he had piqued himself upon, had fail'd. *Envy*—of his Servant's superior Wit—*Distress* —to retrieve the Occasion he had lost. *Shame*—to confess his Folly; and yet a sullen Desire to be reconciled and better advised for the future! What Tragedy ever shew'd us such a Tumult of Passions rising at once in one Bosom! or what buskin'd Heroe standing under the Load of them could have more effectually mov'd his Spectators by the most pathetick Speech, than poor miserable *Nokes* did by this silent Eloquence and piteous Plight of his Features?

His Person was of the middle size, his Voice clear and audible; his natural Countenance grave and sober; but the Moment he spoke the settled Seriousness of his Features was utterly discharg'd, and a dry, drolling, or laughing Levity took such full Possession of him that I can only refer the Idea of him to your Imagination. In some of his low Characters, that became it, he had a shuffling Shamble in his Gait, with so contented an Ignorance in his Aspect and an aukward Absurdity in his Gesture, that had you not known him, you could not have believ'd that naturally he could have had a Grain of common Sense. In a Word, I am tempted to sum up the Character of *Nokes*, as a Comedian, in a Parodie of what *Shakespear's Mark Antony* says of *Brutus* as a Hero.

His Life was Laughter, and the Ludicrous
So mixt in him, that Nature might stand up
And say to all the World—This was an Actor.[1]

Leigh was of the mercurial kind, and though not so strict an Observer of Nature, yet never so wanton in his Performance as to be wholly out of her Sight. In Humour he lov'd to take a full Career, but was careful enough to stop short when just upon the Precipice : He had great Variety in his manner, and was famous in very different Characters : In the canting, grave Hypocrisy of the *Spanish* Friar he stretcht the Veil of Piety so thinly over him, that in

[1] See memoir of James Nokes at end of second volume.

every Look, Word, and Motion you saw a palpable, wicked Slyness shine through it—Here he kept his Vivacity demurely confin'd till the pretended Duty of his Function demanded it, and then he exerted it with a cholerick sacerdotal Insolence. But the Friar is a Character of such glaring Vice and so strongly drawn, that a very indifferent Actor cannot but hit upon the broad Jests that are remarkable in every Scene of it. Though I have never yet seen any one that has fill'd them with half the Truth and Spirit of *Leigh*——*Leigh* rais'd the Character as much above the Poet's Imagination as the Character has some-times rais'd other Actors above themselves! and I do not doubt but the Poet's Knowledge of *Leigh*'s Genius help'd him to many a pleasant Stroke of Nature, which without that Knowledge never might have enter'd into his Conception. *Leigh* was so eminent in this Character that the late Earl of *Dorset* (who was equally an Admirer and a Judge of Thea-trical Merit) had a whole Length of him, in the Friar's Habit, drawn by *Kneller:* The whole Portrait is highly painted, and extremely like him. But no wonder *Leigh* arriv'd to such Fame in what was so compleatly written for him, when Characters that would make the Reader yawn in the Closet, have, by the Strength of his Action, been lifted into the lowdest Laughter on the Stage. Of this kind was the Scrivener's great boobily Son in the *Villain;*[1]

---

[1] " *Coligni,* the character alluded to, at the original representa-tion of this play, was sustained, says Downs, 'by that inimitable

Ralph, a stupid, staring Under-servant, in Sir *Solomon Single*.[1] Quite opposite to those were Sir *Jolly Jumble* in the *Soldier's Fortune*,[2] and his old *Belfond* in the *Squire* of *Alsatia*.[3] In Sir *Jolly* he was all Life and laughing Humour, and when *Nokes* acted

sprightly actor, Mr. Price,—especially in this part.' Joseph Price joined D'Avenant's company on Rhodes's resignation, being one of 'the new actors,' according to the 'Roscius Anglicanus,' who were 'taken in to complete' it. He is first mentioned for *Guildenstern*, in 'Hamlet;' and, in succession, for *Leonel*, in D'Avenant's 'Love and Honour,' on which occasion the Earl of Oxford gave him his coronation-suit; for *Paris*, in 'Romeo and Juliet;' the *Corregidor*, in Tuke's 'Adventures of five hours;' and *Coligni*, as already recorded. In the year 1663, by speaking a 'short comical prologue' to the 'Rivals,' introducing some 'very diverting dances,' Mr. Price 'gained him an universal applause of the town.' The versatility of this actor must have been great, or the necessities of the company imperious, as we next find him set down for *Lord Sands*, in 'King Henry the Eighth.' He then performed *Will*, in the 'Cutter of Coleman-street,' and is mentioned by Downs as being dead, in the year 1673."

The above is Bellchambers's note. He is wrong in stating that Price played the Corregidor in Tuke's "Adventures of Five Hours;" his part was Silvio. He omits, too, to mention one of Price's best parts, Dufoy, in "Love in a Tub," in which Downes specially commends him in this queer couplet :—

"Sir Nich'las, Sir Fred'rick; Widow and Dufoy,
Were not by any so well done, Mafoy."

Price does not seem to have acted after May, 1665, when the theatres closed for the Plague, for his name is never mentioned by Downes after the theatres re-opened in November, 1666, after the Plague and Fire.

[1] "Sir Solomon; or, the Cautious Coxcomb," by John Caryll.

[2] By Otway.

[3] By Shadwell.

with him in the same Play, they returned the Ball so
dexterously upon one another, that every Scene between them seem'd but one continued Rest [1] of Excellence——But alas ! when those Actors were gone,
that Comedy and many others, for the same Reason,
were rarely known to stand upon their own Legs ;
by seeing no more of *Leigh* or *Nokes* in them, the
Characters were quite sunk and alter'd.   In his Sir
William Belfond, Leigh shew'd a more spirited
Variety than ever I saw any Actor, in any one
Character, come up to : The Poet, 'tis true, had here
exactly chalked for him the Out-lines of Nature;
but the high Colouring, the strong Lights and Shades
of Humour that enliven'd the whole and struck our
Admiration with Surprize and Delight, were wholly
owing to the Actor.   The easy Reader might, per-

---

[1] " Rest " is a term used in tennis, and seems to have meant a
quick and continued returning of the ball from one player to the
other—what is in lawn tennis called a "rally."

Cibber uses the word in his " Careless Husband," act iv. sc. 1.

" *Lady Betty* [to Lord Morelove]. Nay, my lord, there's no
standing against two of you.

Lord Foppington. No, faith, that's odds at tennis, my lord : not
but if your ladyship pleases, I'll endeavour to keep your back-
hand a little ; though upon my soul you may safely set me up at
the line : for, knock me down, if ever I saw a rest of wit better
played, than that last, in my life."

In the only dictionary in which I have found this word " Rest,"
it is given as " A match, a game ;" but, as I think I have shown,
this is a defective explanation.   I may add that, since writing the
above, I have been favoured with the opinion of Mr. Julian
Marshall. the distinguished authority on tennis, who confirms my
view.

haps, have been pleased with the Author without discomposing a Feature, but the Spectator must have heartily held his Sides, or the Actor would have heartily made them ach for it.

Now, though I observ'd before that *Nokes* never was tolerably touch'd by any of his Successors, yet in this Character I must own I have seen *Leigh* extremely well imitated by my late facetious Friend *Penkethman*, who, tho' far short of what was inimitable in the Original, yet, as to the general Resemblance, was a very valuable Copy of him : And, as I know *Penkethman* cannot yet be out of your Memory, I have chosen to mention him here, to give you the nearest Idea I can of the Excellence of *Leigh* in that particular Light : For *Leigh* had many masterly Variations which the other cou'd not, nor ever pretended to reach, particularly in the Dotage and Follies of extreme old Age, in the Characters of *Fumble* in the *Fond Husband*,[1] and the Toothless Lawyer[2] in the *City Politicks*, both which Plays liv'd only by the extraordinary Performance of *Nokes* and *Leigh*.

There were two other Characters of the farcical kind, *Geta* in the *Prophetess*, and *Crack* in Sir *Courtly Nice*, which, as they are less confin'd to Nature, the Imitation of them was less difficult to

---

[1] By Durfey.

[2] Bartoline. Genest suggests that this character was intended for the Whig lawyer, Serjeant Maynard. The play was written by Crowne.

Penkethman,[1] who, to say the Truth, delighted more
in the whimsical than the natural ; therefore, when I
say he sometimes resembled *Leigh*, I reserve this
Distinction on his Master's side, that the pleasant
Extravagancies of *Leigh* were all the Flowers of his
own Fancy, while the less fertile Brain of my Friend
was contented to make use of the Stock his Predecessor had left him.   What I have said, therefore, is
not to detract from honest *Pinky*'s Merit, but to do
Justice to his Predecessor——And though, 'tis true,
we as seldom see a good Actor as a great Poet arise
from the bare *Imitation* of another's Genius, yet if
this be a general Rule, *Penkethman* was the nearest
to an Exception from it; for with those who never
knew *Leigh* he might very well have pass'd for a
more than common Original.   Yet again, as my
Partiality for *Penkethman* ought not to lead me from
Truth, I must beg leave (though out of its Place) to
tell you fairly what was the best of him, that the
superiority of *Leigh* may stand in its due Light——
Penkethman had certainly from Nature a great deal
of comic Power about him, but his Judgment was by
no means equal to it; for he would make frequent
Deviations into the Whimsies of an *Harlequin*.   By
the way, (let me digress a little farther) whatever
Allowances are made for the Licence of that Character, I mean of an *Harlequin*, whatever Pretences
may be urged, from the Practice of the ancient
Comedy, for its being play'd in a Mask, resembling

---

[1] See memoir of Pinkethman at end of second volume.

no part of the human Species, I am apt to think the
best Excuse a modern Actor can plead for his continuing it, is that the low, senseless, and monstrous
things he says and does in it no theatrical Assurance could get through with a bare Face : Let me
give you an Instance of even *Penkethman's* being out
of Countenance for want of it : When he first play'd
Harlequin in the *Emperor* of the *Moon*,[1] several
Gentlemen (who inadvertently judg'd by the Rules
of Nature) fancied that a great deal of the Drollery
and Spirit of his Grimace was lost by his wearing
that useless, unmeaning Masque of a black Cat, and
therefore insisted that the next time of his acting
that Part he should play without it : Their Desire
was accordingly comply'd with——but, alas ! in vain
—*Penkethman* could not take to himself the Shame
of the Character without being concealed—he was
no more *Harlequin*—his Humour was quite disconcerted ! his Conscience could not with the same
Effronterie declare against Nature without the cover
of that unchanging Face, which he was sure would
never blush for it ! no ! it was quite another Case !

---

[1] In this farce, written by Mrs. Behn, and produced in 1687,
Jevon was the original Harlequin. Pinkethman played the part
in 1702, and played it without the mask on 18th September,
1702. The "Daily Courant" of that date contains an advertisement in which it is stated that "At the Desire of some Persons of
Quality . . . will be presented a Comedy, call'd, *The Emperor of
the Moon*, wherein Mr. *Penkethman* acts the part of *Harlequin*
without a Masque, for the Entertainment of an *African* Prince
lately arrived here."

without that Armour his Courage could not come up
to the bold Strokes that were necessary to get the
better of common Sense. Now if this Circumstance
will justify the Modesty of *Penkethman*, it cannot
but throw a wholesome Contempt on the low Merit
of an *Harlequin.* But how farther necessary the
Masque is to that Fool's Coat, we have lately had a
stronger Proof in the Favour that the *Harlequin
Sauvage* met with at *Paris*, and the ill Fate that followed the same *Sauvage* when he pull'd off his
Masque in *London.*[1] So that it seems what was Wit
from an *Harlequin* was something too extravagant
from a human Creature. If, therefore, *Penkethman*
in Characters drawn from Nature might sometimes
launch out into a few gamesome Liberties which would
not have been excused from a more correct Comedian,
yet, in his manner of taking them, he always seem'd
to me in a kind of Consciousness of the Hazard he
was running, as if he fairly confess'd that what he
did was only as well as he *could* do——That he was
willing to take his Chance for Success, but if he did
not meet with it a Rebuke should break no Squares;

[1] This refers to "Art and Nature," a comedy by James Miller,
produced at Drury Lane 16th February, 1738. The principal
character in "Harlequin Sauvage" was introduced into it and
played by Theophilus Cibber. The piece was damned the first
night, but it must not be forgotten that the Templars damned
everything of Miller's on account of his supposed insult to them in
his farce of "The Coffee House." Bellchambers says the piece
referred to by Cibber was "The Savage," 8vo, 1736; but this does
not seem ever to have been acted.

he would mend it another time, and would take whatever pleas'd his Judges to think of him in good part; and I have often thought that a good deal of the Favour he met with was owing to this seeming humble way of waving all Pretences to Merit but what the Town would please to allow him. What confirms me in this Opinion is, that when it has been his ill Fortune to meet with a *Disgraccia*, I have known him say apart to himself, yet loud enough to be heard——*Odso!* I believe I *am* a *little wrong here!* which once was so well receiv'd by the Audience that they turn'd their Reproof into Applause.[1]

Now, the Judgment of *Leigh* always guarded the happier Sallies of his Fancy from the least Hazard of Disapprobation: he seem'd not to court, but to

[1] This probably refers to the incident related by Davies in his "Dramatic Miscellanies":—"In the play of the 'Recruiting Officer,' Wilks was the Captain *Plume*, and Pinkethman one of the recruits. The captain, when he enlisted him, asked his name: instead of answering as he ought, Pinkey replied, 'Why! don't you know my name, Bob? I thought every fool had known that!' Wilks, in rage, whispered to him the name of the recruit, *Thomas Appletree*. The other retorted aloud, '*Thomas Appletree?* Thomas Devil! my name is Will Pinkethman:' and, immediately addressing an inhabitant of the upper regions, he said 'Hark you, friend; don't you know my name?'—'Yes, Master Pinkey,' said a respondent, 'we know it very well.' The play-house was now in an uproar: the audience, at first, enjoyed the petulant folly of Pinkethman, and the distress of Wilks; but, in the progress of the joke, it grew tiresome, and Pinkey met with his deserts, a very severe reprimand in a hiss; and this mark of displeasure he changed into applause, by crying out, with a countenance as melancholy as he could make it, in a loud and nasal twang, 'Odso! I fear I am wrong'" (iii. 89).

attack your Applause, and always came off victorious ; nor did his highest Assurance amount to any
more than that just Confidence without which the
commendable Spirit of every good Actor must be
abated ; and of this Spirit *Leigh* was a most perfect
Master. He was much admir'd by King *Charles*, who
us'd to distinguish him when spoke of by the Title
of *his Actor :* Which however makes me imagine
that in his Exile that Prince might have receiv'd his
first Impression of good Actors from the *French*
Stage ; for *Leigh* had more of that farcical Vivacity
than *Nokes ;* but *Nokes* was never languid by his
more strict Adherence to Nature, and as far as my
Judgment is worth taking, if their intrinsick Merit
could be justly weigh'd, *Nokes* must have had the
better in the Balance.   Upon the unfortunate Death
of *Monfort, Leigh* fell ill of a Fever, and dy'd in a
Week after him, in *December* 1692.[1]

Underhil was a correct and natural Comedian, his
particular Excellence was in Characters that may be
called Still-life, I mean the Stiff, the Heavy, and the
Stupid ; to these he gave the exactest and most expressive Colours, and in some of them look'd as if it
were not in the Power of human Passions to alter
a Feature of him.   In the solemn Formality of
Obadiah in the *Committee*, and in the boobily Heavi-
ness of *Lolpoop* in the *Squire of Alsatia*, he seem'd
the immoveable Log he stood for ! a Countenance
of Wood could not be more fixt than his, when the

[1] See memoir of Leigh at end of second volume.

Blockhead of a Character required it: His Face
was full and long; from his Crown to the end of his
Nose was the shorter half of it, so that the Dispro-
portion of his lower Features, when soberly compos'd, with an unwandering Eye hanging over them,
threw him into the most lumpish, moping Mortal
that ever made Beholders merry! not but at other
times he could be wakened into Spirit equally ridiculous——In the course, rustick Humour of Justice
Clodpate, in *Epsome Wells*,[1] he was a delightful Brute!
and in the blunt Vivacity of Sir *Sampson*, in *Love for
Love*, he shew'd all that true perverse Spirit that is
commonly seen in much Wit and Ill-nature. This
Character is one of those few so well written, with
so much Wit and Humour, that an Actor must be
the grossest Dunce that does not appear with an
unusual Life in it: But it will still shew as great a
Proportion of Skill to come near *Underhil* in the
acting it, which (not to undervalue those who soon
came after him) I have not yet seen. He was particularly admir'd too for the Grave-digger in *Hamlet*.
The Author of the *Tatler* recommends him to the
Favour of the Town upon that Play's being acted
for his Benefit, wherein, after his Age had some
Years oblig'd him to leave the Stage, he came on
again, for that Day, to perform his old Part;[2] but,

---

[1] By Shadwell.

[2] Underhill seems to have partially retired about the beginning
of 1707. He played Sir Joslin Jolley on 5th December, 1706,
but Bullock played it on 9th January, 1707, and, two days after,

alas! so worn and disabled, as if himself was to have lain in the Grave he was digging; when he could no more excite Laughter, his Infirmities were dismiss'd with Pity: He dy'd soon after, a superannuated Pensioner in the List of those who were supported by the joint Sharers under the first Patent granted to Sir *Richard Steele*.

The deep Impressions of these excellent Actors which I receiv'd in my Youth, I am afraid may have drawn me into the common Foible of us old Fellows; which is a Fondness, and perhaps a tedious Partiality, for the Pleasures we have formerly tasted, and think are now fallen off because we can no longer enjoy them. If therefore I lie under that Suspicion, tho' I have related nothing incredible or out of the reach of a good Judge's Conception, I

Johnson played Underhill's part of the First Gravedigger. Underhill, however, played in "The Rover" on 20th January, 1707. The benefit Cibber refers to took place on 3rd June, 1709. Underhill played the Gravedigger again on 23rd February, 1710, and on 12th May, 1710, for his benefit, he played Trincalo in "The Tempest." Genest says he acted at Greenwich on 26th August, 1710. The advertisement in the "Tatler" (26th May, 1709) runs: "Mr. Cave Underhill, the famous Comedian in the Reigns of K. Charles ii. K. James ii. K. William and Q. Mary, and her present Majesty Q. Anne; but now not able to perform so often as heretofore in the Play-house, and having had losses to the value of near £2,500, is to have the Tragedy of Hamlet acted for his Benefit, on Friday the third of June next, at the Theatre-Royal in Drury-Lane, in which he is to perform his Original Part, the Grave-Maker. Tickets may be had at the Mitre-Tavern in Fleet-Street." See also memoir of Underhill at end of second volume.

must appeal to those Few who are about my own Age for the Truth and Likeness of these Theatrical Portraicts.

There were at this time several others in some degree of Favour with the Publick, *Powel,*[1] *Verbruggen,*[2] *Williams,*[3] &c. But as I cannot think their best Improvements made them in any wise equal to those I have spoke of, I ought not to range them in the same Class. Neither were *Wilks* or *Dogget* yet come to the Stage; nor was *Booth* initiated till about six Years after them; or Mrs. *Oldfield* known till the Year 1700. I must therefore reserve the four last for their proper Period, and proceed to the Actresses that were famous

---

[1] See memoir of Powel at end of second volume.

[2] John Verbruggen, whose name Downes spells "Vanbruggen," "Vantbrugg," and "Verbruggen," is first recorded as having played Termagant in "The Squire of Alsatia," at the Theatre Royal, in 1688. His name last appears in August, 1707, and he must have died not long after. On 26th April, 1708, a benefit was announced for "a young orphan child of the late Mr. and Mrs. Verbruggen." He seems to have been an actor of great natural power, but inartistic in method. See what Anthony Aston says of him. Cibber unfairly, as we must think, seems carefully to avoid mentioning him as of any importance. "The Laureat," p. 58, says: "I wonder, considering our Author's Particularity of Memory, that he hardly ever mentions Mr. *Verbruggen,* who was in many Characters an excellent Actor. . . . . I cannot conceive why *Verbruggen* is left out of the Number of his excellent Actors; whether some latent Grudge, *alta Mente repostum,* has robb'd him of his Immortality in this Work." See also memoir of Verbruggen at end of second volume.

[3] See memoir of Williams at end of second volume.

with *Betterton* at the latter end of the last Century.

Mrs. *Barry* was then in possession of almost all the chief Parts in Tragedy : With what Skill she gave Life to them you will judge from the Words of *Dryden* in his Preface to *Cleomenes*,[1] where he says,

Mrs. Barry, *always excellent, has in this Tragedy excell'd herself, and gain'd a Reputation beyond any Woman I have ever seen on the Theatre.*

I very perfectly remember her acting that Part ; and however unnecessary it may seem to give my Judgment after *Dryden*'s, I cannot help saying I do not only close with his Opinion, but will venture to add that (tho' *Dryden* has been dead these Thirty Eight Years) the same Compliment to this Hour may be due to her Excellence. And tho' she was then not a little past her Youth, she was not till that time fully arriv'd to her maturity of Power and Judgment : From whence I would observe, That the short Life of Beauty is not long enough to form a complete Actress. In Men the Delicacy of Person is not so absolutely necessary, nor the Decline of it so soon taken notice of. The Fame Mrs. *Barry* arriv'd to is a particular Proof of the Difficulty there is in judging with Certainty, from their first Trials, whether young People will ever make

---

[1] Produced at the Theatre Royal in 1692.

any great Figure on a Theatre. There was, it
seems, so little Hope of Mrs. *Barry* at her first
setting out, that she was at the end of the first
Year discharg'd the Company, among others that
were thought to be a useless Expence to it. I take
it for granted that the Objection to Mrs. *Barry* at
that time must have been a defective Ear, or some
unskilful Dissonance in her manner of pronouncing :
But where there is a proper Voice and Person, with
the Addition of a good Understanding, Experience
tells us that such Defect is not always invincible ; of
which not only Mrs. *Barry*, but the late Mrs. *Oldfield*
are eminent Instances. Mrs. *Oldfield* had been a
Year in the Theatre-Royal before she was observ'd
to give any tolerable Hope of her being an Actress;
so unlike to all manner of Propriety was her Speaking![1] How unaccountably, then, does a Genius for
the Stage make its way towards Perfection ? For,
notwithstanding these equal Disadvantages, both
these Actresses, tho' of different Excellence, made
themselves complete Mistresses of their Art by the
Prevalence of their Understanding. If this Observation may be of any use to the Masters of future
Theatres, I shall not then have made it to no
purpose.[2]

---

[1] In Chapter IX. of this work Cibber gives an elaborate account
of Mrs. Oldfield. He remarks there that, after her joining the
company, " she remain'd about a Twelvemonth almost a Mute,
and unheeded."

[2] See memoir of Mrs. Barry at end of second volume.

Mrs. *Barry*, in Characters of Greatness, had a Presence of elevated Dignity, her Mien and Motion superb and gracefully majestick; her Voice full, clear, and strong, so that no Violence of Passion could be too much for her: And when Distress or Tenderness possess'd her, she subsided into the most affecting Melody and Softness. In the Art of exciting Pity she had a Power beyond all the Actresses I have yet seen, or what your Imagination can conceive. Of the former of these two great Excellencies she gave the most delightful Proofs in almost all the Heroic Plays of *Dryden* and *Lee;* and of the latter, in the softer Passions of *Otway's Monimia* and *Belvidera.*[1] In Scenes of Anger, Defiance, or Resentment, while she was impetuous and terrible, she pour'd out the Sentiment with an enchanting Harmony; and it was this particular Excellence for which *Dryden* made her the above-recited Compliment upon her acting *Cassandra* in his *Cleomenes.* But here I am apt to think his Partiality for that Character may have tempted his Judgment to let it pass for her Master-piece, when he could not but know there were several other Characters in which her Action might have given her a fairer Pretence to the Praise he has bestow'd on her for *Cassandra;* for in no Part of that is there the least ground for Compassion, as in *Monimia*, nor equal cause for Admiration, as in the nobler Love of *Cleopatra*, or the

[1] In "The Orphan," produced at Dorset Garden in 1680, and in "Venice Preserved," produced at the same theatre in 1682

tempestuous Jealousy of *Roxana.*[1] 'Twas in these Lights I thought Mrs. *Barry* shone with a much brighter Excellence than in *Cassandra.* She was the first Person whose Merit was distinguish'd by the Indulgence of having an annual Benefit-Play, which was granted to her alone, if I mistake not, first in King *James*'s time,[2] and which became not common to others 'till the Division of this Company after the Death of King *William*'s Queen *Mary.* This great Actress dy'd of a Fever towards the latter end of Queen *Anne;* the Year I have forgot; but perhaps you will recollect it by an Expression that fell from her in blank Verse, in her last Hours, when she was delirious, *viz.*

Ha, ha! and so they make us Lords, by Dozens![3]

Mrs. *Betterton,* tho' far advanc'd in Years, was so

[1] In "The Rival Queens." Mrs. Marshall was the original Roxana, at the Theatre Royal in 1677. So far as we know, Mrs. Barry had not played Cleopatra (Dryden's "All for Love") when Dryden wrote the eulogy Cibber quotes. Mrs. Boutell originally acted the part, Theatre Royal, 1678.

[2] Bellchambers contradicts Cibber, saying that the Agreement of 14th October, 1681 [see Memoir of Hart], shows that benefits existed then. The words referred to are, "the day the young men or young women play for their own profit only." But this day set aside for the young people playing was, I think, quite a different matter from a benefit to a particular performer. Pepys (21st March, 1667) says, "The young men and women of the house . . . having liberty to act for their own profit on Wednesdays and Fridays this Lent." These were evidently "scratch" performances on "off" nights; and it is to these, I think, that the agreement quoted refers.

[3] As Dr. Doran points out ("Their Majesties' Servants," 1888

great a Mistress of Nature that even Mrs. *Barry*,
who acted the Lady *Macbeth* after her, could not in
that Part, with all her superior Strength and Melody
of Voice, throw out those quick and careless Strokes
of Terror from the Disorder of a guilty Mind, which
the other gave us with a Facility in her Manner
that render'd them at once tremendous and delightful.
Time could not impair her Skill, tho' he had brought
her Person to decay.   She was, to the last, the Admiration of all true Judges of Nature and Lovers of
Shakespear, in whose Plays she chiefly excell'd, and
without a Rival.   When she quitted the Stage
several good Actresses were the better for her Instruction.   She was a Woman of an unblemish'd
and sober life, and had the Honour to teach Queen
Anne, when Princess, the Part of *Semandra* in *Mith-
ridates*, which she acted at Court in King *Charles*'s
time.   After the Death of Mr. *Betterton*, her Husband, that Princess, when Queen, order'd her a Pension for Life, but she liv'd not to receive more than
the first half Year of it.[1]

Mrs. *Leigh*, the Wife of *Leigh* already mention'd,
had a very droll way of dressing the pretty Foibles
of superannuated Beauties.   She had in her self a
good deal of Humour, and knew how to infuse it

edition, i. 160) this does not settle the question so easily as Cibber
supposes.   Twelve Tory peers were created by Queen Anne in
the last few days of 1711, and Mrs. Barry did not die till the end
of 1713.

[1] See memoir of Mrs. Betterton at end of second volume.

into the affected Mothers, Aunts, and modest stale Maids that had miss'd their Market; of this sort were the Modish Mother in the *Chances*, affecting to be politely commode for her own Daughter; the Coquette Prude of an Aunt in Sir *Courtly Nice*, who prides herself in being chaste and cruel at Fifty; and the languishing Lady *Wishfort* in *The Way of the World*: In all these, with many others, she was extremely entertaining, and painted in a lively manner the blind Side of Nature.[1]

Mrs. *Butler*, who had her Christian Name of *Charlotte* given her by King *Charles*, was the Daughter of a decay'd Knight, and had the Honour of that Prince's Recommendation to the Theatre; a provident Restitution, giving to the Stage in kind what he had sometimes taken from it: The Publick at least was oblig'd by it; for she prov'd not only a good Actress, but was allow'd in those Days to sing and dance to great Perfection. In the Dramatick Operas of *Dioclesian* and that of *King Arthur*, she

---

[1] Downes includes Mrs. Leigh among the recruits to the Duke's Company about 1670. He does not give her maiden name, but Genest supposes she may have been the daughter of Dixon, one of Rhodes's Company. As there are two actresses of the name of Mrs. Leigh, and one Mrs. Lee, and as no reliance can be placed on the spelling of names in the casts of plays, it is practically impossible to decide accurately the parts each played. This Mrs. Leigh seems to have been Elizabeth, and her name does not appear after 1707, the Eli. Leigh who signed the petition to Queen Anne in 1709 being probably a younger woman. Bellchambers has a most inaccurate note regarding Mrs. Leigh, stating that she "is probably not a distinct person from Mrs. Mary Lee."

was a capital and admired Performer.   In speaking,
too, she had a sweet-ton'd Voice, which, with her
naturally genteel Air and sensible Pronunciation,
render'd her wholly Mistress of the Amiable in many
serious Characters.   In Parts of Humour, too, she
had a manner of blending her assuasive Softness
even with the Gay, the Lively, and the Alluring.
Of this she gave an agreeable Instance in her Action
of the (*Villiers*) Duke of *Buckingham*'s second *Constantia* in the *Chances*.   In which, if I should say I
have never seen her exceeded, I might still do no
wrong to the late Mrs. *Oldfield*'s lively Performance
of the same Character.   Mrs. *Oldfield*'s Fame may
spare Mrs. *Butler*'s Action this Compliment, without
the least Diminution or Dispute of her Superiority
in Characters of more moment.[1]

Here I cannot help observing, when there was but
one Theatre in *London*, at what unequal Sallaries,
compar'd to those of later Days, the hired Actors were
then held by the absolute Authority of their frugal
Masters the Patentees ; for Mrs. *Butler* had then
but Forty Shillings a Week, and could she have

---

[1] Mrs. Charlotte Butler is mentioned by Downes as entering
the Duke's Company about the year 1673. By 1691 she occupied
an important position as an actress, and in 1692 her name appears
to the part of La Pupsey in Durfey's " Marriage-Hater Matched."
This piece must have been produced early in the year, for Ashbury,
by whom, as Cibber relates, she was engaged for Dublin, opened
his season on 23rd March, 1692. Hitchcock, in his " View of
the Irish Stage," describes her as " an actress of great repute,
and a prodigious favourite with King Charles the Second " (i. 21).

obtain'd an Addition of Ten Shillings more (which was refus'd her) would never have left their Service; but being offer'd her own Conditions to go with Mr. *Ashbury*[1] to *Dublin* (who was then raising a Company of Actors for that Theatre, where there had been none since the Revolution) her Discontent here prevail'd with her to accept of his Offer, and he found his Account in her Value. Were not those Patentees most sagacious Oeconomists that could lay hold on so notable an Expedient to lessen their Charge? How gladly, in my time of being a Sharer, would we have given four times her Income to an Actress of equal Merit?

Mrs. *Monfort*, whose second Marriage gave her the Name of *Verbruggen*, was Mistress of more variety of Humour than I ever knew in any one Woman Actress. This variety, too, was attended with an equal Vivacity, which made her excellent in Characters extremely different. As she was naturally a pleasant Mimick, she had the Skill to make

---

[1] Chetwood gives a long account of Joseph Ashbury. He was born in 1638, and served for some years in the army. By the favour of the Duke of Ormond, then Lord Lieutenant, Ashbury was appointed successively Deputy-Master and Master of the Revels in Ireland. The latter appointment he seems to have received in 1682, though Hitchcock says "1672." Ashbury managed the Dublin Theatre with propriety and success, and was considered not only the principal actor in his time there, but the best teacher of acting in the three kingdoms. Chetwood, who saw him in his extreme old age, pronounced him admirable both in Tragedy and Comedy. He died in 1720, at the great age of eighty-two.

that Talent useful on the Stage, a Talent which may
be surprising in a Conversation and yet be lost when
brought to the Theatre, which was the Case of
Estcourt already mention'd : But where the Elocution
is round, distinct, voluble, and various, as Mrs.
Monfort's was, the Mimick there is a great Assistant
to the Actor. Nothing, tho' ever so barren, if within
the Bounds of Nature, could be flat in her Hands.
She gave many heightening Touches to Characters
but coldly written, and often made an Author vain
of his Work that in it self had but little Merit. She
was so fond of Humour, in what low Part soever to
be found, that she would make no scruple of defacing
her fair Form to come heartily into it ;[1] for when
she was eminent in several desirable Characters of
Wit and Humour in higher Life, she would be in as
much Fancy when descending into the antiquated
Abigail[2] of *Fletcher*, as when triumphing in all the
Airs and vain Graces of a fine Lady ; a Merit that
few Actresses care for. In a Play of *D'urfey*'s, now
forgotten, call'd *The Western Lass*,[3] which Part she
acted, she transform'd her whole Being, Body, Shape,
Voice, Language, Look, and Features, into almost

---

[1] This artistic sense was shown also by Margaret Woffington.
Davies ("Life of Garrick," 4th edition, i. 315) writes : "in Mrs.
Day, in the Committee, she made no scruple to disguise her
beautiful countenance, by drawing on it the lines of deformity and
the wrinkles of old age, and to put on the tawdry habiliments and
vulgar manners of an old hypocritical city vixen."

[2] In "The Scornful Lady."

[3] "The Bath ; or, the Western Lass," produced at Drury Lane
in 1701.

another Animal, with a strong *Devonshire* Dialect, a broad laughing Voice, a poking Head, round Shoulders, an unconceiving Eye, and the most be-diz'ning, dowdy Dress that ever cover'd the untrain'd Limbs of a *Joan Trot*. To have seen her here you would have thought it impossible the same Creature could ever have been recover'd to what was as easy to her, the Gay, the Lively, and the Desirable. Nor was her Humour limited to her Sex; for, while her Shape permitted, she was a more adroit pretty Fellow than is usually seen upon the Stage: Her easy Air, Action, Mien, and Gesture quite chang'd from the Quoif to the cock'd Hat and Cavalier in fashion.[1] People were so fond of seeing her a Man, that when the Part of *Bays* in the *Rehearsal* had for some time lain dormant, she was desired to take it up, which I have seen her act with all the true coxcombly Spirit and Humour that the Sufficiency of the Character required.

But what found most Employment for her whole various Excellence at once, was the Part of *Melantha* in *Marriage-Alamode*.[2] *Melantha* is as finish'd an Impertinent as ever flutter'd in a Drawing-Room, and seems to contain the most compleat System of Female Foppery that could possibly be crowded into

---

[1] It is curious to compare with this Anthony Aston's outspoken criticism on Mrs. Mountfort's personal appearance.

[2] Anthony Aston says "Melantha was her Masterpiece." Dryden's comedy was produced at the Theatre Royal in 1672, when Mrs. Boutell played Melantha.

the tortured Form of a Fine Lady. Her Language,
Dress, Motion, Manners, Soul, and Body, are in a
continual Hurry to be something more than is necessary or commendable. And though I doubt it will
be a vain Labour to offer you a just Likeness of Mrs.
Monfort's Action, yet the fantastick Impression is
still so strong in my Memory that I cannot help
saying something, tho' fantastically, about it. The
first ridiculous Airs that break from her are upon a
Gallant never seen before, who delivers her a Letter
from her Father recommending him to her good
Graces as an honourable Lover.[1]   Here now, one
would think, she might naturally shew a little of the
Sexe's decent Reserve, tho' never so slightly cover'd!
No, Sir; not a Tittle of it; Modesty is the Virtue
of a poor-soul'd Country Gentlewoman; she is too
much a Court Lady to be under so vulgar a Confusion; she reads the Letter, therefore, with a careless,
dropping Lip and an erected Brow, humming it
hastily over as if she were impatient to outgo her
Father's Commands by making a compleat Conquest
of him at once; and that the Letter might not em-
barrass her Attack, crack! she crumbles it at once
into her Palm and pours upon him her whole Artillery of Airs, Eyes, and Motion; down goes her
dainty, diving Body to the Ground, as if she were
sinking under the conscious Load of her own Attractions; then launches into a Flood of fine Language

---

[1] Act ii. scene 1.

and Compliment, still playing her Chest forward in
fifty Falls and Risings, like a Swan upon waving
Water; and, to complete her Impertinence, she is so
rapidly fond of her own Wit that she will not give
her Lover Leave to praise it: Silent assenting Bows
and vain Endeavours to speak are all the share of
the Conversation he is admitted to, which at last he
is relieved from by her Engagement to half a Score
Visits, which she *swims* from him to make, with a
Promise to return in a Twinkling.

If this Sketch has Colour enough to give you any
near Conception of her, I then need only tell you
that throughout the whole Character her variety of
Humour was every way proportionable; as, indeed,
in most Parts that she thought worth her care or
that had the least Matter for her Fancy to work
upon, I may justly say, That no Actress, from her
own Conception, could have heighten'd them with
more lively Strokes of Nature.[1]

[1] Mrs. Mountfort, originally Mrs. (that is Miss) Percival, and
afterwards Mrs. Verbruggen, is first mentioned as the representative of Winifrid, a young Welsh jilt, in "Sir Barnaby Whigg," a
comedy produced at the Theatre Royal in 1681. As Diana, in
"The Lucky Chance" (1687), Genest gives her name as Mrs.
Mountfort, late Mrs. Percival; so that her marriage with Mountfort must have taken place about the end of 1686 or beginning of
1687. Mountfort was killed in 1692, and in 1694 the part of
Mary the Buxom, in "Don Quixote," part first, is recorded by
Genest as played by Mrs. Verbruggen, late Mrs. Mountfort. In
1702, in the "Comparison between the Two Stages," Gildon pronounces her "a miracle." In 1703 she died. She was the
original representative of, among other characters, Nell, in "Devil

I come now to the last, and only living Person, of
all those whose Theatrical Characters I have pro-
mised you, Mrs. *Bracegirdle ;* who, I know, would
rather pass her remaining Days forgotten as an
Actress, than to have her Youth recollected in the
most favourable Light I am able to place it; yet, as
she is essentially necessary to my Theatrical History,
and as I only bring her back to the Company of
those with whom she pass'd the Spring and Summer
of her Life, I hope it will excuse the Liberty I take
in commemorating the Delight which the Publick
received from her Appearance while she was an
Ornament to the Theatre.

Mrs. *Bracegirdle* was now but just blooming to her
Maturity; her Reputation as an Actress gradually
rising with that of her Person; never any Woman
was in such general Favour of her Spectators, which,
to the last Scene of her Dramatick Life, she maintain'd by not being unguarded in her private Character.[1]   This Discretion contributed not a little to

of a Wife;" Belinda, in "The Old Bachelor;" Lady Froth, in
"The Double Dealer;" Charlott Welldon, in "Oroonoko;"
Berinthia, in "Relapse;" Lady Lurewell; Lady Brumpton, in
"The Funeral ;" Hypolita, in "She Would and She Would Not ;"
and Hillaria, in "Tunbridge Walks."

[1] Bellchambers has here a most uncharitable note, which I
quote as curious, though I must add that there is not a shadow of
proof of the truth of it.

"Mrs. Bracegirdle was decidedly not 'unguarded' in her conduct, for though the object of general suspicion, no proof of positive unchastity was ever brought against her.   Her intrigue with
Mountfort, who lost his life in consequence of it, (1) is hardly to

make her the *Cara*, the Darling of the Theatre : For
it will be no extravagant thing to say, Scarce an
Audience saw her that were less than half of them
Lovers, without a suspected Favourite among them :

be disputed, and there is pretty ample evidence that Congreve
was honoured with a gratification of his amorous desires. (2)

---

(1) "'We had not parted with him as many minutes as a man
may beget his likeness in, but who should we meet but Mountfort
the player, looking as pale as a ghost, sailing forward as gently as
a caterpillar 'cross a sycamore leaf, gaping for a little air, like a
sinner just come out of the powdering-tub, crying out as he crept
towards us, "O my back ! Confound 'em for a pack of brimstones :
O my back !"—"How now, *Sir Courtly*," said I, "what the devil
makes thee in this pickle?"—"O, gentlemen," says he, "I am glad
to see you ; but I am troubled with such a weakness in my back,
that it makes me bend like a superannuated fornicator." "Some
strain," said I, "got in the other world, with overheaving yourself."
—"What matters it how 'twas got," says he ; "can you tell me anything that's good for it?" "Yes," said I ; "get a warm girdle and
tie round you ; 'tis an excellent corroborative to strengthen the
loins."—"Pox on you," says he, "for a bantering dog ! how can a
single *girdle* do me good, when a *Brace* was my destruction?"'—
Brown's 'Letters from the Dead to the Living' [1744, ii. 186].

(2) "In one of those infamous collections known by the name of
'Poems on State Affairs' [iv. 49], there are several obvious,
though coarse and detestable, hints of this connexion. Collier's
severity against the stage is thus sarcastically deprecated, in a short
piece called the 'Benefits of a Theatre.'

Shall a place be put down, when we see it affords
Fit wives for great poets, and whores for great lords?
Since *Angelica*, bless'd with a singular grace,
Had, by her fine acting, preserv'd all his plays,
In an amorous rapture, young *Valentine* said,
One so fit for his plays might be fit for his bed.

M

And tho' she might be said to have been the Universal
Passion, and under the highest Temptations, her
Constancy in resisting them served but to increase
the number of her Admirers : And this perhaps you
will more easily believe when I extend not my Encomiums on her Person beyond a Sincerity that can
be suspected; for she had no greater Claim to
Beauty than what the most desirable *Brunette* might
pretend to.   But her Youth and lively Aspect threw
out such a Glow of Health and Chearfulness, that on
the Stage few Spectators that were not past it could
behold her without Desire.   It was even a Fashion
among the Gay and Young to have a Taste or *Tendre*
for Mrs. *Bracegirdle*.   She inspired the best Authors
to write for her, and two of them,[1] when they gave
her a Lover in a Play, seem'd palpably to plead their
own Passions, and make their private Court to her in

" The allusion to Congreve and Mrs. Bracegirdle wants, of course,
no corroboration ; but the hint at their marriage, broached in the
half line I have italicised, is a curious though unauthorized fact.
From the verses I shall continue to quote, it will appear that this
marriage between the parties, though thought to be private, was
currently believed ; it is an expedient that has often been used, in
similar cases, to cover the nakedness of outrageous lust.

> He warmly pursues her, she yielded her charms,
> And bless'd the kind youngster in her kinder arms :
> But at length the poor nymph did for justice implore,
> And *he's married her now*, though he'd —— her before.

"On a subsequent page of the same precious miscellany, there is
a most offensive statement of the cause which detached our great
comic writer from the object of his passion.   The thing is too
filthy to be even described."

[1] Rowe and Congreve.

fictitious Characters. In all the chief Parts she acted, the Desirable was so predominant, that no Judge could be cold enough to consider from what other particular Excellence she became delightful. To speak critically of an Actress that was extremely good were as hazardous as to be positive in one's Opinion of the best Opera Singer. People often judge by Comparison where there is no Similitude in the Performance. So that, in this case, we have only Taste to appeal to, and of Taste there can be no disputing. I shall therefore only say of Mrs. *Bracegirdle*, That the most eminent Authors always chose her for their favourite Character, and shall leave that uncontestable Proof of her Merit to its own Value. Yet let me say, there were two very different Characters in which she acquitted herself with uncommon Applause: If any thing could excuse that desperate Extravagance of Love, that almost frantick Passion of *Lee's Alexander the Great*, it must have been when Mrs. *Bracegirdle* was his *Statira*: As when she acted *Millamant*[1] all the Faults, Follies, and Affectations of that agreeable Tyrant were venially melted down into so many Charms and Attractions of a conscious Beauty. In other Characters, where Singing was a necessary Part of them, her Voice and Action gave a Pleasure which good Sense, in those Days, was not asham'd to give Praise to.

She retir'd from the Stage in the Height of her

---

[1] In Congreve's "Way of the World."

Favour from the Publick, when most of her Cotemporaries whom she had been bred up with were declining, in the Year 1710,[1] nor could she be persuaded to return to it under new Masters upon the most advantageous Terms that were offered her; excepting one Day, about a Year after, to assist her good Friend Mr. *Betterton*, when she play'd *Angelica* in *Love for Love* for his Benefit. She has still the Happiness to retain her usual Chearfulness, and to be, without the transitory Charm of Youth, agreeable.[2]

If, in my Account of these memorable Actors, I

[1] Cibber's chronology is a little shaky here. Mrs. Bracegirdle's name appeared for the last time in the bill of 20th February, 1707. Betterton's benefit, for which she returned to the stage for one night, took place on 7th April, 1709.

[2] Mrs. Anne Bracegirdle made her first appearance on the stage as a very young child. In the cast of Otway's "Orphan," 1680, the part of Cordelio, Polydore's Page, is said to be played by "the little girl," who, Curll ("History," p. 26) informs us, was Anne Bracegirdle, then less than six years of age. In 1688 her name appears to the part of Lucia in "The Squire of Alsatia;" but it is not till 1691 that she can be said to have regularly entered upon her career as an actress. She was the original representative of some of the most famous heroines in comedy: Araminta, in "The Old Bachelor;" Cynthia, in "The Double Dealer;" Angelica, in "Love for Love;" Belinda, in "The Provoked Wife;" Millamant; Flippanta, in "The Confederacy," and many others. Mrs. Bracegirdle appears to have been a good and excellent woman, as well as a great actress. All the scandal about her seems to have had no further foundation than, to quote Genest, "the extreme difficulty with which an actress at this period of the stage must have preserved her chastity." Genest goes on to remark, with delicious *naïveté*, "Mrs. Bracegirdle was perhaps a woman of a cold constitution." Her retirement from the stage

have not deviated from Truth, which, in the least
Article, I am not conscious of, may we not venture
to say, They had not their Equals, at any one Time,
upon any Theatre in *Europe?* Or, if we confine
the Comparison to that of *France* alone, I believe
no other Stage can be much disparag'd by being
left out of the question ; which cannot properly be
decided by the single Merit of any one Actor ;
whether their *Baron* or our *Betterton* might be
the Superior, (take which Side you please) that
Point reaches, either way, but to a thirteenth part of
what I contend for, *viz.* That no Stage, at any one
Period, could shew thirteen Actors, standing all in
equal Lights of Excellence in their Profession : And
I am the bolder, in this Challenge to any other
Nation, because no Theatre having so extended a

when not much over thirty is accounted for by Curll, by a story of
a competition between her and Mrs. Oldfield in the part of Mrs.
Brittle in " The Amorous Widow," in which the latter was the more
applauded.   He says that they played the part on two successive
nights ; but I have carefully examined Dr. Burney's MSS. in the
British Museum for the season 1706-7, and " The Amorous Widow "
was certainly not played twice successively.   I doubt the story
altogether.   That Mrs. Bracegirdle retired because Mrs. Oldfield
was excelling her in popular estimation is most likely, but I can
find no confirmation whatever for Curll's story.   " The Laureat,"
p. 36, attributes her retirement to Mrs. Oldfield's being " preferr'd
to some Parts before her, by our very *Apologist*" ; but though the
reason thus given is probably accurate, the person blamed is as
probably guiltless ; for I do not think Cibber could have sufficient
authority to distribute parts in 1706-7.   Mrs. Bracegirdle died
September, 1748, but was dead to the stage from 1709.   Cibber's
remark on p. 99 had therefore no reference to her.

Variety of natural Characters as the *English*, can have a Demand for Actors of such various Capacities; why then, where they could not be equally wanted, should we suppose them, at any one time, to have existed?

How imperfect soever this copious Account of them may be, I am not without Hope, at least, it may in some degree shew what Talents are requisite to make Actors valuable: And if that may any ways inform or assist the Judgment of future Spectators, it may as often be of service to their publick Entertainments; for as their Hearers are, so will Actors be; worse, or better, as the false or true Taste applauds or discommends them. Hence only can our Theatres improve or must degenerate.

There is another Point, relating to the hard Condition of those who write for the Stage, which I would recommend to the Consideration of their Hearers; which is, that the extreme Severity with which they damn a bad Play seems too terrible a Warning to those whose untried Genius might hereafter give them a good one: Whereas it might be a Temptation to a latent Author to make the Experiment, could he be sure that, though not approved, his Muse might at least be dismiss'd with Decency: But the Vivacity of our modern Criticks is of late grown so riotous, that an unsuccessful Author has no more Mercy shewn him than a notorious Cheat in a Pillory; every Fool, the lowest Member of the Mob, becomes a Wit, and will have a fling at him. They come now to a new Play like Hounds to a Carcase, and are all in a full Cry, sometimes for an Hour together, before the Curtain rises to throw it amongst them. Sure those Gentlemen cannot but allow that a Play condemned after a fair Hearing falls with thrice the Ignominy as when it is refused that common Justice.

But when their critical Interruptions grow so loud, and of so long a Continuance, that the Attention of quiet People (though not so complete Criticks) is terrify'd, and the Skill of the Actors quite disconcerted by the Tumult, the Play then seems rather to fall by Assassins than by a Lawful Sentence.[1] Is it possible that such Auditors can receive Delight, or think it any Praise to them, to prosecute so injurious, so unmanly a Treatment? And tho' perhaps the Compassionate, on the other side (who know they have as good a Right to clap and support, as others have to catcall, damn, and destroy,) may oppose this Oppression; their Good-nature, alas! contributes little to the Redress; for in this sort of Civil War the unhappy Author, like a good Prince, while his Subjects are at mortal Variance, is sure to be a Loser by a Victory on either Side; for still the Commonwealth, his Play, is, during the Conflict, torn to pieces. While this is the Case, while the Theatre is so turbulent a Sea and so infested with Pirates, what

---

[1] Cibber writes here with feeling; for, after his "Nonjuror" abused the Jacobites and Nonjurors, that party took every opportunity of revenging themselves on him by maltreating his plays.

Poetical Merchant of any Substance will venture to
trade in it? If these valiant Gentlemen pretend to
be Lovers of Plays, why will they deter Gentlemen
from giving them such as are fit for Gentlemen to
see? In a word, this new Race of Criticks seem to
me like the Lion-Whelps in the *Tower*, who are so
boisterously gamesome at their Meals that they dash
down the Bowls of Milk brought for their own
Breakfast.[1]

As a good Play is certainly the most rational and
the highest Entertainment that Human Invention
can produce, let that be my Apology (if I need any)
for having thus freely deliver'd my Mind in behalf
of those Gentlemen who, under such calamitous
Hazards, may hereafter be reduced to write for the
Stage, whose Case I shall compassionate from the
same Motive that prevail'd on *Dido* to assist the
Trojans in Distress.

> *Non ignara mali miseris succurrere disco.*   Virg.[2]

Or, as *Dryden* has it,

> *I learn to pity Woes so like my own.*

If those particular Gentlemen have sometimes
made me the humbled Object of their Wit and
Humour, their Triumph at least has done me this
involuntary Service, that it has driven me a Year or
two sooner into a quiet Life than otherwise my own

---

[1] See *ante*, p. 63, for an allusion to this passage by Fielding
in "The Champion."
[2] Æneid, i. 630.

want of Judgment might have led me to :[1]   I left the
Stage before my Strength left me, and tho' I came to
it again for some few Days a Year or two after, my
Reception there not only turn'd to my Account, but
seem'd a fair Invitation that I would make my Visits
more frequent: But to give over a Winner can be
no very imprudent Resolution.[2]

[1] This is a curious statement, and has never, so far as I know,
been commented on ; the cause of Cibber's retirement having
always been considered mysterious.   I suppose this reference to
ill-treatment must be held as confirming Davies's statement that
the public lost patience at Cibber's continually playing tragic parts,
and fairly hissed him off the stage.   Davies (" Dram. Misc.," iii.
471) relates the following incident: " When Thomson's Sophonisba was read to the actors, Cibber laid his hand upon Scipio,
a character, which, though it appears only in the last act, is of
great dignity and importance.   For two nights successively, Cibber
was as much exploded as any bad actor could be.   Williams, by
desire of Wilks, made himself master of the part ; but he, march-
ing slowly, in great military distinction, from the upper part of the
stage, and wearing the same dress as Cibber, was mistaken for
him, and met with repeated hisses, joined to the music of cat-
cals ; but, as soon as the audience were undeceived, they con-
verted their groans and hisses to loud and long continued applause."

[2] Cibber retired in May, 1733.   The reappearance he refers to
was not that he made in 1738, as Bellchambers states.   He no
doubt alludes to his performances in 1734-35, when he played
Bayes, Lord Foppington, Sir John Brute, and other comedy parts.
On the nights he played, the compliment was paid him of putting
no name in the bill but his own.

CHAPTER VI.

The Author's first Step upon the Stage. His Discouragements. The best Actors in Europe ill us'd. A Revolution in their Favour. King William grants them a Licence to act in Lincoln's-Inn Fields. The Author's Distress in being thought a worse Actor than a Poet. Reduc'd to write a Part for himself. His Success. More Remarks upon Theatrical Action. Some upon himself.

HAVING given you the State of the Theatre at my first Admission to it, I am now drawing towards the several Revolutions it suffer'd in my own Time. But (as you find by the setting out of my History) that I always intended myself the Heroe of it, it may be necessary to let you know me in my Obscurity, as well as in my higher Light, when I became one of the Theatrical Triumvirat.

The Patentees,[1] who were now Masters of this united and only Company of Comedians, seem'd to make it a Rule that no young Persons desirous to be Actors should be admitted into Pay under at least half a Year's Probation, wisely knowing that how early soever they might be approv'd of, there could be no great fear of losing them while they had then no other Market to go to. But, alas! Pay was the least of my Concern ; the Joy and Privilege of every Day seeing Plays for nothing I thought was a sufficient Consideration for the best of my Services. So that it was no Pain to my Patience that I waited full three Quarters of a Year before I was taken into a Salary of Ten Shillings *per* Week ;[2] which, with the Assistance of Food and Raiment at my Father's

[1] The original holders of the Patents, Sir William Davenant and Thomas Killigrew, were dead in 1690; and their successors, Alexander Davenant, to whom Charles Davenant had assigned his interest, and Charles Killigrew, seem to have taken little active interest in the management; for Christopher Rich, who acquired Davenant's share in 1691, seems at once to have become managing proprietor.

[2] Davies ("Dramatic Miscellanies," iii. 444) gives the following account of Cibber's first salary: "But Mr. Richard Cross, late prompter of Drury-lane theatre, gave me the following history of Colley Cibber's first establishment as a hired actor. He was known only, for some years, by the name of Master Colley. After waiting impatiently a long time for the prompter's notice, by good fortune he obtained the honour of carrying a message on the stage, in some play, to Betterton. Whatever was the cause, Master Colley was so terrified, that the scene was disconcerted by him. Betterton asked, in some anger, who the young fellow was that had committed the blunder. Downes replied, 'Master Colley.'— 'Master Colley! then forfeit him.'—'Why, sir,' said the prompter,

House, I then thought a most plentiful Accession, and myself the happiest of Mortals.

The first Thing that enters into the Head of a young Actor is that of being a Heroe: In this Ambition I was soon snubb'd by the Insufficiency of my Voice; to which might be added an uninform'd meagre Person, (tho' then not ill made) with a dismal pale Complexion.[1] Under these Disadvantages,[2] I had but a melancholy Prospect of ever playing a Lover with Mrs. *Bracegirdle*, which I had flatter'd my Hopes that my Youth might one Day have recommended me to. What was most promising in me, then, was the Aptness of my Ear; for I was soon allow'd to speak

'he has no salary.'—'No!' said the old man; 'why then put him down ten shillings a week, and forfeit him 5*s*.'"

[1] Complexion is a point of no importance now, and this allusion suggests a theory to me which I give with all diffidence. We know that actresses painted in Pepys's time ("1667, Oct. 5. But, Lord! To see how they [Nell Gwynne and Mrs. Knipp] were both painted would make a man mad, and did make me loathe them"), and we also know that Dogget was famous for the painting of his face to represent old age. If, then, complexion was a point of importance for a lover, as Cibber states, it suggests that young actors playing juvenile parts did not use any "make-up" or paint, but went on the stage in their natural complexion. The lighting of the stage was of course much less brilliant than it afterwards became, so that "make-up" was not so necessary.

[2] "The Laureat" (p. 103) describes Cibber's person thus:— "He was in Stature of the middle Size, his Complexion fair, inclinable to the Sandy, his Legs somewhat of the thickest, his Shape a little clumsy, not irregular, and his Voice rather shrill than loud or articulate, and crack'd extremely, when he endeavour'd to raise it. He was in his younger Days so lean, as to be known by the Name of *Hatchet Face*."

justly, tho' what was grave and serious did not equally become me. The first Part, therefore, in which I appear'd with any glimpse of Success, was the Chaplain[1] in the *Orphan* of *Otway*. There is in this Character (of one Scene only) a decent Pleasantry, and Sense enough to shew an Audience whether the Actor has any himself. Here was the first Applause I ever receiv'd, which, you may be sure, made my Heart leap with a higher Joy than may be necessary to describe; and yet my Transport was not then half so high as at what *Goodman* (who had now left the Stage) said of me the next Day in my hearing. *Goodman* often came to a Rehearsal for Amusement, and having sate out the *Orphan* the Day before, in a Conversation with some of the principal Actors enquir'd what new young Fellow that was whom he had seen in the Chaplain? Upon which *Monfort* reply'd, *That's he, behind you.* *Goodman* then turning about, look'd earnestly at me, and, after some Pause, clapping me on the Shoulder, rejoin'd, *If he does not make a good Actor, I'll be d—'d!* The Surprize of being commended by one who had been himself so eminent on the Stage, and in so positive a manner, was more than I could support; in a Word, it almost took away my Breath, and (laugh, if you please) fairly drew Tears from my Eyes! And, tho' it may be as ridiculous as incredible to tell you what a full Vanity and

---

[1] Bellchambers notes that this part was originally played by Percival, who came into the Duke's Company about 1673.

Content at that time possess'd me, I will still make
it a Question whether *Alexander* himself, or *Charles
the Twelfth* of *Sweden*, when at the Head of their
first victorious Armies, could feel a greater Transport in their Bosoms than I did then in mine, when
but in the Rear of this Troop of Comedians.   You
see to what low Particulars I am forc'd to descend
to give you a true Resemblance of the early and
lively Follies of my Mind. Let me give you another
Instance of my Discretion, more desperate than that
of preferring the Stage to any other Views of Life.
One might think that the Madness of breaking from
the Advice and Care of Parents to turn Player could
not easily be exceeded : But what think you, Sir,
of——Matrimony ? which, before I was Two-and-
twenty, I actually committed,[1] when I had but
Twenty Pounds a Year, which my Father had assur'd to me, and Twenty Shillings a Week from my
Theatrical Labours, to maintain, as I then thought,
the happiest young Couple that ever took a Leap in
the Dark !   If after this, to complete my Fortune, I

---

[1] Of Cibber's wife there is little record. In 1695 the name of
"Mrs. Cibbars" appears to the part of Galatea in "Philaster,"
and she was the original Hillaria in Cibber's "Love's Last Shift"
in 1696 ; but she never made any great name or played any
famous part.   She was a Miss Shore, sister of John Shore, "Ser-
geant-trumpet" of England.   The "Biographia Dramatica"
(i. 117) says that Miss Shore's father was extremely angry at her
marriage, and spent that portion of his fortune which he had intended for her in building a retreat on the Thames which was
called Shore's Folly.

turn'd Poet too, this last Folly indeed had something a better Excuse—Necessity: Had it never been my Lot to have come on the Stage, 'tis probable I might never have been inclin'd or reduc'd to have wrote for it: But having once expos'd my Person there, I thought it could be no additional Dishonour to let my Parts, whatever they were, take their Fortune along with it.—But to return to the Progress I made as an Actor.

Queen *Mary* having commanded the *Double Dealer* to be acted, *Kynaston* happen'd to be so ill that he could not hope to be able next Day to perform his Part of the Lord *Touchwood*. In this Exigence, the Author, Mr. *Congreve*, advis'd that it might be given to me, if at so short a Warning I would undertake it.[1] The Flattery of being thus distinguish'd by so celebrated an Author, and the Honour to act before a Queen, you may be sure made me blind to whatever Difficulties might attend it. I accepted the Part, and was ready in it before I slept; next Day the Queen was present at the Play, and was receiv'd with a new Prologue from the Author, spoken by Mrs. *Barry*, humbly acknowledging the great Honour done to the Stage, and to his Play in particular: Two Lines of it, which tho' I have not since read, I still remember.

But never were in Rome *nor* Athens *seen,*
So fair a Circle, or so bright a Queen.

[1] "The Double Dealer," 1693, was not very successful, and

After the Play, Mr. *Congreve* made me the Compliment of saying, That I had not only answer'd,
but had exceeded his Expectations, and that he
would shew me he was sincere by his saying
more of me to the Masters.——He was as good
as his Word, and the next Pay-day I found my
Sallary of fifteen was then advanc'd to twenty
Shillings a Week. But alas! this favourable Opinion of Mr. *Congreve* made no farther Impression
upon the Judgment of my good Masters; it only
serv'd to heighten my own Vanity, but could not
recommend me to any new Trials of my Capacity;
not a Step farther could I get 'till the Company was
again divided, when the Desertion of the best Actors
left a clear Stage for younger Champions to mount
and shew their best Pretensions to Favour. But it
is now time to enter upon those Facts that immediately preceded this remarkable Revolution of the
Theatre.

You have seen how complete a Set of Actors
were under the Government of the united Patents
in 1690; if their Gains were not extraordinary, what
shall we impute it to but some extraordinary ill
Menagement? I was then too young to be in their
Secrets, and therefore can only observe upon what
I saw and have since thought visibly wrong.

when played at Lincoln's Inn Fields, 18th October, 1718, was
announced as not having been acted for fifteen years; so that this
incident no doubt occurred in the course of the first few nights of
the play, which, Malone says, was produced in November, 1693.

Though the Success of the *Prophetess* [1] and *King Arthur* [2] (two dramatic Operas, in which the Patentees had embark'd all their Hopes) was in Appearance very great, yet their whole Receipts did not so far balance their Expence as to keep them out of a large Debt, which it was publickly known was about this time contracted, and which found Work for the Court of Chancery for about twenty Years following, till one side of the Cause grew weary. But this was not all that was wrong; every Branch of the Theatrical Trade had been sacrific'd to the necessary fitting out those tall Ships of Burthen that were to bring home the *Indies*. Plays of course were neglected, Actors held cheap, and slightly dress'd, while Singers and Dancers were better paid, and embroider'd. These Measures, of course, created Murmurings on one side, and Ill-humour and Contempt on the other. When it became necessary therefore to lessen the Charge, a Resolution was

[1] "The Prophetess," now supposed to be mostly Fletcher's work (see Ward's "English Dramatic Literature," ii. 218), was made into an opera by Betterton, the music by Purcell. It was produced in 1690, with a Prologue written by Dryden, which, for political reasons, was forbidden by the Lord Chamberlain after the first night.

[2] "King Arthur; or, the British Worthy," a Dramatic Opera, as Dryden entitles it, was produced in 1691. In his Dedication to the Marquis of Halifax, Dryden says: "This Poem was the last Piece of Service, which I had the Honour to do, for my Gracious Master, King Charles the Second." Downes says "'twas very Gainful to the Company," but Cibber declares it was not so successful as it appeared to be.

taken to begin with the Sallaries of the Actors ; and what seem'd to make this Resolution more necessary at this time was the Loss of *Nokes*, *Monfort*, and *Leigh*, who all dy'd about the same Year : [1] No wonder then, if when these great Pillars were at once remov'd, the Building grew weaker and the Audiences very much abated.   Now in this Distress, what more natural Remedy could be found than to incite and encourage (tho' with some Hazard) the Industry of the surviving Actors ?   But the Patentees, it seems, thought the surer way was to bring down their Pay in proportion to the Fall of their Audiences.   To make this Project more feasible they propos'd to begin at the Head of 'em, rightly judging that if the Principals acquiesc'd, their Inferiors would murmur in vain.   To bring this about with a better Grace, they, under Pretence of bringing younger Actors forward, order'd several of *Betterton*'s and Mrs. *Barry*'s chief Parts to be given to young *Powel* and Mrs. *Bracegirdle*.   In this they committed two palpable Errors ; for while the best Actors are in Health, and still on the Stage, the Publick is always apt to be out of Humour when those of a lower Class pretend to stand in their Places ; or admitting at this time they might have been accepted, this Project might very probably have lessen'd, but could not possibly mend an Audience, and was a sure Loss of that Time, in studying, which might have

[1] End of 1692.

been better employ'd in giving the Auditor Variety,
the only Temptation to a pall'd Appetite; and
Variety is only to be given by Industry: But
Industry will always be lame when the Actor has
Reason to be discontented. This the Patentees did
not consider, or pretended not to value, while they
thought their Power secure and uncontroulable:
But farther their first Project did not succeed; for
tho' the giddy Head of *Powel* accepted the Parts of
Betterton, Mrs. *Bracegirdle* had a different way of
thinking, and desir'd to be excus'd from those of
Mrs. *Barry*; her good Sense was not to be misled
by the insidious Favour of the Patentees; she knew
the Stage was wide enough for her Success, without
entring into any such rash and invidious Competition with Mrs. *Barry*, and therefore wholly refus'd
acting any Part that properly belong'd to her. But
this Proceeding, however, was Warning enough to
make *Betterton* be upon his Guard, and to alarm
others with Apprehensions of their own Safety, from
the Design that was laid against him: *Betterton*
upon this drew into his Party most of the valuable
Actors, who, to secure their Unity, enter'd with him
into a sort of Association to stand or fall together.[1]
All this the Patentees for some time slighted; but
when Matters drew towards a Crisis, they found it

---

[1] Betterton seems to have been a very politic person. In the
"Comparison between the two Stages" (p. 41) he is called,
though not in reference to this particular matter, "a cunning old
Fox."

adviseable to take the same Measures, and accordingly open'd an Association on their part; both which were severally sign'd, as the Interest or Inclination of either Side led them.

During these Contentions which the impolitick Patentees had rais'd against themselves (not only by this I have mentioned, but by many other Grievances which my Memory retains not) the Actors offer'd a Treaty of Peace; but their Masters imagining no Consequence could shake the Right of their Authority, refus'd all Terms of Accommodation. In the mean time this Dissention was so prejudicial to their daily Affairs, that I remember it was allow'd by both Parties that before *Christmas* the Patent had lost the getting of at least a thousand Pounds by it.

My having been a Witness of this unnecessary Rupture was of great use to me when, many Years after, I came to be a Menager my self. I laid it down as a settled Maxim, that no Company could flourish while the chief Actors and the Undertakers were at variance. I therefore made it a Point, while it was possible upon tolerable Terms, to keep the valuable Actors in humour with their Station; and tho' I was as jealous of their Encroachments as any of my Co-partners could be, I always guarded against the least Warmth in my Expostulations with them; not but at the same time they might see I was perhaps more determin'd in the Question than those that gave a loose to their Resentment, and when they were cool were as apt to recede.[1] I do not remember that ever I made a Promise to any that I did not keep, and therefore was cautious how I made them. This Coldness, tho' it might not please, at least left them nothing to reproach me with ; and if Temper and fair Words could prevent a Disobligation, I was sure never to give Offence or receive it.[2] But as I was but one of three, I could not oblige others to observe the same Conduct. However, by this means I kept many an unreasonable Discontent from breaking out, and both Sides found their Account in it.

How a contemptuous and overbearing manner of treating Actors had like to have ruin'd us in our early Prosperity shall be shewn in its Place.[3] If future Menagers should chance to think my way right, I suppose they will follow it ; if not, when they find what happen'd to the Patentees (who chose to disagree with their People) perhaps they may think better of it.

The Patentees then, who by their united Powers

---

[1] This is no doubt a hit at Wilks, whose temper was extremely impetuous.

[2] "The Laureat," p. 39: "He (Cibber) was always against raising, or rewarding, or by any means encouraging Merit of any kind." He had "many Disputes with *Wilks* on this Account, who was impatient, when Justice required it, to reward the Meritorious."

[3] This is a reference to the secession of seven or eight actors in 1714, caused, according to Cibber, by Wilks's overbearing temper. See Chapter XV.

had made a Monopoly of the Stage, and consequently presum'd they might impose what Conditions they pleased upon their People, did not consider that they were all this while endeavouring to
enslave a Set of Actors whom the Publick (more
arbitrary than themselves) were inclined to support;
nor did they reflect that the Spectator naturally
wish'd that the Actor who gave him Delight might
enjoy the Profits arising from his Labour, without
regard of what pretended Damage or Injustice
might fall upon his Owners, whose personal Merit
the Publick was not so well acquainted with. From
this Consideration, then, several Persons of the
highest Distinction espous'd their Cause, and sometimes in the Circle entertain'd the King with the
State of the Theatre. At length their Grievances
were laid before the Earl of *Dorset*, then Lord
Chamberlain, who took the most effectual Method
for their Relief.[1] The Learned of the Law were

---

[1] Downes and Davies give the following accounts of the transaction :—

"Some time after, a difference happening between the United
Patentees, and the chief *Actors*: As Mr. *Betterton*; Mrs. *Barry*
and Mrs. *Bracegirdle*; the latter complaining of Oppression from
the former; they for Redress, Appeal'd to my Lord of *Dorset*,
then Lord Chamberlain, for Justice; who Espousing the Cause of
the Actors, with the assistance of Sir *Robert Howard*, finding their
Complaints just, procur'd from King *William*, a Seperate License
for Mr. *Congreve*, Mr. *Betterton*, Mrs. *Bracegirdle* and Mrs. *Barry*,
and others, to set up a new Company, calling it the New Theatre
in *Lincolns-Inn-Fields*."—" Roscius Anglicanus," p. 43.

"The nobility, and all persons of eminence, favoured the cause

advised with, and they gave their Opinion that no
Patent for acting Plays, &c. could tie up the Hands
of a succeeding Prince from granting the like Authority where it might be thought proper to trust it.
But while this Affair was in Agitation, Queen *Mary*
dy'd,[1] which of course occasion'd a Cessation of all
publick Diversions. In this melancholy Interim,
Betterton and his Adherents had more Leisure to
sollicit their Redress ; and the Patentees now finding that the Party against them was gathering
Strength, were reduced to make sure of as good a
Company as the Leavings of *Betterton*'s Interest
could form ; and these, you may be sure, would not
lose this Occasion of setting a Price upon their
Merit equal to their own Opinion of it, which was
but just double to what they had before. *Powel*
and *Verbruggen*, who had then but forty Shillings a
Week, were now raised each of them to four Pounds,
and others in Proportion : As for my self, I was then
too insignificant to be taken into their Councils, and
consequently stood among those of little Importance,
like Cattle in a Market, to be sold to the first Bidder.
But the Patentees seeming in the greater Distress
for Actors, condescended to purchase me. Thus,

of the comedians ; the generous Dorset introduced Betterton,
Mrs. Barry, Mrs. Bracegirdle, and others, to the King, who granted
them an audience. . . . William, who had freed all the
subjects of England from slavery, except the inhabitants of the
mimical world, rescued them also from the insolence and tyranny
of their oppressors."—" Dram. Miscellanies," iii. 419.

[1] 28th December, 1694.

without any farther Merit than that of being a scarce
Commodity, I was advanc'd to thirty Shillings a
Week : Yet our Company was so far from being
full,[1] that our Commanders were forced to beat up
for Volunteers in several distant Counties; it was
this Occasion that first brought *Johnson*[2] and *Bullock*[3] to the Service of the Theatre-Royal.

Forces being thus raised, and the War declared
on both Sides, *Betterton* and his Chiefs had the
Honour of an Audience of the *King*, who consider'd
them as the only Subjects whom he had not yet
deliver'd from arbitrary Power, and graciously dismiss'd them with an Assurance of Relief and Support—Accordingly a select number of them were
impower'd by his Royal Licence[4] to act in a separate
Theatre for themselves. This great Point being
obtain'd, many People of Quality came into a voluntary Subscription of twenty, and some of forty Guineas
a-piece, for erecting a Theatre within the Walls of
the Tennis-Court in *Lincoln's-Inn-Fields*.[5] But as

---

[1] The "Comparison between the two Stages" says (p. 7):
" 'twas almost impossible in *Drury-Lane*, to muster up a sufficient
number to take in all the Parts of any Play."

[2] See memoir of Johnson at end of second volume.

[3] See memoir of Bullock at end of second volume.

[4] I do not think that the date of this Licence has ever been
stated. It was 25th March, 1695.

[5] "Comparison between the two Stages," p. 12: "We know
what importuning and dunning the Noblemen there was, what
flattering, and what promising there was, till at length, the in-
couragement they received by liberal Contributions set 'em in a

it required Time to fit it up, it gave the Patentees more Leisure to muster their Forces, who notwithstanding were not able to take the Field till the *Easter-Monday* in *April* following. Their first Attempt was a reviv'd Play call'd *Abdelazar*, or the *Moor's Revenge*, poorly written, by Mrs. *Behn*. The House was very full, but whether it was the Play or the Actors that were not approved, the next Day's Audience sunk to nothing. However, we were assured that let the Audiences be never so low, our Masters would make good all Deficiencies, and so indeed they did, 'till towards the End of the Season, when Dues to Ballance came too thick upon 'em. But that I may go gradually on with my own Fortune, I must take this Occasion to let you know, by the following Circumstance, how very low my Capacity as an Actor was then rated : It was thought necessary at our Opening that the Town should be address'd in a new Prologue ; but to our great Distress, among several that were offer'd, not one was judg'd fit to be spoken. This I thought a favourable Occasion to do my self some remarkable Service, if I should have the good Fortune to produce one that might be accepted. The next (memorable) Day my Muse brought forth her first Fruit that was ever made publick ; how good or bad imports not ; my Prologue was accepted, and resolv'd on to be spoken. This Point being gain'd, I began to stand upon

Condition to go on." This theatre was the theatre in *Little* Lincoln's Inn Fields. See further details in Chap. XIII.

Terms, you will say, not unreasonable; which were, that if I might speak it my self I would expect no farther Reward for my Labour: This was judg'd as bad as having no Prologue at all! You may imagine how hard I thought it, that they durst not trust my poor poetical Brat to my own Care. But since I found it was to be given into other Hands, I insisted that two Guineas should be the Price of my parting with it; which with a Sigh I received, and *Powel* spoke the Prologue: But every Line that was applauded went sorely to my Heart when I reflected that the same Praise might have been given to my own speaking; nor could the Success of the Author compensate the Distress of the Actor. However, in the End, it serv'd in some sort to mend our People's Opinion of me; and whatever the Criticks might think of it, one of the Patentees [1] (who, it is true, knew no Difference between *Dryden* and *D'urfey*) said, upon the Success of it, that insooth! I was an ingenious young Man. This sober Compliment (tho' I could have no Reason to be vain upon it) I thought was a fair Promise to my being in favour. But to Matters of more Moment: Now let us reconnoitre the Enemy.

After we had stolen some few Days March upon them, the Forces of *Betterton* came up with us in terrible Order: In about three Weeks following, the new Theatre was open'd against us with a veteran Company and a new Train of Artillery; or in plainer

---

[1] No doubt, Rich.

English, the old Actors in *Lincoln's-Inn-Fields* began with a new Comedy of Mr. *Congreve's,* call'd
Love for *Love;*[1] which ran on with such extraordinary Success that they had seldom occasion to
act any other Play 'till the End of the Season. This
valuable Play had a narrow Escape from falling
into the Hands of the Patentees; for before the
Division of the Company it had been read and
accepted of at the Theatre-Royal: But while the
Articles of Agreement for it were preparing, the
Rupture in the Theatrical State was so far advanced
that the Author took time to pause before he sign'd
them; when finding that all Hopes of Accommodation were impracticable, he thought it advisable to
let it take its Fortune with those Actors for whom he
had first intended the Parts.

Mr. *Congreve* was then in such high Reputation as
an Author, that besides his Profits from this Play,
they offered him a whole Share with them, which he
accepted;[2] in Consideration of which he oblig'd
himself, if his Health permitted, to give them one
new Play every Year.[3] *Dryden,* in King *Charles's*

[1] Downes says (p. 43), "the House being fitted up from a
Tennis-Court, they Open'd it the last Day of *April,* 1695."

[2] It will be noticed that Downes in the passage quoted by
me (p. 192, note 1) mentions Congreve as if he had been an
original sharer in the Licence; but the statement is probably
loosely made.

[3] Bellchambers has here the following notes, the entire substance
of which will be found in Malone ("Shakespeare," 1821, iii. 170,
et seq.): "In Shakspeare's time the nightly expenses for lights,
supernumeraries, etc., was but forty-five shillings, and having

Time, had the same Share with the King's Company, but he bound himself to give them two Plays every Season. This you may imagine he could not hold long, and I am apt to think he might have

deducted this charge, the clear emoluments were divided into shares, (supposed to be forty in number,) between the proprietors, and principal actors. In the year 1666, the whole profit arising from acting plays, masques, etc., at the King's theatre, was divided into twelve shares and three quarters, of which Mr. Killegrew, the manager, had two shares and three quarters, each share computed to produce about £250, net, per annum. In Sir William D'Avenant's company, from the time their new theatre was opened in Portugal-row, the total receipt, after deducting the nightly expenses, was divided into fifteen shares, of which it was agreed that ten should belong to D'Avenant, for various purposes, and the remainder be divided among the male members of his troops according to their rank and merit. I cannot relate the arrangement adopted by Betterton in Lincoln's-inn-fields, but the share accepted by Congreve was, doubtless, presumed to be of considerable value.

"Dryden had a share and a quarter in the king's company, for which he bound himself to furnish not two, but three plays every season. The following paper, which, after remaining long in the Killegrew family, came into the hands of the late Mr. Reed, and was published by Mr. Malone in his 'Historical Account of the English Stage,' incontestably proves the practice alluded to. The superscription is lost, but it was probably addressed to the lord-chamberlain, or the king, about the year 1678, 'Œdipus,' the ground of complaint, being printed in 1679:

"'Whereas upon Mr. Dryden's binding himself to write three playes a yeere, hee the said Mr. Dryden was admitted and continued as a sharer in the king's playhouse for diverse years, and received for his share and a quarter three or four hundred pounds, communibus annis; but though he received the moneys, we received not the playes, not one in a yeare. After which, the house being burnt, the company in building another, contracted great debts, so that shares fell much short of what they were formerly.

serv'd them better with one in a Year, not so hastily written. Mr. *Congreve*, whatever Impediment he met with, was three Years before, in pursuance to his Agreement, he produced the *Mourning Bride* ;[1]

Thereupon Mr. Dryden complaining to the company of his want of proffit, the company was so kind to him that they not only did not presse him for the playes which he so engaged to write for them, and for which he was paid beforehand, but they did also at his earnest request give him a third day for his last new play called *All for Love;* and at the receipt of the money of the said third day, he acknowledged it as a guift, and a particular kindnesse of the company. Yet notwithstanding this kind proceeding, Mr. Dryden has now, jointly with Mr. Lee, (who was in pension with us to the last day of our playing, and shall continue,) written a play called *Oedipus*, and given it to the Duke's company, contrary to his said agreement, his promise, and all gratitude, to the great prejudice and almost undoing of the company, they being the only poets remaining to us. Mr. Crowne, being under the like agreement with the duke's house, writt a play called *The Destruction of Jerusalem*, and being forced by their refusall of it, to bring it to us, the said company compelled us, after the studying of it, and a vast expence in scenes and cloaths, to buy off their clayme, by paying all the pension he had received from them, amounting to one hundred and twelve pounds paid by the king's company, besides near forty pounds he the said Mr. Crowne paid out of his owne pocket.

" 'These things considered, if notwithstanding Mr. Dryden's said agreement, promise, and moneys freely giving him for his said last new play, and the many titles we have to his writings, this play be judged away from us, we must submit.

(Signed)   " ' Charles Killigrew.

" ' Charles Hart.

" ' Rich. Burt.

" ' Cardell Goodman.

" ' Mic. Mohun.' "

[1] The interval between the two plays cannot have been quite

and if I mistake not, the Interval had been much the same when he gave them the *Way of the World*.[1] But it came out the stronger for the Time it cost him, and to their better support when they sorely wanted it: For though they went on with Success for a Year or two, and even when their Affairs were declining stood in much higher Estimation of the Publick than their Opponents; yet in the End both Sides were great Sufferers by their Separation; the natural Consequence of two Houses, which I have already mention'd in a former Chapter.

The first Error this new Colony of Actors fell into was their inconsiderately parting with *Williams* and Mrs. *Monfort*[2] upon a too nice (not to say severe) Punctilio; in not allowing them to be equal Sharers with the rest; which before they had acted one Play occasioned their Return to the Service of the Patentees. As I have call'd this an Error, I ought to give my Reasons for it. Though the Industry of *Williams* was not equal to his Capacity; for he lov'd his Bottle better than his Business; and though Mrs. *Monfort* was only excellent in Comedy, yet their Merit was too great almost on any Scruples to be added to the Enemy; and at worst, they were certainly much more above those they would have ranked them with than they could possibly be under

three years. The first was produced in April, 1695, the second some time in 1697.

[1] Produced early in 1700.

[2] Mrs. Mountfort was now Mrs. Verbruggen.

those they were not admitted to be equal to. Of this Fact there is a poetical Record in the Prologue to *Love for Love*, where the Author, speaking of the then happy State of the Stage, observes that if, in Paradise, when two only were there, they both fell; the Surprize was less, if from so numerous a Body as theirs, there had been any Deserters.

Abate the Wonder, and the Fault forgive,
If, in our larger Family, we grieve
One falling Adam, and one tempted Eve.[1]

These Lines alluded to the Revolt of the Persons above mention'd.

Notwithstanding the Acquisition of these two Actors, who were of more Importance than any of those to whose Assistance they came, the Affairs of the Patentees were still in a very creeping Condition;[2] they were now, too late, convinced of their Error in having provok'd their People to this Civil

[1] The passage is :—

"The Freedom man was born to, you've restor'd,
And to our World such Plenty you afford,
It seems, like Eden, fruitful of its own accord.
But since, in Paradise, frail Flesh gave Way,
And when but two were made, both went astray ;
Forbear your Wonder, and the Fault forgive,
If, in our larger Family, we grieve
One falling Adam, and one tempted Eve."

[2] In his Preface to "Woman's Wit," Cibber says, "But however a Fort is in a very poor Condition, that (in a Time of General War) has but a Handful of raw young Fellows to maintain it." He also talks of himself and his companions as "an uncertain Company."

War of the Theatre! quite changed and dismal now
was the Prospect before them! their Houses thin,
and the Town crowding into a new one! Actors at
double Sallaries, and not half the usual Audiences to
pay them! And all this brought upon them by those
whom their full Security had contemn'd, and who
were now in a fair way of making their Fortunes
upon the ruined Interest of their Oppressors.

Here, tho' at this time my Fortune depended on
the Success of the Patentees, I cannot help in regard
to Truth remembring the rude and riotous Havock
we made of all the late dramatic Honours of the
Theatre! all became at once the Spoil of Ignorance
and Self-conceit! *Shakespear* was defac'd and tortured in every signal Character—*Hamlet* and *Othello*
lost in one Hour all their good Sense, their Dignity
and Fame. *Brutus* and *Cassius* became noisy Blus-
terers, with bold unmeaning Eyes, mistaken Sentiments, and turgid Elocution! Nothing, sure, could
more painfully regret[1] a judicious Spectator than to
see, at our first setting out, with what rude Confidence
those Habits which actors of real Merit had left
behind them were worn by giddy Pretenders that so
vulgarly disgraced them! Not young Lawyers in
hir'd Robes and Plumes at a Masquerade could be

---

[1] Bellchambers has here this note: " Mr. Cibber's usage of the
verb *regret* here, may be said to confirm the censure of Fielding,
who urged, in reviewing some other of his inadvertencies, that it
was 'needless for a great writer to understand his grammar.'" See
note 1 on page 69.

less what they would seem, or more aukwardly per-
sonate the Characters they belong'd to. If, in all
these Acts of wanton Waste, these Insults upon
injur'd Nature, you observe I have not yet charged
one of them upon myself, it is not from an imaginary
Vanity that I could have avoided them ; but that I
was rather safe, by being too low at that time to be
admitted even to my Chance of falling into the same
eminent Errors : So that as none of those great
Parts ever fell to my Share, I could not be accountable for the Execution of them : Nor indeed could
I get one good Part of any kind 'till many Months
after ; unless it were of that sort which no body else
car'd for, or would venture to expose themselves in.[1]
The first unintended Favour, therefore, of a Part of
any Value, Necessity threw upon me on the following Occasion.

As it has been always judg'd their natural Interest,
where there are two Theatres, to do one another as

---

[1] Genest (ii. 65) has the following criticism of Cibber's statement : "There can be no doubt but that the acting at the
Theatre Royal was miserably inferiour to what it had been—but
perhaps Cibber's account is a little exaggerated—he had evidently
a personal dislike to Powell—everything therefore that he says,
directly or indirectly, against him must be received with some
grains of allowance—Powell seems to have been eager to exhibit
himself in some of Betterton's best parts, whereas a more diffident
actor would have wished to avoid comparisons—we know from
the Spectator that Powell was too apt to tear a passion to
tatters, but still he must have been an actor of considerable reputation at this time, or he would not have been cast for several good
parts before the division of the Company."

much Mischief as they can, you may imagine it could
not be long before this hostile Policy shew'd itself in
Action. It happen'd, upon our having Information
on a *Saturday* Morning that the *Tuesday* after
Hamlet was intended to be acted at the other House,
where it had not yet been seen, our merry menaging
Actors, (for they were now in a manner left to govern
themselves) resolv'd at any rate to steal a March
upon the Enemy, and take Possession of the same
Play the Day before them : Accordingly, *Hamlet*
was given out that Night to be Acted with us on
Monday. The Notice of this sudden Enterprize soon
reach'd the other House, who in my Opinion too
much regarded it; for they shorten'd their first
Orders, and resolv'd that *Hamlet* should to *Hamlet*
be opposed on the same Day ; whereas, had they
given notice in their Bills that the same Play
would have been acted by them the Day after, the
Town would have been in no Doubt which House
they should have reserved themselves for ; ours
must certainly have been empty, and theirs, with
more Honour, have been crowded : Experience,
many Years after, in like Cases, has convinced me
that this would have been the more laudable Conduct. But be that as it may ; when in their *Monday*'s
Bills it was seen that *Hamlet* was up against us, our
Consternation was terrible, to find that so hopeful a
Project was frustrated. In this Distress, *Powel*, who
was our commanding Officer, and whose enterprising
Head wanted nothing but Skill to carry him through

the most desperate Attempts; for, like others of his
Cast, he had murder'd many a Hero only to get into
his Cloaths. This *Powel*, I say, immediately called
a Council of War, where the Question was, Whether
he should fairly face the Enemy, or make a Retreat
to some other Play of more probable Safety? It
was soon resolved that to act *Hamlet* against *Hamlet*
would be certainly throwing away the Play, and
disgracing themselves to little or no Audience;
to conclude, *Powel*, who was vain enough to envy
Betterton as his Rival, proposed to change Plays
with them, and that as they had given out the *Old
Batchelor*, and had chang'd it for *Hamlet* against us,
we should give up our *Hamlet* and turn the *Old
Batchelor* upon them. This Motion was agreed to,
Nemine contradicente; but upon Enquiry, it was
found that there were not two Persons among
them who had ever acted in that Play: But that
Objection, it seems, (though all the Parts were to be
study'd in six Hours) was soon got over; *Powel* had
an Equivalent, *in petto*, that would ballance any
Deficiency on that Score, which was, that he would
play the *Old Batchelor* himself, and mimick *Betterton*
throughout the whole Part. This happy Thought
was approv'd with Delight and Applause, as whatever can be suppos'd to ridicule Merit generally
gives joy to those that want it: Accordingly the
Bills were chang'd, and at the Bottom inserted,

The Part of the Old Batchelor *to be perform'd
in Imitation of the Original.*

O

Printed Books of the Play were sent for in haste, and every Actor had one to pick out of it the Part he had chosen : Thus, while they were each of them chewing the Morsel they had most mind to, some one happening to cast his Eye over the *Dramatis Personæ*, found that the main Matter was still forgot, that no body had yet been thought of for the Part of Alderman *Fondlewife.* Here we were all aground agen ! nor was it to be conceiv'd who could make the least tolerable Shift with it. This Character had been so admirably acted by *Dogget*, that though it is only seen in the Fourth Act, it may be no Dispraise to the Play to say it probably ow'd the greatest Part of its Success to his Performance. But, as the Case was now desperate, any Resource was better than none. Somebody must swallow the bitter Pill, or the Play must die. At last it was recollected that I had been heard to say in my wild way of talking, what a vast mind I had to play *Nykin*, by which Name the Character was more frequently call'd.[1] Notwithstanding they were thus distress'd about the Disposal of this Part, most of them shook their Heads at my being mention'd for it ; yet *Powel*, who was resolv'd at all Hazards to fall upon *Betterton*, and

---

[1] "Old Bachelor," act iv. sc. 4 :—

"*Fondlewife.* Come kiss *Nykin* once more, and then get you in —So—Get you in, get you in. By by.

Lætitia. By, *Nykin.*

Fondlewife. By, Cocky.

Lætitia. By, *Nykin.*

Fondlewife. By, Cocky, by, by."

having no concern for what might become of any one that serv'd his Ends or Purpose, order'd me to be sent for; and, as he naturally lov'd to set other People wrong, honestly said before I came, *If the Fool has a mind to blow himself up at once, let us ev'n give him a clear Stage for it.* Accordingly the Part was put into my Hands between Eleven and Twelve that Morning, which I durst not refuse, because others were as much straitned in time for Study as myself. But I had this casual Advantage of most of them ; that having so constantly observ'd *Dogget's* Performance, I wanted but little Trouble to make me perfect in the Words; so that when it came to my turn to rehearse, while others read their Parts from their Books, I had put mine in my Pocket, and went thro' the first Scene without it; and though I was more abash'd to rehearse so remarkable a Part before the Actors (which is natural to most young People) than to act before an Audience, yet some of the better-natur'd encouraged me so far as to say they did not think I should make an ill Figure in it : To conclude, the Curiosity to see *Betterton* mimick'd drew us a pretty good Audience, and *Powel* (as far as Applause is a Proof of it) was allow'd to have burlesqu'd him very well.[1] As I have question'd

---

[1] Regarding Powell's playing in imitation of Betterton, Chetwood ("History of the Stage," p. 155) says : " Mr. *George Powel*, a reputable Actor, with many Excellencies, gave out, that he would perform the part of Sir *John Falstaff* in the manner of that very excellent *English Roscius*, Mr. *Betterton*. He certainly hit his Manner, and Tone of Voice, yet to make the Picture more like,

the certain Value of Applause, I hope I may venture with less Vanity to say how particular a Share I had of it in the same Play. At my first Appearance one might have imagin'd by the various Murmurs of the Audience, that they were in doubt whether *Dogget* himself were not return'd, or that they could not conceive what strange Face it could be that so nearly resembled him ; for I had laid the Tint of forty Years more than my real Age upon my Features, and, to the most minute placing of an Hair, was dressed exactly like him : When I spoke, the Surprize was still greater, as if I had not only borrow'd his Cloaths, but his Voice too.   But tho' that was the least difficult Part of him to be imitated, they seem'd to allow I had so much of him in every other Requisite, that my Applause was, perhaps, more than proportionable :   For, whether I had done so much where so little was expected, or that the Generosity of my Hearers were more than usually zealous upon so unexpected an Occasion, or from what other Motive such Favour might be pour'd upon me, I cannot say ; but in plain and honest Truth, upon my going off from the first Scene, a much better Actor might have been proud of the Applause that followed me ; after one loud *Plaudit* was ended and sunk into a general Whisper that seem'd still to continue their private Approbation, it reviv'd to a second, and again to a third, still louder than the

he mimic'd the Infirmities of Distemper, old Age, and the afflicting Pains of the Gout, which that great Man was often seiz'd with."

former.   If to all this I add, that *Dogget* himself was
in the Pit at the same time, it would be too rank
Affectation if I should not confess that to see him
there a Witness of my Reception, was to me as
consummate a Triumph as the Heart of Vanity
could be indulg'd with.   But whatever Vanity I
might set upon my self from this unexpected Success,
I found that was no Rule to other People's Judgment of me.   There were few or no Parts of the
same kind to be had ; nor could they conceive, from
what I had done in this, what other sort of Characters I could be fit for.   If I sollicited for any
thing of a different Nature, I was answered, *That
was not in my Way*.   And what *was* in my Way it
seems was not as yet resolv'd upon.   And though I
reply'd, *That I thought any thing naturally written
ought to be in every one's Way that pretended to be an
Actor ;* this was looked upon as a vain, impracticable
Conceit of my own.   Yet it is a Conceit that, in forty
Years farther Experience, I have not yet given up ;
I still think that a Painter who can draw but one sort
of Object, or an Actor that shines but in one Light,
can neither of them boast of that ample Genius which
is necessary to form a thorough Master of his Art :
For tho' Genius may have a particular Inclination,
yet a good History-Painter, or a good Actor, will,
without being at a loss, give you upon Demand a
proper Likeness of whatever nature produces.   If
he cannot do this, he is only an Actor as the Shoe-
maker was allow'd a limited Judge of *Apelles*'s Paint-

ing, but *not beyond his Last.*   Now, tho' to do any
one thing well may have more Merit than we often
meet with, and may be enough to procure a Man
the Name of a good Actor from the Publick;
yet, in my Opinion, it is but still the Name without the Substance.   If his Talent is in such narrow
Bounds that he dares not step out of them to look
upon the Singularities of Mankind, and cannot
catch them in whatever Form they present themselves; if he is not Master of the *Quicquid agunt
homines,*[1] &c. in any Shape Human Nature is fit
to be seen in; if he cannot change himself into
several distinct Persons, so as to vary his whole
Tone of Voice, his Motion, his Look and Gesture,
whether in high or lower Life, and, at the same time,
keep close to those Variations without leaving the
Character they singly belong to; if his best Skill
falls short of this Capacity, what Pretence have we to
call him a complete Master of his Art ?   And tho' I
do not insist that he ought always to shew himself in
these various Lights, yet, before we compliment him
with that Title, he ought at least, by some few
Proofs, to let us see that he has them all in his
Power.   If I am ask'd, who, ever, arriv'd at this
imaginary Excellence, I confess the Instances are
very few; but I will venture to name *Monfort* as
one of them, whose Theatrical Character I have

---

[1]   "Quicquid agunt homines, votum, timor, ira, voluptas,
      Gaudia, discursus, nostri est farrago libelli."

                                        Juvenal, i. 85.

given in my last Chapter: For in his Youth he had
acted Low Humour with great Success, even down
to *Tallboy* in the *Jovial Crew ;* and when he was in
great Esteem as a Tragedian, he was, in Comedy,
the most complete Gentleman that I ever saw upon
the Stage. Let me add, too, that *Betterton*, in his
declining Age, was as eminent in Sir *John Falstaff*,
as in the Vigour of it, in his *Othello.*

While I thus measure the Value of an Actor by
the Variety of Shapes he is able to throw himself
into, you may naturally suspect that I am all this
while leading my own Theatrical Character into your
Favour : Why really, to speak as an honest Man, I
cannot wholly deny it : But in this I shall endeavour
to be no farther partial to myself than known Facts
will make me ; from the good or bad Evidence of
which your better Judgment will condemn or acquit
me. And to shew you that I will conceal no Truth
that is against me, I frankly own that had I been
always left to my own choice of Characters, I am
doubtful whether I might ever have deserv'd an
equal Share of that Estimation which the Publick
seem'd to have held me in : Nor am I sure that it
was not Vanity in me often to have suspected that I
was kept out of the Parts I had most mind to by
the Jealousy or Prejudice of my Cotemporaries;
some Instances of which I could give you, were they
not too slight to be remember'd : In the mean time,
be pleas'd to observe how slowly, in my younger
Days, my Good-fortune came forward.

My early Success in the *Old Batchelor*, of which I
have given so full an Account, having open'd no
farther way to my Advancement, was enough, perhaps, to have made a young Fellow of more Modesty
despair; but being of a Temper not easily dishearten'd,
I resolv'd to leave nothing unattempted that might
shew me in some new Rank of Distinction. Having
then no other Resource, I was at last reduc'd to write a
Character for myself; but as that was not finish'd till
about a Year after, I could not, in the Interim, procure
any one Part that gave me the least Inclination to act
it; and consequently such as I got I perform'd with a
proportionable Negligence. But this Misfortune, if
it were one, you are not to wonder at; for the same
Fate attended me, more or less, to the last Days of
my remaining on the Stage. What Defect in me
this may have been owing to, I have not yet had
Sense enough to find out; but I soon found out as
good a thing, which was, never to be mortify'd at it:
Though I am afraid this seeming Philosophy was
rather owing to my Inclination to Pleasure than
Business. But to my Point. The next Year I produc'd the Comedy of *Love's last Shift;* yet the
Difficulty of getting it to the Stage was not easily
surmounted; for, at that time, as little was expected
from me, as an Author, as had been from my Pretensions to be an Actor. However, Mr. *Southern*,
the Author of *Oroonoko*, having had the Patience to
hear me read it to him, happened to like it so well
that he immediately recommended it to the Patentees,

and it was accordingly acted in *January* 1695.[1] In this Play I gave myself the Part of Sir *Novelty*, which was thought a good Portrait of the Foppery then in fashion. Here, too, Mr. *Southern*, though he had approv'd my Play, came into the common Diffidence of me as an Actor: For, when on the first Day of it I was standing, myself, to prompt the *Prologue*, he took me by the Hand and said, *Young Man ! I pronounce thy Play a good one; I will answer for its Success*,[2] *if thou dost not spoil it by thy own Action*. Though this might be a fair *Salvo* for his favourable Judgment of the Play, yet, if it were his real Opinion of me as an Actor, I had the good Fortune to deceive him: I succeeded so well in both, that People seem'd at a loss which they should give

[1] That is, January, 1696. The cast was :—

"Love's last Shift ; or, the Fool in Fashion."

SIR WILLIAM WISEWOUD . . .	Mr. Johnson.
LOVELESS	Mr. Verbruggen.
SIR NOVELTY FASHION	Mr. Cibber.
ELDER WORTHY	Mr. Williams.
YOUNG WORTHY	Mr. Horden.
SNAP	Mr. Penkethman.
SLY	Mr. Bullock.
LAWYER	Mr. Mills.
AMANDA	Mrs. Rogers.
NARCISSA	Mrs. Verbruggen.
HILLARIA	Mrs. Cibber.
MRS. FLAREIT	Mrs. Kent.
AMANDA'S WOMAN	Mrs. Lucas.

[2] In the Dedication to this play Cibber says that " Mr. *Southern*'s Good-nature (whose own Works best recommend his Judgment) engaged his Reputation for the Success."

the Preference to.[1]   But (now let me shew a little
more Vanity, and my Apology for it shall come after)
the Compliment which my Lord *Dorset* (then Lord-
Chamberlain) made me upon it is, I own, what I had
rather not suppress, *viz. That it was the best First Play
that any Author in his Memory had produc'd ; and
that for a young Fellow to shew himself such an Actor
and such a Writer in one Day, was something extraordinary.*   But as this noble Lord has been celebrated for his Good-nature, I am contented that as
much of this Compliment should be suppos'd to
exceed my Deserts as may be imagin'd to have been
heighten'd by his generous Inclination to encourage
a young Beginner.   If this Excuse cannot soften the
Vanity of telling a Truth so much in my own Favour,
I must lie at the Mercy of my Reader.   But there
was a still higher Compliment pass'd upon me which
I may publish without Vanity, because it was not a
design'd one, and apparently came from my Enemies,
viz. That, to their certain Knowledge, *it was not my
own :* This Report is taken notice of in my Dedication to the Play.[2]   If they spoke Truth, if they knew

---

[1] Gildon praises this play highly in the "Comparison between
the two Stages," p. 25 :—

"*Ramble.* Ay, marry, that Play was the Philosopher's Stone ; I
think it did wonders.

Sullen. It did so, and very deservedly ; there being few Comedies
that came up to't for purity of Plot, Manners and Moral : It's
often acted now a daies, and by the help of the Author's own
good action, it pleases to this Day."

[2] Davies ("Dram. Misc.," iii. 437) says: "So little was hoped

what other Person it really belong'd to, I will at least allow them true to their Trust; for above forty Years have since past, and they have not yet reveal'd the Secret.[1]

The new Light in which the Character of Sir *Novelty* had shewn me, one might have thought were enough to have dissipated the Doubts of what I might now be possibly good for. But to whatever Chance my Ill-fortune was due; whether I had still but little Merit, or that the Menagers, if I had any, were not competent Judges of it; or whether I was not generally elbow'd by other Actors (which I am most inclin'd to think the true Cause) when any fresh Parts were to be dispos'd of, not one Part of any consequence was I preferr'd to 'till the Year following: Then, indeed, from Sir *John Vanbrugh*'s favour-

---

from the genius of Cibber, that the critics reproached him with stealing his play. To his censurers he makes a serious defence of himself, in his dedication to Richard Norton, Esq., of Southwick, a gentleman who was so fond of stage-plays and players, that he has been accused of turning his chapel into a theatre. The furious John Dennis, who hated Cibber for obstructing, as he imagined, the progress of his tragedy called the Invader of his Country, in very passionate terms denies his claim to this comedy: 'When the Fool in Fashion was first acted (says the critic) Cibber was hardly twenty years of age—how could he, at the age of twenty, write a comedy with a just design, distinguished characters, and a proper dialogue, who now, at forty, treats us with Hibernian sense and Hibernian English?'"

[1] This same accusation was made against Cibber on other occasions. Dr. Johnson, referring to one of these, said: "There was no reason to believe that the *Careless Husband* was not written by himself."—Boswell's Johnson, ii. 340.

able Opinion of me, I began, with others, to have a better of myself: For he not only did me Honour as an Author by writing his *Relapse* as a Sequel or Second Part to *Love's last Shift*, but as an Actor too, by preferring me to the chief Character in his own Play, (which from Sir *Novelty*) he had ennobled by the Style of Baron of *Foppington*. This Play (the *Relapse*) from its new and easy Turn of Wit, had great Success, and gave me, as a Comedian, a second Flight of Reputation along with it.[1]

As the Matter I write must be very flat or impertinent to those who have no Taste or Concern for the Stage, and may to those who delight in it, too, be equally tedious when I talk of no body but myself, I shall endeavour to relieve your Patience by a Word or two more of this Gentleman, so far as he lent his Pen to the Support of the Theatre.

Though the *Relapse* was the first Play this agreeable Author produc'd, yet it was not, it seems, the first he had written; for he had at that time by him (more than) all the Scenes that were acted of the *Provok'd Wife;* but being then doubtful whether he should ever trust them to the Stage, he thought no more of it: But after the Success of the *Relapse* he was more strongly importun'd than able to refuse it

[1] "The Relapse; or, Virtue in Danger," was produced at Drury Lane in 1697. Cibber's part in it, Lord Foppington, became one of his most famous characters. The "Comparison between the two Stages," p. 32, says: "*Oronoko, Æsop,* and *Relapse* are Master-pieces, and subsisted *Drury-lane* House, the first two or three Years."

to the Publick.   Why the last-written Play was first acted, and for what Reason they were given to different Stages, what follows will explain.

In his first Step into publick Life, when he was but an Ensign and had a Heart above his Income, he happen'd somewhere at his Winter-Quarters, upon a very slender Acquaintance with Sir *Thomas Skipwith*, to receive a particular Obligation from him which he had not forgot at the Time I am speaking of: When Sir *Thomas*'s Interest in the Theatrical Patent (for he had a large Share in it, though he little concern'd himself in the Conduct of it) was rising but very slowly, he thought that to give it a Lift by a new Comedy, if it succeeded, might be the handsomest Return he could make to those his former Favours ; and having observ'd that in *Love's last Shift* most of the Actors had acquitted themselves beyond what was expected of them, he took a sudden Hint from what he lik'd in that Play, and in less than three Months, in the beginning of *April* following, brought us the *Relapse* finish'd ; but the Season being then too far advanc'd, it was not acted 'till the succeeding Winter.   Upon the Success of the *Relapse* the late Lord *Hallifax*, who was a great Favourer of *Betterton*'s Company, having formerly, by way of Family-Amusement, heard the *Provok'd Wife* read to him in its looser Sheets, engag'd Sir *John Vanbrugh* to revise it and gave it to the Theatre in *Lincoln's-Inn Fields*.   This was a Request not to be refus'd to so eminent a Patron of the Muses as the

Lord *Hallifax*, who was equally a Friend and Admirer of Sir *John* himself.[1]   Nor was Sir *Thomas Skipwith* in the least disobliged by so reasonable a Compliance : After which, Sir *John* was agen at liberty to repeat his Civilities to his Friend Sir *Thomas*, and about the same time, or not long after, gave us the Comedy of *Æsop*, for his Inclination always led him to serve Sir *Thomas*.   Besides, our Company about this time began to be look'd upon in another Light; the late Contempt we had lain under was now wearing off, and from the Success of two or three new Plays, our Actors, by being Originals in a few good Parts where they had not the Disadvantage of Comparison against them, sometimes found new Favour in those old Plays where others had exceeded them.[2]

Of this Good-fortune perhaps I had more than my Share from the two very different chief Characters I had succeeded in; for I was equally approv'd in *Æsop* as the *Lord Foppington*, allowing the Difference to be no less than as Wisdom in a Person deform'd may be less entertaining to the general Taste than

---

[1] "The Provoked Wife" was produced at Lincoln's Inn Fields in 1697 ; and, as Cibber states, "Æsop" was played at Drury Lane in the same year.   It seems (see Prologue to "The Confederacy") that Vanbrugh gave his first three plays as presents to the Companies.

[2] "Comparison between the two Stages," p. 12 : "In the meantime the Mushrooms in *Drury-Lane* shoot up from such a desolate Fortune into a considerable Name ; and not only grappled with their Rivals, but almost eclipst 'em."

Folly and Foppery finely drest: For the Character
that delivers Precepts of Wisdom is, in some sort,
severe upon the Auditor by shewing him one wiser
than himself. But when Folly is his Object he
applauds himself for being wiser than the Coxcomb
he laughs at: And who is not more pleas'd with an
Occasion to commend than accuse himself?

Though to write much in a little time is no Excuse for writing ill; yet Sir *John Vanbrugh*'s Pen is
not to be a little admir'd for its Spirit, Ease, and
Readiness in producing Plays so fast upon the Neck
of one another; for, notwithstanding this quick Dis-
patch, there is a clear and lively Simplicity in his
Wit that neither wants the Ornament of Learning
nor has the least Smell of the Lamp in it. As
the Face of a fine Woman, with only her Locks
loose about her, may be then in its greatest Beauty;
such were his Productions, only adorn'd by Nature.
There is something so catching to the Ear, so easy
to the Memory, in all he writ, that it has been observ'd by all the Actors of my Time, that the Style
of no Author whatsoever gave their Memory less
trouble than that of Sir *John Vanbrugh;* which I
myself, who have been charg'd with several of his
strongest Characters, can confirm by a pleasing Experience. And indeed his Wit and Humour was so
little laboured, that his most entertaining Scenes
seem'd to be no more than his common Conversation
committed to Paper. Here I confess my Judgment
at a Loss, whether in this I give him more or less

than his due Praise? For may it not be more laudable to raise an Estate (whether in Wealth or Fame)
by Pains and honest Industry than to be born to
it? Yet if his Scenes really were, as to me they
always seem'd, delightful, are they not, thus expe-
ditiously written, the more surprising? let the Wit
and Merit of them then be weigh'd by wiser Criticks
than I pretend to be: But no wonder, while his Con-
ceptions were so full of Life and Humour, his Muse
should be sometimes too warm to wait the slow Pace
of Judgment, or to endure the Drudgery of forming
a regular Fable to them: Yet we see the *Relapse*,
however imperfect in the Conduct, by the mere Force
of its agreeable Wit, ran away with the Hearts of its
Hearers; while *Love's last Shift*, which (as Mr. *Congreve* justly said of it) had only in it a great many
things that were *like* Wit, that in reality were *not*
Wit: And what is still less pardonable (as I say of it
myself) has a great deal of Puerility and frothy
Stage-Language in it, yet by the mere moral Delight
receiv'd from its Fable, it has been, with the other,
in a continued and equal Possession of the Stage for
more than forty Years.[1]

As I have already promis'd you to refer your Judgment of me as an Actor rather to known Facts than
my own Opinion (which I could not be sure would
keep clear of Self-Partiality) I must a little farther
risque my being tedious to be as good as my Word.

[1] The last performance of this comedy which Genest indexes
was at Covent Garden, 14th February, 1763.

I have elsewhere allow'd that my want of a strong
and full Voice soon cut short my Hopes of making
any valuable Figure in Tragedy; and I have been
many Years since convinced, that whatever Opinion
I might have of my own Judgment or Capacity
to amend the palpable Errors that I saw our
Tragedians most in favour commit; yet the Auditors who would have been sensible of any such
Amendments (could I have made them) were so very
few, that my best Endeavour would have been but
an unavailing Labour, or, what is yet worse, might
have appeared both to our Actors and to many
Auditors the vain Mistake of my own Self-Conceit:
For so strong, so very near indispensible, is that one
Article of Voice in the forming a good Tragedian,
that an Actor may want any other Qualification
whatsoever, and yet have a better chance for Applause than he will ever have, with all the Skill in the
World, if his Voice is not equal to it.   Mistake me
not; I say, for *Applause* only—but Applause does
not always stay for, nor always follow intrinsick
Merit; Applause will frequently open, like a young
Hound, upon a wrong Scent; and the Majority of
Auditors, you know, are generally compos'd of Bab-
blers that are profuse of their Voices before there is
any thing on foot that calls for them.   Not but, I
grant, to lead or mislead the Many will always stand
in some Rank of a necessary Merit; yet when I say
a good Tragedian, I mean one in Opinion of whose
real Merit the best Judges would agree.

P

Having so far given up my Pretensions to the
Buskin, I ought now to account for my having been,
notwithstanding, so often seen in some particular
Characters in Tragedy, as *Jago*,[1] *Wolsey*, *Syphax*,
Richard the Third, &c.   If in any of this kind I
have succeeded, perhaps it has been a Merit dearly
purchas'd ; for, from the Delight I seem'd to take in
my performing them, half my Auditors have been
persuaded that a great Share of the Wickedness
of them must have been in my own Nature :
If this is true, as true I fear (I had almost said
hope) it is, I look upon it rather as a Praise than
Censure of my Performance.   Aversion there is
an involuntary Commendation, where we are only
hated for being like the thing we *ought* to be like ; a
sort of Praise, however, which few Actors besides
my self could endure : Had it been equal to the
usual Praise given to Virtue, my Cotemporaries
would have thought themselves injur'd if I had pretended to any Share of it : So that you see it has been
as much the Dislike others had to them, as Choice
that has thrown me sometimes into these Characters.
But it may be farther observ'd, that in the Characters
I have nam'd, where there is so much close meditated

---

[1] Davies (" Dram. Misc.," iii. 469) says : " The truth is, Cibber
was endured, in this and other tragic parts, on account of his general
merit in comedy ;" and the author of "The Laureat," p. 41,
remarks : " I have often heard him blamed as a Trifler in that
Part ; he was rarely perfect, and, abating for the Badness of his
Voice and the Insignificancy and Meanness of his Action, he did
not seem to understand either what he said or what he was about."

Mischief, Deceit, Pride, Insolence, or Cruelty, they cannot have the least Cast or Profer of the Amiable in them; consequently, there can be no great Demand for that harmonious Sound, or pleasing round Melody of Voice, which in the softer Sentiments of Love, the Wailings of distressful Virtue, or in the Throws and Swellings of Honour and Ambition, may be needful to recommend them to our Pity or Admiration : So that, again, my want of that requisite Voice might less disqualify me for the vicious than the virtuous Character. This too may have been a more favourable Reason for my having been chosen for them—a yet farther Consideration that inclin'd me to them was that they are generally better written, thicker sown with sensible Reflections, and come by so much nearer to common Life and Nature than Characters of Admiration, as Vice is more the Practice of Mankind than Virtue : Nor could I sometimes help smiling at those dainty Actors that were too squeamish to swallow them ! as if they were one Jot the better Men for acting a good Man well, or another Man the worse for doing equal Justice to a bad one ! 'Tis not, sure, *what* we act, but *how* we act what is allotted us, that speaks our intrinsick Value! as in real Life, the wise Man or the Fool, be he Prince or Peasant, will in either State be equally the Fool or the wise Man—but alas ! in personated Life this is no Rule to the Vulgar ! they are apt to think all before them real, and rate the Actor according to his borrow'd Vice or Virtue.

If then I had always too careless a Concern for false or vulgar Applause, I ought not to complain if I have had less of it than others of my time, or not less of it than I desired : Yet I will venture to say, that from the common weak Appetite of false Applause, many Actors have run into more Errors and Absurdities, than their greatest Ignorance could otherwise have committed :[1] If this Charge is true, it will lie chiefly upon the better Judgment of the Spectator to reform it.

But not to make too great a Merit of my avoiding this common Road to Applause, perhaps I was vain enough to think I had more ways than one to come at it. That, in the Variety of Characters I acted, the Chances to win it were the stronger on my Side —That, if the Multitude were not in a Roar to see me in *Cardinal Wolsey*, I could be sure of them in Alderman *Fondlewife*. If they hated me in *Jago*, in Sir *Fopling* they took me for a fine Gentleman ; if they were silent at *Syphax*, no *Italian* Eunuch was more applauded than when I sung in Sir *Courtly*. If the Morals of *Æsop* were too grave for them, Justice *Shallow* was as simple and as merry an old Rake as the wisest of our young ones could wish me.[2] And

---

[1] "The Laureat," p. 44 : "Whatever the Actors appear'd upon the Stage, they were most of them *Barbarians* off on't, few of them having had the Education, or whose Fortunes could admit them to the Conversation of Gentlemen."

[2] Davies praises Cibber in Fondlewife, saying that he "was much and justly admired and applauded" ("Dram. Misc.," iii.

though the Terror and Detestation raised by King *Richard* might be too severe a Delight for them, yet the more gentle and modern Vanities of a Poet *Bays*, or the well-bred Vices of a Lord *Foppington*, were not at all more than their merry Hearts or nicer Morals could bear.

These few Instances out of fifty more I could give you, may serve to explain what sort of Merit I at most pretended to; which was, that I supplied with Variety whatever I might want of that particular

391); and in the same work (i. 306) he gives an admirable sketch of Cibber as Justice Shallow :—

"Whether he was a copy or an original in Shallow, it is certain no audience was ever more fixed in deep attention, at his first appearance, or more shaken with laughter in the progress of the scene, than at Colley Cibber's exhibition of this ridiculous justice of peace. Some years after he had left the stage, he acted Shallow for his son's benefit. I believe in 1737, when Quin was the Falstaff, and Milward the King. Whether it was owing to the pleasure the spectators felt on seeing their old friend return to them again, *though for that night only*, after an absence of some years, I know not; but, surely, no actor or audience were better pleased with each other. His manner was so perfectly simple, his look so vacant, when he questioned his cousin Silence about the price of ewes, and lamented, in the same breath, with silly surprise, the death of Old Double, that it will be impossible for any surviving spectator not to smile at the remembrance of it. The want of ideas occasions Shallow to repeat almost every thing he says. Cibber's transition, from asking the price of bullocks, to trite, but grave reflections on mortality, was so natural, and attended with such an unmeaning roll of his small pigs-eyes, accompanied with an important utterance of tick ! tick ! tick ! not much louder than the balance of a watch, that I question if any actor was ever superior in the conception or expression of such solemn insignificancy."

Skill wherein others went before me. How this Variety was executed (for by that only is its value to be rated) you who have so often been my Spectator are the proper Judge : If you pronounce my Performance to have been defective, I am condemn'd by my own Evidence; if you acquit me, these Out-lines may serve for a Sketch of my Theatrical Character.

CHAPTER VII.

The State of the Stage continued. The Occasion of Wilks's *commencing Actor. His Success. Facts relating to his Theatrical Talent. Actors more or less esteem'd from their private Characters.*

THE *Lincoln's-Inn-Fields* Company were now, in 1693,[1] a Common-wealth, like that of *Holland,* divided from the Tyranny of *Spain:* But the Similitude goes very little farther; short was the Duration of the Theatrical Power! for tho' Success pour'd in so fast upon them at their first Opening

---

[1] I presume Cibber means 1695. The Company was self-governed from its commencement in 1695, and the disintegration seems to have begun in the next season. See what Cibber says of Dogget's defection a few pages on.

that every thing seem'd to support it self, yet Experience in a Year or two shew'd them that they had
never been worse govern'd than when they govern'd
themselves! Many of them began to make their
particular Interest more their Point than that of the
general : and tho' some Deference might be had to
the Measures and Advice of *Betterton*, several of
them wanted to govern in their Turn, and were
often out of Humour that their Opinion was not
equally regarded—But have we not seen the same
Infirmity in Senates? The Tragedians seem'd to
think their Rank as much above the Comedians as
in the Characters they severally acted; when the
first were in their Finery, the latter were impatient
at the Expence, and look'd upon it as rather laid out
upon the real than the fictitious Person of the Actor;
nay, I have known in our own Company this ridiculous sort of Regret carried so far, that the Tragedian
has thought himself injured when the *Comedian* pretended to wear a fine Coat! I remember *Powel*, upon
surveying my first Dress in the *Relapse*, was out of
all temper, and reproach'd our Master in very rude
Terms that he had not so good a Suit to play *Cæsar
Borgia*[1] in! tho' he knew, at the same time, my Lord
Foppington fill'd the House, when his bouncing
Borgia would do little more than pay Fiddles and
Candles to it: And though a Character of Vanity

---

[1] In Lee's tragedy of "Cæsar Borgia," originally played at
Dorset Garden in 1680. Borgia was Betterton's part, and was
evidently one of those which Powell laid violent hands on.

might be supposed more expensive in Dress than possibly one of Ambition, yet the high Heart of this heroical Actor could not bear that a Comedian should ever pretend to be as well dress'd as himself. Thus again, on the contrary, when *Betterton* proposed to set off a Tragedy, the Comedians were sure to murmur at the Charge of it: And the late Reputation which *Dogget* had acquired from acting his *Ben* in *Love* for *Love*, made him a more declared Male-content on such Occasions; he over-valued Comedy for its being nearer to Nature than Tragedy, which is allow'd to say many fine things that Nature never spoke in the same Words; and supposing his Opinion were just, yet he should have consider'd that the Publick had a Taste as well as himself, which in Policy he ought to have complied with. *Dogget*, however, could not with Patience look upon the costly Trains and Plumes of Tragedy, in which knowing himself to be useless, he thought were all a vain Extravagance: And when he found his Singularity could no longer oppose that Expence, he so obstinately adhered to his own Opinion, that he left the Society of his old Friends, and came over to us at the *Theatre-Royal:* And yet this Actor always set up for a Theatrical Patriot. This happened in the Winter following the first Division of the (only) Company.[1] He came time enough to the *Theatre-Royal* to act the Part of *Lory* in the *Relapse,*

[1] Among the Lord Chamberlain's Papers is a curious Decision, dated 26 Oct. 1696, regarding this desertion. By it, Dogget, who

an arch Valet, quite after the *French* cast, pert and familiar. But it suited so ill with *Dogget*'s dry and closely-natural Manner of acting, that upon the second Day he desired it might be disposed of to another ; which the Author complying with, gave it to *Pen-kethman*, who, tho' in other Lights much his Inferior, yet this Part he seem'd better to become. *Dogget* was so immovable in his Opinion of whatever he thought was right or wrong, that he could never be easy under any kind of Theatrical Government, and was generally so warm in pursuit of his Interest that he often out-ran it ; I remember him three times, for some Years, unemploy'd in any Theatre, from his not being able to bear, in common with others, the disagreeable Accidents that in such Societies are unavoidable.[1] But whatever Pretences he had form'd for this first deserting from *Lincoln's-Inn-Fields*, I always thought his best Reason for it was, that he look'd upon it as a sinking Ship; not only from the melancholy Abatement of their Profits, but likewise from the Neglect and Disorder in their Government :   He plainly saw that their extraordinary Success at first had made them too confident of its Duration, and from thence had slacken'd their Industry—by which he observ'd, at the same time, the old House, where

is stated to have been seduced from Lincoln's Inn Fields, is permitted to act where he likes.

[1] Genest's list of Dogget's characters shows that he was apparently not engaged 1698 to 1700, both inclusive; for the seasons 1706-7 and 1707-8 ; and for the season 1708-9. This would make the three occasions mentioned by Cibber.

there was scarce any other Merit than Industry, began to flourish. And indeed they seem'd not enough to consider that the Appetite of the Publick, like that of a fine Gentleman, could only be kept warm by Variety; that let their Merit be never so high, yet the Taste of a Town was not always constant, nor infallible : That it was dangerous to hold their Rivals in too much Contempt;[1] for they found that a young industrious Company were soon a Match for the best Actors when too securely negligent: And negligent they certainly were, and fondly fancied that had each of their different Schemes been follow'd, their Audiences would not so suddenly have fallen off.[2]

But alas! the Vanity of applauded Actors, when they are not crowded to as they may have been, makes them naturally impute the Change to any Cause rather than the true one, Satiety: They are mighty loath to think a Town, once so fond of them, could ever be tired; and yet, at one time or other, more or less thin Houses have been the certain Fate

---

[1] Dryden, in his Address to Granville on his tragedy of "Heroic Love" in 1698, says of the Lincoln's Inn Fields Company :—

> "Their setting sun still shoots a glimmering ray,
> Like ancient Rome, majestic in decay ;
> And better gleanings their worn soil can boast,
> Than the crab-vintage of the neighbouring coast."

[2] "Comparison between the two Stages," p. 13 : "But this [the success of 'Love for Love'] like other things of that kind, being only nine Days wonder, and the Audiences, being in a little time sated with the Novelty of the *New-house*, return in Shoals to the Old."

of the most prosperous Actors ever since I remember the Stage! But against this Evil the provident Patentees had found out a Relief which the new House were not yet Masters of, *viz.* Never to pay their People when the Money did not come in; nor then neither, but in such Proportions as suited their Conveniency. I my self was one of the many who for six acting Weeks together never received one Day's Pay; and for some Years after seldom had above half our nominal Sallaries: But to the best of my Memory, the Finances of the other House held it not above one Season more, before they were reduced to the same Expedient of making the like scanty Payments.[1]

Such was the Distress and Fortune of both these Companies since their Division from the *Theatre-Royal*; either working at half Wages, or by alternate Successes intercepting the Bread from one another's Mouths;[2] irreconcilable Enemies, yet without Hope

---

[1] Cibber says nothing of his having been a member of the Lincoln's Inn Fields Company. But he was, for he writes in his Preface to "Woman's Wit": "during the Time of my writing the two first Acts I was entertain'd at the New Theatre. . . . In the Middle of my Writing the Third Act, not liking my Station there, I return'd again to the Theatre Royal." Cibber must have joined Betterton, I should think, about the end of 1696. It is curious that he should in his "Apology" have entirely suppressed this incident. It almost suggests that there was something in it of which he was in later years somewhat ashamed.

[2] "Comparison between the two Stages," p. 14: "The Town . . . chang'd their Inclinations for the two Houses, as they found 'emselves inclin'd to Comedy or Tragedy: If they desir'd a

of Relief from a Victory on either Side; sometimes both Parties reduced, and yet each supporting their Spirits by seeing the other under the same Calamity.

During this State of the Stage it was that the lowest Expedient was made use of to ingratiate our Company in the Publick Favour : Our Master, who had sometime practised the Law,[1] and therefore loved a Storm better than fair Weather (for it was his own Conduct chiefly that had brought the Patent into these Dangers) took nothing so much to Heart as that Partiality wherewith he imagined the People of Quality had preferr'd the Actors of the other House to those of his own : To ballance this Misfortune, he was resolv'd, at least, to be well with their Domes- ticks, and therefore cunningly open'd the upper Gallery to them *gratis :* For before this time no Footman was ever admitted, or had presum'd to come into it, till after the fourth Act was ended : This additional Privilege (the greatest Plague that ever Play-house had to complain of) he conceived would not only incline them to give us a good Word in the respective Families they belong'd to, but would natu- rally incite them to come all Hands aloft in the Crack

Tragedy, they went to *Lincolns-Inn-Fields* ; if to Comedy, they flockt to *Drury-lane*."

[1] Christopher Rich, of whom the " Comparison between the two Stages " says (p. 15): " *Critick*. In the other House there's an old snarling Lawyer Master and Sovereign; a waspish, ignorant, pettifogger in Law and Poetry ; one who understands Poetry no more than Algebra ; he wou'd sooner have the Grace of God than do everybody Justice."

of our Applauses : And indeed it so far succeeded,
that it often thunder'd from the full Gallery above,
while our thin Pit and Boxes below were in the
utmost Serenity. This riotous Privilege, so craftily
given, and which from Custom was at last ripen'd
into Right, became the most disgraceful Nusance
that ever depreciated the Theatre.[1] How often have
the most polite Audiences, in the most affecting
Scenes of the best Plays, been disturb'd and insulted
by the Noise and Clamour of these savage Spectators ? From the same narrow way of thinking, too,
were so many ordinary People and unlick'd Cubs of
Condition admitted behind our Scenes for Money,
and sometimes without it: The Plagues and Incon-
veniences of which Custom we found so intolerable,
when we afterwards had the Stage in our Hands,
that at the Hazard of our Lives we were forced to
get rid of them ; and our only Expedient was by
refusing Money from all Persons without Distinction
at the Stage-Door; by this means we preserved to
ourselves the Right and Liberty of chusing our own
Company there : And by a strict Observance of this
Order we brought what had been before debas'd
into all the Licenses of a Lobby into the Decencies
of a Drawing-Room.[2]

[1] This privilege seems to have been granted about 1697 or 1698.
It was not abolished till 1737. On 5th May, 1737, footmen having
been deprived of their privilege, 300 of them broke into Drury Lane
and did great damage. Many were, however, arrested, and no
attempt was made to renew hostilities.

[2] Queen Anne issued several Edicts forbidding persons to be

About the distressful Time I was speaking of, in the Year 1696,[1] *Wilks*, who now had been five Years in great Esteem on the *Dublin* Theatre, return'd to that of *Drury-Lane*; in which last he had first set out, and had continued to act some small Parts for one Winter only. The considerable Figure which he so lately made upon the Stage in *London*, makes me imagine that a particular Account of his first commencing Actor may not be unacceptable to the Curious; I shall, therefore, give it them as I had it from his own Mouth.

In King *James*'s Reign he had been some time employ'd in the Secretary's Office in *Ireland* (his native Country) and remain'd in it till after the Battle of the *Boyn*, which completed the Revolution. Upon that happy and unexpected Deliverance, the People of *Dublin*, among the various Expressions of their Joy, had a mind to have a Play; but the Actors being dispersed during the War, some private Persons agreed in the best Manner they were able to give one to the Publick *gratis* at the *Theatre*. The Play was *Othello*, in which *Wilks* acted the *Moor*; and the Applause he received in it warm'd him to so strong an Inclination for the Stage, that he imme-

admitted behind the scenes, and in the advertisements of both theatres there appeared the announcement, " By Her Majesty's Command no Persons are to be admitted behind the Scenes." Cibber here, no doubt, refers to the Sign Manual of 13 Nov. 1711, a copy of which is among the Chamberlain's Papers.

[1] Cibber is probably incorrect here. It seems certain from the bills that Wilks did not re-appear in London before 1698.

diately prefer'd it to all his other Views in Life : for
he quitted his Post, and with the first fair Occasion
came over to try his Fortune in the (then only) Company of Actors in *London.* The Person who supply'd his Post in *Dublin*, he told me, raised to himself from thence a Fortune of fifty thousand Pounds.
Here you have a much stronger Instance of an extravagant Passion for the Stage than that which I
have elsewhere shewn in my self ; I only quitted my
Hopes of being preferr'd to the like Post for it ; but
Wilks quitted his actual *Possession* for the imaginary
Happiness which the Life of an Actor presented to
him. And, though possibly we might both have
better'd our Fortunes in a more honourable Station,
yet whether better Fortunes might have equally
gratify'd our Vanity (the universal Passion of Mankind) may admit of a Question.

Upon his being formerly received into the *Theatre-
Royal* (which was in the Winter after I had been initiated) his Station there was much upon the same Class
with my own ; our Parts were generally of an equal
Insignificancy, not of consequence enough to give
either a Preference : But *Wilks* being more impatient
of his low Condition than I was, (and, indeed, the
Company was then so well stock'd with good Actors
that there was very little hope of getting forward)
laid hold of a more expeditious way for his Advancement, and returned agen to *Dublin* with Mr. *Ashbury*,
the Patentee of that Theatre, to act in his new Company there : There went with him at the same time

Mrs. *Butler*, whose Character I have already given, and *Estcourt*, who had not appeared on any Stage, and was yet only known as an excellent Mimick: *Wilks* having no Competitor in *Dublin*, was immediately preferr'd to whatever parts his Inclination led him, and his early Reputation on that Stage as soon raised in him an Ambition to shew himself on a better. And I have heard him say (in Raillery of the Vanity which young Actors are liable to) that when the News of *Monfort's* Death came to *Ireland*, he from that time thought his Fortune was made, and took a Resolution to return a second time to *England* with the first Opportunity; but as his Engagements to the Stage where he was were too strong to be suddenly broke from, he return'd not to the *Theatre-Royal* 'till the Year 1696.[1]

Upon his first Arrival, *Powel*, who was now in Possession of all the chief Parts of *Monfort*, and the only Actor that stood in *Wilks's* way, in seeming Civility offer'd him his choice of whatever he thought fit to make his first Appearance in; though, in reality, the Favour was intended to hurt him. But *Wilks* rightly judg'd it more modest to accept only of a Part of *Powel's*, and which *Monfort* had never acted, that of *Palamede* in *Dryden's Marriage Alamode*. Here, too, he had the Advantage of having the Ball play'd into his Hand by the inimitable Mrs. *Monfort*, who was then his *Melantha* in the same Play: Whatever Fame *Wilks* had brought

---

[1] See note on page 235.

with him from *Ireland*, he as yet appear'd but a very
raw Actor to what he was afterwards allow'd to be :
His Faults, however, I shall rather leave to the
Judgments of those who then may remember him,
than to take upon me the disagreeable Office of being
particular upon them, farther than by saying, that in
this Part of *Palamede* he was short of *Powel*, and miss'd
a good deal of the loose Humour of the Character,
which the other more happily hit.[1]   But however he
was young, erect, of a pleasing Aspect, and, in the
whole, gave the Town and the Stage sufficient Hopes
of him.   I ought to make some Allowances, too, for
the Restraint he must naturally have been under
from his first Appearance upon a new Stage.   But
from that he soon recovered, and grew daily more
in Favour, not only of the Town, but likewise of
the Patentee, whom *Powel*, before *Wilks*'s Arrival,
had treated in almost what manner he pleas'd.

Upon this visible Success of *Wilks*, the pretended
Contempt which *Powel* had held him in began to
sour into an open Jealousy ; he now plainly saw he
was a formidable Rival, and (which more hurt him)
saw, too, that other People saw it ; and therefore
found it high time to oppose and be troublesome to
him.   But *Wilks* happening to be as jealous of his

---

[1] "The Laureat," p. 44 : "*Wilks*, in this Part of *Palamede*,
behav'd with a modest Diffidence, and yet maintain'd the Spirit of
his Part." The author says, on the same page, that Powel never
could appear a Gentleman. "His Conversation, his Manners, his
Dress, neither on nor off the Stage, bore any Similitude to that
Character."

Fame as the other, you may imagine such clashing Candidates could not be long without a Rupture : In short, a Challenge, I very well remember, came from *Powel*, when he was hot-headed ; but the next Morning he was cool enough to let it end in favour of *Wilks*. Yet however the Magnanimity on either Part might subside, the Animosity was as deep in the Heart as ever, tho' it was not afterwards so openly avow'd : For when *Powel* found that intimidating would not carry his Point ; but that *Wilks*, when provok'd, would really give Battle,[1] he (*Powel*) grew so out of Humour that he cock'd his Hat, and in his Passion walk'd off to the Service of the Company in *Lincoln's-Inn Fields*. But there finding more Competitors, and that he made a worse Figure among them than in the Company he came from, he stay'd but one Winter with them[2] before he return'd to his old Quarters in *Drury-Lane* ; where, after these unsuccessful Pushes of his Ambition, he at last became a Martyr to Negligence, and quietly submitted to the Advantages and Superiority which (during his late Desertion) *Wilks* had more easily got over him.

[1] " The Laureat," p. 44 : " I believe he (Wilks) was obliged to fight the Heroic *George Powel*, as well as one or two others, who were piqued at his being so highly encouraged by the Town, and their Rival, before he cou'd be quiet."

[2] Powell seems to have been at Lincoln's Inn Fields for two seasons, those of 1702 and 1703, and for part of a third, 1703-4. He returned to Drury Lane about June, 1704. For the arbitrary conduct of the Lord Chamberlain, in allowing him to desert to Lincoln's Inn Fields (or the Haymarket), but arresting him when he deserted back again to Drury Lane, see after, in Chap. X.

However trifling these Theatrical Anecdotes may seem to a sensible Reader, yet, as the different Conduct of these rival Actors may be of use to others of the same Profession, and from thence may contribute to the Pleasure of the Publick, let that be my Excuse for pursuing them. I must therefore let it be known that, though in Voice and Ear Nature had been more kind to *Powel*, yet he so often lost the Value of them by an unheedful Confidence, that the constant wakeful Care and Decency of *Wilks* left the other far behind in the publick Esteem and Approbation. Nor was his Memory less tenacious than that of *Wilks*; but *Powel* put too much Trust in it, and idly deferr'd the Studying of his Parts, as School-boys do their Exercise, to the last Day, which commonly brings them out proportionably defective. But *Wilks* never lost an Hour of precious Time, and was, in all his Parts, perfect to such an Exactitude, that I question if in forty Years he ever five times chang'd or misplac'd an Article in any one of them. To be Master of this uncommon Diligence is adding to the Gift of Nature all that is in an Actor's Power; and this Duty of Studying perfect whatever Actor is remiss in, he will proportionably find that Nature may have been kind to him in vain, for though *Powel* had an Assurance that cover'd this Neglect much better than a Man of more Modesty might have done, yet, with all his Intrepidity, very often the Diffidence and Concern for what he was to *say* made him lose the Look of what he was to *be:* While, therefore, *Powel* presided, his idle Example made this Fault so common to others, that I cannot but confess, in the general Infection, I had my Share of it; nor was my too critical Excuse for it a good one, *viz.* That scarce one Part in five that fell to my Lot was worth the Labour. But to shew Respect to an Audience is worth the best Actor's Labour, and, his Business consider'd, he must be a very impudent one that comes before them with a conscious Negligence of what he is about.[1] But *Wilks* was never known to make any of these venial Distinctions, nor, however barren his Part might be, could bear even the Self-Reproach of favouring his Memory: And I have been astonished to see him swallow a Volume of Froth and Insipidity in a new Play that we were

[1] Cibber is here somewhat in the position of Satan reproving sin, if Davies's statements ("Dram. Misc.," iii. 480) are accurate. He says:—

"This attention to the gaming-table would not, we may be assured, render him [Cibber] fitter for his business of the stage. After many an unlucky run at Tom's Coffee-house [in Russell Street], he has arrived at the playhouse in great tranquillity; and then, humming over an opera-tune, he has walked on the stage not well prepared in the part he was to act. Cibber should not have reprehended Powell so severely for neglect and imperfect representation: I have seen him at fault where it was least expected; in parts which he had acted a hundred times, and particularly in Sir Courtly Nice; but Colley dexterously supplied the deficiency of his memory by prolonging his ceremonious bow to the lady, and drawling out 'Your humble servant, madam,' to an extraordinary length; then taking a pinch of snuff, and strutting deliberately across the stage, he has gravely asked the prompter, what is next?"

sure could not live above three Days, tho' favour'd
and recommended to the Stage by some good person
of Quality. Upon such Occasions, in Compassion
to his fruitless Toil and Labour, I have sometimes
cry'd out with *Cato*——*Painful Præeminence!* So
insupportable, in my Sense, was the Task, when the
bare Praise of not having been negligent was sure to
be the only Reward of it. But so indefatigable was
the Diligence of *Wilks*, that he seem'd to love it, as
a good Man does Virtue, for its own sake; of which
the following Instance will give you an extraordinary
Proof.

In some new Comedy he happen'd to complain of
a crabbed Speech in his Part, which, he said, gave
him more trouble to study than all the rest of it had
done; upon which he apply'd to the Author either
to soften or shorten it. The Author, that he might
make the Matter quite easy to him, fairly cut it all
out. But when he got home from the Rehearsal,
Wilks thought it such an Indignity to his Memory
that any thing should be thought too hard for it,
that he actually made himself perfect in that Speech,
though he knew it was never to be made use of.
From this singular Act of Supererogation you may
judge how indefatigable the Labour of his Memory
must have been when his Profit and Honour were
more concern'd to make use of it.[1]

---

[1] "The Laureat," p. 45: "I have known him (Wilks) lay a
Wager and win it, that he wou'd repeat the Part of *Truewitt* in
the *Silent Woman*, which consists of thirty Lengths of Paper, as

But besides this indispensable Quality of Diligence, *Wilks* had the Advantage of a sober Character in private Life, which *Powel*, not having the least Regard to, labour'd under the unhappy Disfavour, not to say Contempt, of the Publick, to whom his licentious Courses were no Secret : Even when he did well that natural Prejudice pursu'd him ; neither the Heroe nor the Gentleman, the young *Ammon*[1] nor the *Dorimant*,[2] could conceal from the conscious Spectator the True *George Powel*. And this sort of Disesteem or Favour every Actor will feel, and, more or less, have his Share of, as he *has*, or has *not*, a due Regard to his private Life and Reputation. Nay, even false Reports shall affect him, and become the Cause, or Pretence at least, of undervaluing or treating him injuriously. Let me give a known Instance of it, and at the same time a Justification of myself from an Imputation that was laid upon me not many Years before I quitted the Theatre, of which you will see the Consequence.

After the vast Success of that new Species of Dramatick Poetry, the *Beggars Opera*,[3] The Year following I was so stupid as to attempt something of the same Kind, upon a quite different Foundation, that

they call 'em, (that is, one Quarter of a Sheet on both Sides to a Length) without misplacing a single Word, or missing an (*and*) or an (*or*)."

[1] Alexander in "The Rival Queens."
[2] In "The Man of the Mode ; or, Sir Fopling Flutter."
[3] Produced at Lincoln's Inn Fields, 29th January, 1728.

of recommending Virtue and Innocence; which I
ignorantly thought might not have a less Pretence
to Favour than setting Greatness and Authority in
a contemptible, and the most vulgar Vice and
Wickedness, in an amiable Light. But behold how
fondly I was mistaken! *Love in a Riddle*[1] (for so
my new-fangled Performance was called) was as
vilely damn'd and hooted at as so vain a Presumption
in the idle Cause of Virtue could deserve. Yet this

[1] "Love in a Riddle." A Pastoral. Produced at Drury Lane,
7th January, 1729.

ARCAS	Mr. Mills.
ÆGON	Mr. Harper.
AMYNTAS	Mr. Williams.
IPHIS	Mrs. Thurmond.
PHILAŪTUS, a conceited Corinthian courtier	Mr. Cibber.
CORYDON	Mr. Griffin.
CIMON	Mr. Miller.
MOPSUS	Mr. Oates.
DAMON	Mr. Ray.
IANTHE, daughter to Arcas	Mrs. Cibber.
PASTORA, daughter to Ægon	Mrs. Lindar.
PHILLIDA, daughter to Corydon	Mrs. Raftor.

Mrs. Raftor (at this time *Miss* was not generally used) was
afterwards the famous Mrs. Clive. Chetwood, in his "History of
the Stage," 1749 (p. 128), says: "I remember the first night of *Love
in a Riddle* (which was murder'd in the same Year) a Pastoral
Opera wrote by the *Laureat*, which the Hydra-headed Multitude
resolv'd to worry without hearing, a Custom with Authors of Merit,
when Miss *Raftor* came on in the part of *Phillida*, the monstrous
Roar subsided. A Person in the Stage-Box, next to my Post,
called out to his Companion in the following elegant Style—
'Zounds! *Tom!* take Care! or this charming little Devil will
save all.'" Chetwood's "Post" was that of Prompter.

is not what I complain of; I will allow my Poetry
to be as much below the other as Taste or Criticism
can sink it : I will grant likewise that the applauded
Author of the *Beggars Opera* (whom I knew to be
an honest good-natur'd Man, and who, when he had
descended to write more like one, in the Cause of
Virtue, had been as unfortunate as others of that
Class ;) I will grant, I say, that in his *Beggars Opera*
he had more skilfully gratify'd the Publick Taste
than all the brightest Authors that ever writ before
him ; and I have sometimes thought, from the
Modesty of his Motto, *Nos hæc novimus esse nihil*,[1]
that he gave them that Performance as a Satyr upon
the Depravity of their Judgment (as *Ben. Johnson* of
old was said to give his *Bartholomew-Fair* in Ridicule of the vulgar Taste which had disliked his
Sejanus[2]) and that, by artfully seducing them to be
the Champions of the Immoralities he himself detested,
he should be amply reveng'd on their former Severity
and Ignorance. This were indeed a Triumph ! which
even the Author of *Cato* might have envy'd, *Cato!*
'tis true, succeeded, but reach'd not, by full forty Days,
the Progress and Applauses of the *Beggars Opera*.
Will it, however, admit of a Question, which of the
two Compositions a good Writer would rather wish
to have been the Author of ? Yet, on the other
side, must we not allow that to have taken a whole
Nation, High and Low, into a general Applause,

[1] Martial, xiii. 2, 8.
[2] Cibber should have written *Catiline.*

has shown a Power in Poetry which, though often attempted in the same kind, none but this one Author could ever yet arrive at ? By what Rule, then, are we to judge of our true National Taste ? But to keep a little closer to my Point,

The same Author the next Year had, according to the Laws of the Land, transported his Heroe to the *West-Indies* in a Second Part to the *Beggars Opera* ;[1] but so it happen'd, to the Surprize of the Publick, this Second Part was forbid to come upon the Stage! Various were the Speculations upon this act of Power : Some thought that the Author, others that the Town, was hardly dealt with ; a third sort, who perhaps had envy'd him the Success of his first Part, affirm'd, when it was printed, that whatever the Intention might be, the Fact was in his Favour, that he had been a greater Gainer by Subscriptions to his Copy than he could have been by a bare Theatrical Presentation. Whether any Part of these Opinions were true I am not concerned to determine or consider. But how they affected me I am going to tell you. Soon after this Prohibition,[2] my Performance was to come upon the Stage, at a time when many

---

[1] This second part was called "Polly." In his Preface Gay gives an account of its being vetoed. The prohibition undoubtedly was in revenge for the political satire in "The Beggar's Opera." " Polly" was published by subscription, and probably brought the author more in that way than its production would have done. It was played for the first time at the Haymarket, 19th June, 1777. It is, as Genest says, miserably inferior to the first part.

[2] "Polly" was officially prohibited on 12th December, 1728.

People were out of Humour at the late Disappointment, and seem'd willing to lay hold of any Pretence
of making a Reprizal. Great Umbrage was taken
that I was permitted to have the whole Town to my
self, by this absolute Forbiddance of what they had
more mind to have been entertain'd with. And,
some few Days before my Bawble was acted, I was
inform'd that a strong Party would be made against
it: This Report I slighted, as not conceiving why
it should be true ; and when I was afterwards told
what was the pretended Provocation of this Party, I
slighted it still more, as having less Reason to suppose any Persons could believe me capable (had I
had the Power) of giving such a Provocation. The
Report, it seems, that had run against me was this :
That, to make way for the Success of my own Play,
I had privately found means, or made Interest, that
the Second Part of the *Beggars Opera* might be
suppressed. What an involuntary Compliment did
the Reporters of this falshood make me ? to suppose
me of Consideration enough to Influence a great
Officer of State to gratify the Spleen or Envy of a
Comedian so far as to rob the Publick of an innocent Diversion (if it were such) that none but that
cunning Comedian might be suffered to give it
them.[1]   This is so very gross a Supposition that it

---

[1] I know only one case in which a new piece is said to have
been prohibited because the other house was going to play one on
the same subject. This is Swiney's " Quacks; or, Love's the
Physician," produced at Drury Lane on 18th March, 1705, after

needs only its own senseless Face to confound it; let that alone, then, be my Defence against it. But against blind Malice and staring inhumanity whatever is upon the Stage has no Defence! There they knew I stood helpless and expos'd to whatever they might please to load or asperse me with. I had not considered, poor Devil! that from the Security of a full Pit Dunces might be Criticks, Cowards valiant, and 'Prentices Gentlemen! Whether any such were concern'd in the Murder of my Play I am not certain, for I never endeavour'd to discover any one of its Assassins; I cannot afford them a milder Name, from their unmanly manner of destroying it. Had it been heard, they might have left me nothing to say to them: 'Tis true it faintly held up its wounded Head a second Day, and would have spoke for Mercy, but was not suffer'd. Not even the Presence of a Royal Heir apparent could protect it. But then I was reduced to be serious with them; their Clamour then became an Insolence, which I thought it my Duty by the Sacrifice of any Interest of my own to put an end to. I therefore quitted the Actor for the Author, and, stepping forward to the Pit, told them, *That since I found they were not inclin'd that this Play should go forward, I gave them my Word that after this Night it should never be acted agen: But that, in the mean time, I hop'd they would consider in whose Presence they were, and for*

being twice vetoed. Swiney in his Preface gives the above as the reason for the prohibition.

that Reason at least would suspend what farther
Marks of their Displeasure they might imagine I had
deserved. At this there was a dead Silence; and
after some little Pause, a few civiliz'd Hands signify'd
their Approbation. When the Play went on, I observ'd about a Dozen Persons of no extraordinary
Appearance sullenly walk'd out of the Pit. After
which, every Scene of it, while uninterrupted, met
with more Applause than my best Hopes had expected. But it came too late : Peace to its *Manes !*
I had given my Word it should fall, and I kept it by
giving out another Play for the next Day, though I
knew the Boxes were all lett for the same again.
Such, then, was the Treatment I met with : How
much of it the Errors of the Play might deserve I
refer to the Judgment of those who may have Curiosity and idle time enough to read it.[1] But if I had
no occasion to complain of the Reception it met with
from its *quieted* Audience, sure it can be no great
Vanity to impute its Disgraces chiefly to that severe
Resentment which a groundless Report of me had
inflam'd : Yet those Disgraces have left me something to boast of, an Honour preferable even to the
Applause of my Enemies : A noble Lord came
behind the Scenes, and told me, from the Box, where
he was in waiting, *That what I said to quiet the*
Audience was extremely well taken there ; and that I
had been commended for it in a very obliging manner.

[1] Cibber afterwards formed the best scenes of "Love in a
Riddle" into a Ballad Opera, called "Damon and Phillida."

Now, though this was the only Tumult that I have known to have been so effectually appeas'd these fifty Years by any thing that could be said to an Audience in the same Humour, I will not take any great Merit to myself upon it ; because when, like me, you will but humbly submit to their doing you all the Mischief they can, they will at any time be satisfy'd.

I have mention'd this particular Fact to inforce what I before observ'd, That the private Character of an Actor will always more or less affect his Publick Performance. And if I suffer'd so much from the bare *Suspicion* of my having been guilty of a base Action, what should not an Actor expect that is hardy enough to think his whole private Character of no consequence ? I could offer many more, tho' less severe Instances of the same Nature. I have seen the most tender Sentiment of Love in Tragedy create Laughter, instead of Compassion, when it has been applicable to the real Engagements of the Person that utter'd it. I have known good Parts thrown up, from an humble Consciousness that something in them might put an Audience in mind of— what was rather wish'd might be forgotten : Those remarkable Words of *Evadne*, in the *Maid's Tragedy*— *A Maidenhead*, Amintor, *at my Years ?*—have sometimes been a much stronger Jest for being a true one. But these are Reproaches which in all Nations the Theatre must have been us'd to, unless we could suppose Actors something more than Human Creatures, void of Faults or Frailties. 'Tis a Misfortune at least not limited to the *English* Stage. I have seen the better-bred Audience in *Paris* made merry even with a modest Expression, when it has come from the Mouth of an Actress whose private Character it seem'd not to belong to. The Apprehension of these kind of Fleers from the Witlings of a Pit has been carry'd so far in our own Country, that a late valuable Actress[1] (who was conscious her Beauty was not her greatest Merit) desired the Warmth of some Lines might be abated when they have made her too remarkably handsome : But in this Discretion she was alone, few others were afraid of undeserving the finest things that could be said to them. But to consider this Matter seriously, I cannot but think, at a Play, a sensible Auditor would contribute all he could to his being well deceiv'd, and not suffer his Imagination so far to wander from the well-acted Character before him, as to gratify a frivolous Spleen by Mocks or personal Sneers on the Performer, at the Expence of his better Entertainment. But I must now take up *Wilks* and *Powel* again where I left them.

Though the Contention for Superiority between

[1] Bellchambers notes that this was probably Mrs. Oldfield. But I think this more than doubtful, for this lady not only was fair, but also, as Touchstone says, "had the gift to know it." It is, of course, impossible to say decidedly to whom Cibber referred ; but I fancy that Mrs. Barry is the actress who best fulfils the conditions, though, of course, I must admit that her having been dead for a quarter of a century weakens my case.

them seem'd about this time to end in favour of the
former, yet the Distress of the Patentee (in having
his Servant his Master, as *Powel* had lately been),
was not much reliev'd by the Victory ; he had only
chang'd the Man, but not the Malady : For *Wilks*,
by being in Possession of so many good Parts, fell
into the common Error of most Actors, that of over-
rating their Merit, or never thinking it is so thoroughly consider'd as it ought to be, which generally
makes them proportionably troublesome to the
Master, who they might consider only pays them to
profit by them.   The Patentee therefore found it as
difficult to satisfy the continual Demands of *Wilks*
as it was dangerous to refuse them ; very few were
made that were not granted, and as few were granted
as were not grudg'd him : Not but our good Master
was as sly a Tyrant as ever was at the Head of a
Theatre ; for he gave the Actors more Liberty, and
fewer Days Pay, than any of his Predecessors : He
would laugh with them over a Bottle, and bite[1] them
in their Bargains : He kept them poor, that they might
not be able to rebel ; and sometimes merry, that they
might not think of it : All their Articles of Agreement had a Clause in them that he was sure to creep
out at, *viz.* Their respective Sallaries were to be paid
in such manner and proportion as others of the same

---

[1] A " bite " is what we now term a " sell."   In "The Spectator,"
Nos. 47 and 504, some account of " Biters " is given : " a Race
of Men that are perpetually employed in laughing at those Mis-
takes which are of their own Production."

Company were paid; which in effect made them all, when he pleas'd, but limited Sharers of Loss, and himself sole Proprietor of Profits; and this Loss or Profit they only had such verbal Accounts of as he thought proper to give them. 'Tis true, he would sometimes advance them Money (but not more than he knew at most could be due to them) upon their Bonds; upon which, whenever they were mutinous, he would threaten to sue them. This was the Net we danc'd in for several Years: But no wonder we were Dupes, while our Master was a Lawyer. This Grievance, however, *Wilks* was resolv'd, for himself at least, to remedy at any rate; and grew daily more intractable, for every Day his Redress was delay'd. Here our Master found himself under a Difficulty he knew not well how to get out of: For as he was a close subtle Man, he seldom made use of a Confident in his Schemes of Government :[1] But here the old Expedient of Delay would stand him in no longer stead; *Wilks* must instantly be comply'd with, or *Powel* come again into Power! In a word, he was push'd so home, that he was reduc'd even to take my Opinion into his Assistance: For he knew I was a Rival to neither of them; perhaps, too, he had fancy'd that, from the Success of my first Play, I might know as much of the Stage, and what made an Actor valuable, as either of them : He saw, too, that tho' they had each of them five good Parts to my one, yet the Applause which in my few I had

[1] This is a capital sketch of Christopher Rich.

met with, was given me by better Judges than as
yet had approv'd of the best they had done. They
generally measured the goodness of a Part by the
Quantity or Length of it : I thought none bad for
being short that were closely-natural ; nor any the
better for being long, without that valuable Quality.
But in this, I doubt, as to their Interest, they judg'd
better than myself; for I have generally observ'd
that those who do a great deal not ill, have been
preferr'd to those who do but little, though never so
masterly. And therefore I allow that, while there
were so few good Parts, and as few good Judges of
them, it ought to have been no Wonder to me, that
as an Actor I was less valued by the Master or the
common People than either of them : All the Advantage I had of them was, that by not being troublesome I had more of our Master's personal Inclination than any Actor of the male Sex ; [1] and so much
of it, that I was almost the only one whom at that
time he us'd to take into his Parties of Pleasure ;
very often *tete à tete,* and sometimes in a *Partie
quarrèe.* These then were the Qualifications, however good or bad, to which may be imputed our
Master's having made choice of me to assist him in
the Difficulty under which he now labour'd. He

---

[1] Cibber's hint of Rich's weakness for the fair sex is corroborated
by the "Comparison between the two Stages," page 16: "*Critick.*
He is Monarch of the Stage, tho' he knows not how to govern one
Province in his Dominion, but that of Signing, Sealing, and something else, that shall be nameless."

was himself sometimes inclin'd to set up *Powel* again
as a Check upon the over-bearing Temper of *Wilks:*
Tho' to say truth, he lik'd neither of them, but was
still under a Necessity that one of them should
preside, tho' he scarce knew which of the two Evils
to chuse. This Question, when I happen'd to be
alone with him, was often debated in our Evening
Conversation ; ,nor, indeed, did I find it an easy
matter to know which Party I ought to recommend
to his Election. I knew they were neither of them
Well-wishers to me, as in common they were
Enemies to most Actors in proportion to the Merit
that seem'd to be rising in them. But as I had the
Prosperity of the Stage more at Heart than any
other Consideration, I could not be long undeter-
mined in my Opinion, and therefore gave it to our
Master at once in Favour of *Wilks.* I, with all the
Force I could muster, insisted, " That if *Powel* were
" preferr'd, the ill Example of his Negligence and
" abandon'd Character (whatever his Merit on the
" Stage might be) would reduce our Company to
" Contempt and Beggary; observing, at the same
" time, in how much better Order our Affairs went
" forward since *Wilks* came among us, of which I
" recounted several Instances that are not so neces-
" sary to tire my Reader with. All this, though he
" allow'd to be true, yet *Powel*, he said, was a better
" Actor than *Wilks* when he minded his Business
" (that is to say, when he was, what he seldom was,
" sober). But *Powel*, it seems, had a still greater

R

" Merit to him, which was, (as he observ'd) that
" when Affairs were in his Hands, he had kept the
" Actors quiet, without one Day's Pay, for six
" Weeks together, and it was not every body could
" do that ; for you see, said he, *Wilks* will never be
" easy unless I give him his whole Pay, when others
" have it not, and what an Injustice would that be
" to the rest if I were to comply with him ? How
" do I know but then they may be all in a Mutiny,
" and *mayhap* (that was his Expression) with *Powel*
" at the Head of 'em ?" By this Specimen of our
Debate, it may be judg'd under how particular and
merry a Government the Theatre then labour'd.
To conclude, this Matter ended in a Resolution to
sign a new Agreement with *Wilks*, which entitled
him to his full Pay of four Pounds a Week without
any conditional Deductions. How far soever my
Advice might have contributed to our Master's settling
his Affairs upon this Foot, I never durst make the
least Merit of it to *Wilks*, well knowing that his
great Heart would have taken it as a mortal Affront
had I (tho' never so distantly) hinted that his
Demands had needed any Assistance but the Justice of them. From this time, then, *Wilks* became
first Minister, or Bustle-master-general of the Company.[1] He now seem'd to take new Delight in

---

[1] "The Laureat," p. 48 : " If *Minister Wilks* was now alive to
hear thee prate thus, Mr. *Bayes*, I would not give one Half-penny
for thy Ears ; but if he were alive, thou durst not for thy Ears
rattle on in this affected *Matchiavilian* stile."

keeping the Actors close to their Business, and got
every Play reviv'd with Care in which he had acted
the chief Part in *Dublin :* 'Tis true, this might be
done with a particular View of setting off himself to
Advantage; but if at the same time it served the
Company, he ought not to want our Commendation:
Now, tho' my own Conduct neither had the Appearance of his Merit, nor the Reward that follow'd his
Industry, I cannot help observing that it shew'd me,
to the best of my Power, a more cordial Common-
wealth's Man : His first Views in serving himself
made his Service to the whole but an incidental
Merit; whereas, by my prosecuting the Means to
make him easy in his Pay, unknown to him, or without asking any Favour for my self at the same time,
I gave a more unquestionable Proof of my preferring
the Publick to my Private Interest : From the same
Principle I never murmur'd at whatever little Parts
fell to my Share, and though I knew it would not
recommend me to the Favour of the common
People, I often submitted to play wicked Characters rather than they should be worse done by
weaker Actors than my self: But perhaps, in all this
Patience under my Situation, I supported my Spirits
by a conscious Vanity : For I fancied I had more
Reason to value myself upon being sometimes the
Confident and Companion of our Master, than *Wilks*
had in all the more publick Favours he had extorted
from him. I imagined, too, there was sometimes as
much Skill to be shewn in a short Part, as in the

most voluminous, which he generally made choice
of; that even the coxcombly Follies of a Sir *John
Daw* might as well distinguish the Capacity of an
Actor, as all the dry Enterprizes and busy Conduct
of a *Truewit*.[1] Nor could I have any Reason to
repine at the Superiority he enjoy'd, when I consider'd at how dear a Rate it was purchased, at the
continual Expence of a restless Jealousy and fretful
Impatience——These were the Passions that, in
the height of his Successes, kept him lean to his last
Hour, while what I wanted in Rank or Glory was
amply made up to me in Ease and Chearfulness.
But let not this Observation either lessen his Merit
or lift up my own; since our different Tempers were
not in our Choice, but equally natural to both of us.
To be employ'd on the Stage was the Delight of
his Life; to be justly excused from it was the Joy
of mine: I lov'd Ease, and he Pre-eminence: In
that, he might be more commendable. Tho' he
often disturb'd me, he seldom could do it without
more disordering himself:[2] In our Disputes, his
Warmth could less bear Truth than I could support
manifest Injuries: He would hazard our Undoing
to gratify his Passions, tho' otherwise an honest

---

[1] Characters in Ben Jonson's "Silent Woman."

[2] "The Laureat," p. 49: "Did you not, by your general Mis-
behaviour towards Authors and Actors, bring an *Odium* on your
Brother *Menagers*, as well as yourself; and were not these, with
many others, the Reasons, that sometimes gave Occasion to *Wilks*,
to chastise you, with his Tongue only."

Man ; and I rather chose to give up my Reason, or not see my Wrong, than ruin our Community by an equal Rashness. By this opposite Conduct our Accounts at the End of our Labours stood thus : While he lived he was the elder Man, when he died he was not so old as I am : He never left the Stage till he left the World : I never so well enjoy'd the World as when I left the Stage : He died in Posses-sion of his Wishes ; and I, by having had a less cholerick Ambition, am still tasting mine in Health and Liberty. But as he in a great measure wore out the Organs of Life in his incessant Labours to gratify the Publick, the Many whom he gave Plea-sure to will always owe his Memory a favourable Report—Some Facts that will vouch for the Truth of this Account will be found in the Sequel of these Memoirs. If I have spoke with more Freedom of his quondam Competitor *Powel*, let my good Inten-tions to future Actors, in shewing what will so much concern them to avoid, be my Excuse for it : For though *Powel* had from Nature much more than *Wilks* ; in Voice and Ear, in Elocution in Tragedy, and Humour in Comedy, greatly the Advantage of him ; yet, as I have observ'd, from the Neglect and Abuse of those valuable Gifts, he suffer'd *Wilks* to be of thrice the Service to our Society. Let me give another Instance of the Reward and Favour which, in a Theatre, Diligence and Sobriety seldom fail of : *Mills* the elder [1] grew into the Friendship of

[1] See memoir of John Mills at end of second volume.

Wilks with not a great deal more than those useful Qualities to recommend him : He was an honest, quiet, careful Man, of as few Faults as Excellencies, and *Wilks* rather chose him for his second in many Plays, than an Actor of perhaps greater Skill that was not so laboriously diligent. And from this constant Assiduity, *Mills*, with making to himself a Friend in *Wilks*, was advanced to a larger Sallary than any Man-Actor had enjoy'd during my time on the Stage.[1] I have yet to offer a more happy Recommendation of Temperance, which a late celebrated Actor was warn'd into by the mis-conduct of *Powel*. About the Year that *Wilks* return'd from *Dublin*, *Booth*, who had commenced Actor upon that Theatre, came over to the Company in *Lincolns-Inn-Fields* :[2] He was then but an Under-graduate of the Buskin, and, as he told me himself, had been for some time too frank a Lover of the Bottle; but having had the Happiness to observe into what Contempt and Distresses *Powel* had plung'd himself by the same Vice, he was so struck with the Terror of his Example, that he fix'd a Resolution (which

[1] John Mills, in the advertisement issued by Rich, in 1709, in the course of a dispute with his actors, is stated to have a salary of " £4 a week for himself, and £1 a week for his wife, for little or nothing." This advertisement is quoted by me in Chap. XII. Mills's salary was the same as Betterton's. No doubt Cibber, Wilks, Dogget, and Booth had ultimately larger salaries, but they, of course, were managers as well as actors.

[2] Booth seems to have joined the Lincoln's Inn Fields Company in 1700.

from that time to the End of his Days he strictly
observ'd) of utterly reforming it ; an uncommon Act
of Philosophy in a young Man ! of which in his
Fame and Fortune he afterwards enjoy'd the Reward and Benefit. These Observations I have not
merely thrown together as a Moralist, but to prove
that the briskest loose Liver or intemperate Man
(though Morality were out of the Question) can
never arrive at the necessary Excellencies of a good
or useful Actor.

CHAPTER VIII.

The Patentee of Drury-Lane *wiser than his Actors. His particular Menagement. The Author continues to write Plays. Why. The best dramatick Poets censured by* J. Collier, *in his* Short View of the Stage. *It has a good Effect. The Master of the Revels, from that time, cautious in his licensing new Plays. A Complaint against him. His Authority founded upon Custom only. The late Law for fixing that Authority in a proper Person, considered.*

THOUGH the Master of our Theatre had no Conception himself of Theatrical Merit either in Authors or Actors, yet his Judgment was govern'd by a saving Rule in both : He look'd into his Receipts for the Value of a Play, and from common Fame he judg'd of his Actors. But by whatever Rule he was govern'd, while he had prudently reserv'd to himself a Power of not paying them more than their Merit could get, he could not be much deceived by their being over or under-valued.   In a Word, he had with great Skill inverted the Constitution of the Stage, and quite changed the Channel of Profits arising from it ; formerly, (when there was but one Company) the Proprietors punctually paid the Actors their appointed Sallaries, and took to themselves only the clear Profits : But our wiser Proprietor took first out of every Day's Receipts two Shillings in the Pound to himself; and left their Sallaries to be paid only as the less or greater Deficiencies of acting (according to his own Accounts) would permit.   What seem'd most extraordinary in these Measures was, that at the same time he had persuaded us to be contented with our Condition, upon his assuring us that as fast as Money would come in we should all be paid our Arrears : And that we might not have it always in our Power to say he had never intended to keep his Word, I remember in a few Years after this time he once paid us nine Days in one Week : This happen'd when the *Funeral*, or *Grief à la Mode*,[1] was first acted, with more than expected Success.   Whether this well-tim'd Bounty was only allow'd us to save Appearances I will not say : But if that was his real Motive for it, it was too costly a frolick to be repeated, and was at least the only Grimace of its kind he vouchsafed us ; we

[1] Steele's comedy was produced at Drury Lane in 1702.   Cibber played Lord Hardy.

never having received one Day more of those Arrears in above fifteen Years Service.

While the Actors were in this Condition, I think I may very well be excused in my presuming to write Plays : which I was forced to do for the Support of my encreasing Family, my precarious Income as an Actor being then too scanty to supply it with even the Necessaries of Life.

It may be observable, too, that my Muse and my Spouse were equally prolifick ; that the one was seldom the Mother of a Child, but in the same Year the other made me the Father of a Play : I think we had a Dozen of each Sort between us ; of both which kinds, some died in their Infancy, and near an equal Number of each were alive when I quitted the Theatre—But it is no Wonder, when a Muse is only call'd upon by Family Duty, she should not always rejoice in the Fruit of her Labour. To this Necessity of writing, then, I attribute the Defects of my second Play, which, coming out too hastily the Year after my first, turn'd to very little Account. But having got as much by my first as I ought to have expected from the Success of them both, I had no great Reason to complain : Not but, I confess, so bad was my second, that I do not chuse to tell you the Name of it ; and that it might be peaceably forgotten, I have not given it a Place in the two Volumes of those I publish'd in Quarto in the Year 1721.[1] And

---

[1] The play was called "Woman's Wit ; or, the Lady in Fashion." It was produced at Drury Lane in 1697. It must have been in

whenever I took upon me to make some dormant
Play of an old Author to the best of my Judgment
fitter for the Stage, it was honestly not to be idle
that set me to work; as a good Housewife will mend
old Linnen when she has not better Employment:
But when I was more warmly engag'd by a Subject
entirely new, I only thought it a good Subject when
it seem'd worthy of an abler Pen than my own, and
might prove as useful to the Hearer as profitable to
my self : Therefore, whatever any of my Productions
might want of Skill, Learning, Wit, or Humour, or
however unqualify'd I might be to instruct others who
so ill govern'd my self : Yet such Plays (entirely my
own) were not wanting, at least, in what our most
admired Writers seem'd to neglect, and without
which I cannot allow the most taking Play to be in-

the early months of that year, for in his Preface Cibber says, to
excuse its failure, that it was hurriedly written, and that "rather
than lose a Winter" he forced himself to invent a fable. "The
Laureat," p. 50, stupidly says that the name of the play was
"*Perolla* and *Isadora.*" The cast was :—

LORD LOVEMORE	Mr. Harland.
LONGVILLE	Mr. Cibber.
MAJOR RAKISH	Mr. Penkethman.
JACK RAKISH	Mr. Powel.
MASS JOHNNY, Lady Manlove's Son,	
a schoolboy	Mr. Dogget.
FATHER BENEDIC	Mr. Smeaton.
LADY MANLOVE	Mrs. Powel.
LEONORA	Mrs. Knight.
EMILIA	Mrs. Rogers.
OLIVIA	Mrs. Cibber.
LETTICE	Mrs. Kent.

trinsically good, or to be a Work upon which a Man of Sense and Probity should value himself: I mean when they do not, as well *prodesse* as *delectare*,[1] give Profit with Delight! The *Utile Dulci*[2] was, of old, equally the Point; and has always been my Aim, however wide of the Mark I may have shot my Arrow. It has often given me Amazement that our best Authors of that time could think the Wit and Spirit of their Scenes could be an Excuse for making the Looseness of them publick. The many Instances of their Talents so abused are too glaring to need a closer Comment, and are sometimes too gross to be recited. If then to have avoided this Imputation, or rather to have had the Interest and Honour of Virtue always in view, can give Merit to a Play, I am contented that my Readers should think such Merit the All that mine have to boast of—Libertines of meer Wit and Pleasure may laugh at these grave Laws that would limit a lively Genius: But every sensible honest Man, conscious of their Truth and Use, will give these Ralliers Smile for Smile, and shew a due Contempt for their Merriment.

But while our Authors took these extraordinary Liberties with their Wit, I remember the Ladies were then observ'd to be decently afraid of venturing bare-fac'd to a new Comedy 'till they had been

[1] "Aut prodesse volunt aut delectare poetae."
Hor. *Ars Poetica*, 333.

[2] "Omne tulit punctum qui miscuit utile dulci."
Hor. *Ars Poetica*, 343.

assur'd they might do it without the Risque of an
Insult to their Modesty—Or, if their Curiosity were
too strong for their Patience, they took Care, at
least, to save Appearances, and rarely came upon the
first Days of Acting but in Masks, (then daily worn
and admitted in the Pit, the side Boxes, and Gallery[1])
which Custom, however, had so many ill Consequences attending it, that it has been abolish'd these
many Years.

These Immoralities of the Stage had by an avow'd
Indulgence been creeping into it ever since King
Charles his Time ; nothing that was loose could then
be too low for it : The *London Cuckolds*, the most
rank Play that ever succeeded,[2] was then in the
highest Court-Favour : In this almost general Corruption, *Dryden*, whose Plays were more fam'd for
their Wit than their Chastity, led the way, which he
fairly confesses, and endeavours to excuse in his
Epilogue to the *Pilgrim*, revived in 1700 for his

---

[1] Pepys (12th June, 1663) records that the Lady Mary Cromwell at the Theatre, "when the House began to fill, put on her
vizard, and so kept it on all the play ; which of late is
become a great fashion among the ladies, which hides their whole
face." Very soon, however, ladies gave up the use of the mask,
and "Vizard-mask" became a synonym for "Prostitute." In
this sense it is frequently used in Dryden's Prologues and
Epilogues.

[2] Compare with Cibber's condemnation Genest's opinion of this
play. He says (i. 365): "If it be the province of Comedy, not to
retail morality to a yawning pit, but to make the audience laugh,
and to keep them in good humour, this play must be allowed to be
one of the best comedies in the English language."

Benefit,[1] in his declining Age and Fortune—The following Lines of it will make good my Observation.

Perhaps the Parson[2] *stretch'd a Point too far,*
When with our Theatres he wag'd a War.
He tells you that this very moral Age
Receiv'd the first Infection from the Stage.
But sure, a banish'd Court, with Lewdness fraught,
The Seeds of open Vice returning brought.
Thus lodg'd (as vice by great Example thrives)
It first debauch'd the Daughters, and the Wives.
London, *a fruitful Soil, yet never bore*
So plentiful a Crop of Horns before.
The Poets, who must live by Courts or starve,
Were proud so good a Government to serve.
And mixing with Buffoons and Pimps profane,
Tainted the Stage for some small snip of Gain.
For they, like Harlots under Bawds profest,
Took all th'ungodly Pains, and got the least.
Thus did the thriving Malady prevail,

[1] To " The Pilgrim," revived in 1700, as Cibber states, Dryden's " Secular Masque " was attached. Whether the revival took place before or after Dryden's death (1st May, 1700) is a moot point. See Genest, ii. 179, for an admirable account of the matter. He thinks it probable that the date of production was 25th March, 1700. Cibber is scarcely accurate in stating that " The Pilgrim " was revived for Dryden's benefit. It seems, rather, that Vanbrugh, who revised the play, stipulated that, in consideration of Dryden's writing " The Secular Masque," and also the Prologue and Epilogue, he should have the usual author's third night. The B. M. copy of " The Pilgrim " is dated, in an old handwriting, " Monday, the 5 of May."

[2] Jeremy Collier.

The Court it's Head, the Poets but the Tail.
The Sin was of our native Growth, 'tis true,
The Scandal of the Sin was wholly new.
Misses there were, but modestly conceal'd ;
White-hall *the naked* Venus *first reveal'd.*
Who standing, as at Cyprus, *in her Shrine,*
The Strumpet was ador'd with Rites divine, &c.

This Epilogue, and the Prologue to the same Play,
written by *Dryden,* I spoke myself, which not being
usually done by the same Person, I have a mind,
while I think of it, to let you know on what Occasion they both fell to my Share, and how other
Actors were affected by it.

Sir *John Vanbrugh,* who had given some light
touches of his Pen to the *Pilgrim* to assist the
Benefit Day of *Dryden,* had the Disposal of the
Parts, and I being then as an Actor in some Favour
with him, he read the Play first with me alone, and
was pleased to offer me my Choice of what I might
like best for myself in it. But as the chief Characters
were not (according to my Taste) the most shining,
it was no great Self-denial in me that I desir'd he
would first take care of those who were more difficult
to be pleased ; I therefore only chose for myself two
short incidental Parts, that of *the stuttering Cook* [1]
and *the mad Englishman.* In which homely Characters I saw more Matter for Delight than those that

---

[1] Genest notes (ii. 181) that in the original play the Servant in
the 2nd act did not stutter.

might have a better Pretence to the Amiable : And
when the Play came to be acted I was not deceiv'd
in my Choice.   Sir *John*, upon my being contented
with so little a Share in the Entertainment, gave me
the Epilogue to make up my Mess; which being
written so much above the Strain of common Authors,
I confess I was not a little pleased with.   And
Dryden, upon his hearing me repeat it to him, made
me a farther Compliment of trusting me with the
Prologue.   This so particular Distinction was looked
upon by the Actors as something too extraordinary.
But no one was so impatiently ruffled at it as *Wilks*,
who seldom chose soft Words when he spoke of any
thing he did not like.   The most gentle thing he
said of it was, that he did not understand such
Treatment; that for his Part he look'd upon it as an
Affront to all the rest of the Company, that there
shou'd be but one out of the Whole judg'd fit to
speak either a Prologue or an Epilogue! to quiet
him I offer'd to decline either in his Favour, or both,
if it were equally easy to the Author : But he was
too much concern'd to accept of an Offer that had
been made to another in preference to himself, and
which he seem'd to think his best way of resenting
was to contemn.   But from that time, however, he
was resolv'd, to the best of his Power, never to let
the first Offer of a Prologue escape him : Which
little Ambition sometimes made him pay too dear
for his Success : The Flatness of the many miserable
Prologues that by this means fell to his Lot, seem'd

wofully unequal to the few good ones he might have Reason to triumph in.

I have given you this Fact only as a Sample of those frequent Rubs and Impediments I met with when any Step was made to my being distinguish'd as an Actor ; and from this Incident, too, you may partly see what occasion'd so many Prologues, after the Death of *Betterton*, to fall into the Hands of one Speaker : But it is not every Successor to a vacant Post that brings into it the Talents equal to those of a Predecessor. To speak a good Prologue well is, in my Opinion, one of the hardest Parts and strongest Proofs of sound Elocution, of which, I confess, I never thought that any of the several who attempted it shew'd themselves, by far, equal Masters to *Betterton*. *Betterton*, in the Delivery of a good Prologue, had a natural Gravity that gave Strength to good Sense, a temper'd Spirit that gave Life to Wit, and a dry Reserve in his Smile that threw Ridicule into its brightest Colours. Of these Qualities, in the speaking of a Prologue, *Booth* only had the first, but attain'd not to the other two : *Wilks* had Spirit, but gave too loose a Rein to it, and it was seldom he could speak a grave and weighty Verse harmoniously : His Accents were frequently too sharp and violent, which sometimes occasion'd his eagerly cutting off half the Sound of Syllables that ought to have been gently melted into the Melody of Metre : In Verses of Humour, too, he would sometimes carry the Mimickry farther than the hint would bear, even to

a trifling Light, as if himself were pleased to see it
so glittering.   In the Truth of this Criticism I have
been confirm'd by those whose Judgment I dare more
confidently rely on than my own : *Wilks* had many
Excellencies, but if we leave Prologue-Speaking out
of the Number he will still have enough to have
made him a valuable Actor.   And I only make this
Exception from them to caution others from imitating
what, in his time, they might have too implicitly
admired—   But I have a Word or two more to say
concerning the Immoralities of the Stage.   Our
Theatrical Writers were not only accus'd of Immorality, but Prophaneness ; many flagrant Instances
of which were collected and published by a Nonjuring Clergyman, *Jeremy Collier*, in his *View of the
Stage*, &c. about the Year 1697.[1]   However just his
Charge against the Authors that then wrote for it
might be, I cannot but think his Sentence against
the Stage itself is unequal ; Reformation he thinks
too mild a Treatment for it, and is therefore for
laying his Ax to the Root of it : If this were to be a
Rule of Judgment for Offences of the same Nature,

---

[1]   Collier's famous work, which was entitled "A Short View of
the Immorality and Profaneness of the English Stage : together
with the sense of Antiquity upon this Argument," was published
in 1698.   Collier was a Nonjuring clergyman.   He was born on
23rd September, 1650, and died in 1726.   The circumstance to
which Cibber alludes in the second paragraph from the present,
was Collier's attending to the scaffold Sir John Friend and Sir
William Perkins, who were executed for complicity in plots
against King William in 1696.

what might become of the Pulpit, where many a seditious and corrupted Teacher has been known to cover the most pernicious Doctrine with the Masque of Religion ? This puts me in mind of what the noted *Jo. Hains*,[1] the Comedian, a Fellow of a wicked Wit, said upon this Occasion ; who being ask'd what could transport Mr. *Collier* into so blind a Zeal for a general Suppression of the Stage, when only some particular Authors had abus'd it ? Whereas the Stage, he could not but know, was generally allow'd, when rightly conducted, to be a delightful Method of mending our Morals ? " For that Reason, reply'd " *Hains: Collier* is by Profession a Moral-mender " himself, and two of Trade, you know, can never " agree."[2]

[1] The facetious Joe Haines was an actor of great popularity, and seems to have excelled in the delivery of Prologues and Epilogues, especially of those written by himself. He was on the stage from about 1672 to 1700 or 1701, in which latter year (on the 4th of April) he died. He was the original Sparkish in Wycherley's " Country Wife," Lord Plausible in the same author's " Plain Dealer," and Tom Errand in Farquhar's " Constant Couple." Davies (" Dram. Misc.," iii. 284) tells, on Quin's authority, an anecdote of Haines's pretended conversion to Romanism during James the Second's reign. He declared that the Virgin Mary appeared to him in a vision. " Lord Sunderland sent for Joe, and asked him about the truth of his conversion, and whether he had really seen the Virgin ?—Yes, my Lord, I assure you it is a fact.—How was it, pray?—Why, as I was lying in my bed, the Virgin appeared to me, and said, *Arise, Joe !*—You lie, you rogue, said the Earl ; for, if it had really been the Virgin herself, she would have said *Joseph*, if it had been only out of respect to her husband." For an account of Haines, see also Anthony Aston.

[2] " The Laureat " (p. 53) states that soon after the publication

The Authors of *the old Batchelor* and of the *Relapse* were those whom *Collier* most labour'd to convict of Immorality; to which they severally published their Reply; the first seem'd too much hurt to be able to defend himself, and the other felt him so little that his Wit only laugh'd at his Lashes.[1]

My first Play of the *Fool in Fashion*, too, being then in a Course of Success; perhaps for that Reason only, this severe Author thought himself oblig'd to attack it; in which I hope he has shewn more Zeal than Justice, his greatest Charge against it is, that it sometimes uses the Word *Faith!* as an Oath, in the Dialogue: But if *Faith* may as well signify our given Word or Credit as our religious Belief, why might not his Charity have taken it in the less criminal Sense? Nevertheless, Mr. *Collier*'s Book was upon the whole thought so laudable a Work, that King

of Collier's book, informers were placed in different parts of the theatres, on whose information several players were charged with uttering immoral words. Queen Anne, however, satisfied that the informers were not actuated by zeal for morality, stopped the inquisition. These informers were paid by the Society for the Reformation of Manners.

[1] Congreve's answer to Collier was entitled "Amendments of Mr. Collier's false and imperfect Citations, &c. from the Old Batchelour, Double Dealer, Love for Love, Mourning Bride. By the Author of those Plays." Vanbrugh called his reply, "A Short Vindication of the Relapse and the Provok'd Wife, from Immorality and Prophaneness. By the Author." Davies says, regarding Congreve ("Dram. Misc.," iii. 401): "Congreve's pride was hurt by Collier's attack on plays which all the world had admired and commended; and no hypocrite showed more rancour and resentment, when unmasked, than this author, so greatly celebrated for sweetness of temper and elegance of manners."

William, soon after it was publish'd, granted him a *Nolo Prosequi* when he stood answerable to the Law for his having absolved two Criminals just before they were executed for High Treason. And it must be farther granted that his calling our Dramatick Writers to this strict Account had a very wholesome Effect upon those who writ after this time. They were now a great deal more upon their guard; Indecencies were no longer Wit; and by Degrees the fair Sex came again to fill the Boxes on the first Day of a new Comedy, without Fear or Censure. But the Master of the Revels,[1] who then licens'd all Plays for the Stage, assisted this Reformation with a more zealous Severity than ever. He would strike out whole Scenes of a vicious or immoral Character, tho' it were visibly shewn to be reform'd or punish'd; a severe Instance of this kind falling upon my self may be an Excuse for my relating it : When *Richard the Third* (as I alter'd it from *Shakespear*)[2] came from his Hands to the Stage, he expung'd the whole first Act without sparing a Line of it. This extraordinary Stroke of a *Sic volo* occasion'd my applying to him for the small Indulgence of a Speech or two, that the other four Acts might limp on with a little less Absurdity ! no ! he had not leisure to consider what might be separately inoffensive. He had an Objec-

---

[1] Charles Killigrew, who died in 1725, having held the office of Master of the Revels for over forty years.

[2] Produced at Drury Lane in 1700. For some account of Cibber's playing of Richard, see *ante*, pp. 139, 140.

tion to the whole Act, and the Reason he gave for it
was, that the Distresses of King *Henry the Sixth*,
who is kill'd by *Richard* in the first Act, would put
weak People too much in mind of King *James* then
living in *France*; a notable Proof of his Zeal for the
Government![1] Those who have read either the
Play or the History, I dare say will think he strain'd
hard for the Parallel. In a Word, we were forc'd,
for some few Years, to let the Play take its Fate
with only four Acts divided into five; by the Loss of
so considerable a Limb, may one not modestly suppose it was robbed of at least a fifth Part of that
Favour it afterwards met with? For tho' this first
Act was at last recovered, and made the Play whole
again, yet the Relief came too late to repay me for
the Pains I had taken in it. Nor did I ever hear
that this zealous Severity of the Master of the Revels
was afterwards thought justifiable. But my good
Fortune, in Process of time, gave me an Opportunity
to talk with my Oppressor in my Turn.

The Patent granted by his Majesty King *George*
the First to Sir *Richard Steele* and his Assigns,[2] of
which I was one, made us sole Judges of what Plays

---

[1] Chalmers ("Apology for the Believers in the Shakspeare
Papers," page 535) comments unfavourably on Cibber's method
of stating this fact, saying, "Well might Pope cry out, *modest
Cibber!*" But Chalmers is unjust to Colley, who is not expressing his own opinion of his play's importance, but merely reporting
the opinion of Killigrew.

[2] Steele's name first appears in a License granted 18th October,
1714. His Patent was dated 19th January, 1715.

might be proper for the Stage, without submitting them to the Approbation or License of any other particular Person. Notwithstanding which, the Master of the Revels demanded his Fee of Forty Shillings upon our acting a new One, tho' we had spared him the Trouble of perusing it. This occasion'd my being deputed to him to enquire into the Right of his Demand, and to make an amicable End of our Dispute.[1] I confess I did not dislike the Office; and told him, according to my Instructions, That I came not to defend even our own Right in prejudice to his; that if our Patent had inadvertently superseded the Grant of any former Power or Warrant whereon he might ground his Pretensions, we would not insist upon our Broad Seal, but would readily answer his Demands upon sight of such his Warrant, any thing in our Patent to the contrary notwithstanding. This I had reason to think he could not do; and when I found he made no direct Reply to my Question, I repeated it with greater Civilities

[1] Chalmers ("Apology for the Believers," page 536) says: "The patentees sent Colley Cibber, as envoy-extraordinary, to negotiate an amicable settlement with the Sovereign of the Revels. It is amusing to hear, how this flippant negotiator explained his own pretensions, and attempted to invalidate the right of his opponent; as if a subsequent charter, under the great seal, could supersede a preceding grant under the same authority. Charles Killigrew, who was now sixty-five years of age, seems to have been oppressed by the insolent civility of Colley Cibber." But this is an undeserved hit at Cibber, who had suffered the grossest injustice at Killigrew's hands regarding the licensing of " Richard III." See *ante*, p. 275. The dispute regarding fees must have occurred about 1715.

and Offers of Compliance, 'till I was forc'd in the
end to conclude with telling him, That as his Pretensions were not back'd with any visible Instrument
of Right, and as his strongest Plea was Custom, we
could not so far extend our Complaisance as to continue his Fees upon so slender a Claim to them:
And from that Time neither our Plays or his Fees
gave either of us any farther trouble. In this Nego-
tiation I am the bolder to think Justice was on our
Side, because the Law lately pass'd,[1] by which the

---

[1] The Licensing Act of 1737. This Act was passed by Sir
Robert Walpole's government, and gave to the Lord Chamberlain
the power to prohibit a piece from being acted at all, by making
it necessary to have every play licensed. This power, however,
had practically been exercised by the Chamberlain before, as in
the case of Gay's "Polly," which Cibber has already mentioned.
The immediate cause of this Act of 1737 was a piece called "The
Golden Rump," which was so full of scurrility against the powers
that were, that Giffard, the manager to whom it was submitted, carried it to Walpole. In spite of the opposition of Lord Chesterfield,
who delivered a famous speech against it, the Bill was passed,
21st June, 1737. The "Biographia Dramatica" hints plainly that
"The Golden Rump" was written at Walpole's instigation to
afford an excuse for the Act. Bellchambers has the following
note on this passage :—

"The Abbé Le Blanc,* who was in England at the time this
law passed, has the following remarks upon it in his correspon-
dence :—

"'This act occasioned an universal murmur in the nation, and
was openly complained of in the public papers: in all the coffee-
houses of London it was treated as an unjust law, and manifestly
contrary to the liberties of the people of England. When winter
came, and the play-houses were opened, that of Covent-garden

---

* Mr. Garrick, when in Paris, refused to meet this writer, on account of the
irreverence with which he had treated Shakspeare.

Power of Licensing Plays, &c. is given to a proper
Person, is a strong Presumption that no Law had
ever given that Power to any such Person before.
My having mentioned this Law, which so immediately affected the Stage, inclines me to throw out a

began with three new pieces, which had been approved of by the
Lord Chamberlain. There was a crowd of spectators present at
the first, and among the number myself. The best play in the
world would not have succeeded the first night.* There was a
resolution to damn whatever might appear, the word *hiss* not
being sufficiently expressive for the English. They always say, to
damn a piece, to *damn* an author, &c. and, in reality, the word is
not too strong to express the manner in which they receive a play
which does not please them. The farce in question was damned
indeed, without the least compassion : nor was that all, for the
actors were driven off the stage, and happy was it for the author
that he did not fall into the hands of this furious assembly.

" ' As you are unacquainted with the customs of this country, you
cannot easily devise who were the authors of all this disturbance.
Perhaps you may think they were schoolboys, apprentices, clerks,
or mechanics. No, sir, they were men of a very grave and genteel
profession ; they were lawyers, and please you ; a body of gentlemen, perhaps less honoured, but certainly more feared here than
they are in France. Most of them live in colleges,† where, conversing always with one another, they mutually preserve a spirit of
independency through the body, and with great ease form cabals.
These gentlemen, in the stage entertainments of London, behave
much like our footboys, in those at a fair. With us, your party-
coloured gentry are the most noisy ; but here, men of the law have
all the sway, if I may be permitted to call so those pretended pro-
fessors of it, who are rather the organs of chicanery, than the inter-

* The action was interrupted almost as soon as begun, in presence of a
numerous assembly, by a cabal who had resolved to overthrow the first effect
of this act of parliament, though it had been thought necessary for the regulation of the stage.

† Called here Inns of Court, as the two Temples, Lincoln's Inn, Gray's Inn,
Doctor's Commons, &c.

few Observations upon it : But I must first lead
you gradually thro' the Facts and natural Causes
that made such a Law necessary.

Although it had been taken for granted, from Time

preters of justice. At Paris the cabals of the pit are only among
young fellows, whose years may excuse their folly, or persons of
the meanest education and stamp; here they are the fruit of deli-
berations in a very grave body of people, who are not less formidable to the minister in place, than to the theatrical writers.

"'The players were not dismayed, but soon after stuck up bills
for another new piece : there was the same crowding at Covent-
garden, to which I again contributed. I was sure, at least, that if
the piece advertised was not performed, I should have the pleasure
of beholding some very extraordinary scene acted in the pit.

"'Half an hour before the play was to begin, the spectators gave
notice of their dispositions by frightful hisses and outcries, equal,
perhaps, to what were ever heard at a Roman amphitheatre. I
could not have known, but by my eyes only, that I was among an
assembly of beings who thought themselves to be reasonable. The
author, who had foreseen this fury of the pit, took care to be
armed against it. He knew what people he had to deal with, and,
to make them easy, put in his prologue double the usual dose of
incense that is offered to their vanity; for there is an established
tax of this kind, from which no author is suffered to dispense
himself. This author's wise precaution succeeded, and the men
that were before so redoubtable grew calm; the charms of flattery,
more strong than those of music, deprived them of all their fierce-
ness.

"'You see, sir, that the pit is the same in all countries : it loves
to be flattered, under the more genteel name of being complimented. If a man has tolerable address at panegyric, they swallow
it greedily, and are easily quelled and intoxicated by the draught.
Every one in particular thinks he merits the praise that is given to
the whole in general; the illusion operates, and the prologue is
good, only because it is artfully directed. Every one saves his own
blush by the authority of the multitude he makes a part of, which

immemorial, that no Company of Comedians could act Plays, *&c.* without the Royal License or Protection of some legal Authority, a Theatre was, notwithstanding, erected in *Goodman's-Fields* about

is, perhaps, the only circumstance in which a man can think himself not obliged to be modest.

" 'The author having, by flattery, begun to tame this wild audience, proceeded entirely to reconcile it by the first scene of his performance. Two actors came in, one dressed in the English manner very decently, and the other with black eyebrows, a ribbon of an ell long under his chin, a bag-peruke immoderately powdered, and his nose all bedaubed with snuff. What Englishman could not know a Frenchman by this ridiculous picture! The common people of London think we are indeed such sort of folks, and of their own accord, add to our real follies all that their authors are pleased to give us. But when it was found, that the man thus equipped, being also laced down every seam of his coat, was nothing but a cook, the spectators were equally charmed and surprised. The author had taken care to make him speak all the impertinencies he could devise, and for that reason, all the impertinencies of his farce were excused, and the merit of it immediately decided. There was a long criticism upon our manners, our customs, and above all, upon our cookery. The excellence and virtues of English beef were cried up, and the author maintained, that it was owing to the qualities of its juice, that the English were so courageous, and had such a solidity of understanding, which raised them above all the nations in Europe : he preferred the noble old English pudding beyond all the finest ragouts that were ever invented by the greatest geniuses that France has produced ; and all these ingenious strokes were loudly clapped by the audience.

" ' The pit, biassed by the abuse that was thrown on the French, forgot that they came to damn the play, and maintain the ancient liberty of the stage. They were friends with the players, and even with the court itself, and contented themselves with the privilege left them, of lashing our nation as much as they pleased, in the room of laughing at the expense of the minister. The license of

seven Years ago,[1] where Plays, without any such
License, were acted for some time unmolested and
with Impunity. After a Year or two, this Playhouse
was thought a Nusance too near the City: Upon
which the Lord-Mayor and Aldermen petition'd the
Crown to suppress it: What Steps were taken in
favour of that Petition I know not, but common
Fame seem'd to allow, from what had or had not
been done in it, that acting Plays in the said Theatre
was not evidently unlawful.[2]   However, this Question of Acting without a License a little time after
came to a nearer Decision in *Westminster-Hall*; the
Occasion of bringing it thither was this: It happened that the Purchasers of the Patent, to whom

authors did not seem to be too much restrained, since the court
did not hinder them from saying all the ill they could of the
French.

"'Intractable as the populace appear in this country, those who
know how to take hold of their foibles, may easily carry their
point.   Thus is the liberty of the stage reduced to just bounds,
and yet the English pit makes no farther attempt to oppose the
new regulation. The law is executed without the least trouble, all
the plays since having been quietly heard, and either succeeded,
or not, according to their merit.'"

See article in Mr. Archer's "About the Theatre," p. 101, and
Parliamentary Reports, 1832 and 1866.

[1] The theatre in Goodman's Fields was opened in October,
1729, by Thomas Odell, who was afterwards Deputy Licenser
under the 1737 Act. Odell, having no theatrical experience,
entrusted the management to Henry Giffard. Odell's theatre
seems to have been in Leman Street.

[2] I can find no hint that plays were ever stopped at Odell's
theatre. There is a pamphlet, published in 1730, with the following title: "A Letter to the Right Honourable Sir Richard

Mr. *Booth* and Myself had sold our Shares,[1] were at variance with the Comedians that were then left to their Government, and the Variance ended in the chief of those Comedians deserting and setting up for themselves in the little House in the *Hay-Market*, in 1733, by which Desertion the Patentees were very much distressed and considerable Losers. Their Affairs being in this desperate Condition, they were advis'd to put the Act of the Twelfth of Queen *Anne* against Vagabonds in force against these Deserters, then acting in the *Hay-Market* without License. Accordingly, one of their chief Performers[2] was taken from the Stage by a Justice of Peace his Warrant, and committed to *Bridewell* as one within the Penalty of the said Act. When the Legality of this Commitment was disputed in *West-minster-Hall*, by all I could observe from the learned Pleadings on both Sides (for I had the Curiosity to

Brocas, Lord Mayor of London. By a Citizen," which demands the closing of the theatre, but I do not suppose any practical result followed. In 1733 an attempt by the Patentees of Drury Lane and Covent Garden to silence Giffard's Company, then playing at his new theatre in Goodman's Fields, was unsuccessful. This theatre was in Ayliffe Street.

[1] Half of Booth's share of the Patent was purchased by High-more, who also bought the whole of Cibber's share. Giffard was the purchaser of the remainder of Booth's share.

[2] This was John Harper. Davies ("Life of Garrick," i. 40) says that "The reason of the Patentees fixing on Harper was in consequence of his natural timidity." His trial was on the 20th November, 1733. Harper was a low comedian of some ability, but of no great note.

hear them) it did not appear to me that the Comedian so committed was within the Description of the said Act, he being a Housekeeper and having a Vote for the *Westminster* Members of Parliament. He was discharged accordingly, and conducted through the Hall with the Congratulations of the Crowds that attended and wish'd well to his Cause.

The Issue of this Trial threw me at that time into a very odd Reflexion, *viz.* That if acting Plays without License did not make the Performers Vagabonds unless they wandered from their Habitations so to do, how particular was the Case of Us three late Menaging Actors at the *Theatre-Royal*, who in twenty Years before had paid upon an Averidge at least Twenty Thousand Pounds to be protected (as Actors) from a Law that has not since appeared to be against us. Now, whether we might certainly have acted without any License at all I shall not pretend to determine; but this I have of my own Knowledge to say, That in Queen *Anne*'s Reign the Stage was in such Confusion, and its Affairs in such Distress, that Sir *John Vanbrugh* and Mr. *Congreve*, after they had held it about one Year, threw up the Menagement of it as an unprofitable Post, after which a License for Acting was not thought worth any Gentleman's asking for, and almost seem'd to go a begging, 'till some time after, by the Care, Application, and Industry of three Actors, it became so prosperous, and the Profits so considerable, that it created a new Place, and a *Sine-cure* of a Thousand

Pounds a Year,[1] which the Labour of those Actors
constantly paid to such Persons as had from time to
time Merit or Interest enough to get their Names inserted as Fourth Menagers in a License with them
for acting Plays, &c. a Preferment that many a Sir
Francis Wronghead would have jump'd at.[2] But to
go on with my Story. This Endeavour of the
Patentees to suppress the Comedians acting in the
Hay-Market proving ineffectual, and no Hopes of a
Reunion then appearing, the Remains of the Company left in *Drury-Lane* were reduced to a very low
Condition. At this time a third Purchaser, *Charles
Fleetwood*, Esq., stept in ; who judging the best Time
to buy was when the Stock was at the lowest Price,
struck up a Bargain at once for Five Parts in Six of
the Patent ;[3] and, at the same time, gave the revolted
Comedians their own Terms to return and come
under his Government in *Drury-Lane*, where they
now continue to act at very ample Sallaries, as I am
informed, in 1738.[4] But (as I have observ'd) the late

---

[1] Cibber again alludes to this in Chap. XIII.

[2] Sir Francis Wronghead is a character in " The Provoked Husband," a country squire who comes to London to seek a place at
Court. In Act iv. Sir Francis relates his interview with a certain
great man : " Sir Francis, says my lord, pray what sort of a place
may you ha' turned your thoughts upon ? My lord, says I,
beggars must not be chusers ; but ony place, says I, about a thousand a-year, will be well enough to be doing with, till something
better falls in—for I thowght it would not look well to stond hag-
gling with him at first."

[3] Giffard seems to have retained his sixth part.

[4] Some account of the entire dispute between Highmore and
his actors will be found in my Supplement to this book.

Cause of the prosecuted Comedian having gone so strongly in his Favour, and the House in *Goodman's-Fields*, too, continuing to act with as little Authority unmolested; these so tolerated Companies gave Encouragement to a broken Wit to collect a fourth Company, who for some time acted Plays in the *Hay-Market*, which House the united *Drury-Lane* Comedians had lately quitted: This enterprising Person, I say (whom I do not chuse to name,[1] unless it could be to his Advantage, or that it were of Importance) had Sense enough to know that the best Plays with bad Actors would turn but to a very poor Account; and therefore found it necessary to give the Publick some Pieces of an extraordinary Kind, the Poetry of which he conceiv'd ought to be so strong that the greatest Dunce of an Actor could not spoil it: He knew, too, that as he was in haste to

---

[1] This "broken Wit" was Henry Fielding, between whom and Cibber there was war to the knife, Fielding taking every opportunity of mocking at Colley and attacking his works.

Mr. Austin Dobson, in his "Fielding," page 66, writes: "When the *Champion* was rather more than a year old, Colley Cibber published his famous *Apology*. To the attacks made upon him by Fielding at different times he had hitherto printed no reply—perhaps he had no opportunity of doing so. But in his eighth chapter, when speaking of the causes which led to the Licensing Act, he takes occasion to refer to his assailant in terms which Fielding must have found exceedingly galling. He carefully abstained from mentioning his name, on the ground that it could do him no good, and was of no importance; but he described him as 'a broken Wit,'" &c.

Mr. Dobson, on page 69, gives his approval to the theory that "Fielding had openly expressed resentment at being described by Cibber as 'a broken wit,' without being mentioned by name."

get Money, it would take up less time to be intrepidly abusive than decently entertaining; that to draw the Mob after him he must rake the Channel[1] and pelt their Superiors; that, to shew himself somebody, he must come up to *Juvenal's* Advice and stand the Consequence:

Aude aliquid brevibus Gyaris, & carcere dignum
Si vis esse aliquis ——   Juv. Sat. I.[2]

Such, then, was the mettlesome Modesty he set out with; upon this Principle he produc'd several frank and free Farces that seem'd to knock all Distinctions of Mankind on the Head: Religion, Laws, Government, Priests, Judges, and Ministers, were all laid flat at the Feet of this *Herculean* Satyrist! This *Drawcansir* in Wit,[3] that spared neither Friend nor Foe! who to make his Poetical Fame immortal, like another *Erostratus*, set Fire to his Stage by writing up to an Act of Parliament to demolish it.[4]   I shall

[1] The use of "channel," meaning "gutter," is obsolete in England; but I am sure that I have heard it used in that sense in Scotland.   Shakespeare in "King Henry the Sixth," third part, act ii. sc. 2, has,

"As if a channel should be called the sea."

And in Marlowe's "Edward the Second," act i. sc. 1, occur the lines:—

"Throw off his golden mitre, rend his stole,
And in the channel christen him anew."

[2] Juvenal, i. 73.

[3] Mr. Dobson ("Fielding," page 67) says: "He [Cibber] called him, either in allusion to his stature, or his pseudonym in the *Champion*, a '*Herculean* Satyrist,' a '*Drawcansir* in Wit.'"

[4] Fielding's political satires, in such pieces as "Pasquin" and

not give the particular Strokes of his Ingenuity a
Chance to be remembred by reciting them; it may
be enough to say, in general Terms, they were so
openly flagrant, that the Wisdom of the Legislature
thought it high time to take a proper Notice of
them,[1]

Having now shewn by what means there came
to be four Theatres, besides a fifth for Operas, in
London, all open at the same time, and that while
they were so numerous it was evident some of them
must have starv'd unless they fed upon the Trash
and Filth of Buffoonry and Licentiousness; I now
come, as I promis'd, to speak of that necessary Law
which has reduced their Number and prevents the
Repetition of such Abuses in those that remain open
for the Publick Recreation.

"The Historical Register for 1736," contributed largely to the passing of the Act of 1737, although "The Golden Rump" was the
ostensible cause.

[1] Fielding, in the "Champion" for Tuesday, April 22nd, 1740,
says of Cibber's refusal to quote from "Pasquin"—"the good
Parent seems to imagine that he hath produced, as well as my
Lord *Clarendon*, a Κρῆμα ἐς ἀεὶ; for he refuses to quote anything
out of *Pasquin*, lest he should *give it a chance of being remembered*."

Mr. Dobson ("Fielding," page 69) says Fielding "never seems
to have wholly forgotten his animosity to the actor, to whom there
are frequent references in *Joseph Andrews*; and, as late as 1749,
he is still found harping on 'the withered laurel' in a letter to
Lyttelton. Even in his last work, the *Voyage to Lisbon*, Cibber's
name is mentioned. The origin of this protracted feud is obscure;
but, apart from want of sympathy, it must probably be sought for
in some early misunderstanding between the two in their capacities of manager and author."

While this Law was in Debate a lively Spirit and uncommon Eloquence was employ'd against it.[1]   It was urg'd That *one* of the greatest Goods we can enjoy is *Liberty*.   (This we may grant to be an incontestable Truth, without its being the least Objection to this Law.)   It was said, too, That to bring the Stage under the Restraint of a Licenser was leading the way to an Attack upon the Liberty of the Press.   This amounts but to a Jealousy at best, which I hope and believe all honest *Englishmen* have as much Reason to think a groundless, as to fear it is a just Jealousy: For the Stage and the Press, I shall endeavour to shew, are very different Weapons to wound with.   If a great Man could be no more injured by being personally ridicul'd or made contemptible in a Play, than by the same Matter only printed and read against him in a Pamphlet or the strongest Verse; then, indeed, the Stage and the Press might pretend to be upon an equal Foot of Liberty: But when the wide Difference between these two Liberties comes to be explain'd and consider'd, I dare say we shall find the Injuries from one capable of being ten times more severe and formidable than from the other: Let us see, at least, if the Case will not be vastly alter'd.   Read what Mr. *Collier* in his *Defence* of his *Short View of the Stage*, &c. Page 25, says to this Point; he sets this Difference in a clear Light.   These are his Words:

----

[1] By Lord Chesterfield.

" The Satyr of a *Comedian* and another *Poet*, have
" a different effect upon Reputation. A Character
" of Disadvantage upon the *Stage*, makes a stronger
" Impression than elsewhere. Reading is but Hear-
" ing at the second Hand ; Now Hearing at the best,
" is a more languid Conveyance than Sight.   For as
" *Horace* observes,

> *Segnius irritant animos demissa per aurem,*
> *Quam quæ sunt oculis subjecta fidelibus.*[1]

" The Eye is much more affecting, and strikes
" deeper into the Memory than the Ear.   Besides,
" Upon the *Stage* both the Senses are in Conjunc-
" tion.   The Life of the Action fortifies the Object,
" and awakens the Mind to take hold of it.   Thus
" a dramatick Abuse is rivetted in the Audience, a
" Jest is improv'd into an Argument, and Rallying
" grows up into Reason': Thus a Character of Scandal
" becomes almost indelible, a Man goes for a Block-
" head upon *Content*; and he that's made a Fool in
" a *Play*, is often made one for his Life-time.   'Tis
" true he passes for such only among the prejudiced
" and unthinking; but these are no inconsiderable
" Division of Mankind. For these Reasons, I humbly
" conceive the *Stage* stands in need of a great deal
" of Discipline and Restraint : To give them an un-
" limited Range, is in effect to make them Masters
" of all Moral Distinctions, and to lay Honour and
" Religion at their Mercy.   To shew Greatness ridi-

---

[1] Horace, *Ars Poetica*, 180.

" culous, is the way to lose the use, and abate the
" value of the Quality. Things made little in jest,
" will soon be so in earnest: for Laughing and
" Esteem, are seldom bestow'd on the same Object."

If this was Truth and Reason (as sure it was)
forty Years ago, will it not carry the same Conviction
with it to these Days, when there came to be a much
stronger Call for a Reformation of the Stage, than
when this Author wrote against it, or perhaps than
was ever known since the *English* Stage had a Being?
And now let us ask another Question! Does not
the general Opinion of Mankind suppose that the
Honour and Reputation of a Minister is, or ought
to be, as dear to him as his Life? Yet when the
Law, in Queen *Anne*'s Time, had made even an
unsuccessful Attempt upon the Life of a Minister
capital, could any Reason be found that the Fame
and Honour of his Character should not be under
equal Protection? Was the Wound that *Guiscard*
gave to the late Lord *Oxford*, when a Minister,[1] a
greater Injury than the Theatrical Insult which was
offer'd to a later Minister, in a more valuable Part,
his Character? Was it not as high time, then, to
take this dangerous Weapon of mimical Insolence
and Defamation out of the Hands of a mad Poet,
as to wrest the Knife from the lifted Hand of a
Murderer? And is not that Law of a milder Nature
which *prevents* a Crime, than that which *punishes* it
after it is committed? May not one think it amazing

---

[1] Guiscard's attack on Harley occurred in 1711.

that the Liberty of defaming lawful Power and Dignity should have been so eloquently contended for? or especially that this Liberty ought to triumph in a Theatre, where the most able, the most innocent, and most upright Person must himself be, while the Wound is given, defenceless? How long must a Man so injur'd lie bleeding before the Pain and Anguish of his Fame (if it suffers wrongfully) can be dispell'd? or say he had deserv'd Reproof and publick Accusation, yet the Weight and Greatness of his Office never can deserve it from a publick Stage, where the lowest Malice by sawcy Parallels and abusive Inuendoes may do every thing but name him: But alas! Liberty is so tender, so chaste a Virgin, that it seems not to suffer her to do irreparable Injuries with Impunity is a Violation of her! It cannot sure be a Principle of Liberty that would turn the Stage into a Court of Enquiry, that would let the partial Applauses of a vulgar Audience give Sentence upon the Conduct of Authority, and put Impeachments into the Mouth of a *Harlequin?* Will not every impartial Man think that Malice, Envy, Faction, and Mis-rule, might have too much Advantage over lawful Power, if the Range of such a Stage-Liberty were unlimited and insisted on to be enroll'd among the glorious Rights of an *English* Subject?

I remember much such another ancient Liberty, which many of the good People of *England* were once extremely fond of; I mean that of throwing

Squibs and Crackers at all Spectators without Distinction upon a Lord-Mayor's Day ; but about forty
Years ago a certain Nobleman happening to have
one of his Eyes burnt out by this mischievous Merriment, it occasion'd a penal Law to prevent those
Sorts of Jests from being laugh'd at for the future :
Yet I have never heard that the most zealous Patriot
ever thought such a Law was the least Restraint
upon our Liberty.

If I am ask'd why I am so voluntary a Champion
for the Honour of this Law that has limited the
Number of Play-Houses, and which now can no
longer concern me as a Professor of the Stage ? I
reply, that it being a Law so nearly relating to the
Theatre, it seems not at all foreign to my History to
have taken notice of it ; and as I have farther pro-
mised to give the Publick a true Portrait of my
Mind, I ought fairly to let them see how far I am,
or am not, a Blockhead, when I pretend to talk of
serious Matters that may be judg'd so far above my
Capacity : Nor will it in the least discompose me
whether my Observations are contemn'd or applauded.
A Blockhead is not always an unhappy Fellow, and
if the World will not flatter us, we can flatter ourselves ; perhaps, too, it will be as difficult to convince
us we are in the wrong, as that you wiser Gentlemen
are one Tittle the better for your Knowledge. It is
yet a Question with me whether we weak Heads have
not as much Pleasure, too, in giving our shallow
Reason a little Exercise, as those clearer Brains have

that are allow'd to dive into the deepest Doubts and
Mysteries ; to reflect or form a Judgment upon remarkable things *past* is as delightful to me as it is to
the gravest Politician to penetrate into what is *present*,
or to enter into Speculations upon what is, or is not
likely to come. Why are Histories written, if all
Men are not to judge of them ? Therefore, if my
Reader has no more to do than I have, I have a
Chance for his being as willing to have a little more
upon the same Subject as I am to give it him.

When direct Arguments against this Bill were
found too weak, Recourse was had to dissuasive
ones : It was said that *this Restraint upon the Stage
would not remedy the Evil complain'd of: That a
Play refus'd to be licensed would still be printed, with
double Advantage, when it should be insinuated that it
was refused for some Strokes of Wit, &c. and would
be more likely then to have its Effect among the People.*
However natural this Consequence may seem, I
doubt it will be very difficult to give a *printed* Satyr
or Libel half the Force or Credit of an *acted* one.
The most artful or notorious Lye or strain'd Allusion
that ever slander'd a great Man, may be read by
some People with a Smile of Contempt, or, at worst,
it can impose but on one Person at once : but when
the Words of the same plausible Stuff shall be repeated on a Theatre, the Wit of it among a Crowd
of Hearers is liable to be over-valued, and may unite
and warm a whole Body of the Malicious or Ignorant
into a Plaudit ; nay, the partial Claps of only *twenty*

ill-minded Persons among several hundreds of silent
Hearers shall, and often have been, mistaken for a
general Approbation, and frequently draw into their
Party the Indifferent or Inapprehensive, who rather
than be thought not to understand the Conceit, will
laugh with the Laughers and join in the Triumph!
But alas! the *quiet* Reader of the same ingenious
Matter can only like for *himself*; and the Poison has
a much slower Operation upon the Body of a People
when it is so retail'd out, than when sold to a full
Audience by wholesale.   The *single* Reader, too,
may happen to be a sensible or unprejudiced Person;
and then the merry Dose, meeting with the Antidote
of a sound Judgment, perhaps may have no Operation
at all : With such a one the Wit of the most ingenious
Satyr will only by its intrinsick Truth or Value
gain upon his Approbation; or if it be worth an
Answer, a printed Falshood may possibly be con-
founded by printed Proofs against it.   But against
Contempt and Scandal, heighten'd and colour'd by
the Skill of an *Actor* ludicrously infusing it into a
Multitude, there is no immediate Defence to be
made or equal Reparation to be had for it; for it
would be but a poor Satisfaction at last, after lying
long patient under the Injury, that Time only is to
shew (which would probably be the Case) that the
Author of it was a desperate Indigent that did it for
Bread.   How much less dangerous or offensive, then,
is the *written* than the *acted* Scandal?   The Impression the Comedian gives to it is a kind of double

Stamp upon the Poet's Paper, that raises it to ten
times the intrinsick Value. Might we not strengthen
this Argument, too, even by the Eloquence that
seem'd to have opposed this Law? I will say for
my self, at least, that when I came to read the printed
Arguments against it, I could scarce believe they were
the same that had amaz'd and raised such Admiration
in me when they had the Advantage of a lively
Elocution, and of that Grace and Spirit which gave
Strength and Lustre to them in the Delivery!

Upon the whole; if the Stage ought ever to have
been reform'd; if to place a Power *somewhere* of
restraining its Immoralities was not inconsistent with
the Liberties of a civiliz'd People (neither of which,
sure, any moral Man of Sense can dispute) might it
not have shewn a Spirit too poorly prejudiced, to
have rejected so rational a Law only because the
Honour and Office of a Minister might happen, in
some small Measure, to be protected by it.[1]

But however little Weight there may be in the
Observations I have made upon it, I shall, for my
own Part, always think them just; unless I should
live to see (which I do not expect) some future Set
of upright Ministers use their utmost Endeavours to
repeal it.

---

[1] Genest (iii. 521) remarks, "If the power of the Licenser had
been laid *under proper regulations*, all would have been right."
The whole objection to the Licenser is simply that he is under no
regulations whatever. He is a perfectly irresponsible authority,
and one from whose decisions there is no appeal.

And now we have seen the Consequence of what
many People are apt to contend for, Variety of Play-
houses! How was it possible so many could honestly
subsist on what was fit to be seen? Their extraordinary Number, of Course, reduc'd them to live
upon the Gratification of such Hearers as they knew
would be best pleased with publick Offence; and
publick Offence, of what kind soever, will always be
a good Reason for making Laws to restrain it.

To conclude, let us now consider this Law in a
quite different Light; let us leave the political Part
of it quite out of the Question; what Advantage
could either the Spectators of Plays or the Masters
of Play-houses have gain'd by its having never been
made? How could the same Stock of Plays supply
four Theatres, which (without such additional Entertainments as a Nation of common Sense ought to be
ashamed of) could not well support two? Satiety
must have been the natural Consequence of the
same Plays being twice as often repeated as now
they need be; and Satiety puts an End to all Tastes
that the Mind of Man can delight in. Had therefore
this Law been made seven Years ago, I should not
have parted with my Share in the Patent under a
thousand Pounds more than I received for it[1]——So
that, as far as I am able to judge, both the Publick
as Spectators, and the Patentees as Undertakers,

[1] Cibber received three thousand guineas from Highmore for
his share in the Patent. (See Victor's " History," i. 8).

are, or might be, in a way of being better entertain'd
and more considerable Gainers by it.

I now return to the State of the Stage, where I
left it, about the Year 1697, from whence this Pursuit
of its Immoralities has led me farther than I first
design'd to have follow'd it.

CHAPTER IX. .

A small Apology for writing on. The different State of the two
Companies. Wilks *invited over from* Dublin. Estcourt, *from*
the same Stage, the Winter following. Mrs. Oldfield's *first*
Admission to the Theatre-Royal. *Her Character. The great*
Theatre in the Hay-Market *built for* Betterton's *Company. It*
Answers not their Expectation. Some Observations upon it. A
Theatrical State Secret.

I NOW begin to doubt that the *Gayeté du Cœur*
in which I first undertook this Work may have
drawn me into a more laborious Amusement than I
shall know how to away with : For though I cannot
say I have yet jaded my Vanity, it is not impossible
but by this time the most candid of my Readers may
want a little Breath ; especially when they consider

that all this Load I have heap'd upon their Patience
contains but seven Years of the forty three I pass'd
upon the Stage, the History of which Period I have
enjoyn'd my self to transmit to the Judgment (or
Oblivion) of Posterity.[1]   However, even my Dulness
will find somebody to do it right; if my Reader is
an ill-natur'd one, he will be as much pleased to find
me a Dunce in my old Age as possibly he may have
been to prove me a brisk Blockhead in my Youth :
But if he has no Gall to gratify, and would (for his
simple Amusement) as well know how the Play-
houses went on forty Years ago as how they do now,
I will honestly tell him the rest of my Story as well
as I can.   Lest therefore the frequent Digressions
that have broke in upon it may have entangled his
Memory, I must beg leave just to throw together the
Heads of what I have already given him, that he
may again recover the Clue of my Discourse.

Let him then remember, from the Year 1660 to
1682,[2] the various Fortune of the (then) King's and
Duke's two famous Companies ; their being reduced
to one united ; the Distinct Characters I have given

---

[1] "The Laureat," page 72 : "Indeed, *Laureat*, notwithstanding
what thou may'st dream of the Immortality of this Work of thine,
and bestowing the same on thy Favourites by recording them
here ; thou mayst, old as thou art, live to see thy precious Labours
become the vile Wrappers of Pastry-Grocers and Chandlery
Wares."   The issue of the present edition of Cibber's "Apology"
is sufficient commentary on "The Laureat's" ill-natured pro-
phecy.

[2] Cibber prints 1684, repeating his former blunder. (See p. 96.)

of thirteen Actors, which in the Year 1690 were the
most famous then remaining of them; the Cause of
their being again divided in 1695, and the Consequences of that Division 'till 1697; from whence I
shall lead them to our Second Union in——Hold!
let me see——ay, it was in that memorable Year
when the two Kingdoms of *England* and *Scotland*
were made one.   And I remember a Particular that
confirms me I am right in my Chronology; for the
Play of *Hamlet* being acted soon after, *Estcourt*,
who then took upon him to say any thing, added a
fourth Line to *Shakespear's* Prologue to the Play, in
that Play which originally consisted but of three, but
Estcourt made it run thus :

> *For Us, and for our Tragedy,*
> *Here stooping to your Clemency;*
> [This being a Year of Unity,]
> *We beg your Hearing patiently.*[1]

This new Chronological Line coming unexpectedly
upon the Audience, was received with Applause,
tho' several grave Faces look'd a little out of
Humour at it.   However, by this Fact, it is plain
our Theatrical Union happen'd in 1707.[2]   But to
speak of it in its Place I must go a little back again.

---

[1] The first play acted by the United Company was "Hamlet."
In this Estcourt is cast for the Gravedigger, so that if Cibber's
anecdote is accurate, as no doubt it is, Estcourt must have
"doubled" the Gravedigger and the speaker of the Prologue.

[2] The first edition reads "1708," and in the next chapter Cibber
says 1708. In point of fact, the first performance by the United
Company took place 15th January, 1708. This does not make Est-

From 1697 to this Union both Companies went
on without any memorable Change in their Affairs,
unless it were that *Betterton's* People (however good
in their Kind) were most of them too far advanc'd in
Years to mend; and tho' we in *Drury-Lane* were
too young to be excellent, we were not too old to be
better. But what will not Satiety depreciate? For
though I must own and avow that in our highest
Prosperity I always thought we were greatly their
Inferiors; yet, by our good Fortune of being seen in
quite new Lights, which several new-written Plays
had shewn us in, we now began to make a considerable Stand against them. One good new Play to
a rising Company is of inconceivable Value. In
Oroonoko[1] (and why may I not name another, tho'
it be my own?) in *Love's last Shift*, and in the Sequel
of it, the *Relapse*, several of our People shew'd themselves in a new Style of Acting, in which Nature had
not as yet been seen. I cannot here forget a Misfortune that befel our Society about this time, by
the loss of a young Actor, *Hildebrand Horden*,[2] who

court's "gag" incorrect, for though we now should not consider
May, 1707, and the following January in the same year, yet up to
1752, when the style was changed in England, they were so.

[1] Southerne's "Oroonoko" was produced at Drury Lane in
1696.

[2] Of Horden we know little more than Cibber tells us. He
seems to have been on the stage only for a year or two; and
during 1696 only, at Drury Lane, does his name appear to important parts. Davies ("Dram. Misc.," iii. 443) says Horden "was
bred a Scholar: he complimented George Powell, in a Latin encomium on his Treacherous Brothers."

was kill'd at the Bar of the *Rose-Tavern*,[1] in a frivolous, rash, accidental Quarrel ; for which a late Resi-
dent at *Venice*, Colonel *Burgess*, and several other
Persons of Distinction, took their Tryals, and were
acquitted. This young Man had almost every natural Gift that could promise an excellent Actor ; he
had besides a good deal of Table-wit and Humour,
with a handsome Person, and was every Day rising

"The London News-Letter," 20th May, 1696, says: "On
Monday Capt. *Burges* who kill'd Mr. *Fane*, and was found guilty
of Manslaughter at the *Old Baily*, kill'd Mr. *Harding* a Comedian in a Quarrel at the *Rose* Tavern in *Hatton* [should be
Covent] *Garden*, and is taken into custody."

In "Luttrell's Diary," on Tuesday, 19th May, 1696, is noted :
"Captain Burgesse, convicted last sessions of manslaughter for
killing Mr. Fane, is committed to the Gatehouse for killing Mr.
Horden, of the Playhouse, last night in Covent Garden."

And on Tuesday, 30th November, 1697, "Captain Burgesse, who
killed Mr. Horden the player, has obtained his majesties pardon."

[1] This tavern seems to have been very near Drury Lane
Theatre, and to have been a favourite place of resort after the
play. In the Epilogue to the "Constant Couple" the Rose
Tavern is mentioned :—

> "Now all depart, each his respective way,
> To spend an evening's chat upon the play ;
> Some to Hippolito's ; one homeward goes,
> And one with loving she, retires to th' Rose."

In the "Comparison between the two Stages" one scene is
laid in the Rose Tavern, and from it we gather that the house was
of a very bad character :—

"*Ramb.* Defend us ! what a hurry of Sin is in this House !

Sull. Drunkenness, which is the proper Iniquity of a Tavern, is
here the most excusable Sin ; so many other Sins over-run it, 'tis
hardly seen in the crowd. .   .   .   .

Sull. This House is the very Camp of Sin ; the Devil sets up

into publick Favour. Before he was bury'd, it was observable that two or three Days together several of the Fair Sex, well dress'd, came in Masks (then frequently worn) and some in their own Coaches, to visit this Theatrical Heroe in his Shrowd. He was the elder Son of Dr. *Horden*, Minister of *Twickenham*, in *Middlesex*. But this Misfortune was soon repair'd by the Return of *Wilks* from *Dublin* (who upon this young Man's Death was sent for over) and liv'd long enough among us to enjoy that Approbation from which the other was so unhappily cut off. The Winter following,[1] *Estcourt*, the famous Mimick, of whom I have already spoken, had the same Invitation from *Ireland*, where he had commenc'd Actor: His first Part here, at the *Theatre-Royal*, was the *Spanish Friar*, in which, tho' he had remembred every Look and Motion of the late *Tony Leigh* so far as to put the Spectator very

his black Standard in the Faces of these hungry Harlots, and to enter into their Trenches is going down to the Bottomless Pit according to the letter."—*Comp.*, p. 140.

Pepys mentions the Rose more than once. On 18th May, 1668, the first day of Sedley's play, "The Mulberry Garden," the diarist, having secured his place in the pit, and feeling hungry, "did slip out, getting a boy to keep my place; and to the Rose Tavern, and there got half a breast of mutton, off the spit, and dined all alone. And so to the play again."

[1] Cibber's chronology cannot be reconciled with what we believe to be facts. Horden was killed in 1696; Wilks seems to have come to England not earlier than the end of 1698, while it is, I should say, certain that Estcourt did not appear before 1704. I can only suppose that Cibber, who is very reckless in his dates, is here particularly confused.

much in mind of him, yet it was visible through the
whole, notwithstanding his Exactness in the Out-
lines, the true Spirit that was to fill up the Figure
was not the same, but unskilfully dawb'd on, like a
Child's Painting upon the Face of a *Metzo-tinto:* It
was too plain to the judicious that the Conception
was not his own, but imprinted in his Memory by
another, of whom he only presented a dead Likeness.[1] But these were Defects not so obvious to
common Spectators; no wonder, therefore, if by his
being much sought after in private Companies, he
met with a sort of Indulgence, not to say Partiality,
for what he sometimes did upon the Stage.

In the Year 1699, Mrs. *Oldfield* was first taken
into the House, where she remain'd about a Twelvemonth almost a Mute[2] and unheeded, 'till Sir *John
Vanbrugh*, who first recommended her, gave her the
Part of *Alinda* in the *Pilgrim* revis'd. This gentle
Character happily became that want of Confidence
which is inseparable from young Beginners, who,
without it, seldom arrive to any Excellence: Notwithstanding, I own I was then so far deceiv'd in my
Opinion of her, that I thought she had little more
than her Person that appear'd necessary to the
forming a good Actress; for she set out with so
extraordinary a Diffidence, that it kept her too de-

---

[1] For Leigh's playing of this character, see *ante*, p. 145.

[2] Curll, in his "Life of Mrs. Oldfield," says that the only part she
played, previous to appearing as Alinda, was Candiope in "Secret
Love." She played Alinda in 1700.

spondingly down to a formal, plain (not to say) flat manner of speaking. Nor could the silver Tone of her Voice 'till after some time incline my Ear to any Hope in her favour. But Publick Approbation is the warm Weather of a Theatrical Plant, which will soon bring it forward to whatever Perfection Nature has design'd it. However, Mrs. *Oldfield* (perhaps for want of fresh Parts) seem'd to come but slowly forward 'till the Year 1703.[1] Our Company that Summer acted at the *Bath* during the Residence of Queen *Anne* at that Place. At that time it happen'd that Mrs. *Verbruggen*, by reason of her last Sickness (of which she some few Months after dy'd) was left in *London* ; and though most of her Parts were, of course, to be dispos'd of, yet so earnest was the Female Scramble for them, that only one of them fell to the Share of Mrs. *Oldfield*, that of *Leonora* in Sir *Courtly Nice* ; a Character of good plain Sense, but not over elegantly written. It was in this Part Mrs. *Oldfield* surpris'd me into an Opinion of her having all the innate Powers of a good Actress, though they were yet but in the Bloom of what they promis'd. Before she had acted this Part I had so cold an Expectation from her Abilities, that she could scarce prevail with me to rehearse with her the Scenes she was chiefly concern'd in with Sir *Courtly*, which I then acted. However, we ran them over with a mutual

---

[1] In 1702, Gildon, in the "Comparison between the two Stages" (p. 200), includes Mrs. Oldfield among the " meer Rubbish that ought to be swept off the Stage with the Filth and Dust."

Inadvertency of one another. I seem'd careless, as concluding that any Assistance I could give her would be to little or no purpose; and she mutter'd out her Words in a sort of mifty[1] manner at my low Opinion of her. But when the Play came to be acted, she had a just Occasion to triumph over the Error of my Judgment, by the (almost) Amazement that her unexpected Performance awak'd me to; so forward and sudden a Step into Nature I had never seen; and what made her Performance more valuable was, that I knew it all proceeded from her own Understanding, untaught and unassisted by any one more experienc'd Actor.[2] Perhaps it may not be unacceptable, if I enlarge a little more upon the Theatrical Character of so memorable an Actress.[3]

Though this Part of *Leonora* in itself was of so little value, that when she got more into Esteem it was one

[1] "Miff," a colloquial expression signifying "a slight degree of resentment."

[2] Cibber is pleasantly candid in allowing that he had no share in Mrs. Oldfield's success. The temptation to assume some credit for teaching her something must have been great.

[3] Mrs. Anne Oldfield, born about 1683, was introduced to Vanbrugh by Farquhar, who accidentally heard her reading aloud, and was struck by her dramatic style. Cibber gives so full an account of her that it is only necessary to add that she made her last appearance on 28th April, 1730, at Drury Lane, and that she died on the 23rd October in the same year. It was of Mrs. Oldfield that Pope wrote the often-quoted lines ("Moral Essays," Epistle I., Part iii.):—

"Odious! in woollen! 'twould a saint provoke
(Were the last words that poor Narcissa spoke),
No, let a charming chintz and Brussels lace
Wrap my cold limbs, and shade my lifeless face:

of the several she gave away to inferior Actresses; yet
it was the first (as I have observ'd) that corrected my
Judgment of her, and confirm'd me in a strong Belief
that she could not fail in very little time of being what
she was afterwards allow'd to be, the foremost Ornament of our Theatre. Upon this unexpected Sally,
then, of the Power and Disposition of so unforeseen
an Actress, it was that I again took up the two first
Acts of the *Careless Husband*, which I had written the
Summer before, and had thrown aside in despair of
having Justice done to the Character of Lady *Betty
Modish* by any one Woman then among us; Mrs. *Verbruggen* being now in a very declining state of Health,
and Mrs. *Bracegirdle* out of my Reach and engag'd in
another Company: But, as I have said, Mrs. *Oldfield*
having thrown out such new Proffers of a Genius, I
was no longer at a loss for Support; my Doubts
were dispell'd, and I had now a new Call to finish it:
Accordingly, the *Careless Husband*[1] took its Fate

> One would not, sure, be frightful when one's dead—
> And—Betty—give this cheek a little red."

I may note that, though Cibber enlarges chiefly on her comedy
acting, she acted many parts in tragedy with the greatest success.

[1] Produced 7th December, 1704, at Drury Lane.

"The Careless Husband."

LORD MORELOVE	Mr. Powel.
LORD FOPPINGTON	Mr. Cibber.
SIR CHARLES EASY	Mr. Wilks.
LADY BETTY MODISH	Mrs. Oldfield.
LADY EASY	Mrs. Knight.
LADY GRAVEAIRS	Mrs. Moore.
MRS. EDGING	Mrs. Lucas.

upon the Stage the Winter following, in 1704. Whatever favourable Reception this Comedy has met with from the Publick, it would be unjust in me not to place a large Share of it to the Account of Mrs. *Oldfield*; not only from the uncommon Excellence of her Action, but even from her personal manner of Conversing. There are many Sentiments in the Character of Lady *Betty Modish* that I may almost say were originally her own, or only dress'd with a little more care than when they negligently fell from her lively Humour : Had her Birth plac'd her in a higher Rank of Life, she had certainly appear'd in reality what in this Play she only excellently acted, an agreeably gay Woman of Quality a little too conscious of her natural Attractions. I have often seen her in private Societies, where Women of the best Rank might have borrow'd some part of her Behaviour without the least Diminution of their Sense or Dignity. And this very Morning, where I am now writing at the *Bath, November* 11, 1738, the same Words were said of her by a Lady of Condition, whose better Judgment of her Personal Merit in that Light has embolden'd me to repeat them. After her Success in this Character of higher Life, all that Nature had given her of the Actress seem'd to have risen to its full Perfection : But the Variety of her Power could not be known 'till she was seen in variety of Characters ; which, as fast as they fell to her, she equally excell'd in. Authors had much more from her Performance than they had reason to hope for from what they had written for her; and none had less than another, but as their Genius in the Parts they allotted her was more or less elevated.

In the Wearing of her Person she was particularly fortunate; her Figure was always improving to her Thirty-sixth Year; but her Excellence in acting was never at a stand: And the last new Character she shone in (*Lady Townly*) was a Proof that she was still able to do more, if more could have been done for *her*.[1] She had one Mark of good Sense, rarely known in any Actor of either Sex but herself. I have observ'd several, with promising Dispositions, very desirous of Instruction at their first setting out; but no sooner had they found their least Account in it, than they were as desirous of being left to their own Capacity, which they then thought would be disgrac'd by their seeming to want any farther Assistance. But this was not Mrs. *Oldfield's* way of thinking; for, to the last Year of her Life, she never undertook any Part she lik'd without being importunately desirous of having all the Helps in it that another could possibly give her. By knowing so much herself, she found how much more there was of Nature yet needful to be known. Yet it was a hard matter to give her any Hint that she was not able to take or improve.

---

[1] Mrs. Oldfield played Lady Townly in the "Provoked Husband," 10th January, 1728. I presume that Cibber means that this was her last *important* original part, for she was the original representative of Sophonisba (by James Thomson) and other characters after January, 1728.

With all this Merit she was tractable and less presuming in her Station than several that had not half
her Pretensions to be troublesome : But she lost
nothing by her easy Conduct ; she had every thing
she ask'd, which she took care should be always
reasonable, because she hated as much to be *grudg'd*
as *deny'd* a Civility. Upon her extraordinary Action
in the *Provok'd Husband*,[1] the Menagers made her a
Present of Fifty Guineas more than her Agreement,
which never was more than a Verbal one ; for they
knew she was above deserting them to engage upon
any other Stage, and she was conscious they would
never think it their Interest to give her cause of
Complaint. In the last two Months of her Illness,
when she was no longer able to assist them, she

[1]   "The Provoked Husband."

LORD TOWNLY	Mr. Wilks.
LADY TOWNLY	Mrs. Oldfield.
LADY GRACE.	Mrs. Porter.
MR. MANLEY.	Mr. Mills, sen.
SIR FRANCIS WRONGHEAD . .	Mr. Cibber, sen.
LADY WRONGHEAD	Mrs. Thurmond.
SQUIRE RICHARD	Young Wetherelt.
MISS JENNY	Mrs. Cibber.
JOHN MOODY.	Mr. Miller.
COUNT BASSET	Mr. Bridgewater.
MRS. MOTHERLY . . .	Mrs. Moore.
MYRTILLA.	Mrs. Grace.
MRS. TRUSTY	Mrs. Mills.

Vanbrugh left behind him nearly four acts of a play entitled
"A Journey to London," which Cibber completed, calling the
finished work "The Provoked Husband." It was produced at
Drury Lane on 10th January, 1728.

declin'd receiving her Sallary, tho' by her Agreement
she was entitled to it.   Upon the whole she was, to
the last Scene she acted, the Delight of her Spectators : Why then may we not close her Character
with the same Indulgence with which *Horace* speaks
of a commendable Poem :

> *Ubi plura nitent—non ego paucis*
> *Offendar maculis*————[1]

> *Where in the whole such various Beauties shine,*
> *'Twere idle upon Errors to refine.*[2]

What more might be said of her as an Actress may
be found in the Preface to the *Provok'd Husband*, to
which I refer the Reader.[3]

[1]   " Verum ubi plura nitent in carmine, non ego paucis
       Offendar maculis."—Horace, *Ars Poetica*, 351.

[2] " The Laureat," p. 57 : " But I can see no Occasion you have
to mention any Errors.   She had fewer as an Actress than any ;
and neither you, nor I, have any Right to enquire into her Conduct
any where else."

[3] The following is the passage referred to :—

"But there is no doing right to Mrs. Oldfield, without putting
people in mind of what others, of great merit, have wanted to
come near her—'Tis not enough to say, she here outdid her usual
excellence.   I might therefore justly leave her to the constant
admiration of those spectators who have the pleasure of living
while she is an actress.   But as this is not the only time she has
been the life of what I have given the public, so, perhaps, my
saying a little more of so memorable an actress, may give this
play a chance to be read when the people of this age shall be
ancestors—May it therefore give emulation to our successors of
the stage, to know, that to the ending of the year 1727, a co-
temporary comedian relates, that Mrs. Oldfield was then in her
highest excellence of action, happy in all the rarely found requisites
that meet in one person to complete them for the stage.   She was

With the Acquisition, then, of so advanc'd a Comedian as Mrs. *Oldfield*, and the Addition of one so much in Favour as *Wilks*, and by the visible Improvement of our other Actors, as *Penkethman*, *Johnson*, *Bullock*, and I think I may venture to name myself in the Number (but in what Rank I leave to the Judgment of those who have been my Spectators)

in stature just rising to that height, where the graceful can only begin to show itself; of a lively aspect, and a command in her mien, that like the principal figure in the finest painting, first seizes, and longest delights, the eye of the spectators. Her voice was sweet, strong, piercing, and melodious; her pronunciation voluble, distinct, and musical; and her emphasis always placed, where the spirit of the sense, in her periods, only demanded it. If she delighted more in the higher comic, than in the tragic strain, 'twas because the last is too often written in a lofty disregard of nature. But in characters of modern practised life, she found occasion to add the particular air and manner which distinguished the different humours she presented; whereas, in tragedy, the manner of speaking varies as little as the blank verse it is written in.—She had one peculiar happiness from nature, she looked and maintained the agreeable, at a time when other fine women only raise admirers by their understanding—The spectator was always as much informed by her eyes as her elocution; for the look is the only proof that an actor rightly conceives what he utters, there being scarce an instance, where the eyes do their part, that the elocution is known to be faulty. The qualities she had acquired, were the genteel and the elegant; the one in her air, and the other in her dress, never had her equal on the stage; and the ornaments she herself provided (particularly in this play) seemed in all respects the *paraphernalia* of a woman of quality. And of that sort were the characters she chiefly excelled in; but her natural good sense, and lively turn of conversation, made her way so easy to ladies of the highest rank, that it is a less wonder if, on the stage, she sometimes was, what might have become the finest woman in real life to have supported." [Bell's edition.]

the Reputation of our Company began to get ground; Mrs. *Oldfield* and Mr. *Wilks*, by their frequently playing against one another in our best Comedies, very happily supported that Humour and Vivacity which is so peculiar to our *English* Stage. The *French*, our only modern Competitors, seldom give us their Lovers in such various Lights: In their Comedies (however lively a People they are by nature) their Lovers are generally constant, simple Sighers, both of a Mind, and equally distress'd about the Difficulties of their coming together; which naturally makes their Conversation so serious that they are seldom good Company to their Auditors: And tho' I allow them many other Beauties of which we are too negligent, yet our Variety of Humour has Excellencies that all their valuable Observance of Rules have never yet attain'd to. By these Advantages, then, we began to have an equal Share of the politer sort of Spectators, who, for several Years, could not allow our Company to stand in any comparison with the other. But Theatrical Favour, like Publick Commerce, will sometimes deceive the best Judgments by an unaccountable change of its Channel; the best Commodities are not always known to meet with the best Markets. To this Decline of the Old Company many Accidents might contribute; as the too distant Situation of their Theatre, or their want of a better, for it was not then in the condition it now is, but small, and poorly fitted up within the Walls of a Tennis *Quaree* Court, which is of the

lesser sort.[1] *Booth*, who was then a young Actor
among them, has often told me of the Difficulties
Betterton then labour'd under and complain'd of:
How impracticable he found it to keep their Body to
that common Order which was necessary for their
Support;[2] of their relying too much upon their intrinsick Merit; and though but few of them were young
even when they first became their own Masters, yet
they were all now ten Years older, and consequently
more liable to fall into an inactive Negligence, or
were only separately diligent for themselves in the
sole Regard of their Benefit-Plays; which several of
their Principals knew, at worst, would raise them
Contributions that would more than tolerably subsist
them for the current Year. But as these were too
precarious Expedients to be always depended upon,
and brought in nothing to the general Support of

---

[1] Mr. Julian Marshall, in his "Annals of Tennis," p. 34,
describes the two different sorts of tennis courts—"that which was
called *Le Quarré*, or the Square; and the other with the *dedans*,
which is almost the same as that of the present day." Cibber is
thus correct in mentioning that the court was one of the lesser sort.

[2] Interesting confirmation of Cibber's statement is furnished by
an edict of the Lord Chamberlain, dated 11th November, 1700, by
which Betterton is ordered "to take upon him y⸰ sole management"
of the Lincoln's Inn Fields company, there having been great dis-
orders, "for want of sufficient authority to keep them to their
duty." See David Craufurd's Preface to "Courtship à la Mode"
(1700), for an account of the disorganized state of the Lincoln's
Inn Fields Company. He says that though Betterton did his
best, some of the actors neither learned their parts nor attended
rehearsals; and he therefore withdrew his comedy and took it to
Drury Lane, where it was promptly produced.

the Numbers who were at Sallaries under them, they
were reduc'd to have recourse to foreign Novelties ;
L'Abbeè, *Balon*, and Mademoiselle *Subligny*,[1] three
of the then most famous Dancers of the *French*
Opera, were, at several times, brought over at extraordinary Rates, to revive that sickly Appetite which
plain Sense and Nature had satiated.[2] But alas!
there was no recovering to a sound Constitution by
those mere costly Cordials ; the Novelty of a Dance
was but of a short Duration, and perhaps hurtful in
its consequence; for it made a Play without a Dance
less endur'd than it had been before, when such
Dancing was not to be had. But perhaps their ex-

[1] Mons. Castil-Blaze, in his "La Danse et les Ballets," 1832,
p. 153, writes : "Ballon danse avec énergie et vivacité ; mademoiselle de Subligny se fait généralement admirer pour sa danse
noble et gracieuse." Madlle. Subligny was one of the first women
who were dancers by profession. "La demoiselle Subligny parut
peu de temps après la demoiselle Fontaine [1681], et fut aussi fort
applaudie pour sa danse ; mais elle quitta le théâtre, en 1705, et
mourut après l'année 1736."—"Histoire de l'Opéra." Of Mons.
L'Abbé I have been unable to discover any critical notice.

[2] Downes ("Roscius Anglicanus," p. 46) says : "In the space
of Ten Years past, Mr. *Betterton* to gratify the desires and Fancies
of the Nobility and Gentry; procur'd from Abroad the best Dances
and Singers, as Monsieur *L'Abbe*, Madam *Sublini*, Monsieur *Balon*,
Margarita Delpine, *Maria Gallia* and divers others; who being
Exhorbitantly Expensive, produc'd small Profit to him and his
Company, but vast Gain to themselves."

Gildon, in the "Comparison between the two Stages," alludes
to some of these dancers :—

"*Sull.* The Town ran mad to see him [Balon], and the prizes
were rais'd to an extravagant degree to bear the extravagant rate
they allow'd him " (p. 49).

hibiting these Novelties might be owing to the Success we had met with in our more barbarous introducing of *French* Mimicks and Tumblers the Year before; of which Mr. *Rowe* thus complains in his Prologue to one of his first Plays:

Must Shakespear, Fletcher, *and laborious* Ben,
Be left for Scaramouch *and* Harlequin ?[1]

While the Crowd, therefore, so fluctuated from one House to another as their Eyes were more or less regaled than their Ears, it could not be a Question much in Debate which had the better Actors; the Merit of either seem'd to be of little moment; and the Complaint in the foregoing Lines, tho' it might be just for a time, could not be a just one for ever, because the best Play that ever was writ may tire by being too often repeated, a Misfortune naturally attending the Obligation to play every Day; not that

" *Crit.* There's another Toy now [Madame Subligny]—Gad, there's not a Year but some surprizing Monster lands: I wonder they don't first show her at *Fleet-bridge* with an old Drum and a crackt Trumpet " (p. 67).

[1] In the Prologue to " The Ambitious Stepmother," produced at Lincoln's Inn Fields in 1701 (probably), Rowe writes :—

"The Stage would need no Farce, nor Song nor Dance,
Nor Capering Monsieur brought from Active France."

And in the Epilogue (not Prologue, as Cibber says) :—

" Show but a Mimick Ape, or French Buffoon,
You to the other House in Shoals are gone,
And leave us here to Tune our Crowds alone.
Must Shakespear, Fletcher, and laborious Ben,
Be left for Scaramouch and Harlaquin ?"

whenever such Satiety commences it will be any
Proof of the Play's being a bad one, or of its being
ill acted.   In a word, Satiety is seldom enough consider'd by either Criticks, Spectators, or Actors, as
the true, not to say just Cause of declining Audiences
to the most rational Entertainments : And tho' I
cannot say I ever saw a good new Play not attended
with due Encouragement, yet to keep a Theatre daily
open without sometimes giving the Publick a bad
old one, is more than I doubt the Wit of human
Writers or Excellence of Actors will ever be able to
accomplish.   And as both Authors and Comedians
may have often succeeded where a sound Judgment
would have condemn'd them, it might puzzle the
nicest Critick living to prove in what sort of Excellence the true Value of either consisted : For if their
Merit were to be measur'd by the full Houses they
may have brought ; if the Judgment of the Crowd
were infallible ; I am afraid we shall be reduc'd to
allow that the *Beggars Opera* was the best-written
Play, and Sir *Harry Wildair*[1] (as *Wilks* play'd it)
was the best acted Part, that ever our *English*
Theatre had to boast of.   That Critick, indeed, must
be rigid to a Folly that would deny either of them
their due Praise, when they severally drew such
Numbers after them ; all their Hearers could not be
mistaken ; and yet, if they were all in the right, what
sort of Fame will remain to those celebrated Authors

[1] In "The Constant Couple," and its sequel, "Sir Harry
Wildair."

and Actors that had so long and deservedly been
admired before these were in Being. The only Distinction I shall make between them is, That to
write or act like the Authors or Actors of the latter
end of the last Century, I am of Opinion will be
found a far better Pretence to Success than to imitate
these who have been so crowded to in the beginning
of this. All I would infer from this Explanation is,
that tho' we had then the better Audiences, and
might have more of the young World on our Side,
yet this was no sure Proof that the other Company
were not, in the Truth of Action, greatly our Superiors. These elder Actors, then, besides the Disadvantages I have mention'd, having only the fewer
true Judges to admire them, naturally wanted the
Support of the Crowd whose Taste was to be pleased
at a cheaper Rate and with coarser Fare. To recover them, therefore, to their due Estimation, a new
Project was form'd of building them a stately Theatre
in the *Hay-Market*,[1] by Sir *John Vanbrugh*, for
which he raised a Subscription of thirty Persons of
Quality, at one hundred Pounds each, in Consideration whereof every Subscriber, for his own Life, was
to be admitted to whatever Entertainments should
be publickly perform'd there, without farther Payment for his Entrance. Of this Theatre I saw the

---

[1] This theatre, opened 9th April, 1705, was burnt down 17th
June, 1788; rebuilt 1791; again burnt in 1867. During its ex-
istence it has borne the name of Queen's Theatre, Opera House,
King's Theatre, and its present title of Her Majesty's Theatre.

first Stone laid, on which was inscrib'd *The little Whig*, in Honour to a Lady of extraordinary Beauty, then the celebrated Toast and Pride of that Party.[1]

In the Year 1706,[2] when this House was finish'd, *Betterton* and his Co-partners dissolved their own Agreement, and threw themselves under the Direction of Sir *John Vanbrugh* and Mr. *Congreve*, imagining, perhaps, that the Conduct of two such eminent Authors might give a more prosperous Turn to their Condition; that the Plays it would now be their Interest to write for them would soon recover the Town to a true Taste, and be an Advantage that no other Company could hope for; that in the Interim, till such Plays could be written, the Grandeur of their House, as it was a new Spectacle, might allure the Crowd to support them: But if these were their Views, we shall see that their Dependence upon them was too sanguine. As to their Prospect of new Plays, I doubt it was not enough consider'd that good ones were Plants of a slow Growth; and tho' Sir *John Vanbrugh* had a

[1] The beautiful Lady Sunderland. Mr. Percy Fitzgerald ("New History," i. 238) states that it was said that workmen, on 19th March, 1825, found a stone with the inscription: "April 18th, 1704. This corner-stone of the Queen's Theatre was laid by his Grace Charles Duke of Somerset."

[2] Should be 1705. Downes (p. 47) says: "About the end of 1704, Mr. *Betterton* Assign'd his License, and his whole Company over to Captain *Vantbrugg* to *Act* under HIS, at the Theatre in the *Hay Market*." Vanbrugh opened his theatre on 9th April, 1705.

very quick Pen, yet Mr. *Congreve* was too judicious
a Writer to let any thing come hastily out of his
Hands: As to their other Dependence, the House,
they had not yet discover'd that almost every proper
Quality and Convenience of a good Theatre had
been sacrificed or neglected to shew the Spectator a
vast triumphal Piece of Architecture! And that the
best Play, for the Reasons I am going to offer, could
not but be under great Disadvantages, and be less
capable of delighting the Auditor here than it could
have been in the plain Theatre they came from.
For what could their vast Columns, their gilded
Cornices, their immoderate high Roofs avail, when
scarce one Word in ten could be distinctly heard in
it? Nor had it then the Form it now stands in,
which Necessity, two or three Years after, reduced it
to: At the first opening it, the flat Ceiling that is
now over the Orchestre was then a Semi-oval Arch
that sprung fifteen Feet higher from above the Cor-
nice: The Ceiling over the Pit, too, was still more
raised, being one level Line from the highest back
part of the upper Gallery to the Front of the Stage:
The Front-boxes were a continued Semicircle to the
bare Walls of the House on each Side: This extraordinary and superfluous Space occasion'd such an
Undulation from the Voice of every Actor, that
generally what they said sounded like the Gabbling
of so many People in the lofty Isles in a Cathedral
—The Tone of a Trumpet, or the Swell of an
Eunuch's holding Note, 'tis true, might be sweeten'd

by it, but the articulate Sounds of a speaking Voice
were drown'd by the hollow Reverberations of one
Word upon another. To this Inconvenience, why
may we not add that of its Situation ; for at that time
it had not the Advantage of almost a large City,
which has since been built in its Neighbourhood :
Those costly Spaces of *Hanover*, *Grosvenor*, and
Cavendish Squares, with the many and great adja-
cent Streets about them, were then all but so many
green Fields of Pasture, from whence they could
draw little or no Sustenance, unless it were that of a
Milk-Diet. The City, the Inns of Court, and the
middle Part of the Town, which were the most constant Support of a Theatre, and chiefly to be relied
on, were now too far out of the Reach of an easy
Walk, and Coach-hire is often too hard a Tax upon
the Pit and Gallery.[1] But from the vast Increase of
the Buildings I have mention'd, the Situation of that
Theatre has since that Time received considerable
Advantages ; a new World of People of Condition
are nearer to it than formerly, and I am of Opinion
that if the auditory Part were a little more reduced
to the Model of that in *Drury-Lane*, an excellent

[1] In Dryden's Prologue at the opening of Drury Lane in 1674,
in comparing the situation of Drury Lane with that of Dorset
Garden, which was at the east end of Fleet Street, he talks of

". . . . . a cold bleak road,
Where bears in furs dare scarcely look abroad."

This is now the Strand and Fleet Street! No doubt the road
westward to the Haymarket was equally wild.

Company of Actors would now find a better Account in it than in any other House in this populous City.[1] Let me not be mistaken, I say an excellent Company, and such as might be able to do Justice to the best of Plays, and throw out those latent Beauties in them which only excellent Actors can discover and give Life to. If such a Company were now there, they would meet with a quite different Set of Auditors than other Theatres have lately been used to : Polite Hearers would be content with polite Entertainments ; and I remember the time when Plays, without the Aid of Farce or Pantomime, were as decently attended as Opera's or private Assemblies, where a noisy Sloven would have past his time as uneasily in a Front-box as in a Drawing-room ; when a Hat upon a Man's Head there would have been look'd upon as a sure Mark of a Brute or a Booby : But of all this I have seen, too, the Reverse, where in the Presence of Ladies at a Play common Civility has been set at defiance, and the Privilege of being a rude Clown, even to a Nusance, has in a manner been demanded as one of the Rights of *English* Liberty : Now, though I grant that Liberty is so precious a Jewel that we ought not to suffer the least Ray of its Lustre to be diminish'd, yet methinks the Liberty of seeing a Play in quiet has as laudable a Claim to Protection as the Privilege of not suffering you to do it has to Impunity. But since we are so

---

[1] This experiment was never tried. From the time Cibber wrote, the house was used as an Opera House.

X

happy as not to have a certain Power among us, which in another Country is call'd the *Police*, let us rather bear this Insult than buy its Remedy at too dear a Rate; and let it be the Punishment of such wrong-headed Savages, that they never will or can know the true Value of that Liberty which they so stupidly abuse: Such vulgar Minds possess their Liberty as profligate Husbands do fine Wives, only to disgrace them. In a Word, when Liberty boils over, such is the Scum of it. But to our new erected Theatre.

Not long before this Time the *Italian* Opera began first to steal into *England*,[1] but in as rude a disguise and unlike it self as possible; in a lame, hobling Translation into our own Language, with false Quantities, or Metre out of Measure to its original Notes, sung by our own unskilful Voices, with Graces misapply'd to almost every Sentiment, and with Action lifeless and unmeaning through every Character: The first *Italian* Performer that

[1]
> "to Court,
> Her seat imperial Dulness shall transport.
> Already Opera prepares the way,
> The sure fore-runner of her gentle sway."
> > "Dunciad," iii. verses 301-303.
> "When lo! a harlot form soft sliding by,
> With mincing step, small voice, and languid eye;
> Foreign her air, her robe's discordant pride
> In patchwork fluttering, and her head aside;
> By singing peers upheld on either hand,
> She tripp'd and laugh'd, too pretty much to stand."
> > "Dunciad," iv. verses 45-50.

made any distinguish'd Figure in it was *Valentini*, a true sensible Singer at that time, but of a Throat too weak to sustain those melodious Warblings for which the fairer Sex have since idoliz'd his Successors. However, this Defect was so well supply'd by his Action, that his Hearers bore with the Absurdity of his singing his first Part of *Turnus* in *Camilla* all in *Italian*, while every other Character was sung and recited to him in *English*.[1] This I have mention'd to shew not only our Tramontane Taste, but that the crowded Audiences which follow'd it to *Drury-Lane* might be another Occasion of their growing thinner in *Lincolns-Inn-Fields*.

To strike in, therefore, with this prevailing Novelty, Sir *John Vanbrugh* and Mr. *Congreve* open'd their new *Hay-Market Theatre* with a translated Opera to *Italian* Musick, called the *Triumph of Love*, but this not having in it the Charms of *Camilla*, either from the Inequality of the Musick or Voices, had but a cold Reception, being perform'd but three Days, and those not crowded. Immediately upon the Failure of this *Opera*, Sir *John Vanbrugh* produced his Comedy call'd the *Confede-*

---

[1] Salvini, the great Italian actor, played in America with an English company, he speaking in Italian, they answering in English. I have myself seen a similar polyglot performance at the Edinburgh Lyceum Theatre, where the manager, Mr. J. B. Howard, acted Iago (in English), while Signor Salvini and his company played in Italian. I confess the effect was not so startling as I expected.

racy,[1] taken (but greatly improv'd) from the *Bour-geois à la mode* of *Dancour*: Though the Fate of this Play was something better, yet I thought it was not equal to its Merit:[2] For it is written with an uncommon Vein of Wit and Humour; which confirms me in my former Observation, that the difficulty of hearing distinctly in that then wide Theatre was no small Impediment to the Applause that might have followed the same Actors in it upon every other Stage; and indeed every Play acted there before the House was alter'd seemed to suffer from the same Inconvenience: In a Word, the Prospect of Profits from this Theatre was so very barren, that Mr. *Congreve* in a few Months gave up his Share and Interest in the Government of it wholly to Sir *John Vanbrugh*.[3] But Sir *John*, being sole Proprietor of the House, was at all Events oblig'd to do his utmost to support it. As he had a happier Talent of throwing the *English* Spirit into his Translation of *French* Plays than any former Author who had borrowed from them, he in the same Season gave the Publick three more of that kind, call'd the *Cuckold in Conceit*, from the *Cocu imaginaire* of *Moliere*;[4] *Squire Trelooby*,

---

[1] "The Confederacy" was not produced till the following season —30th October, 1705.

[2] It was acted ten times.

[3] Genest (ii. 333) says that Congreve resigned his share at the close of the season 1704-5.

[4] Cibber should have said "The Confederacy." "The Cuckold in Conceit" has never been printed, and Genest doubts if it is by Vanbrugh. Besides, it was not produced till 22nd March, 1707.

from his *Monsieur de Pourceaugnac*, and the *Mistake*, from the *Dépit Amoureux* of the same Author.[1] Yet all these, however well executed, came to the Ear in the same undistinguish'd Utterance by which almost all their Plays had equally suffered : For what few could plainly hear, it was not likely a great many could applaud.

It must farther be consider'd, too, that this Company were not now what they had been when they first revolted from the Patentees in *Drury-Lane*, and became their own Masters in *Lincolns-Inn-Fields*. Several of them, excellent in their different Talents, were now dead ; as *Smith*, *Kynaston*, *Sandford*, and *Leigh :* Mrs. *Betterton* and *Underhil* being, at this time, also superannuated Pensioners whose Places were generally but ill supply'd : Nor could it be expected that *Betterton* himself, at past seventy, could retain his former Force and Spirit ; though he was yet far distant from any Competitor. Thus, then, were these Remains of the best Set of Actors that I believe were ever known at once in *England*, by Time, Death, and the Satiety of their Hearers, mould'ring to decay.

It was now the Town-talk that nothing but a Union of the two Companies could recover the Stage to its former Reputation,[2] which Opinion was certainly

---

[1] " The Mistake " was produced 27th December, 1705. "Squire Trelooby," which was first played in 1704, was revived 28th January, 1706, with a new second act.

[2] A junction of the companies seems to have been talked of as

true : One would have thought, too, that the Patentee
of *Drury-Lane* could not have fail'd to close with it,
he being then on the Prosperous Side of the Question, having no Relief to ask for himself, and little
more to do in the matter than to consider what he
might safely grant : But it seems this was not his
way of counting; he had other Persons who had
great Claims to Shares in the Profits of this Stage,
which Profits, by a Union, he foresaw would be too
visible to be doubted of, and might raise up a new
Spirit in those Adventurers to revive their Suits at
Law with him; for he had led them a Chace in
Chancery several Years,[1] and when they had driven
him into a Contempt of that Court, he conjur'd up a
Spirit, in the Shape of Six and eight Pence a-day,
that constantly struck the Tipstaff blind whenever
he came near him : He knew the intrinsick Value of
Delay, and was resolv'd to stick to it as the surest
way to give the Plaintiffs enough on't.   And by this
Expedient our good Master had long walk'd about
at his Leisure, cool and contented as a Fox when
the Hounds were drawn off and gone home from

early as 1701. In the Prologue to "The Unhappy Penitent"
(1701), the lines occur :—

> "But now the peaceful tattle of the town,
> Is how to join both houses into one."

[1] In "The Post-Boy Rob'd of his Mail," p. 342, some curious
particulars of the negotiations for a Union are given. One of
Rich's objections to it is that he has to consider the interests of
his Partners, with some of whom he has already been compelled
to go to law on monetary questions.

him.   But whether I am right or not in my Conjec-
tures, certain it is that this close Master of *Drury-
Lane* had no Inclination to a Union, as will appear
by the Sequel.[1]

Sir *John Vanbrugh* knew, too, that to make a
Union worth his while he must not seem too hasty
for it; he therefore found himself under a Necessity,
in the mean time, of letting his whole Theatrical
Farm to some industrious Tenant that might put it
into better Condition.   This is that Crisis, as I observed in the Eighth Chapter, when the Royal
Licence for acting Plays, *&c.* was judg'd of so little
Value as not to have one Suitor for it.   At this time,
then, the Master of *Drury-Lane* happen'd to have a
sort of primier Agent in his Stage-Affairs, that seem'd
in Appearance as much to govern the Master as the
Master himself did to govern his Actors : But this
Person was under no Stipulation or Sallary for the
Service he render'd, but had gradually wrought him-
self into the Master's extraordinary Confidence and
Trust, from an habitual Intimacy, a cheerful Humour,

---

[1] In July, 1705, Rich was approached on behalf of Vanbrugh
regarding a Union, and the Lord Chamberlain supported the
latter's proposal. Rich, in declining, wrote : "I am concern'd
with above forty Persons in number, either as Adventurers under
the two Patents granted to Sir *William Davenant*, and *Tho. Killigrew*, Esq.; or as Renters of *Covent-Garden* and *Dorset Garden*
Theatres. . . . . I am a purchaser under the Patents, to above
the value of two Thousand Pounds (a great part of which was
under the Marriage-Settlements of Dr. *Davenant*)."—"The Post-
Boy Rob'd of his Mail," p. 344.

and an indefatigable Zeal for his Interest. If I
should farther say, that this Person has been well
known in almost every Metropolis in *Europe*; that
few private Men have, with so little Reproach, run
through more various Turns of Fortune; that, on
the wrong side of Three-score, he has yet the open
Spirit of a hale young Fellow of five and twenty;
that though he still chuses to speak what he thinks
to his best Friends with an undisguis'd Freedom, he
is, notwithstanding, acceptable to many Persons of
the first Rank and Condition; that any one of them
(provided he likes them) may now send him, for their
Service, to *Constantinople* at half a Day's Warning;
that Time has not yet been able to make a visible
Change in any Part of him but the Colour of his
Hair, from a fierce coal-black to that of a milder
milk-white: When I have taken this Liberty with
him, methinks it cannot be taking a much greater if
I at once should tell you that this Person was Mr.
Owen Swiney,[1] and that it was to him Sir *John*

[1] Owen Swiney, or Mac Swiney, was an Irishman. As is related
by Cibber in this and following chapters, he leased the Haymarket
from Vanbrugh from the beginning of the season 1706-7. At the
Union, 1707-8, the Haymarket was made over to him for the
production of operas; and when, at the end of 1708-9, Rich was
ordered to silence his company at Drury Lane, Swiney was allowed
to engage the chief of Rich's actors to play at the Haymarket,
where they opened September, 1709. At the beginning of season
1710-11, Swiney and his partners became managers of Drury
Lane, but Swiney was forced at the end of that season to resume
the management of the operas. After a year of the Opera-house
(end of 1711-12), Swiney was ruined and had to go abroad. He

Vanbrugh, in this Exigence of his Theatrical Affairs, made an Offer of his Actors, under such Agreements of Sallary as might be made with them; and of his House, Cloaths, and Scenes, with the Queen's License to employ them, upon Payment of only the casual Rent of five Pounds upon every acting Day, and not to exceed 700*l.* in the Year. Of this Proposal Mr. *Swiney* desir'd a Day or two to consider; for, however he might like it, he would not meddle in any sort without the Consent and Approbation of his Friend and Patron, the Master of *Drury Lane.* Having given the Reasons why this Patentee was averse to a Union, it may now seem less a Wonder why he immediately consented that *Swiney* should take the *Hay-Market* House, *&c.* and continue that Company to act against him; but the real Truth was, that he had a mind both Companies should be clandestinely under one and the same Interest, and yet in so loose a manner that he might declare his Verbal Agreement with *Swiney* good, or null and void, as he might best find his Account in either. What flatter'd him that he had this wholsom

---

remained abroad some twenty years. On 26th February, 1735, he had a benefit at Drury Lane, at which Cibber played for his old friend. The "Biographia Dramatica" says that he received a place in the Custom House, and was made Keeper of the King's Mews. He died 2nd October, 1754, leaving his property to Mrs. Woffington. Davies, in his "Dramatic Miscellanies" (i. 232), tells an idle tale of a scuffle between Swiney and Mrs. Clive's brother, which Bellchambers quotes at length, though it has no special reference to anything.

Project, and *Swiney* to execute it, both in his Power, was that at this time *Swiney* happen'd to stand in his Books Debtor to Cash upwards of Two Hundred Pounds : But here, we shall find, he over-rated his Security. However, *Swiney* as yet follow'd his Orders; he took the *Hay-Market* Theatre, and had, farther, the private Consent of the Patentee to take such of his Actors from *Drury-Lane* as either from Inclination or Discontent, might be willing to come over to him in the *Hay-Market*. The only one he made an Exception of, was myself : For tho' he chiefly depended upon his Singers and Dancers,[1] he said it would be necessary to keep some one tolerable Actor with him, that might enable him to set those Machines a going. Under this Limitation of not entertaining me, *Swiney* seem'd to acquiesce 'till after he had open'd with the so recruited Company in the *Hay-Market :* the Actors that came to him from *Drury-Lane* were *Wilks, Estcourt,*[2] *Mills, Keen,*[3] *Johnson, Bullock,* Mrs. *Oldfield,* Mrs. *Rogers,* and some few others of less note : But I must here let you know that this Project was form'd and put in Execution all in very few Days, in the Summer-

---

[1] At Drury Lane this season (1706-7) very few plays were acted, Rich relying chiefly on operas.

[2] Cibber seems to be wrong in including Estcourt in this list. His name appears in the Drury Lane bills for 1706-7, and his great part of Sergeant Kite (" Recruiting Officer ") was played at the Haymarket by Pack. On 30th November, 1706, it was advertised that " the true Sergeant Kite is performed at Drury Lane."

[3] See memoir of Theophilus Keen at end of second volume.

Season, when no Theatre was open. To all which I
was entirely a Stranger, being at this time at a
Gentleman's House in *Gloucestershire*, scribbling, if
I mistake not, the *Wife's Resentment*.[1]

The first Word I heard of this Transaction was
by a Letter from *Swiney*, inviting me to make One
in the *Hay-Market* Company, whom he hop'd I
could not but now think the stronger Party. But I
confess I was not a little alarm'd at this Revolution:
For I consider'd, that I knew of no visible Fund to
support these Actors but their own Industry ; that all
his Recruits from *Drury-Lane* would want new
Cloathing ; and that the warmest Industry would be
always labouring up Hill under so necessary an Expence, so bad a Situation, and so inconvenient a
Theatre. I was always of opinion, too, that in
changing Sides, in most Conditions, there generally
were discovered more unforeseen Inconveniencies
than visible Advantages ; and that at worst there
would always some sort of Merit remain with Fidelity,
tho' unsuccessful. Upon these Considerations I was

[1] Downes (p. 50) gives the following account of the transaction :—

"In this Interval Captain *Vanbrugg* by Agreement with Mr.
Swinny, and by the Concurrence of my Lord Chamberlain, Trans-
ferr'd and Invested his License and Government of the Theatre
to Mr. *Swinny*; who brought with him from Mr. *Rich*, Mr. *Wilks*,
Mr. *Cyber*, Mr. *Mills*, Mr. *Johnson*, Mr. *Keene*, Mr. *Norris*, Mr.
Fairbank, Mrs. *Oldfield* and others; United them to the Old
Company ; Mr. *Betterton* and Mr. *Underhill*, being the only remains of the Duke of *York's* Servants, from 1662, till the Union
in *October* 1706."

only thankful for the Offers made me from the *Hay-Market*, without accepting them, and soon after came to Town towards the usual time of their beginning to act, to offer my Service to our old Master. But I found our Company so thinn'd that it was almost impracticable to bring any one tolerable Play upon the Stage.[1] When I ask'd him where were his Actors, and in what manner he intended to proceed ? he reply'd, *Don't you trouble yourself, come along, and I'll shew you*. He then led me about all the By-places in the House, and shew'd me fifty little Back-doors, dark Closets, and narrow Passages ; in Altera-tions and Contrivances of which kind he had busied his Head most part of the Vacation; for he was scarce ever without some notable Joyner, or a Brick-layer extraordinary, in pay, for twenty Years. And there are so many odd obscure Places about a Theatre, that his Genius in Nook-building was never out of Employment; nor could the most vain-headed Author be more deaf to an Interruption in reciting his Works, than our wise Master was while enter-taining me with the Improvements he had made in his invisible Architecture ; all which, without thinking any one Part of it necessary, tho' I seem'd to ap-prove, I could not help now and then breaking in upon his Delight with the impertinent Question of

---

[1] The chief actors left at Drury Lane were Estcourt, Pinketh-man, Powell, Capt. Griffin, Mrs. Tofts, Mrs. Mountfort (that is, the great Mrs. Mountfort's daughter), and Mrs. Cross : a miser-ably weak company.

——*But, Master, where are your Actors?* But it seems I had taken a wrong time for this sort of Enquiry; his Head was full of Matters of more moment, and (as you find) I was to come another time for an Answer: A very hopeful Condition I found myself in, under the Conduct of so profound a Vertuoso and so considerate a Master! But to speak of him seriously, and to account for this Disregard to his Actors, his Notion was that Singing and Dancing, or any sort of Exotick Entertainments, would make an ordinary Company of Actors too hard for the best Set who had only plain Plays to subsist on. Now, though I am afraid too much might be said in favour of this Opinion, yet I thought he laid more Stress upon that sort of Merit than it would bear; as I therefore found myself of so little Value with him, I could not help setting a little more upon myself, and was resolv'd to come to a short Explanation with him. I told him I came to serve him at a time when many of his best Actors had deserted him; that he might now have the Refusal of me; but I could not afford to carry the Compliment so far as to lessen my Income by it; that I therefore expected either my casual Pay to be advanced, or the Payment of my former Sallary made certain for as many Days as we had acted the Year before.—No, he was not willing to alter his former Method; but I might chuse whatever Parts I had a mind to act of theirs who had left him. When I found him, as I thought, so insensible or impregnable, I look'd gravely in his

Face, and told him—He knew upon what Terms I was willing to serve him, and took my leave. By this time the *Hay-Market* Company had begun acting to Audiences something better than usual, and were all paid their full Sallaries, a Blessing they had not felt in some Years in either House before. Upon this Success *Swiney* press'd the Patentee to execute the Articles they had as yet only verbally agreed on, which were in Substance, That *Swiney* should take the *Hay-Market* House in his own Name, and have what Actors he thought necessary from *Drury-Lane*, and after all Payments punctually made, the Profits should be equally divided between these two Under-takers. But soft and fair! Rashness was a Fault that had never yet been imputed to the Patentee; certain Payments were Methods he had not of a long, long time been us'd to; that Point still wanted time for Consideration. But *Swiney* was as hasty as the other was slow, and was resolv'd to know what he had to trust to before they parted; and to keep him the closer to his Bargain, he stood upon his Right of having *Me* added to that Company if I was willing to come into it. But this was a Point as absolutely refus'd on one side as insisted on on the other. In this Contest high Words were exchang'd on both sides, 'till, in the end, this their last private Meeting came to an open Rupture: But before it was pub-lickly known, *Swiney*, by fairly letting me into the whole Transaction, took effectual means to secure me in his Interest. When the Mystery of the Patentee's

Indifference to me was unfolded, and that his slighting me was owing to the Security he rely'd on of *Swiney's* not daring to engage me, I could have no further Debate with my self which side of the Question I should adhere to. To conclude, I agreed, in two Words, to act with *Swiney*,[1] and from this time every Change that happen'd in the Theatrical Government was a nearer Step to that twenty Years of Prosperity which Actors, under the Menagement of Actors, not long afterwards enjoy'd. What was the immediate Consequence of this last Desertion from *Drury-Lane* shall be the Subject of another Chapter.

[1] Swiney's company began to act at the Haymarket on 15th October, 1706. Cibber's first appearance seems to have been on 7th November, when he played Lord Foppington in "The Careless Husband."

END OF VOL. I.

* 9 7 8 3 3 3 7 4 1 5 3 5 8 *